SOMETIMES
IN THE FALL

BAEN BOOKS
by JOHN VAN STRY

Summer's End
Sometimes in the Fall

SOMETIMES IN THE FALL

JOHN VAN STRY

SOMETIMES IN THE FALL

A Baen Books Original

Baen Publishing Enterprises
P.O. Box 1403
Riverdale, NY 10471
www.baen.com

ISBN: 978-1-6680-7247-9

Cover art by Sam R. Kennedy

First printing, March 2025

Distributed by Simon & Schuster
1230 Avenue of the Americas
New York, NY 10020

Library of Congress Cataloging-in-Publication Data

Names: Van Stry, John, author.
Title: Sometimes in the fall / John Van Stry.
Description: Riverdale, NY : Baen Publishing Enterprises, 2025.
Identifiers: LCCN 2024056826 (print) | LCCN 2024056827 (ebook) | ISBN
    9781668072479 (trade paperback) | ISBN 9781964856032 (ebook)
Subjects: LCGFT: Science fiction. | Novels.
Classification: LCC PS3622.A585737 S66 2025   (print) | LCC PS3622.A585737
    (ebook) | DDC 813/.6—dc23/eng/20241126
LC record available at https://lccn.loc.gov/2024056826
LC ebook record available at https://lccn.loc.gov/2024056827

Printed in the United States of America
10 9 8 7 6 5 4 3 2 1

SOMETIMES IN THE FALL

Triton—Lassell Orbital

"HOW GOES THE UNLOADING, EMIL?" I ASKED IN A LOW VOICE AS I walked over to where she was supervising the unloading of the TEUs, or Twenty-foot Equivalent Units, from our ship, the *Iowa Hill*. The cargo containers that shipping had settled on centuries ago.

"Not as fast as I'd like, but we're getting there. Thank god we're not taking on any cargo this time! Hopefully we can get out of this garbage-hole in the next hour. I swear I'm gonna have words with Kacey if she ever sends us here again."

"Yeah, I thought it was bad last time we were here, but if at all possible it seems to have gotten even worse. Still, they did pay a premium for our cargo."

"Probably because no one else wants to come here," Emiliana, who was both our cook and our cargo master, complained.

"As soon as we're done, call me or Hank if anything comes up and get the doors closed quick."

"Oh, I'll be doing that, alright!"

I went over to where Kei, one of our two "new" able spacers was keeping an eye on things, a large rifle of which model I hadn't the slightest clue was cradled in her arms.

When I'd been here thirty minutes ago, it'd been slung on her back.

1

"Something up?" I asked her.

"Why would something be up?"

"You unslung your rifle."

"Oh! I do that every ten or fifteen minutes so the boys down on the floor below don't forget that I got it. Wouldn't want any more 'misunderstandings,' right, boss?"

I shook my head and rolled my eyes. The last time we were here there'd been a few inappropriate advances made and Yuri had broken some idiot's collarbone with a short metal club she'd been hiding someplace on her body. The male-to-female ratio here wasn't the best. Lassell Orbital was the oldest orbital out in Neptune's space, orbiting its largest moon. Other than dockworkers and a few supporting businesses, no one lived on it anymore and rumor was that one of these days they were going to dump it into the planet.

"Just make sure no one comes onboard, and don't let Emil get out of your line of sight, got it?"

"Sure thing, boss."

That done, I went back to Engineering and checked on Nick, my assistant, and the status of our reactors.

"Trouble, Dave?"

I shook my head. "Nope, but Emil's even more unhappy than normal with the progress of the loaders. They're definitely dragging their feet."

"Any idea why?"

"Hank said they had a crew change after we'd unloaded the more expensive rare earths."

"What for?"

"That buyer had their own crew. All that stuff we brought in was shifted out to another ship."

"Then why the hell did they have us land in an internal hold this time?"

I shrugged. "Maybe the second crew here isn't vac certified?"

"With how run-down this place is, I can believe it," Nick said with a shake of his head. "This used to be a company orbital, didn't it?"

"I think it still is."

"That would go a long ways toward explaining things."

"Let's get the preflight checklist done and start warming up the gravity engines. If E's unhappy you can be sure Chris wants to pull out ASAP."

Nick agreed and we started checking the reactors and all the rest of our instruments. We'd been doing a triangle run for the last five months, starting with meeting the *Astro Gerlitz* in deep space, then coming here to off-load, then on to Mars to drop the rest of our cargo and take on stuff for Marcus and the "Let Bees" who were hiding out on Eris.

After our next meetup with the *Astro Gerlitz* it'd be home to Ceres to sell what we got from them there—Kacey's promise to her mother, Maureen, to not sell any more materials on the market there to avoid softening prices having expired by then.

"Dave, come up to the bridge please," our captain, Chris called over the ship's intercom a half hour or so later.

"Keep an eye on things," I told Nick and quickly made my way up to the top deck and onto the bridge.

"What's up?" I asked.

"They want us to take a specialty cargo to Mars," Chris said, giving me a look that told me he wasn't happy about it.

"Are they paying?"

"That's not the problem."

"What is?"

"They won't let us inspect the container."

"So tell them no."

"They won't open the cargo bay doors to let us leave if we don't take the container."

I frowned at him. "They *what*?"

"We're being held hostage until we take the container," Chris said, giving me a very unhappy look.

"And on what grounds are they claiming to be allowed to do *that*? Not that I believe whatever they're telling us is legal."

"They're claiming that it's a medical emergency, that the container contains specialty compounds used to create drugs for the treatment of Versac's disease that are made out here in deep space. Which of course is why we're not allowed to go inside, or we'll contaminate it."

"What the hell is Versac's disease?"

"I looked it up, it's a rare form of lymphoma only found on Mars, and apparently the treatment uses some pretty rare compounds that are specially made."

I shook my head and sighed. "How much are they paying us?"

"They said we'll be paid on delivery."

"Yeah, get back on the radio and tell them we want cash up front. We're not a charity service and we demand to be paid. Dig in your heels, we want cash, not credits, and see just how much they're willing to pay. Let me know what they settle on."

"How much should I charge them?"

"Start off with five times the going rate. Remember: cash, not credits."

Chris gave me a look. "Why is that important?"

"I want them to think we're trying to pad our own pockets. Credits would go to the company. Cash goes to you and the cargo handler. Make up some story about having been told by the head office that we're not allowed to add anything without their approval and how that'll take a week or some shit like that."

"Again, why is this important?"

"Because if they're on the up-and-up, they'll insist on credits and a standard rate. They'll be okay with going through our main office. If they're not"—I smiled—"they'll offer cash, though I'm sure they'll dicker you down, which is fine. Now, I gotta go find Hank."

Chris went back to the radio and started telling them he wanted cash as I left the bridge. As soon as I was out of there I pulled out my tablet and pinged Hank to find out where he was. Then joined him on the mid cargo deck.

"What's up, Dave?"

"They're forcing us to take a cargo, claiming it's some sort of medical emergency."

"To where?" he asked with a concerned look.

"Mars."

Hank snorted. "Ooookay. So they want us to smuggle something for them."

I nodded. "That's my first thought, but not my only one."

"What's the other one?"

"That maybe someone is unhappy with Yuri laying somebody out last time we were here? With us not 'sharing' our women? I mean, why else not allow us to inspect it, right? It's full of contraband and once we're within Mars's orbit they can just drop a comm on us and then we get hauled in by the Mars Navy for smuggling."

"Or it goes boom," Hank said frowning at me.

I sighed. I hadn't thought about *that*. "Or it goes boom. I figure we prep it for jettison as soon as we close the cargo doors, and the moment we're out of range we open the starboard-side door and dump it."

Hank nodded. "Tell Emil to have it loaded up on the third level. I'll grab Chaz and Yuri and we'll stage the gear just inside the aft hatch to the bay so we can rig it quick. Tell Chris to start pumping down the hold the minute the hatches close so we don't have any issues with opening the bay door."

I nodded. "Will do."

That done, I jogged over to the cargo bay ladder, slid down to the first level, and walked over to Emil, who was looking even less happy than before. There was some sort of officious-looking man standing by her that Kei was keeping a close eye on, her gun very conspicuously pointed in his direction.

"You talk to Chris?" Emil asked as I came up to them.

"Yup. Once they pay us we'll be putting it on the top level."

"Why up there?"

"So it's out of the way of our other stuff. Who knows how long it'll take whoever is getting it to show up. This way it won't slow down our unloading the other gear and cause management to start asking questions."

"This is an emergency!" the man said, turning to me. "You'd extort money from us?"

"Look," I said, turning to face him, "we can't ship anything without the head office approving it. You want to talk to them, feel free! But it'll be a week before they'd get back to you. Me? I get paid just as much sitting here in the dock or while underway, so I'm good either way. But if you want us to take it? Well, this ship doesn't move for free, so if you want it gone, best you grease the skids, if you know what I mean," I said, giving him a wink.

He frowned at me a moment, then got out his phone.

"But if we pay, you'll take it?"

"As long as we don't get in trouble with our bosses, of course we will!" I told him with a big smile. "After all, shipping freight is what we do. Now, go talk to your boss," I said and motioned for him to leave the ship.

"What's going on here?" Emil whispered once he'd climbed down out of sight.

"Later. This isn't a good time or place."

Just then my tablet pinged; they'd settled on twice the usual rate, but we'd only get half of it up front. I frowned at that.

"What's wrong?"

"Everything."

Ten minutes later, the man came back with a small overnight bag and handed it to me. I looked inside and sure enough, it was full of cash. I noticed the bag was made of some kind of heavy material, which of course worried me even more.

"Thanks," I told him. "Happy to do business with you. Now, please get off the ship. We're going to be leaving as soon as we have your container aboard."

Smiling, he nodded and left rather quickly.

That didn't sit well with me either.

"Talk to Hank about how to set it down," I told Emil. "The moment their crane is clear, seal the door and get your butt off the deck. Kei, get your ass in your suit and join the rest of us on the top deck."

"Why do I need my suit?"

"Because we'll be pumping down the cargo hold the moment the doors latch." And with that I jogged off the bottom deck through the bottom hatch and into Engineering.

"Nick, prepare to lift ship. Captain's gonna order the hold pumped down as soon as the doors are closed. Get a head count on where everyone is, but don't announce it. I gotta suit up and get back out there."

"What's going on?"

"I think we're getting a little payback for that tune-up Yuri administered the last time we were here."

"Got it."

I left him then and went into my quarters, stripped off my ship-suit, and got into my pressure suit. Grabbing the helmet, I quickly made my way up to the top deck and opened the hatch up there to peek out and see what was going on. The container in question was painted a bright white and was a full-size forty-foot double TEU, the standard size most used. The cargo doors were closing, the top one folded down and the bottom one still moving up—blocking the view of anyone down on the outside deck. Hank had the inside crane latched to the unit and was turning it ninety degrees to face the starboard side hatch, which had remained closed during loading.

"What's up?" I asked, walking over to him.

"Emil pinged me. She said the container was shifting as they were hauling it aboard."

"Shifting?" I asked, giving him a look.

"Like something inside was moving."

"How'd she notice that?"

"There's a level bob on the hoist where it pivots. She had to tell the crane operator to stop and back out because the end wasn't steady. That's when she noticed it wasn't the guy on the crane, it was the unit itself." Hank turned as Chaz ran up to him dragging a couple of heavy chains and a couple of ratchet chain binders. "Okay, the second I drop this onto the ground, run those through the door stays and ratchet them down tight. After that, we'll run a pair of cables around the entire container, just in case."

"Aye-aye," Chaz said with a serious look on his face, so I just stood back and watched as they worked. I noticed that Yuri was holding the kind of weapon that Kei usually favored and already had her helmet on. Kei joined us a minute later with an even bigger gun, surprising me only in that I hadn't known we had anything like that onboard.

When the unit hit the deck, Chaz and Hank quickly ran two chains across the end door, then ratcheted them down as fast as they could.

"Cargo hold sealed, prepare to lift ship!" Chris called and I put my helmet on as I felt the pressure starting to drop. Hank and Chaz grabbed theirs and ran back through the aft hatch to where we stored a lot of the ship's gear. They were both back in less than a minute, helmets on and each carrying a large coil of heavy cable. Working together, they first ran one around the unit about three feet up from the floor, then a second one about four feet above that, then winched both of them down tight.

"Up ship!" Chris's voice sounded over our suit comms.

Touching my helmet to Hank's, I turned my microphone off. "What's going on?"

"I think there's people inside."

"People? Why the hell would they want to smuggle people?"

"Now that would depend on what they look like and how well they're armed, wouldn't it?"

"Shit. No wonder they were willing to pay."

"Prepare for maneuvering. All hands, prepare for maneuvering!" Chris called over the comm. So grabbing on to the cable, I carefully put my helmet up against the side of the container and listened.

Now a cargo hold with a vacuum in it is a pretty quiet place; however, there were a lot of mechanical noises that the _Iowa Hill_ made while it was underway. Sounds from the reactor cooling pumps, environmental fans, water pumps, sewage pumps, the hums from power transformers—a hundred different things. But as the ship's engineer, I knew them all. I listened to them every night when I lay in bed, and sometimes in the silence of a solo shift down in Engineering.

Noises were coming from the container. There were things moving inside and I even thought I heard a muttered voice or two. Pulling my helmet away from it, I walked carefully over to Kei as the maneuvering of the ship made it feel like the deck was rolling under my feet.

"I want you to bring all the explosives you've got up here—now," I said after I touched my helmet to hers.

"But I don't have any—"

"Kei?"

"Yes, boss?"

"I'm not asking, I'm ordering."

"Umm, actually, Yuri's the one who smuggled them onboard."

"I didn't need to know that. Now grab her and go."

I pointed to Chaz and motioned him to stay here and keep an eye on things, then beckoned to Hank to follow me through the air lock to the forward section of the ship where we all lived.

"What's the plan?" Hanks asked as soon as we got into atmosphere and could take off our helmets.

"I sent the girls to fetch their explosives. With the front of that facing the cargo doors, I figure we put a shaped charge on the back of it, and if worse comes to worst, we blow everyone in the container out into space."

Hank nodded slowly. "That'd work if they're pirates. But what if they're just a bunch of folks who they're trying to smuggle into Mars—or worse yet, people who they're just trying to keep on ice for a while because they stole their ships? They could even be workers who are trying to break their contracts."

I bit my lip as I thought about that.

"It's possible. But when he handed me that bag full of cash I got the distinct feeling that he was expecting to get it back."

"I'm not all that big on cold-blooded murder, Dave," Hank said, looking me in the eye.

I sighed. "Yeah, you got a point. I don't want to be that guy anymore either. Suggestions?"

"There's a couple of paddocks on the stern of the ship. We go into free fall, move the container out of the hold and tow it behind us, about twenty meters. Slap a couple of transducers on the sides and we ask them who they are and what they're up to."

"And then what?"

"We call the Mars Navy and tell 'em what's up, and ask for them to come take them off our hands, that's what."

"We're thirty days out, Hank."

"They run patrols out past Jupiter, Dave. We'd probably have someone here in a week, if not less. They're in warships. They go a lot faster than we do."

"Point," I said, nodding. "But I still want to rig that thing so we can blow it if worse comes to worst."

"Agreed. How'd you know Yuri had explosives?"

"Actually, I thought Kei did. But let's be honest, Hank. You didn't hire them for their good looks."

"Actually I did."

"Huh? I though you weren't into women?"

Hank laughed. "A couple of hot young women showing as much skin as they like to walking around? Trust me, suddenly no one's looking for contraband and *everyone* stops and looks."

"I'd ask what you and Chaz are smuggling, but I don't think I want to know."

"It's not smuggling."

"Oh? It's not?"

"Nope, just creative resource relocation!" Hank said, grinning at me.

"I'll go tell Chris the plan, you go set it up."

"Don't mention the explosives."

"Why not?"

"I've noticed that captains tend to get a little twitchy about bombs onboard."

"Noted."

❖   ❖   ❖

Less than twenty minutes later, Chris came over the comms again.

"All hands, prepare for maneuvering! All hands, prepare for zero gravity!"

I was seated at the control panel for Engineering, with the seat belts holding me in place. As Chris cut our acceleration to zero, I started to dial back the reactors. While the twin SS12G Pressurized Water Reactors didn't have any issues with zero gravity, the lack of convection air currents around the hotter parts of the cooling systems could lead to other issues in the engineering spaces.

Setting one of the monitors to the outside starboard camera, I saw the warning lights on my console show that the starboard cargo hatch had unlocked. Using thrusters, Chris gently maneuvered us port-ward and the container, which was no longer secured to the deck, just stayed in place as we "floated" away from it.

Next, Hank and Chaz set up the tow cable. Chris had made it clear he only wanted one line between the container and the ship to prevent any oscillations that might occur due to uneven lines, as the *Iowa Hill* was not set up for towing. Apparently, Chris had some experience with these things from his mining-boat days before getting his captain certificates.

Once they had it all hooked up, he used the thrusters to slowly push us forward as the cargo bay door closed and was re-latched. Slowly taking up slack on the towline.

"Dave, I'm going to bring the gravity up first, then I'll start accelerating us slowly," Chris called down from the bridge. "Please bring the reactors back up to power."

"Aye-aye, Captain!" I called back and dialed the reactors to full power.

"All hands, secure from maneuvering," Chris called over the comms several minutes later after we were back to normal gravity.

"Captain, now that the ship's noise isn't interfering I'm starting to pick up some conversation," Paul, our first mate, replied over the command circuit. He was stationed currently in the ship's computer room, which was in the aft portion of the ship, on the other side of the cargo bay.

"What are they saying?"

"Well, they don't seem too happy. It's mostly men's voices, though I'm getting women's voices as well. Oh! They're ordering to gear up and take the ship!"

I switched to the aft camera on my display. This was likely going to become interesting.

"Captain, I think it might be best if we let them know they're no longer onboard the ship," Hank said. He was stationed with Paul right now, as was Yuri. It was their job to sever the tow cable if it became necessary.

"I concur. Paul, inform them of their situation."

I zoomed the camera in on the container. Chaz had rigged the sling so that when the tow cable was attached to it, the container was orientated such that the acceleration we were pulling would go through the "floor" of the container. This gave the people inside a tenth of a *g*, or gravity, inside due to our acceleration. He'd done this in case they had been innocents. He and Hank had agreed that it would be safer that way.

"I've informed them, Captain. I think they're trying to open the door."

"Make sure they know that they're now in a vacuum."

"Already told them, Captain."

There was a pause then before Chris, our captain, came back on the line.

"Katy just picked up an incoming ship that's overhauling us from behind. She makes it as moving at point-six gees."

"Point six? How big is it?" Hank commed.

"Hard to tell, our radar isn't the best back there. Best guess would put it at a hundred feet?"

"Why the second ship?" Paul asked.

"Probably has the replacement crew," Hank answered almost immediately.

"They're hailing us, demanding we heave to," Chris said next.

"I would suggest telling them we have the container with their buddies in it under tow," I interjected.

"Katy's doing so as we speak."

"Good. As the owner's representative, I would urge you to cut our towline."

"I concur. Bosun, sever our tow."

"On it, Captain," Hank replied.

I continued to watch the white container that was just twenty meters behind us, waiting for Hank to cut it loose.

"Hank, what's the delay?" I asked after several minutes had ticked by.

"I want to be sure they're close enough to see the container so they'll slow down to rescue their friends."

"Do you think they will?" I asked.

"I don't think they can take us without them, so I'm hoping yes."

"I see them," Yuri called out on the radio. Zooming the camera back from the container I saw them as well; they were slowing down to match speeds with us. It quickly resolved into something that looked like an ore boat, which would explain its speed as it was undoubtedly empty.

"Severing the line!" Hank reported and I saw the line whipping back toward the container as the tension came off it. We started accelerating away from it now that it was no longer attached to the ship.

"They're moving to rescue it," Yuri reported.

"Well, hopefully by the time they get everyone secured we'll be too far ahead for them to find us," Chris said.

"We'll see," Hank replied.

"Dave, how much more acceleration do you think you can wring out of our drives without causing any damage?"

"We can run at point two if I kill the gravity. We might make point three, but we can't do that for more than an hour or we'll start blowing panels," I told him as I watched the ship quickly moving over to the container, which was slowly tumbling from the force of the towline striking it.

I had to admit that the pilot was pretty good as I watched them match the yaw. The cargo bay slid open and then they just moved the ship up around the container. At the rate they were taking it onboard, we weren't going to be getting away from them, that was for sure. They'd probably have it tied down and be after us again in only a few minutes.

The doors had only just started closing when one end of the container lit up in a bright flash!

"What was that?" Chris exclaimed suddenly.

"Someone inside the container must have tried to blow the doors open," Hank replied. "I guess they weren't talking to their friends in the ship!"

I watched as a couple of larger explosions touched off inside the cargo bay and the entire ship started to tumble, suited bodies and body parts being ejected out of the now destroyed container and cargo bay.

The navigation lights all went dead suddenly and the cockpit windows went dark.

"Guess we won't have to worry about them following us after all, Captain," I said.

"Should we do something?" Paul asked.

"They're pirates. Not our problem," Chris replied. "We'll record the location and the trajectories, and we'll turn that over to the Mars Navy when we get there."

"I wonder what caused it to blow up?" Nick asked over my shoulder.

I shrugged. I hadn't told Chris about the explosives I'd had Hank rig, and I didn't see any reason to tell him now. I was just happy that the transmitter had enough range to set them off.

I tracked Hank down the next day as we continued on our way to Mars, having settled down into our normal routine.

"How much explosives did Yuri put on the back of that thing?"

"Not that much, actually. But they must have had their oxygen bottles, plus who knows what else, mounted back there. Those old ore boats aren't armored on the inside so I'm guessing we just got lucky with those secondary explosions."

I nodded. "Yeah, we were lucky, alright. I just wonder: were they after us because of what happened the last time we were here, or because of some other reason?"

Hank shrugged. "I don't think they're tied into the VMC, if that's what you're thinking. But we have brought in a couple of rich cargoes."

"So just garden variety pirates?"

"Considering that the folks in charge of the station had to be in on it, I'm not so sure they were of the 'garden variety,'" Hank said with a shake of his head.

"So what do we do about it?"

"Other than telling all of the proper authorities, I'm not sure how much we *can* do about it."

"Well, I'm going to make sure that Paul lets our friends know all about it the next time we see them. They've got the people to look into it. But, I have to ask: Do we need to lay in some weapons?"

"I'm not sure that's the answer here, Dave."

"Then what is? I'm not so sure this group would have given us a chance to abandon ship. *That's* what's worrying me. If we lose the ship, well, we've got insurance and while it'd hurt, we'd all still be alive."

"Yeah, I hear you on that. The only thing I can think of is maybe we need to change the ship's name."

"Does that actually work?"

Hank chuckled and shrugged. "It might. It depends on if the ship is getting a reputation for carrying rich cargoes."

I bit my lip and shook my head. "I need to talk to Kacey when we get back. We need to start being careful about what we're off-loading."

"We also need to pick our ports of call with a bit more care. But look on the bright side."

"There's a bright side?"

"Sure there is! The odds of a ship being hit by pirates is something like one in a hundred thousand and now that we've been hit twice, we should be safe for a good long time!" Hank replied, grinning at me.

I gave him a look that made it clear I didn't think that was funny.

"The first time was a setup, Hank, that didn't count."

"This time was a setup as well. Piracy usually is. The odds of successfully finding a ship this far out from the sun at random with something worth stealing are almost zero. Even with the advanced search-and-tracking radar on most warships it's still pretty hard to find someone if you haven't got an idea of where they are."

"So how do they find you, then?"

"Usually by following you out of port, outside our own ship's radar range, which on most cargo ships isn't made to look that far behind us. Or they sneak on a beacon, bribe a crew member, or even do what this last bunch did and smuggle a team onboard."

"And people fall for that?" I asked, surprised.

"Go ask Chris or Emil if they would have thought there were people onboard that container before you raised their suspicions. Honestly, if we'd taken on a load there, they probably would have just swapped that container with another and we'd have been none the wiser."

I nodded and thought about that. I also realized suddenly that the bag we'd gotten that money in hadn't been normal looking at all.

"I need to go look into something. I also think I should talk to Chris about lifeboat drills. Oh, and make sure Yuri gets paid back for whatever she used. We can take it out of the money they gave us."

"What are you going to do with that, anyway?"

"Give you and the rest of the deck crew a bonus. I think you all earned it."

"Don't forget Emil."

"I won't."

TWO

Iowa Hill—Mars Space

I SWUNG MY LEGS OFF THE BED IN THE CHIEF ENGINEER'S CABIN and put them on the floor as I sat up and yawned. Reaching over, I hit the cancel on the alarm before it could go off and looked up at the repeater on the wall. The two Siz-gees were looking well within specs. Same for the three gravity generators, two of which were two-twenties, the third one being a fifteen hundred.

I ran down all the other systems with a look. Everything was well within bounds, or "all systems nominal" as I've been told they used to say. Looking back at the bed, the other half of which was empty, I sighed and got up to put on my shipsuit. I'd hit the fresher later; for now, I needed a cup of caffeine and some food.

Stepping out of my quarters, I saw Kei was walking down the passageway wearing nothing other than a pair of panties and a camisole that barely went past her chest.

"Kei, I thought I told you not to walk around half naked?" I said with a sigh while shaking my head.

"Sorry, Dave! Just making a quick trip to the bathroom."

"Head, it's called a head shipboard."

"Why?"

"Look, just don't go walking around the ship like that. If Emil saw you, well, I don't think she'd take it all that well."

17

Kei snorted. "She's got Chris, what's she worried about? Plus it's not like she comes down here. So why?"

"May I remind you just who it is that prepares your food? As for coming down here, with Kacey having to stay back home to finish college, Emil's now the quartermaster as well. So she'll be down here."

"No, I mean why's it called a head?"

"Ask Hank, I sure as hell don't know." I sighed again and watched as she shrugged and bounced off for her room, red hair and all. I wondered if she would have put on that show if Kacey were onboard.

"Probably," I snorted softly to myself. Kei and Yuri could be incredibly clueless at times and I still wasn't sure just how much of the dunce act was actually an act. So far, I'd only had to bail them out once, back on Ceres. Thankfully, that little problem at the Lassell Orbital hadn't landed them in jail. It wasn't that they started trouble, it was just that they acted so clueless at times that trouble seemed to find them, and when it did, they were more than happy to beat it into the ground.

I sighed yet again as I made my way up to the top deck. Hank hadn't been able to stop laughing when he dragged me down to the police station to bail them out. Apparently they only *looked* harmless. Which of course had been very helpful when Judge Pimm took one look at them and threw the whole case out of court.

"Morning, Dave," Emil said as I came over to the counter and took the tray of food she handed me.

"Morning," I said and then went and sat by Chris.

"Morning, Dave."

"Morning. When are we landing?"

"Deimos Control has us set up for a sixteen hundred approach into Vance Spaceport."

I nodded and looked back over at Emil. "Has the buyer for our shipment been contacted?"

"Yup. We should be off-loaded within twenty-four hours of landing. But our outbound cargo is going to take a couple days to be delivered and stowed."

I nodded again and started in on my breakfast. This was the last big cargo that we'd be taking to Marcus's people. After we'd delivered this one to the *Astro Gerlitz,* they'd load us up with the last of the ore they had warehoused and then we wouldn't be seeing them again for a year.

So it'd be back to Ceres and I'd get to see Kacey, whom I hadn't seen in over six months. I was very much looking forward to being with my wife again.

"That's fine," I told her. "I think everyone could use a little leave."

"I thought we were going to wait until we got back home for that?"

I shook my head. "I have a meeting with my grandfather, who's due to show up a few days after we land. So we'll probably be in port at least five days."

"When did you find out?" she asked with a scowl.

"Last night, before I went to bed, as we were going by one of the traffic control relays." I sighed, shaking my head.

"I thought those weren't for personal messages?"

"When you've got more money than god and hold the note on the solar system, apparently exceptions can be made."

Emil snorted. "Well, I guess I can't complain, then. I can spend the time looking to see if I can land any high-value cargoes for Ceres while we're waiting."

"Any idea what your grandfather wants to talk about?" Chris asked.

"Probably wants to know if Ben's uncovered the secrets of the universe yet," I said with a wry grin. "I mean, it's been six months! Surely we must be ready to go to production already!"

Chris laughed. "Well, even if he *has* figured it all out, we haven't been home to find out in all that time."

"I need to set Nick up for his Engineer Fourth exam, as long as we're going to be there a while," I said between bites. "He's got the time in now. Hell, he's halfway to third on the hours."

"That's what, three thousand total?"

"For third? Yeah. He's well past two now."

"You gonna stop shipping with us once he gets his engineer third?" Emil asked as Hank and Chaz came into the mess.

I shook my head. "No, but I need to start studying for *my* next cert. As that's a big one, I need someone I can push a lot of my duties off to, so I'll have more time to study."

"When are you up for Engineer Second?" Hank asked as Emil started serving him and Chaz.

"I've got about five hundred more hours and two and a half more years in grade before I can sit for it."

"Gonna hit Marcus up for more crew?" Chaz asked as Hank moved off to the other table and Emil served him.

I shrugged. "No idea. This is the only ship that his people are going to do business with, so maybe when Kacey gets us another ship and I move to set that one up? I mean if he offers I'll probably take him up on it. Why? Do you know something I don't know?"

Chaz laughed and taking his food went to join Hank. "If I know my sister, she's probably halfway through negotiations on another freighter already."

"Ugh, that reminds me, I need to get my fusion reactor cert upgraded too."

"What for?"

"Because the cert I've got is only good for APUs, not the big ones. At least it's not that big a test."

"No, I mean why do you need it?"

"In case the next ship has 'em, of course."

We spent the next few minutes discussing the advantages of swapping out fission pressure vessel reactors for the new fusion ones, even one of the older used military fusion reactors. Hank, being former Mars Navy, had more experience with those than the fission ones we had on board.

After finishing up breakfast, I hit the fresher and got cleaned up. Going into Engineering, I started on the process of preparing us for landing. Mars had a weaker gravity than Earth did; it was a bit more than a third of Earth's, so the ship wouldn't be under as much of a strain as when we'd landed there. But even with that I'd still advised Chris to play it safe when we landed the last time we'd been here. Point-three-seven gee was still a lot when you considered what we normally dealt with and the ship was old, so why take chances?

Six hours later, we were down, the cargo doors were open, and unloading had begun. I sent Nick off to take his test, and spent the next several hours doing paperwork up in the mess with Chris.

"Ah, the glamour of being a ship owner and chief engineer." I sighed as I finished the last of my paperwork. "How's Emil doing on the unloading?"

Chris looked at his tablet. "They've got almost half the mid-deck cleared. So if there's no problems, we should be empty in about twenty more hours."

"I can take the second watch if you want to grab her and the others and go into town for dinner."

"Sure, that'll work. But first we need to get Hank and head over to port operations."

I frowned. "What for?"

"Remember those pirates we dealt with?" Chris asked, looking up at me from his tablet.

"Oh. Right."

"You have to be the only person I know who'd forget about a pirate attack," Chris said with a bemused snort.

"In all fairness, that was almost four weeks ago."

"Uh-huh. Well, let me send in our declarations and customs forms and then we can see about getting a ride over there."

I hit SEND on my tablet and got up from the table.

"I'll meet you outside," I told him. "I just need to put on some better shoes and grab my airmask."

"Grab your parka too. I think it's winter outside now."

"Oh?"

"From the number of complaints about the cold Emil keeps sending me? Has to be!"

I laughed and went down to my quarters to get my things.

When we got to the operations center for the spaceport, we were quickly shown into a conference room with three Mars Navy members in it. All of whom immediately jumped to their feet and saluted.

Hank returned their salute with a smile and the senior one of the three spoke up before any of us could say anything.

"I'm Chief Petty Officer Owens. These are Petty Officer McNurtle, and Petty Officer Williams."

We all nodded hello.

"Now, we'll be breaking you up into three different rooms for the interview. We've reviewed the report as well as the videos you sent us. I'll be talking with Bosun Smith, McNurtle will interview you, Captain Doyle, and Williams will be interviewing you, Engineer Doyle."

"That will be fine," Chris said and he followed McNurtle out as

I followed Williams. If I was reading the rank right, Williams and McNurtle were third class and I was a bit surprised that Owens, being senior, didn't take Chris, as Chris was the captain. Then again, Hank was former Mars Navy, so that probably explained it.

Petty Officer Williams guided me to a seat as we walked into a small office.

"Do you have any problems with this interview being recorded?" she asked.

I shook my head. "Not a one."

"Okay, this is Petty Officer Williams interviewing Engineer Third Class David Doyle, acting chief engineer on the cargo ship *Iowa Hill*."

"I'm also part owner," I added.

"I'll make a note of that," she said with a smile. "Now, please start by recounting what happened in your own words."

I nodded and did just that, not leaving anything out. When I got to the part about the explosives she stopped me.

"Engineer Doyle, are you saying that you are the one that ordered the mining of the container with explosives?"

I nodded. "Yes, that was me. Please don't tell the captain. The bosun and I both agreed that he didn't need to know that."

"Bosun Smith?"

"Yes."

"As owner and chief engineer you outrank the bosun."

"Hank's got a lot more experience sailing than I do, plus he's former Mars Navy. You don't ignore advice from a man with that kind of experience."

Petty Officer Williams laughed at that. "No, sir. You don't. Was it your plan from the beginning to set off the charges?"

"Actually, no. Hank advised that we needed to be positive about just who and what was inside that container before we took any deadly action. In fact, it was his suggestion that we put it under tow, and question the people inside remotely."

"And after that?"

"Contact the Mars Navy once we knew what was going on and let you guys deal with it. Honestly, once we had them off the ship I thought the problem was dealt with."

She nodded and made a few notes on the tablet she'd put on the desk.

"Please, continue."

I did so and when we got to the point where the container exploded she stopped me again.

"Did you give the order to detonate the explosives once the pirate boat had taken the container onboard?"

I shook my head. "No. I'd forgotten about them at that point and was discussing with the captain just how much acceleration we'd be able to get out of the ship in our attempt to get away from them."

"Do you have any idea as to *why* they decided to try and hijack your ship?"

"No," I said, shaking my head again. "It could be they were mad at us because the last time we'd been in port, three months earlier, one of the dockworkers put his hands on one of my crew and she beat him into the deck. Or it could be because we brought in two premium cargoes and they wanted to know where we were getting them from."

"Could it have been because of who your grandfather is?"

I looked at her wide-eyed. "Excuse me?"

"Your grandfather Alistair Morgan is the head of the Morgan family, is he not?"

"Umm, yeah, he is," I said, still a bit shocked that she knew that. "I'm just surprised that you knew that. Hell, I'm surprised that *anyone* knows that!"

"Our records are rather thorough, Engineer Doyle. Also there was a bit of a stir in the gossip columns over what happened on the Earth's Moon, as well as what happened with your brother."

"Great," I sighed, shaking my head.

"People on Earth do love their gossip, especially when it involves the elites and one of their black sheep."

"Did they mention I changed my last name?" I asked, just a little bit worried.

"No, but your picture did make the rounds."

"Well, that's a relief. But honestly, if they'd been looking to grab me, I would have expected them to do it on the docks. Whoever sent that ship after us obviously has a lot of power back there."

"Why would you say that?"

"Because they forced us to take that container. They weren't going to open the hanger doors and let us leave until we took that container."

"The report says that they claimed it was an emergency and that you had to take it under maritime laws."

I snorted. "Then why didn't they contact our head office? If we'd been docked outside I would have told the captain to disengage and leave, assuming he didn't decide to do that on his own. I'm not a very trusting man, Petty Officer Williams."

"Well, after reviewing your records I can understand that."

She asked me a few more questions then, about what, if anything else, I'd observed. I had, rather pointedly, left out the part about the bag the money had come in. Also the money itself. I'd been rather surprised to find that the bag *had* contained a low-powered beacon sewn into the lining. Which I'd dismantled after learning how it worked. From that point forward I'd added a few procedures to the ship's standing orders to scan all those beacon frequencies when leaving port to avoid any such plants in the future.

The interview over, I was escorted out to the main room, where I found Chris, and we both waited another half hour or so until all three of the petty officers escorted Hank out, shook hands, saluted, and then went back into their office.

"Old friend?" I asked Hank as he joined us. The chief petty officer had seemed rather happy when he'd left.

"Eh, just recounting a few stories and swapping lies, an old bosun's tradition."

"Well, let's see if we can cage a ride back to the ship," I said and motioned toward the doors.

"Already done."

"Lead on!" I said with a smile and as Chris and I followed Hank out of the building I noticed that Chris was giving Hank a thoughtful look. I'd have to ask him about that later; for now, I got out my tablet and started reviewing off-loading procedures. If I was going to be taking over the off-load watch, I wanted to be sure I didn't make any stupid mistakes. Usually Emil, Hank, or Chaz handled the off-loads. But if I was going to cut them all loose for dinner, then as both the chief engineer as well as an owner I could legally supervise. Not that there was typically much supervision that was needed.

Six hours later and I was just standing around and watching as each container came off, making a note of the ID tag on the side and getting a picture of it with my tablet so it got entered on the manifest as "unloaded." As jobs went it was boring.

And I was enjoying every last minute of being bored.

The last two years had been pretty hectic at times—true, maybe not as crazy when I was a dumbass thirteen-year-old with the world's biggest chip on my shoulder and a complete lack of morals, ethics, or any other guiding principles beyond what my fellow gang-bangers believed in.

But back then I was immortal and untouchable. The first due to the ignorance of teenagers everywhere. The second due to a mistake of birth that had left me with a lot of baggage to unpack.

Now? Now I had a wife, a company, a decent job, and a grandfather who not only had more money than God, but who apparently liked me.

I think that last bit was a lot harder to come to terms with than everything else that had happened—but at least I could ignore it and pretend it didn't exist. Or I'd thought I could. In a few days I'd have to sit down with my grandfather and talk about whoever the hell knows what. I know he had plans. Hell, *I* had plans! But just what those plans were, I had no idea. I'm sure he was banking on my stepbrother, Ben having cracked the problem of the century, the one everybody had been trying to solve. I'm sure Ben was hoping he could crack it too.

Me? Other than wanting to see my brother be successful because I knew it'd make him happy, I didn't care. Faster-than-light travel didn't matter to me. Seeing new worlds, new star systems? None of that mattered. I hadn't gotten Ben off Earth so he could make himself famous, or our family rich—I'd done it because he'd asked me to. Because he was my brother and he wanted to go into space. Because he'd helped *me* get into space.

"Dave! Dave Walker!" someone called out. Turning, I noticed that there were two people, a guy and a gal, on the platform that the unloading crew used to get up into the cargo bay. One of the shortcomings of the old Argon-class ships is that you have to go through the ship to get to the cargo bay, and with the change in intra-solar customs laws, nobody allowed folks to use that access anymore.

"Who are you and what do you want?" I asked, putting my right hand in the hip pocket of my shipsuit, the one where I had my pistol.

"Hi! I'm Chet Huntley from Mars One News and we were wondering if we could interview you?"

That was when I noticed the gal had a camera and it was pointed at me.

"First off, I'm not Dave Walker. Second, *no!* Now, get off the ship and get out of here. You're not cleared to be in this area during cargo operations. This is a restricted area and you could get somebody hurt."

"Surely you could spare us a few minutes, Mr. Walker!" the guy replied.

I walked over to the edge of the bay and flagged the foreman. "Call the police!" I yelled when he looked up at me. "These folks are trespassing!" He nodded and got out his phone. I turned back to Chet. "My name isn't Walker. Now, get out of here, you're in the way."

With that I focused my attention on the unloading. The workers were slinging another container and I needed to get a picture of the barcode on it for the records.

"If you step off that platform onto my ship, I *will* arrest you, confiscate all of your gear, and destroy it," I warned as he opened the safety gate on the platform.

"You can't do that!"

"Can and will. Go check up on maritime law. This is a Ceres-registered ship and once you set foot on her, you're in Ceres's jurisdiction. Also, I already told you, my name *isn't* Walker. You're talking to the wrong man. Now, shoo!"

I was bluffing on the being able to arrest them bit. With the doors open that wasn't at all true. But I was hoping he didn't know that. The cameraman did grab his arm and she had some harsh words with him. So *she* at least believed me and didn't want to see her gear destroyed.

Smiling, I ignored them and went back to work. Next time I looked back there, the platform had been lowered, so it wasn't my problem anymore. When the shift change came, I went down and checked in with the foreman before he left.

"Who were those folks?" I asked after he got done talking with the supervisor for the next shift.

"Reporters," he said with a shrug. "Never seen 'em around here before, but I did recognize the guy."

"So he's really a reporter?"

He nodded and I just shook my head.

"So are you really Dave Walker?" he asked.

"Nope, Dave Doyle"—I pointed to the company logo we'd had painted on the side of the *Iowa Hill* when we'd registered the ship on Ceres—"of Doyle Shipping, of the Doyle clan on Ceres. Even says so on my engineer's certs."

He looked down at his tablet.

"Says so on the manifest as well. Guess they must have gotten their wires crossed."

"So any idea who this Walker guy is?" I asked out of a morbid sense of curiosity.

"Not a clue. You need to get back up top, looks like Jean's team is ready to start shipping containers," he said, motioning back up at the ship.

"Thanks," I said, giving him a nod, and headed back up to the cargo bay. I checked my watch: it was just a few minutes after midnight. I just hoped I didn't end up here until the end of this shift as well, but I did offer to give everyone some time off so I only had myself to blame.

THREE

Vance Spaceport, Mars

I STUMBLED INTO THE MESS ABOUT NOON. EMILIANA HAD RELIEVED me when she came on shift at eight. Paul and Katy Healy—our first and second mates, respectively—were there.

"Did you really stay up all night supervising the unloading?" Paul asked with a laugh as his wife, Katy, took pity on me and went behind the counter to start making me lunch.

"I thought you might all want a night off after the last three months," I said and yawned, looking around for a clean mug so I could get some coffee.

"You could have called me or Kat to come down and take over you know."

"You're both certi..." I started and then face-palmed—making sure not to use the hand now holding the mug. Of course they were certified. They were the first and second mates onboard.

Kat laughed as she popped something in the micro to warm it up. Knowing Emiliana, she'd put something together for lunch, after making everyone breakfast and going off to relieve me.

"You forgot, didn't you?" she said accusingly, and still laughing.

"In my defense, when I started out on this ship, we had a much smaller crew," I muttered as I went over to the large urn of coffee that was bolted to its own special table.

"Any problems?" Paul asked.

I shook my head as I filled my cup. "Other than some journo who wanted to interview Dave Walker, nope."

"Oh? What'd you tell them?" Katy asked.

"That my name wasn't Walker and no one by that name worked here."

"And they bought it?"

"That or the police got here before they left on their own," I said with a shrug and added some nondairy-type creamer and sugar to my coffee. I never could drink it black.

Kat looked over as I did that and made a face.

"I'm weak, don't judge me," I grumbled as the microwave beeped. She got out my lunch and passed it across the counter to me. Grabbing it, I navigated my way over to the table and sat down. "So how was last night?"

"It was nice. Hank took us to one of his favorite places. The food was good, not too crowded, and when we hit the adjoining bar afterward a bunch of his friends and former Navy shipmates dropped by and they all told outrageous stories about each other." Paul shrugged as Katy sat back down next to him. "The usual."

"And Yuri and Kei stayed out of trouble?"

Katy snorted. "I think they both realized that these were not the kinds of people you want to start anything with. Not that any of Hank's friends were anything but friendly. When he tried to set up a knife-throwing contest between Yuri and one of them, they laughed and said they'd rather hold onto their money."

"Just as long as I don't have to bail anyone out of jail," I said and started in on my lunch.

"Oh, that's the captain's job; I wouldn't worry about that none!" Katy said with a laugh.

"The last time Kei and Yuri got in trouble he told me that 'you hired them, so you get to bail them out.'"

"Why'd he do a thing like that?"

"Because the judge is Chris's uncle," Chaz said, coming into the mess, "and would have definitely fined him for it."

"He didn't tell me that," I complained.

"Probably figured you already knew. Anyway, Emil just told me that they should be done and have everything locked up in an hour. Chris is gonna cut us all loose for leave not too much longer after that. So go hit the shower and get dressed. I got Hank to offer to take sightseeing whoever wants to go."

"Sure beats sitting here on the ship," I said and looked over at Paul and Katy, who both nodded.

"We're in," Paul said.

"Great. I'll let Hank know," Chaz said and headed out of the mess in the direction of the cargo deck.

"Anything I need to know about Mars before we head out?" I asked Paul.

"Beats me, this is our first time taking leave here as well. Just keep an eye out for the gravity transition warnings."

"What're those?"

"Most of the buildings have grav panels set for standard 'g.' I think inside the city proper they have those in a lot of places outside as well. But once you get away from that, everything outside is Mars normal, so they have these transition pads you walk across so you don't just cross a hard line."

"I'll be sure to remember that," I said as I quickly finished my lunch. Then I headed down to the bottom deck to get my stuff and hit the shower. I still had that hat Dot, the *Iowa Hill*'s previous chief engineer, had made me a few years back, though I hadn't worn it since. I debated taking it with me, just in case there were people who wanted to talk to me and I didn't want to talk to them.

Then again, I had no idea why that journo had come around last night. Maybe they'd heard about the pirates? Whatever it was, there wasn't a stream of them trying to beat down the doors, so it was probably just a slow news day and somebody needed a story and the name "Walker" came up.

But in any case, with the sole exception of Kacey, every time someone had "taken an interest" in me, it hadn't been all that much fun. So when I finished with my shower, after I got dressed I grabbed the hat and put it on. Grabbing my airmask, I then headed to the air lock to wait for Hank and whomever else was going.

Nick showed up right after I got there, Kei and Yuri not long after. Paul, Katy, Chaz, and Hank all showed up together.

"Are Chris and Emil coming?" I asked.

"No, they've both been to Mars before and are meeting some friends later on," Chaz said. We all put our masks on and then cycled out through the lock.

The pressure outside was, of course, lower, hence the airmasks, which had small compressors in them to bring up the pressure and therefore the oxygen level, so you didn't pass out. You could also hook up a small bottle of oxygen and then it would function more like a rebreather, but they'd been terraforming Mars for enough centuries now that the free oxygen in the air was a lot closer to Earth normal. Add to that the massive solar structure that had been put in orbit directly between the Sun and Mars to cut down on the amount of solar wind, and other such things that had stripped away Mars's atmosphere in the past due to its lack of a magnetic field, and the atmosphere here was now dense enough that you could survive without a mask. It just wouldn't be all that enjoyable as most people tended to pass out.

A small van was waiting for us outside; Hank led us over to it and we all got inside. I sat up front with the driver, Hank. Chaz and Nick sat behind me, with Paul and Katy in the next row, Yuri and Kei taking the last.

"I figured we'd start off with a driving tour of the city," Hank said. "I'll point out a few of the famous landmarks, then we'll hit the Founders' Museum, dinner, and whatever y'all feel like doing after that."

No one had any problems with that and so off we went.

To be honest, being a tourist was a nice change of pace for me. Earth was supposedly full of sights to see and places to go, but as a prole I'd never been to any of them. The city itself was a bit unexpected. All the buildings had enclosed walkways connecting them at what was either the second or third story, so traffic could pass underneath without any issues.

"So you can get around without having to go outside?" I asked and motioned toward one of the walkways.

"If you don't mind walking. There's also a subway and tunnel network underneath the city that has a line all the way out to the spaceport. If we hadn't been able to borrow the van for the day, I would have just taken us in that way," Hank told me.

We drove by the town center then, where there were two obviously very old spaceships sitting on their landing gear, their noses pointed toward the open sky, a third one lying on its side: a partially crushed steel tube with the edges peeled outward at the bottom, signs of an obvious explosion.

"What's that?" I asked, pointing.

"That's Point Alpha, where the first rockets from Earth landed."

"And they're still here?" I asked, a little surprised.

"The crashed one hasn't moved since it suffered a gear failure on landing and tipped over, killing half the crew. The other two were moved here about a century ago from the breakers when the city council decided we needed some sort of reminder of how we got to where we are today."

"I wonder if those were built in Boca Chica," I said as I remembered where I'd seen that design before. There was a static display of one just outside the spaceport.

"Oh, right, your dad worked there, didn't he?"

"I went to college there too," I said giving the three ships a second look. "Kinda weird to be on the other side of things. I just can't imagine anybody actually crazy enough to want to actually *fly* in something like that."

"They are kinda small, aren't they," Chaz agreed.

"With chemical rockets," Katy added. "But desperate people will do desperate things, right?"

I had to snort at that. I knew all about desperate.

We ended up in a nice restaurant after the museum. The museum had been interesting—the people who lived here were obviously pretty proud of their history and, as a lot of the exhibits had shown, it wasn't an easy one. A lot of the early settlers died young.

"I got this," I told the others when the waitress brought out the check.

"You sure?" Paul asked.

"I'm sure Kacey will figure out a way to write it off, so yeah, I'm sure," I said with a smile and handed my card to the waitress, who smiled and ran off with it.

When she came back several minutes later she looked embarrassed.

"Don't tell me it didn't clear?" I asked her with a frown.

"Oh, no! It's not that, sir! I was wondering if I could get your autograph!"

And with that she set down a small case, the kind that was used to hold vid-cartridges. The title read *Walking Out* and under it there was a small picture that was obviously *me*. I even recognized where it was taken, when I was in court on the Moon.

"What the hell?" I said, looking at it, then I looked up at her. "Where'd you get that?"

"Don't you know?" she said, looking at me in surprise.

I shook my head.

"It's the big new docudrama that's selling all over Mars! It's all about how you outwitted the elites on Earth and smuggled your brother right out from under their noses!"

I closed my eyes for a moment. Somebody was going to die when I got my hands on them. I just didn't know *who*.

"Is it true you were captured by pirates and actually got away?"

I opened my eyes and looked at her. "I'm sure it was nothing at all like they said in the... whatever that is."

"So, will you?" she asked hopefully and offered me a marker.

Sighing, I took it and signed the case. She smiled brightly and then handed me the bill, which I also signed. I almost didn't tip her, but I figured Kacey would smack me one when she got the bill if I didn't.

"Is it really that popular?" Katy asked.

"We're not in it, are we?" Hank followed up.

"Yes, it's very popular. I think all of my friends have watched it! They didn't mention anyone else's names, though I'm sure that more than a few of us recognized you, Mr. Smith. But then I got your autograph when you came to my school, when you were still in the Navy!"

I noticed everyone looked at Hank then. Well, everyone but Chaz, who just looked insufferably pleased with himself.

"I think we need to leave before they all start queuing up to get Dave's autograph," Hank said, standing up.

"Yes, let's," I agreed and, pulling out my hat, I put it on while turning on the power.

"Where'd you get that?" Katy asked, looking at me as we headed out. "It definitely makes you look different."

"Friend of mine made it back when I was having *other* problems," I told her.

"So, going to buy a copy?" Chaz asked with a grin.

"No. And if you buy one, I don't want to see it or even know what's in it."

"How bad can it be?" Nick asked.

"Very," Hank said. "Trust me on that."

"Well, whoever did it must have liked you," Paul pointed out, "otherwise they wouldn't be looking for your signature."

"There is that," I agreed. "And now I know why that reporter showed up last night while we were off-loading."

"So what are our plans for the next few days?" Paul asked.

"That depends on when my grandfather gets here, and what he wants." I sighed. "Also if Emil finds any extra cargoes that'll be worth bringing back to Ceres."

"So we've got leave until then?"

"Until my grandfather shows up. Once he's here, I want everyone to be ready to leave as soon as I'm done meeting with him. We *do* have a schedule to keep."

"Got it."

The rest of the trip back to the *Iowa Hill* was mostly the others talking about what they'd seen at the museum and in town. I was more focused on what, if any, problems this new documentary would be bringing me, and if it was just popular on Mars, or if it was popular everywhere.

As much as I hated to, I just might have to ask my grandfather to look into it. Probably Marcus's people too. If I got too famous, I'd be risking *their* secrecy as well.

I was thinking about that, when I suddenly noticed Hank was also being quiet. While Hank wasn't exactly boisterous, when there was a group chat going on he was usually a part of it and I could see that Chaz was pretty much "covering" for him. As much as I would have liked to ignore it, Hank worked for *me* and I'd learned enough about leadership to know that sometimes you had to have a talk with somebody.

When we got back to the ship, I put my hand on Hank's arm as everyone started heading inside. He looked at me and I gave a nod to the side.

"Go on up, Chaz, I'll be there in a few," Hank said, when Chaz got to the ship's ladder and looked back at him.

"Sure thing, Hank."

"So what's up, Dave?" Hank asked after everyone had gone back aboard as I checked my mask.

"Let's go for a walk."

"Oh, one of *those* talks, is it?" Hank asked with a wry grin.

"Hey, I'm the boss now, which means I get to do all the fun stuff." I sighed. "So, want to talk about it?"

"You're sure there's something to talk about, aren't you?"

"I got *that* impression when I saw the look Chris gave you when all of those Mars Navy NCOs saluted you. But I didn't feel it was any of my business."

"But now it is?"

"Hank, the only reason no one else noticed you were brooding on the way back to the ship was because Chaz was talking enough for the two of you. Now if you don't want to talk about it, that's fine, but this is one of those things where I *know* I have to make the offer, because you work for me and this ain't just a job, this is family, *you're* family, and family takes the time to listen when there's something that needs to be said."

"One of the reasons I left Mars is because I'm famous here."

"Yeah, our server kinda gave that away."

"I'd kinda hoped that it'd die down after a few years. Apparently it hasn't."

We walked another minute before he continued.

"About nine years ago, I was serving on a small frigate. Honestly, it was so small it barely qualified for that title. We only had one officer, he was a jaygee—experienced, though, knew his stuff. We were doing an anti-pirate patrol as part of a larger group. Mars Navy has these 'fleet carriers' as they like to call 'em. They can haul about twenty of these small frigates and we'll string out to cover a really large area. We got some weapons, one hell of a detection suite, and we're all trained in ship boarding and fighting.

"The idea is, we find something and we either track it, board it, or cripple it, while the rest of the fleet comes out and gives us support. It's a fairly effective tactic when you consider the sheer vastness of space.

"Well, we were out of the outside wing of one of the arms of the string when we encountered something *sketchy*. So we turned and burned for it, fired off a notice to the next ship in line to be passed back to fleet." Hank paused a moment. "Oh yeah, it was *sketchy*, alright. We hit a lash-up."

"What's a lash-up?" I asked.

"A point in space where a group of pirates have decided to meet and trade stock, money, slaves, you name it. There were seven of them, and *one* of us. Help was ten or twenty minutes behind us when seconds counted.

"They attacked us immediately—those that could, of course. It takes time for the ships to unlock from each other and most of them were lying their with their power down to mins and the engines cool so they didn't stand out to the deep space sensors on the cruisers.

"So we're in it with two of them immediately and we were slugging it out. A couple of the ships were big enough that we were worried they were slavers, so we couldn't just paste 'em, and almost *all* of them are firing on us. We tagged one of the two pretty good; the other one, however, was holding its own. By this point, our own grav drives are damaged and we're using thrusters and everything else to keep it moving.

"And the captain, our jaygee, tells me to ram the other ship."

I blinked. "You can do that?"

"Yup. I got them amidships, right in their cargo bay, and he orders all hands to board, we're taking the ship." Hank shook his head, "Lieutenant Geuirmo was something else. It took us probably five minutes to kill everyone on the pirate ship, but it felt like an eternity. Geuirmo ordered me to take the conn, and ram another ship so we could board that one. He did that before we'd even finished securing the one we were on.

"Well, by the time I rammed the second ship, the lieutenant was dead; I hadn't even realized he was wounded when he'd ordered me on. Enough other men were dead or wounded that I was now the senior NCO."

"What'd you do?"

"Followed orders. We took *that* ship, and using that one I rammed *another* ship. We got that one in the drives, so we didn't bother boarding it, plus the one we were on was still moving, so I aimed for the biggest one there, figuring if there were any slaves on any of the ships, that was the one, and I rammed it in the lifeboat bays.

"The fighting on that one was particularly vicious. Turns out there were a *lot* of slaves on board. It was the 'pirate chief's' boat and it had most of the loot, and the best fighters of the lot of them. We were down to thirteen effectives and I have no idea how many were dead or seriously wounded when we finally won that battle, and all of us were wounded. I ran to the cockpit, radioed the other big ship that we'd killed those Marsie bastards but we needed help, we needed to transfer the gold and the slaves before the rest of the Navy got there—and those bastards fell for it, and warped right up to us and docked."

Hank was quiet then for the next several minutes.

"Six of us survived. Just six out of a crew of forty-one. We were all wounded, but not a single one of those slaving bastards got away. We all got medals. We all got a *lot* of medals. But I was the one who was leading us and of the ones that stormed that last pirate ship, I was the only one left alive. So I got the Mars Medal of Honor and one hell of a lot of publicity.

"I didn't mind at first, because it helped everyone to remember the rest of our crew, to know what they'd died for. It also helped recruitment. Battles like that are rare these days and we did free almost a hundred slaves, mostly women. All of whom had suffered horribly. So yeah, I didn't mind at first. I wanted to get more sailors out there to find and kill all of those scum." Hank lifted his mask away for a moment to spit on the ground. "But eventually? I just wanted to go back to being me. Just a bosun who did his job, went out drinking with his buds, and told outrageous lies with his friends about what he'd been doing.

"But once you're famous, once they've all but made you into an icon, you can't do that anymore."

I nodded. "You got a documentary too, didn't you?"

"Worse. We all wore cameras when we did 'boarding actions.' I'm in a dozen training films, along with the rest of the crew, as an example of just what a motivated sailor can do when facing overwhelming odds."

I laughed, I couldn't help it, and Hank just shook his head and snorted.

"The hero-worship thing, I guess, was what finally got me to take a 'leave of absence' and start sailing all the lanes again."

"Leave of absence?" I asked.

"Medal of Honor holders in the Mars Navy are never considered 'retired' or 'separated.' You're on the active duty roster until the day you die and you can call on your rank as necessary."

"So they could call you back to duty?"

He shook his head. "I fulfilled my obligation years ago. But if I showed up in uniform? They'd put me right back to work."

I thought about that a moment, then I had a realization.

"That's why they'll come if we call for them, isn't it? Because you're on the crew?"

"I'd have to be the one making the call, but yeah, that. If you called with a pirate problem, they'll come if they can. If I call? They'll come. Because they're all hoping that there'll be a fight."

"Miss it?"

"Used to, not so much anymore, though."

"Why not?"

Hank turned and I could see the smile on his face through the mask. "Because one of these days there's going to be a big-ass war with the Venusian Moral Collective and I'm gonna be able to brag about how I was helpin' the 'Let Bees' and was already a part of it before all those Johnny-come-latelies came on board."

"You really think it'll come to that?" I asked, a little concerned.

"Bet money on it. Sooner or later they're going to need a new monster to keep the people in line. Marcus and his people are disappearing. There's less and less of them for the VMC to find every year. Even if they find out where they all ran to, it's too far away to carry on the fight. The only question is, who will they turn their eye to next?"

"Earth?"

Hank shook his head. "Not at first—Earth's too big and Mars is too strong. They'll probably start with some of the asteroid groups that have moved inside Earth's orbit. But, yeah, sooner or later they're going to decide that their particular brand of crazy will work with all of those dolers back on Earth, and that's when things will get nasty."

"Let's go back to the ship," I said, and thought about that. I wondered if my grandfather knew. I'd be surprised if he didn't. But it just might be worth bringing up when we met.

"Compared to Earth, Venus is pretty small, population-wise. Do you really think they'd try it?" I asked when we finally got back to the *Iowa Hill*.

"Study Earth history. It's been tried before. More than once. The scary part is how far they often get and how many people die before they finally get beaten back."

"Guess I shouldn't be surprised," I said with a sigh.

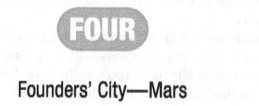

FOUR

Founders' City—Mars

"GRANDFATHER," I SAID, WALKING INTO THE PRIVATE ROOM.

"David." He smiled and stood, sticking out his hand. I shook hands and then figured *why not?* and gave him a hug.

"Well, *this* is a surprise, Grandson."

"The Doyle clan is very demonstrative and, well, maybe we need a bit more of that ourselves."

"Something on your mind, then?"

"Someone pointed out to me that sooner or later the VMC are going to invade Earth."

His grandfather sighed as he sat back down. "Nice to know there are other people who feel the same way."

"The doles are ripe for them, aren't they?"

"Not quite, but if we don't watch out, they will be. Still, I'm surprised you care, seeing as you've put that all behind you."

"More like I'm worried that if they got Earth, who would be next."

"Ah!" His grandfather said with a laugh. "A much more understandable sentiment! But now perhaps you understand why there are many of us who are willing to help your friends and look the other way when others do so."

"They paid you rather handsomely for that help, I might point out."

41

"Yes, they did. But we *could* have sold it to any number of other groups, including those wonderful people at the VMC for twice as much."

"Why would the VMC need something like that?"

"Because they've focused all their efforts on shipbuilding—so much so that their own defenses have become neglected. Also, with the loss of some of their most talented people, their technology is no longer on par with that of Earth's."

"Well, I guess that's a relief. So, why did you want to meet, Grandfather?"

"Because you're a family member and I need to be *seen* keeping in touch with you so others will keep that in mind. Also, because I do enjoy our times together, however brief they may be."

"Ah, so this isn't about Ben, then?" I asked with a scowl.

"It's been, what, six months? No, I won't start bugging you about him for at least another year. However, I did want to discuss business."

"Oh? What kind of business?"

"We need to start construction of a shipyard on Ceres, obviously."

"Ben hasn't even started his research yet! Isn't it a bit early to start building a shipyard?"

"It's a risk, I admit, David. But how long do you think it will take to construct it? Just *finding* a place on Ceres to do so will take months, if not years. Then there's the matter of construction, staffing, all of that. It could take your brother years, the rest of his life, I understand that, or he could have the answer next week."

I nodded slowly as he said that. It made sense.

"Still, what do I do with a shipyard until he *does* figure it out?"

"Oh, I don't know...build ships?" Grandfather said with a smile. "You're going to need to learn how that's done *now* with *current* technology before you can even start to understand how to use whatever it is that your brother comes up with."

"So why not just hire another shipyard to build our ships?"

"Because then they'll have access to the drives and they'll have all the knowledge of how to install them. They may even learn how to build them."

"I'm sure they'll figure out the drives soon enough," I pointed out.

"Maybe yes, maybe no. But every year we have a monopoly on their production is another year we are the only ones making money. It's another year where we are advancing our production methods and abilities. It means that when someone *else* finally figures it out, we'll still be able to produce them faster, cheaper, and with a higher level of quality than them.

"That's an edge that will take decades for other companies to catch up with. The only way to do so quickly would require large expenditures of capital that their board members probably won't be willing to make."

I nodded again. "I need to bring Kacey the next time we talk. She's the one that really understands business."

"I'll be looking forward to it. I also want to discuss using your ships to do some of our transportation and shipping."

"Why?"

"Because we don't own a shipping company, but as you're family we now have ties to yours. That means we can count on certain allowances and priorities in return for granting you certain exclusive rights."

"That's definitely something Kacey needs to discuss with you."

Grandfather chuckled at that. "I'll send the proposals with you, as well as the other agreements for the shipyards."

"This is definitely spiraling far beyond anything I ever expected."

"These are all the consequences of your freeing your brother Ben. If you weren't my grandson, other interests would be moving in and wanting to talk with you. Their offers would not be so generous either."

I didn't doubt that at all.

"Now, how about we order some dinner and talk about something other than business? Give that whole 'family' thing a try?"

I smiled at him. "I'd like that."

We were just finishing up dinner when Havier quickly came into the room and handed my grandfather a piece of paper.

"Oh, this isn't good," Grandfather said, looking up at me.

"What?"

"Ben was kidnapped several hours ago and smuggled aboard a ship that is taking him back to Earth."

"*What?!*" I said jumping to my feet. "Do you have an ID on the ship? Registration? Any of that?"

"Actually we do, it's a newer model General Ship Designs Xenon freighter, the *New Market*. It's on a least-time course to Earth, according to the note."

Walking over to my grandfather, I took the note and read it over.

"The Xenon class are about twice the size of the *Iowa Hill*," I said. "They're only point-one-gee ships, but if they're running empty they can probably get point three out of her." I looked up at my grandfather. "Just how fast is the ship you came here in?"

"The *Valkyrie*? It's a converted Earth Guard Navy destroyer."

"How old is it?"

"What? Do you really think your grandfather, a *Morgan*, would buy a used ship?" he said with a smile.

"Where's it parked?"

"Vance Spaceport, berth Zulu One-Five. Havier can show you where it is."

I hugged my grandfather. "Thank you. Hopefully this won't take long. Havier," I said, standing up, "please take me there."

Havier nodded and I followed him out of the room while pulling out my tablet. I buzzed Hank.

"What's up, Dave?"

"Grab my pressure suit, your suit, the girls, any and all weapons that you or they want to lug along. Meet me at Zulu One-Five. Someone kidnapped my brother and we're getting him back. Tell Chris he's gonna be here until we return. Make sure Paul knows the next shipment is going to be delayed a bit."

"On it!"

"You're not thinking of doing what I think you are, are you?" Havier asked as we went outside to a rather nice Martian land car.

"Oh no, this'll be a lot worse, I'm sure," I growled. "Any idea what house is behind this?"

"Why?"

"Because I thought we were done with this and I'm guessing it's time to send a message. A very loud message. Do you know if this ship has any weapons?"

Havier snorted. "It's your grandfather's—of course it has weapons. No missiles, though, and only one rail gun. The rest of the weapons are short-range lasers."

I nodded and, pulling my tablet back out, I looked at the current state of the planets. Thankfully, Mars wasn't in opposition to Ceres right now; however, Earth was definitely closer to it than we were.

The driver got us to my grandfather's ship in record time; I guess Havier had clued him in. I was too busy sending messages to Kacey and my father to pay much attention to that. When I got out, I saw that Hank was there already, along with Chaz—which surprised me. Kei and Yuri were both there and from the size of the gear bags they were hauling, I guess they'd brought *all* the goodies they owned.

"Let me introduce you to the captain, then I need to get back to your grandfather," Havier said.

"Fine. Follow me, guys!" I said and followed Havier up onto the ship.

"What's going on?" A man in a captain's uniform asked as soon as we got through the air lock.

"Captain Trandell, allow me to introduce Dave Doyle, Alistair Morgan's grandson. You will follow his orders in all things and understand he has his grandfather's blessings."

"This is highly irregular, Havier," Captain Trandell, said looking me over.

"Yes, well, there's the hatch, you can either quit or you can do as you're told. Mr. Morgan will clean up any issues, as always, and I'm sure there'll be bonuses for all involved. Also, don't underestimate David here. Good luck, Dave," Havier said, turning to me as Hank and Chaz cycled through the air lock.

"Thanks. Oh, make sure those documents from my grandfather make it onto my ship. I forgot them."

"Got it!" Havier said and cycled out.

"If you have your own ship, why do you need mine?"

"First off, it's not *yours*," I said, turning to the captain. "It's my grandfather's—or more to the point, *mine* now. Second, cargo ships aren't all that fast and we need to catch somebody."

Just then Kei and Yuri cycled through.

"And who are all these people?"

I smiled. "Captain Trandell, allow me to introduce some of my crew. This is Bosun Hank Smith, and able spacers Chaz, Yuri, and Kei. They are here to help for when we get to our goal. Now, we need to up ship immediately and I need to use your comms so I can get the most up-to-date information on the ship we're hunting."

Captain Trandell frowned a moment, then sighed. "Very well, follow me to the bridge."

It wasn't very far from the hatch we'd come in, as the bridge was in the center of the ship. I noticed Hank was looking around at the control stations with a critical eye.

"Janet, please get clearance and raise ship," Trandell said, going over to a woman in the pilot's seat.

"Sure thing, Captain, where are we going?"

"Mr. Morgan's grandson here is going to supply us with that information."

"Janet, I'm Dave," I said looking her over. Janet was probably midthirties, with short blond hair and a trim figure. I figured if she flew my grandfather's private yacht she probably knew what she was doing and hadn't been hired on looks alone. "We need to intercept a Xenon-class cargo ship on a least-time orbit from Ceres to Earth."

"That's not a lot to go on," she said, then hit the intercom. "Grace, bring up the fusactors! We're leaving!"

"On it!" came back over the intercom.

"I'm waiting on their departure vector; I'm guessing the most they're going to pull is point three. How much can this pull?"

"Two point five in an emergency."

"Well, once I get updated, we'll head out at two." I turned to Hank. "You any good at plotting intercepts?"

"Sure you don't want our pilot, Janet, to do it?"

"Actually I want you *both* to do it, as well as anyone else who's got the skill."

"Dave, that's the comms center," Hank said, pointing. "Why don't you call who you have to call, and let the captain worry about everything else?"

"Sorry," I said with a heavy sigh while shaking my head. "I thought this shit was over, and now . . . this."

"And just what would that be?" Captain Trandell asked.

"Freeing his brother from a life of slavery," Hank said. "They just kidnapped a citizen of Ceres."

"Why would anyone do that?"

"Because they want to be richer than they already are," Hank told them as I plugged my tablet into the comm center. I waited for a response from Ceres as I sent out several additional requests of my own to both Kacey and Paul, to be forwarded to the proper people while I started debating if I needed to send a message to Dot as well.

That one I knew wouldn't be cheap, I was sure.

"Raising ship!" Janet called out.

"Let me plot a least time from Ceres to Earth," the captain said, "so we'll have an initial vector at least." After a minute, he said, "If they're making point three, it'll take them ten days to get to Earth. It'll take us a hair under seventy hours to intercept their course, going at what their estimated speed will be at that point. *However...*"

"Yes?" I asked, turning to look at him.

"I think it'd be safer to plot them at point two and then come up from behind them at point five to point eight. We don't want to overshoot them."

"That sounds good to me. Once I have some sort of departure vector on them, I'll give it to you so you can update."

"You know, once we catch them, you're still going to have to board them."

"Yup, and having been on a ship that was taken by pirates once already, I've got a pretty good idea of just how to do this."

Thinking about what I just said, I went and actually downloaded a copy of the Xenon class's floor plan. I also got all the specifications, and whatever else I could think of while we were still in range of Mars's information networks. While I had been aboard several of them when working as a tech at Boca Chica, as well as studied them in college, it would be best to have something to show the others so we could make plans.

Also, I was worried about that rear hatch. Under the law you weren't allowed to lock it, but even if they hadn't found a way to do so, the full crew would be on board and they'd be prepared to repel boarders. And the last thing I wanted to do was give them a fair chance. As it was, I wasn't looking forward to the possibility that I might end up killing some or possibly even *all* of them.

But I needed to send a message and for years that was the only kind of message I knew how to send.

We were an hour out of Mars when I finally got a message from Kacey that had all the information on the *New Market*. Better still, several ore boats had gotten fixes on it for the first several hours of its flight. While it had started out at point three, they'd backed off to point two once they were two hours out and no one had called them on comms to accuse them of kidnapping.

Sighing, I leaned back in the seat and looked around the bridge. It was only the captain, Janet, and myself at this point.

"Captain, sorry to be an ass about this, but this is my *brother* we're dealing with."

"I'm surprised that anyone would kidnap a Morgan," Trandell replied.

"He's not. He's my stepbrother, actually."

"Then why is any of this happening?" he asked, looking confused.

"Because my brother Ben may just have figured out the secret to faster-than-light travel and I want to see *him* get the credit as well as the rewards. *Not* some group of elies who will treat him like a slave and make sure he never sees a dime or gets the credit."

"And keep all the profits in the Morgan family as well?" he asked, surprising me.

"I brought my grandfather in because I thought that would prevent something like this from happening. That whichever family this is, Clark or McVay, would give up and leave us alone."

"Assuming that is who's behind this."

"Yes, assuming. Once we've got my brother back, there will be more than a few questions for the others on that ship until I find out just who."

I stood up then. "I need to get some food and talk to my crew. Bosun Smith has dealt with pirates before, from back when he was in the Navy. I'm sure he can tell us what to do."

"These are hardly pirates, David."

"They kidnapped someone tied into the Morgan family, and worth trillions. I can't think of any other definition *than* pirate. Can you?"

I left him shaking his head as I went in search of the mess.

"Ah, you found us!" Chaz said after I'd finally found the mess, which was more like a dining room in this case. The place looked like it probably cost more than the *Iowa Hill* had back when it was first christened.

"Where do I order...?" I asked, looking around.

"Sit, someone will ask," Chaz said, motioning to the open seat at the table.

Looking around, I went over and sat with him and Hank. The girls were nowhere to be seen.

"So what's the plan?" Hank asked.

I shook my head. "I haven't made one yet. I downloaded the deck plans for that class of ship, but once we get there?" I took a deep breath. "I think I need to do something over the top, but honestly? I'm not so sure I want to kill anybody, Hank. Well, not unless they force me to."

"Send me the plans?" Hank said.

"Me too," Chaz added. I got my tablet out and did that just as another woman came over to the table.

"What would you like to eat?" she asked me.

"Something good, not too fancy, and lots of it," I said, looking up at her. "That's not too vague, is it?"

"Not at all," she said and waltzed off. She was definitely a looker.

"Other than the captain, does my grandfather have *any* men working on board this ship?" I asked, looking back and forth between Hank and Chaz.

"Doesn't appear so," Hank said, swiping through pages on his tablet. "I wonder how many crew they've got on board?"

"Probably three engineers, captain, first and second mates, cook, cook's aide, a couple of spacers, probably the crew that grabbed Ben as well," I said, shaking my head. "And there's what? Four of us? Ow. Five?" I said when Chaz kicked me under the table.

"Most of those aren't going to be combatants, and I'm sure that they're not at all comfortable with their bosses kidnapping someone."

"Do you think we'll be able to just use the rear boarding hatch?" Chaz asked. "Or will they have it locked down?"

"It would make more sense for them to leave it be and ambush us as we tried to enter the ship," I said with a shake of my head. "What do you think, Hank?"

"That you're probably right. If they have a snatch-and-grab team on board, those folks are going to be armed and they're going to he ready to fight."

"Think we can ram them?" I asked with a chuckle.

"Easily. Problem is, *where*? We hit them in the wrong place, and it's a long walk home."

I thought about that a moment. "We could ram the starboard-side loading hatches. They're not structural, so there won't be any heavy-duty bracing, they have to move so they need to be low mass."

"You know they'll try to cut and run as soon as you ram them," Chaz said.

"How?" I asked.

"Well, there's the ship's boat in the back, and the two life-boats up top."

"Also if they blow the cargo doors, the force of the escaping air will push us back out and the swinging doors will do even more damage," Hank added.

I took a deep breath and thought about that a moment.

"I know we've got a rail gun and lasers for close-in defenses. How about we put a round through the ship's boat when we're coming up from behind as a warning shot, then we tell them to stop? That takes the boat out of the equation."

"Do you think they'll stop?" Chaz asked.

I shook my head no. "After that I think we'll put a shot across the cargo decks next, that'd blow a hole in both cargo doors and depressurize the entire hold. Just like what happened to us when we got stopped."

"Which would make it harder to move their people from the front to the back," Hank said, skimming over the plans for the ship again.

"We have Yuri and Kei run up to the lifeboats and stop anybody from trying to board them, while we have some words with the captain, then, I guess?" I said, looking at Hank.

"I'm surprised you don't want to come up from underneath and put a round or two through their keel and take out their grav drive."

I shook my head. "I don't want to leave them dead and unable to maneuver. They'll be accelerating and that could cause them to go Dutchman. The odds of hitting just one of the drives and nothing else important aren't all that good."

"Plus if it becomes a protracted fight we can just throw a bunch of explosives down there and cripple the ship," Hank said, looking thoughtful. "Still, if we send the girls to deal with the lifeboats, that leaves the three of us to deal with the snatch team, any security, as well as dealing with the rest of the crew."

"Well, if you have a better idea, have at it," I told Hank. "Because this isn't anything I'm experienced at."

"Okay, as long as we're careful with ramming the ship and keep any damage when we board to a minimum, we'll have your grandfather's toy here to use."

I nodded. "Yeah, I would like to take this back to Mars."

"They won't expect it, so it'll give us the advantage of surprise and they'll be forced to kill their drive and go to zero gee or it'll blow out their panels, right?"

I nodded again.

"Further, if they use any of the lifeboats, we'll be able to catch up with them easily. They're not very fast and they're intentionally made to be easy to find. So we catch up and destroy their engine with one of the lasers. After that, we board at our leisure, and get your brother back. Assuming that they get their act together quickly enough to drag him off the ship and onto one of the lifeboats."

"Why don't we just shoot the lifeboats after we shoot the ship's boat?" Chaz asked.

"Because they may not be able to fly after we crash through the cargo doors with the nose of our ship. Depending on how much cargo they're carrying, we could end up bending their spine," I replied.

"You sure this ship can handle it?" Chaz asked, a little worried.

"This is a warship, it'll handle it, don't worry," Hank told him. "But cargo ships aren't built to withstand the kinds of lateral forces like we're about to apply to it."

I nodded in agreement. "Well, we got what, two days? Let's work out the details, then we can tell everyone else what their part in this is."

FIVE

Ceres / Earth Deep Space Intercept

"SO, IS THAT IT?" I ASKED, LOOKING OVER HANK'S SHOULDER AS he ran the radar and imaging detection gear.

"Well, it's a GSD Xenon freighter and they're not running their transponder, because I've tried to ping it twice now. They're also running with their navigation lights off, and running at point two, which is twice what they're rated for."

"I wonder how many of their panels have burned out so far?"

"I wonder how many trips *this* ship has made," Hank said, looking over his shoulder at me.

"What, you think this is its initial voyage?"

"How many cargo ships does your family own?"

I thought about what my grandfather had said. "Zero."

"And this *is* an act of piracy. They've kidnapped someone, someone important. How many shipping companies would be okay with that?"

I snorted. "Ones you could trust? Still, it's, what, a hundred million credits for a ship like that one? Maybe twice that?"

"And just how much money do you think they stand to make off of your brother if he solves the FTL issue?"

"What comes after trillions?"

"Well after trillions, I'm sure. Plus, being a new ship, it'll take a lot more abuse, and it won't be in a lot of the shipping databases yet, so no one will know just *who* owns it—well, no one outside of Earth, Mars, and probably Venus. They get the updates first. For everyone else, it just kind of trickles out there."

I thought about that for a minute. If this was the only ship that whatever family was behind this owned, that meant the crew was either just some group of people hired to do the job—which probably wasn't likely considering the sensitive and financial nature of it—or...Or this was a crew made up of well-paid family loyalists, or retainers, possibly even family members.

I said as much to Hank.

"Yup, the captain may be an actual family member. The pilots and maybe even the engineers are going to be family retainers. Everyone else? Anybody's guess."

"Think they know we're here?"

"If they had their transponder on, they would have known when we pinged it. As it is, we haven't come into *their* radar range yet, and they're probably only looking to see what's ahead of them. When we get closer, however..."

"Don't they have any kind of threat detection gear?" I asked.

Hank turned and gave me a look. "Oh, like we do on *your* ship?"

I blushed. "Okay, stupid question. Still, knowing what they were going to be doing, you'd think they might have."

"Then when they put in at Ceres they would have stood out."

"Good point."

I turned to Captain Trandell. "Well, Captain, as much as it pains me to tell you to do this—because I'm sure you hate having some young kid ordering you about—I hearby order you, as the ship's owner, to execute the plans we've briefed everyone on."

I was surprised to see the captain smile. "Mr. Doyle, I see only a pirate ship before us, as you have made clear. We are rescuing hostages, a noble cause no matter the person in charge. Now, let us be about it.

"Monalisa?" the captain said, turning toward his weapons officer.

"Yes, Captain?"

"Power up the rail gun, we will put a shot through their ship's pinnace when I give the command. Janet, bring us up directly behind, as briefed, be prepared for them to either cut power or try to maneuver."

"Yes, Captain," Janet said, then triggered her own intercom. "Prepare for maneuvering, Grace. Captain's given us the order."

"Understood!"

Captain Trandell hit the all hands button on his command chair.

"Everyone, prepare for battle. Get your helmets on. We don't believe they're armed, but it's best to be prepared. Boarding team, to your station."

We continued to overtake quickly, though once we were about a thousand meters out, Janet slowed us down fast enough that I had to grab onto one of the handholds on the bridge.

"They've seen us," Hank said, looking at his console.

"Monalisa, fire," the captain said, and an instant later the small hanger door that covered the ship's boat suddenly sprouted a hole. Followed a moment later by a stream of gases, probably atmosphere, spewing out of the new opening.

"Attention, captain and crew of the *New Market*, you are hereby ordered to shut down your grav drive. Repeat: You are ordered to shut down your grav drive and prepare for boarding."

"This is the *New Market*, who do you think you are?"

"This is Captain Trandell of the *Valkyrie*. You stand accused of piracy—we know you have prisoners aboard and we will be sending an armed team to recover them and take you prisoner. I suggest you surrender," the captain said in a calm voice.

"Janet, move along side and prepare for ramming," he said after he released the broadcast key. "Monalisa, prepare to fire a shot through the cargo decks."

"We are not stopping! We do not recognize your authority! This is an Earth-registered vessel!" came back over the coms.

"This is your last chance, Captain. We are an Earthgov *destroyer* and we are *armed*. Now, heave to!"

"Earthgov?" I asked after Captain Trandell released the microphone key.

"I hold a reserve commission and this *is* an emergency," he said smiling, his eyes still on the displays. "Also, I do believe this ship *is* a member of the reserve fleet—part of the agreements Alistair, your grandfather, had to make to buy it."

"They're moving away from us, Captain!" Janet reported.

"Monalisa, fire."

The jet of gases coming out of the hole in the cargo door

was a lot more pronounced as the cargo hold had a lot more air inside it.

"I believe you two need to go join the boarding party?"

"Yes, sir!" I said and left the bridge, putting my helmet on as Hank followed me. Apparently, ramming ships is something that destroyers actually do, as the nose of this one was heavily reinforced. On most destroyers, there were also two hatches three meters aft of the prow. Unfortunately for us, as this ship was primarily meant to be a yacht for an overly rich man, so those hatches didn't exist.

However, Hank and Kelly, the *Valkyrie*'s bosun, had come up with a solution.

"All hands, prepare for ramming."

Hank and I secured ourselves in the restraints we rigged just hours ago. Chaz, Yuri, and Kei were there, as were Kelly and Natasha, another member of the *Valkyrie*'s crew. The two of them would remain aboard the ship and make sure that no one other than us boarded when this was over. Both were heavily armed.

Janet's voice came over the all hands next. "Contact in... three...two...one...Contact!"

There was an initial jolt, the sound of shearing metal, a second jolt, a twisting sensation, and then it got quiet.

"Boarding crew! Board!" Captain Trandell's voice commanded.

Kelly, as bosun, got to do the honors of triggering the "improved" jet axe that had been attached to the outer hull of the *Valkyrie*. A jet axe is a large rectangular ring of shaped charges that is used to blow holes through bulkheads in emergencies when a hatch has been damaged or jammed.

Working together, Hank and Kelly had "upgraded" this one to be able to cut through the side of the hull.

There was a very loud *bang* as the charges all went off together and then the force of the air in the compartment blew the large rectangle of hull metal into the cargo hold of the *New Market*. Hank was the first to the "hatch" and, stepping carefully over the still glowing edges of the hole, he entered the *New Market*'s cargo hold. We all quickly followed him into the ship.

"We're on the third level! Yuri! Rear guard! Let's move to the forward ladder and take the bridge!" I called out. Looking around, I could see the entire level was empty. The Xenon class had one more level than the *Iowa Hill*'s Argon class. It was also half again as wide and almost twice as long. The floors were grates like on the *Iowa Hill* and from what I could see, there wasn't any cargo at all aboard the ship on the other levels.

We'd just gotten to the ladder when the gravity went out. Pulling ourselves up it, we came to the hatch that led between the front crew spaces and the lifeboats.

"Kei!" Hank called, and she ran up, slapped a small charge on it, and we all got out of the way as she blew the hatch's locking mechanism. The atmosphere on the other side was now the only thing holding the door closed, but we had prepared for that. Chaz and I held a hydraulic door breacher up against the hatch as Yuri and Hank spot-welded it to the bulkhead on both sides of the door. As soon as that was done, Chaz triggered the breacher and it pushed the door open. After the first few inches, we could manhandle it ourselves and we all quickly pushed through against the out-rushing air, then let the hatch slam close behind us.

We felt the ship rock slightly.

"Captain?" I called over my helmet comms.

"One lifeboat launched. We're tracking."

"Well, let's see what we're left with," I grumbled as Hank, with his rifle out front, led us into the mess, which had gravity, albeit at perhaps a half g.

Several people ran into the mess as we got there. They immediately all raised their hands and slid to a stop.

"On your knees facing the wall! NOW!" Hank yelled at them.

All six immediately complied.

"Yuri, Chaz, keep them under guard. Anyone else shows up, they do the same. Anybody starts anything, put a bullet in them. If that doesn't stop them, kill them."

"Yes, sir!" Yuri said as she and Chaz moved to flanking positions.

"How many are there on board?" Hank asked, turning on a young woman who looked like the cook.

"Nine crew, two passengers, and the...umm...ops team."

"And just how many are on that team?"

"Four."

"Great. Cooperate and I'm sure none of you will be hanged."

"*Hanged?*" she said with a gulp, but Hank was already leading me and Kei down the passageway to the bridge. Overall, the crew section of the Xenon class wasn't any different from the Argon class as it didn't take any more people to run it than it did on the Argons.

When we got to the bridge, there were two people on it.

"Cut the grav drives, now," I ordered, putting my pistol to the back of the head of what looked like the captain.

"Who do—"

I lifted up the pistol and slammed the handgrip down, hard, on the top of his head, knocking him to the deck. "You kidnapped my brother; don't think I won't kill you."

"Grav drive is cut," said the other person, who was obviously the pilot.

"Great. Tell Engineering to put us on minimum life support and go to the mess and no surprises, unless they want us to start stacking bodies."

"Harry, put us on min life support, then go to the mess."

"And turn on the navigation lights," Hank added.

The pilot flipped a few switches.

"There aren't any kidnapped people on board my ship!" The captain groaned, his hands going to the top of his head, which was bleeding heavily.

"Yeah, tell you what, we're going to go after that lifeboat after we secure all of you. How about we make a little wager? If my brother is aboard it, I come back here and kill all of you?"

I looked up at the pilot, who was pale as a ghost.

"I don't think your pilot there wants any part of that bet. So tell me," I said looking up at the pilot. "Who's on the lifeboat?"

"Don't te—" The captain shut up then as I kicked him in the face.

"How many?"

"The four men who kidnapped your brother, your brother, and some gal they were using to keep your brother in line."

"Using, how?"

"By threatening to kill her or by hurting her in front of him."

I looked down at the captain. "Hank, would it be wrong of me to just kill this piece of shit on the floor, here and now?"

I heard Hank sigh, heavily. "As much as I want to tell you to do it, I think we need to haul him back to Mars. Tie him up. Drag him back to the mess. You"—Hank pointed to the pilot—"keep your hands up. We're going back to the mess with the rest of the crew. Kei, with me. And Dave, don't think I'm leaving you alone so you can kill him."

"Got it," I replied. I grabbed the heavy zip ties I had on my belt—we'd all brought a bunch—and quickly bound the dazed captain.

"Now, before we join the rest of your crew, care to tell me who you work for?"

"I ain't telling you shit!"

"Oh, so you really *are* a pirate! Wow, guess you won't have to worry about them assassinating you for failing at your job! Just that hangman's noose on Mars," I told him as I gagged him. That done, I picked him up and carried him to the mess.

"So what have we learned?" I asked as I came in and dropped the captain on the floor. I could see that all of the crew were now bound and gagged.

"They work for the McVay family," Chaz told me.

"We need to clear the ship."

"Why?" Hank asked.

"Because we need to get after that lifeboat. Transferring everyone right now will take too much time. So we'll have to come back for them, which means leaving them tied up in here with someone guarding them."

"And you're worried that there may be someone hiding out?"

"Yup."

"Ah." Hank turned toward the crew. "Okay, listen up. We're going to search the ship. Anyone we find we are just going to shoot dead. No surrenders, no mercy, because they're planning to ambush us, which is why they're hiding. Oh! And we'll pick one of you at random and shoot you too.

"So, before we go, where are they?"

Several of the guys, and the cook, started to shake their heads and make noises. Going over to the cook, Hank undid her gag.

"Melissa McVay is aboard! She was sent here to supervise! She's hiding someplace!"

"Thanks! Now, who knows where?"

One of the men made a noise so while Hank redid her gag I undid his.

"She's hiding in the gear locker, down by the able spacers' rooms. We tossed the extra gear into one of the empty rooms to make space for her."

"Well, let's go get her," I said, looking at Hank, who nodded.

As soon as we were out of the mess, I started checking the crew quarters and the two staterooms on the main deck.

"What are you doing?"

"Looking for her room," I said as I opened the first stateroom. It definitely had that lived-in look.

"Looks like you found it."

"Yup," I said, and then checked the one across the hall; it *also* had that lived-in look.

Hank laughed. "I can't believe they lied to us."

"I'm not sure that they did. Could be the head of the grab team was staying here. But I'm just too damn paranoid to take any of these people at their word."

Hank nodded. "Well, let's make it quick."

We found four more rooms that had been occupied than we had crew upstairs. One had been my brother's and I could see he hadn't been alone in it.

That was something I'd have to ask him about.

When we got to the locker, I stopped Hank and held up my hand.

"Well, that's it, crew's off-loaded, nobody's left. I'll call for them to pump down the atmosphere and shut down the fusion reactors. Maybe we can come back in a few months and get a salvage claim."

"Assuming someone doesn't try to use it for target practice," Hank agreed loudly.

A loud banging started coming from the closet.

"You hear something?" Hank asked.

"I think that's Chaz starting the pumps, better close our helmets!"

There was a screech then and a lot more noise until the doors to the gear closet opened and a woman in a set of ship's coveralls tumbled out.

"Oh look, a stowaway!" Hank said, lowering his rifle to point at Melissa. She gathered herself up on her hands and knees, then looked up at the two of us.

"Do you know who I am?" she demanded.

"The way I'm getting Ben back alive," I told her. "Otherwise, you're no good to me and I'd just as happily kick your ass out the air lock as shoot you."

"You wouldn't!"

I smiled. "You may have heard of me? David Walker? The murderous bastard black sheep grandson of Alistair Morgan?"

I smiled even wider as she blanched.

"Great, now, let's get you in a pressure suit, then we're going to trade you for my brother. Just remember, if he dies, you die."

"So how do you want to proceed?" Captain Trandell asked me as we closed on the lifeboat. As they were made to be seen, finding it was not hard at all.

"I think we need to damage the heat sink on their power unit. That'll cause it to overheat and shut down—along with their gravity, life support, and almost everything else. Our new friend Melissa here"—I motioned to Melissa, who had her hands bound behind her back and was wearing a blindfold, more to keep her "off balance" than induce any fears about seeing anything—"will tell them over the radio that if Ben or the other hostage are killed, she'll be killed. And then they'll *all* die.

"But if they give us Ben and the other one, everyone gets to live."

"Sounds like a plan. Monalisa, if you would be so kind as to target their heat sink with one of the lasers as Janet brings us alongside."

"Aye-aye, Captain," Monalisa said, and as I watched Janet not only brought us close, but barrel-rolled the ship around the lifeboat as they tried to dodge. During which time Monalisa used one of the short-range lasers to partially slag the heat sink.

The lifeboat went dead in the water almost immediately.

"Attention lifeboat, prepare to be boarded!" the captain said, keying his microphone.

"You board us, and we'll kill the hostages!" came back.

"Melissa?" I said and pushed her head down over the microphone. "Please talk a little sense into them."

"Gil! This is Melissa McVay! It has been made quite clear to me that if you hurt either of those hostages they'll not only kill *you* but they'll kill *me* as well! As my father is the one paying you, and I don't feel like dying today, you will not harm anyone. You will allow the destroyer to dock and you will release the prisoners."

"And then what? We go to Mars and get hanged?"

"I'm perfectly fine letting them stay aboard the lifeboat," I said. "I don't care about the lackeys, I just want Ben."

"Did you hear that?" Melissa asked.

"How do I know you won't shoot us?"

"This really is an Earthgov ship, with an Earthgov officer at the helm," I replied. "I don't think they'd let me do such a thing."

The captain spoke up then. "As much as it will pain me to let you go, once I have, to shoot a lifeboat *is* a serious offense. Now you have your orders. We will be docking with you shortly, and we will have armed crew members at the hatch, so do not think you can storm the ship, or you *will* be killed."

"Do as the captain said, Gil! You keep me from getting killed and I *promise* that I won't let my father hurt you, and that you'll all be paid, even if I have to pay you myself!"

"Fine" was all the response we got.

"Well, let's get down to the docking bay," I told Yuri. Hank had stayed aboard the *New Market* with Chaz and Kei to keep an eye on the crew.

When we got down to the hatch, I removed the blindfold from Melissa, though I left her hands tied behind her back. Kelly and Natasha were there, and both were well armed. All of us had our helmets on, just in case, however I'd clearly left Melissa's off to make it clear that if they tried to dump atmosphere, she'd die. Or if they forced *us* to dump atmosphere, she'd die.

I did have her helmet clipped to the back of her pressure suit, on the off chance that there was an accident, as I really didn't want her to die. But we were playing hardball here and as much as I might not enjoy the game anymore, I still knew how to play.

"Now, remember, everyone behaves and you get to go home alive. Or at least back to Mars."

"You don't think they'll prosecute me, do you?" she asked with a snort.

I shook my head. "Mars? No. I'm sure your family has enough pull to keep you from doing anything but the bare minimum for the proles and doles to see. But if we took you to Ceres? Oh, trust me, you wouldn't like that."

"Like what you did to Captain Marshall back onboard my ship?"

"Melissa, the only reason I haven't beaten you black and blue is because I was taught never to hit a lady," I confessed. "Beating and threatening to kill a woman to make my brother comply is one of those things that a lot of us have issues with, and that's the crime that'll probably get Marshall hanged."

"He didn't order it, and he had no control over Gil or Gil's men."

"Doesn't matter, he was the captain," Yuri said in a soft voice. "As ship owner, you're responsible as well. And, while *I* have no problems with hitting a woman, it's clear that we need you for this exchange."

I tried not to smile as she turned and gave Yuri a glare.

"Oh, and if anything does happen, I'll shoot you first," Yuri said with a wink.

A loud *clang* sounded as the docking mechanism on the side of the ship engaged the lifeboat. As a ship's engineer I knew exactly how the system worked. After the boat was engaged, it was pulled in against an inflatable rubber bumper that was used to ensure an airtight seal should the lifeboat be damaged.

Next the area between the two hatches would be pressure tested. If necessary, the docking bay, which is where I was, could be pumped down to a lower pressure or no pressure at all. In extreme cases where they could not make a seal, they had what was known as the HAL method, though I have no idea where the name came from. That involved pumping down the docking bay and using the air pressure in the lifeboat to more or less shoot everyone into the bay. The doors would then slam close and there would be an emergency repressurization.

I'd told the captain that I did not want to do that today, even if it was a technique often used with pirates.

"Sealed and secure!" Natasha said from where she was standing by one of the control panels.

"Opening the hatch," someone commed over my headset, and I watched as it quickly split in two, one half going up, the other sliding down. We were then looking at the hatch for the lifeboat. There was a window in it and I could see a face looking out of it. So I moved Melissa into the center of the room.

Then I put a gun to her head.

"Do you have to?" she whispered, and for the first time, I heard fear in her voice.

"Have to? Yes," I whispered back from inside my open helmet. "Want to? No. I don't want to kill you, Melissa. I don't want to kill anybody, anymore. But you people keep pushing me and I'll tell you right now, it's not going to end well for anybody. What I can't understand is how someone as beautiful and young as you ended up so ugly inside."

"I am not ugly inside," she growled back as the door started to open on the lifeboat.

"Takes one to know one," I said and, moving behind Melissa, I called for lights.

"Hey! What are you doing?" the man at the door yelled as the lights around the docking ring lit up and gave us a clear view into the lifeboat.

"You saw we had Melissa, now I want to see that you have Ben and whoever else," I replied, loudly.

One of the things about the lifeboats is that they were clearly designed so that you couldn't hide anything from view. I could see the other three, who all had their weapons pointed up. One was holding Ben, and another one was holding a young woman, who I really couldn't see well, but she did look bruised.

"How would you like it if I did to you what they did to her?" I growled in Melissa's ear. Then moving my head a bit back I raised my voice. "Send Ben and the girl over."

"Let go of Melissa, first!"

"Like I'm gonna trust you?" I called back. "You beat defenseless women!" I urged Melissa forward and pointed my pistol at the man—Gil, I assumed. "Understand I can just start picking the four of you off, nice and safe, from behind the body of your boss."

"Gil! Send them out! *Now!*" Melissa yelled as suddenly targeting lasers from Yuri's, Natasha's, and Kelly's rifles started sweeping over the men's faces. "Or I swear when this is over I'll tell my father to kill your ass!"

"Send out the kid," Gil said, looking back over his shoulder.

The guy holding Ben gave him a push and Ben stumbled forward. With the power mostly out on the lifeboat, the already less-than-normal gravity on it was close to zero, and when Ben crossed the threshold into the ship, he stumbled again and fell to his knees, swearing. At least they had him in a pressure suit.

"Crawl toward me, Ben," Yuri said over her suit speaker and Ben started doing just that.

"Okay, give us Melissa."

"You've still got the girl!" I called. "So no!"

As soon as Ben was out of sight of Gil, Yuri grabbed him, dragged him into the air lock out of the room, hit the close button, and retook her position. Melinda, the ship's doctor, was on the other side along with Michelle, the steward. They'd take care of him.

"Gil!" Melissa warned.

"Ted, bring the girl up!" Gil yelled to the guy holding her. It was about then that I noticed she was barely conscious.

"What the hell did you do to her?" I said and pressed the pistol into the back of Melissa's skull.

"Ben was being stubborn! He wouldn't head for the lifeboat! We needed to encourage him!" Melissa said hurriedly. "I wanted you to go after the lifeboat! I wanted you to leave me alone! I wanted you to get them!" she said, waving her hand at Gil and the others. "Not *me*! Please don't hurt me! *Please!*"

The look that Gil was focusing on Melissa was not a good one. I guess the other guy, the one carrying the abused girl, didn't hear what Melissa had just said, as he all but tossed the girl into the ship.

"Here, take her! That bitch is all used up, anyway! Haven't had any fun with her in days!" he said while laughing.

I couldn't help it. I shot him in the balls as the girl hit the floor and slid into the hanger. Then putting my foot square in the back of Melissa, I yelled, "Here, why don't you play with *this* one instead?"

I pushed with all of my might, sending her stumbling forward.

"Nooooo! I don't want to go with them!" Melissa screamed just as she hit the gravity terminator line and flew all the way into the lifeboat.

"Close the hatch! Blow the boat!" I yelled and dropped to the floor as someone started shooting. The door slammed shut almost instantly and a second later I felt it as the locks disengaged and the inflatable ring effectively jettisoned the lifeboat from the *Valkyrie*.

"Wow, think they got their hatch closed in time?" Yuri asked, picking herself up from the floor where she'd gone prone.

"It's spring-loaded," Kelly said, running over to the downed girl, Natasha was already there. "The second the pressure started to drop it slammed closed. Now whether or not that bastard David shot was able to get out of the way or got cut in half, that's a question this girl would love to know the answer to."

Picking myself up, I went to look at the barely conscious woman on the floor. "How bad is it?"

"I need to get her to the sickbay," Natasha said. "Next time, use a bigger caliber. I'm not sure you blew both of his balls off."

Yuri snorted and Kelly laughed.

"Help me pick her up, Dave," Natasha said.

"Yes, ma'am."

Aboard the *Valkyrie*

"HOW IS SHE, DOC?" I ASKED AS THE *VALKYRIE* MADE ITS WAY back to the *New Market* to pick up our crew and our prisoners.

"Someone put one hell of a beating on that poor girl. Recently too."

"They said they were beating her to get my brother to go on the lifeboat."

"Oh, they were beating her a lot more recently than that. I suspect when we took out their power plant she also got a beating. I can just imagine what kinds of things they were doing to her on the way *out* to get your brother. At least one of those men was a sick bastard."

"So, physically, how is she?"

"Physically, I'll have her all but normal by the time we get back to Mars."

"Huh? How is that even possible?"

"Because Alistair spent a hundred million credits on the medbay?" Melinda said, smiling at me. "Dave, do you really think your grandfather just hired us because of our pretty faces?"

"Not really, no."

"Damn right he didn't. I'm his personal physician and normally I go wherever he goes. Carol's his personal cook; Natasha is both a nurse and one of his personal bodyguards, like Havier. He only has men working in positions where he figures a woman would get too much resistance."

"I have to admit, I find that rather curious."

"A lot of the elitist families have a tendency to overlook women, even their own. The ones that do rise to power tend to be real pieces of work, like that Melissa was."

"You know about her?"

"We were all listening in to what was going on. You left your mic on."

"Umm, yeah."

"And if you weren't married, trust me: all of the girls on board would be chasing you."

"Huh?"

"You went to war over a woman you've never met, never laid eyes on, never knew, all because some scum was abusing her. Oh, you're not half as ugly inside as you think you are. Besides, we all like the bad boys, that's why we work for Alistair."

I coughed, "*What?* My grandfather, a *bad boy?*"

"Oh, he may not be on *your* level, but trust me, among the elites? There are those who won't even sit in the same room as him because they're just too damn afraid. He loaned you his personal private yacht, which from what the captain tells me you did quite the number on, ramming that freighter."

"I thought they built these things to take that?"

"They built them to be able to do it"—Melinda smiled and held up a finger—"once."

"Okay, now you're just messing with me," I said with a side-long look at her as she laughed.

"Go see your brother. I think he's mad at you."

"Me? What did I do?"

"I make it a rule never to get in the middle of family arguments. Now, go, shoo!"

Smiling at her, I left the room and headed off to the examination room across the passageway. Opening the door, I stepped in and smiled.

"Hi, Ben," I said, and hugged him as he scowled at me.

"I'm not falling for that, Dave," he said, frowning as he pushed me back.

"Yes, the doc warned me you were mad, but I'm still happy

to see you! And why the hell are you mad at me? I just saved your life!"

"And killed two people in the process!"

"Two? I only shot that one guy! And don't try telling me he didn't deserve it! I *saw* how badly beaten that girl was!"

"That wasn't his fault! It was mine!"

"Oh, don't you *dare* fall for that shit in front of me!" I yelled back at him. "You didn't beat her! *They* did!"

"Only because I wasn't doing what they told me—"

I cut him off. "Dammit, Ben! They beat her because they were sick fucks who didn't have the brains or the brawn to force you to comply!"

"But!"

"No! No fucking buts! Would *I*, the meanest bastard you've ever known, have done that? Picked on some innocent woman?"

"They couldn't have me showing up beaten and bruised!"

"Sure they could! But how many beatings would they have had to give you? Not as many as they gave her! I don't want to hear that shit coming out of your mouth again and I don't even want you thinking it. Go read some books on coercion! You're the damn genius! Even Donde didn't beat or rape our sister to get me to cooperate!"

I had the pleasure of seeing Ben look guilty for a moment, but then he was right back at me.

"You shouldn't have put Melissa with them! They'll kill her!"

"Why the hell would they do that?" I asked, looking at him a bit surprised. "They kill her, and her father will kill them slowly!"

"How long do you think it will be before they realize that they're in a lifeboat with no drive? That they can't go anywhere with it, and that they'll all suffocate when the air runs out?"

"Umm…" I thought about that for an instant. "When I kicked Melissa into the lifeboat I was kinda hoping they'd do to her the same stuff they'd done to that poor girl."

"*What?*" Ben yelled at me.

"Hey, they answered to her, so it's just as much her responsibility as it was those guys'," I said with a guilty look. "But they're in a lifeboat, it's got a beacon, it shows up on every radar out there! They're on a course for Earth! They'll get picked up!" I said, waving my hands.

"And just how long until they get there? And how fast will they be going? The ship was still accelerating when we left and was nowhere near the top velocity!"

I sighed. "You want me to do something, don't you?"

"I want you to stop killing people, Dave! You keep sliding back into your old ways! I mean really, did you have to shoot that guy, even?"

I looked Ben in the eyes. "Yeah, I did. I've got a wife now and one of these days I'm gonna have kids, and the way that guy was acting, treating that gal like she was trash and deserved what he'd done to her? Yeah, he's lucky I only shot him in the balls. The gals wanted him hurt a lot more."

Ben blinked at me. "You're serious?"

I rolled my eyes. "Ben, doesn't it bother you what they did to that girl?"

"Aurelia, her name is Aurelia." He looked down and shook his head. "And yeah, it bothered me, that's why I did what they told me to. But she'll get better, they can fix everything these days."

"Ben!" I said, throwing my hands up in the air with a look of exasperation. "What about her mind? You put someone through that kind of torture and do you really think they'll just be *all right* when it's over? Hell, why they'd pick her?"

"They thought I was sweet on her," Ben said in a soft voice. Suddenly, I remembered that Ben was a lot younger than I was. He'd literally only just turned eighteen a few weeks ago and he'd lived through his own special hell for years now.

"One of the girls you were doing routines for, who was more than happy to sleep with you?"

I could see his face turning red. "Yes," he said in a strangled voice, still looking at the floor.

I sighed and gave him another hug, because damn if *I* didn't need one myself at that point.

"Do you like her?"

"You sound like Mom..."

I barked out a laugh, "Yeah. I think we both have a pretty poor track record when it comes to women—well, I used to. Thank god for Kacey. But did you like her? Seriously—give, Ben."

"Yeah, I like her. She's not as dumb as a lot of the others. I mean, she understood the whole 'deal' thing with the cheerleading squad, but she kept coming by and hanging out after the season had ended and they'd won Nationals. She liked talking about math and other stuff like that with me. I enjoyed having her around."

"Okay, two things." I turned to the intercom and thumbed the button for the bridge.

"Captain here."

"Captain, it's Dave. It occurred to me that we probably should alert the Earth and Mars navies about the lifeboat containing five pirates, one of which is a member of a very wealthy family. Along with their course data."

"Don't want to leave them to random chance?"

"Let's just say I don't want the McVay family to accuse me of murdering Melissa."

"True. I'll notify everyone and let the lifeboat know that someone will be along to rescue them."

"Thanks, Captain."

"Just doing my job."

I took my finger off the intercom.

"What's the second thing?" Ben asked, looking at me suspiciously.

"You need to spend every waking moment sitting with your girlfriend and holding her hand and comforting her when she wakes up."

"She's not my girlfriend!" Ben protested.

"She is now. Ben, they put her through a world of hurt, and they did it because of you. You said you liked her and right now, I suspect she could stand to have someone she knows and has slept with and *likes* holding her hand and soothing her fears. Like it or not, you have an obligation to her.

"Besides, who knows? Maybe if you treat her like a human being and not a sex object you'll find out you like her—" I *oof*ed then as Ben punched me in the gut.

"What was that for?"

"Being right," Ben said and sighed. "I'm really not a very nice person myself, am I?"

I snorted. "Compared to me, you're a saint."

"That's not saying much, Dave."

"Yeah, well, you're becoming an adult, growing up. Remember when I told you how no one likes a kid telling them they're wrong?"

"What's that got to do with *this*?"

"It's time to stop looking at women as something just to drag into bed and have fun with. It's time to start looking at them as *people*. Trust me, that changes everything."

"Oh? And when did you learn this?"

"I think it was when I met Kacey and I found someone who was as ruthless as I was, just in a different way."

"Kacey's not ruthless, Dave."

"Oh? Try getting between her and something she wants. She won't kill you, or probably even hurt you, but you'll know it when she just rolls right over you."

Ben snorted. "Thanks for telling the captain to do that. Melissa might be a bit of a bitch, but she was raised that way. She doesn't deserve what they did to Auri. No one deserves that."

"You might change your mind after she opens up to you, Ben."

He shook his head. "No, Melissa may have turned a blind eye, but she's not the one who actually did it. You know, they debated exchanging me for her, while you were docking with them just now. They figured as long as I was alive, her father wouldn't give a damn if she died. They were just bluffing about wanting her, looking for an opportunity to take the ship."

"They thought they could take the ship?" I laughed. "Sounds delusional."

"I think when the laser sights from the girls' rifles started hitting them in the eyes they realized just how much trouble they were in."

"Go see Auri. Be nice. Talk. Listen to her and don't be afraid to tell her things. Might be time to finally have someone other than family to start caring about."

Ben nodded, and getting up he clapped me on the shoulder as he left and went to go see Aurelia.

"You know," Melinda said, coming into the room, "any chance you might be interested in a mistress?" she asked with a chuckle.

"You heard?" I groaned.

"Every word. Your brother may be the family genius, but you've definitely got a way with people, Dave."

"Only when I'm not killing them," I replied, shaking my head. "I probably shouldn't have kicked Melissa into the lifeboat."

"Maybe, maybe not. But I can't say as she didn't deserve it. Who knows, maybe it'll make her a better person?"

❖   ❖   ❖

It took us four hours to get back to the *New Market* and for the ship to dock with the rear hatch. I went aboard with Yuri, while Kelly and Natasha again watched the hatch. Until I'd confirmed that everything was as we left it, nobody was taking any chances.

Once I had, it took us an hour to move everyone into the holding area aboard the *Valkyrie*, which was just the docking deck, with a warning that if anyone started anything, the hatch would be opened and they'd all die.

"So, now what?" Hank asked me as we made a second sweep of the ship, with Yuri and Kei helping, just in case we'd missed something important—or somebody.

I shrugged. "Go back to Mars, and go home."

"Aren't you forgetting something?"

I stopped and looked at him. "Huh?"

Hank smiled at me. "What did you do the *last* time you left an untended and damaged ship?"

"Umm, isn't that stealing?"

"'Stealing' is such a poor choice of words. Right now, this ship is headed to Earth space. With no crew. Think of just how dangerous that would be! No, we're just thinking of others and putting this ship in a safer orbit. All for the good of those poor blighted people on Earth!"

"And what do we tell the folks who own it?"

"Do you really think they're going to admit to what just happened? I'm sure the owners are going to keep their mouths shut. They may not even report it to their insurance company—not that any insurance company would pay off when you consider what they were doing."

I hit the switch for the *Valkyrie* on my helmet comm. "Captain, could you send either Christine or Janet over, along with Chaz."

"What's up?"

"I want to program a new course into the ship's computers before we leave. Letting this fly through Earth Space untended just wouldn't be safe."

I heard a snort of laughter. "I'll send them over."

"I guess I need to go program the fusion reactors," I said, shaking my head. "Do you think you can fix the doors so the software will let us fly?"

"Already checked them. When we drilled through the upper

door we didn't break any of the locks. Right now, those two doors are jammed tight. Couldn't open them even if we blew the latching mechanisms."

"Well, that's one less thing to worry about."

"Looks like Kacey's getting another cargo ship for her birthday!" Hank said, laughing.

"Looks like," I said, looking around the ship with a critical eye for the first time. Hank had been right, this ship had never seen a load of cargo and half the equipment down in Engineering had never even been out of the lockers.

I'd definitely be updating my fusion reactor certs when I got back to Ceres.

SEVEN

Vance Spaceport, Mars

THE PORT AUTHORITIES CAME AND TOOK OUR PRISONERS OFF our hands within minutes of landing. I'd had us land near the *Iowa Hill* so I could move Ben off without anyone noticing. Or at least that was what I hoped.

"So now what?" Ben asked as I watched the last of the *New Market* crew get marched off, by armed guards, to a large bus of some sort.

"Now I get to tell my grandfather that I totaled his yacht," I replied with a chuckle.

"Some paint, some Bondo, it's all good," Ben said with a chuckle of his own.

"This ain't a stolen car we took for a joy ride, bro."

"I wonder if anyone's found Melissa yet?"

I shrugged. "Not my problem. How's Aurelia doing?"

"And that's the problem..." he said with a sigh.

"Oh, this I gotta hear," I said, turning and smiling at him. Aurelia, even bruised, was one beautiful woman, and in the four days it'd taken for us to get back here, she'd gone from that bed in the sickbay straight to my brother's. He'd taken my advice to heart and sat with her until Melinda had declared her fit enough to leave the med bay. She had not, however, wanted to leave Ben's presence and all but glued herself to him. This was the first time I'd seen him alone.

Ben frowned at me.

"What? She's a beautiful woman! And it's obvious she has a thing for you, which I believe you even hinted was from before all of this happened?"

"She wants to stay with me. She doesn't want to go home. She doesn't think it'd be safe, that they might blame her."

"Hmm, that could be a bit of a problem," I admitted.

"Yeah, I—*what*?" Ben said doing a double take.

"I said it could be a bit of a problem."

"David! This is where you're supposed to reassure your younger brother that you know people and that you can get the fine folks at Ceres to allow her to stay rather than deport her back to Earth!"

I blinked. It'd been a while since I'd seen Ben be that forceful about *anything*, much less a girl.

"Hold on, you *want* her to come with you?" I asked.

"Of course I do! Remember how I said she wasn't dumb?"

I nodded slowly.

"Well, it turns out that when we got to talking, *really* talking, she admitted that she'd been chasing me because *I* wasn't boring or stupid like all those other guys who only wanted her for her looks."

"Ben," I said giving him a look, "*you* only wanted her for her looks."

"Well, yeah, at first. I mean, she's gorgeous. But I never stopped her from coming back long after most girls moved on. I mean, I was surprised she kept coming back, most girls didn't, especially after I started spending so much time in that damn chair." He blushed then.

"Yeah, I guess I was using her, but she confessed she was hoping that when I got to the development stage I'd put her on my team because while she's no genius, she still found what I was doing fascinating."

I looked at him. "She understands your work?"

"She's got her master's. It's MIT, Dave, all those girls on the cheerleading teams are smart. She's just smarter than most."

"And a lot better built."

I laughed as Ben blushed again. "Yeah, there's that too."

"So how'd she end up with those guys?"

Ben sighed. "She wanted to get me back. She's a bit like Mom. She figured if she attached herself to me, gave me everything I wanted, I'd take care of her and give her the kind of life *she* wanted. She had no idea they were going to beat her, or torture her, none of that. She cried about that. She had no idea the McVays could be that cruel."

"So she was willing to do anything she had to, to get you, even if it meant bringing you back to Earth, against your will?"

"She didn't really understand what I was running from," Ben said, shaking his head. "She's smart, but sometimes she's obviously clueless. But after what they did to her?" He looked up at me. "She told me straight out that she's more than willing to spend the rest of her life making it up to me."

"And?"

Ben gave me a look. "David, it's like our mom all over again! She sees a better life for herself, and yeah, for her kids, if she goes with me. If I take her and make her my wife. She knows I won't abuse her or treat her bad. She knows that I actually care. Yeah, she thought she was being sly and it bit her on the ass but good. Back then, she was looking at me not all that differently than I was looking at her, if you want to be honest.

"But now that we've *actually* talked and cleared the air? It's nice to have someone who's read my paper and understands what I'm talking about."

I thought about that a moment. I wasn't the universe's most knowledgeable man when it came to the opposite sex, but Kacey had gone after me even more ruthlessly than Aurelia had gone after Ben. But once we'd actually *talked* to each other, that was when it had clicked for us and I suddenly realized that there just might be something more there than a good time.

It sounded like Aurelia and Ben finally did the same thing.

"Okay, here's the problem," I said. "We have a shipment that's going to those people I've been working with, the 'Let-Bees' as people call them."

"And that's a problem, why?"

"It's a problem because I was going to send *you* with the shipment."

"*What?*" Ben said, giving me a wild look.

"Ben, almost no one knows about them, and other than *me*, nobody knows where they are! Oh, I'm sure you'll figure it out as soon as you get there, but if I send you there, you'll be safe! No one will be able to grab you!"

"You'd stick your own brother out in some refugee camp?" he said, still giving me that look again.

"Ben! If it wasn't for *you*—well, you and Kacey—I would have *stayed* out there! They're good people! And they're building one hell of a place to live! I'm pretty sure if I ask them to take you in, they will. But you're gonna have to work, they're like Ceres, no freeloaders."

"What about my research? I mean, shit, Dave! What am I going to do for lab gear?"

"You're going to make up a list, right now, and we'll get it all packed onboard to take with you. As for your research? Ben, do you really think you're going to solve this next month? Next *year*? I'd rather see you off someplace safe, hopefully with someone you care about, where you got the same choices the rest of us mere mortals got. Besides, someone with your brains could probably make a big difference to them."

"I don't know, Dave..."

"Look, give it a year, okay? That'll hopefully give the McVays and everyone else time to forget about you and move on. Then I could bring you back and you could go back to your research."

Ben thought about that for a few moments.

"What about those shipyards you told me about?"

"Those are going to take years to get built. You don't need to be there for that."

"If they won't let me take Auri, I'm not going, Dave. I honestly think she's the one."

"You need to find out if she's okay with living in a dark hab in the middle of nowhere and possibly spending the rest of her life there."

"Yeah, that is a lot to take in, isn't it?"

"She also needs to understand that if she ever tells anybody where the place you're going to is, she'll be killed."

"I'll make sure she understands all about keeping faith."

"Well, let's get the two of you settled in on the *Iowa Hill* and you can write up your list and give it to Emiliana while I go apologize to my grandfather for trashing his yacht."

"Oh, I doubt it's that bad!" Ben said with a laugh. "I mean, it got us back here, right?"

I shook my head and went to find a couple of respirator masks that would conceal their faces, plus a couple of hats to hide their hair. Michelle, the steward, had already found a couple of extra pairs of ships coveralls that did a good job of hiding what was inside them.

Once I got them both suited up, I went and found Hank, Chaz, Yuri, and Yei.

"Okay, we're going over to the *Iowa Hill*. Keep everyone—and I do mean *everyone*—well away from Ben and Auri. I don't want anyone getting any pictures if we can avoid it. We're all just a group of people going from one ship to another."

"Well we better get a move on, then," Hank said, "because the press is definitely on their way."

"Great, let's go." I'd already thanked everyone on the crew while we were landing for their help. So we went down the stairs to the ground.

"Hank, take over, I want a quick look at the front of the *Valkyrie*."

"Sure thing, Dave!"

It was a couple-hundred-meter walk to the bow, and as I got close I could see there were ripples in the hull metal. When I actually *got* to the front, the once-pointed nose was crushed in on the sides, the hull metal torn and peeled back in spots like papier-mâché. I could see the hole we'd cut in the side, which was a lot farther back than I'd realized. In all the excitement of taking the *New Market* and then chasing after the lifeboat, I'd never really stopped to look at all the damage.

"Quite a mess, isn't it?" Captain Trandell said, walking over to me. I'd been so taken in by the wreckage that I hadn't even noticed him.

"How bad is it?"

"Oh, it doesn't look like any of the structural beams are bent. Those are made from specially blended and reinforced metals. The hull plates, however, are just steel, like the door we rammed, so I'm not surprised to see some of those got peeled back. I suspect they'll have it all repaired in a month."

"That fast?"

"Warships getting damaged is something everyone expects. So being able to turn them around quickly is important."

I nodded; it made sense. "Well, I guess I need to apologize

to my grandfather for not only trashing his yacht, but for getting him stranded here."

"Oh, he's not here."

"What?" I said, looking back at the captain.

"He left Mars shortly after you did. While everyone thought he was on board with you, he was actually on one of the regular passenger liners that ply the route between Earth and Mars."

"Smart," I said, nodding slowly. "Can't be guilty if he wasn't with us."

"Very much that. Though I suspect he wanted to be ready to fend off any claims that the McVay family might make."

I nodded again. "Thanks again, Captain. Sorry for ruining your ship. Oh, has there been any word on that lifeboat?"

"The Earthgov Navy sent out one of their destroyers and picked them all up yesterday. Once word got around as to just *who* was aboard it, they got their asses in high gear."

"Well, guess I won't be blamed for their deaths, at least. What do you think will happen to the crew we turned over?"

"They'll all be stripped of their ratings, at least for when they're in Mars space. I doubt any of them will be hanged or jailed—everybody knows just who they were working for. The only interesting thing will be is if the McVays pay for them to be able to go back home, or if they just get abandoned here on Mars to rot."

"Well, I need to get back to my day job. Later, Captain," I said with a wave as I turned and headed off to the *Iowa Hill*. While I was a bit pissed at that one captain for allowing Auri to be abused while aboard his ship, there probably really hadn't been anything he could have done about it, and I now felt bad for having kicked him in the face. I'm sure it sucked for the rest of the crew to all lose their ratings. I don't doubt that they'd spent years earning them.

Then again, I had no idea if the Earth authorities would follow suit and pull them as well. Shaking my head again, I went up the ladder and back into my ship. I had other things I needed to think about, as I was sure right about now Ben was passing a list of things he needed over to Emiliana, who would then either yell at me or ask me for money.

Probably both.

✧   ✧   ✧

We'd been underway for almost three days. Nick and I had just finished rebuilding a panel that had burned out just after dinner. I'd be a lot happier when he got his engineer third certification and his panel rebuilding certification. It would mean less work for me. While Nick was good at his job and didn't shirk, I had picked up enough of Dot's mannerisms that until Nick actually had those certificates in hand, I wasn't going to be trusting him to do the work without me supervising.

So I was sitting in the mess having a cup of coffee—Emiliana always left a pot on—when Aurelia came in, wearing a bathrobe of all things, saw me, then stopped and looked at me a little warily.

"Married, remember?" I said, holding up my left hand and wiggling the fingers to show off the ring.

"It's not that," she said hesitating a moment before coming in and making a beeline for the coffee pot.

"Oh? Then what is it?"

"I've heard the...stories...about you."

I sighed. "Oh god, don't tell me, the documentary?"

She nodded. "Also, Ben has admitted to me that you were both in a gang and I *saw* you shoot Ted"—she shivered—"not that he didn't deserve it, he was the worst of them."

"And?"

"And I'm afraid of you."

"You're my brother's girlfriend. Don't be."

"Still..."

I looked up at her and she had a torn look on her face.

"Have you had a tour of the ship yet?" I asked her, standing up.

"Huh?"

"A tour, of the ship?"

She shook her head.

"Okay, grab your cup and come along," I said, picking up my own cup and going over to her.

"Umm, do I have to?"

I shook my head. "No, you don't. But you look like someone who has something to say, and this isn't exactly the most private space on board."

"Oh," she said in a soft voice. Taking her by the elbow, I steered her toward the cargo bay.

"So, this is the top level of the cargo bay. It's three levels here, unlike the *New Market,* which was four. Now, the ship's gym is through the back here," I said, leading her across the deck.

"There's a gym?"

"Yup. Most of the crew likes to exercise and while it's not all that big, there aren't a lot of us."

"What's it going to be like?"

"What's what going to be like?"

"Living with these people you want to send us to. The documentary said they were pirates, but Ben told me they're not?"

"No, they're just people who got a raw deal and are trying to start over, somewhere far away from everyone else. They're good people, but as things go, they don't have a lot of luxuries."

She'd been shivering a little in the cargo bay. When we went into the aft section it was warmer and she took a moment to warm up as I showed her the gym.

"You know, you don't have to go, if you don't want to. We can take you to Ceres with us."

She shook her head and sighed, looking up at me. "I have to go with Ben."

"Oh? Why?"

"Because the Clark family was paying me to play up to him, and seduce him and make sure when we got back that they got their hands on him and not the McVays," she said, and took a step back from me with a scared look on her face as I frowned.

"Does Ben know about this?"

She nodded quickly. "I told him everything. Back in the sickbay when he sat with me. I . . . I didn't want to lie to him anymore."

"Oh?"

Aurelia sighed and looked down at her feet. "He asked me why I did it. Part of it was the money, and part of it was I really do like him. He's so damn smart. I mean, I used to think I was smart, I got my master's degree in like a year, and while everyone thought it was because I was sleeping with the professors, it wasn't. I've just always been the smartest person in any of my classes.

"Then one of the older men from the Clark family came along and told me that they'd pay me to date Ben, and well"—she looked up at me and blushed—"he wasn't all that hard to reel in. It didn't hurt that I liked him, and when the cheerleading thing ended we kept seeing each other.

"Then of course he *left,*" she said with a frown.

I couldn't help it, I laughed.

"It's not funny!" she grumbled. "First guy I meet who's way smarter than I am, and he dumps me! So when they asked me to help get him back I made them promise that I'd be on his research team."

"And you believed them?"

She sighed, crestfallen. "Right up until they started to beat me."

"Did Melissa know you were working for the Clarks?"

"I don't know... I don't think so? But I doubt she would have cared if she had. Ted told me more than once that after they got Ben back to Earth he was going to have a 'party' with me and the other three would just laugh every time he did. Like they knew something I didn't." She shivered again. "Then when you caught the lifeboat and started docking with it, they started talking about trying to take the ship and Gil said it didn't matter if anything happened to Melissa. That if they could use her as a hostage, to do so, and if she died, as long as they got Ben her father wouldn't care. I suddenly realized that Ted hadn't been lying about his plans for me, that he was planning on raping and killing me."

She shivered again, wrapping her arms around herself. I stepped closer and gave her a hug, because she obviously needed one.

"So yeah, I messed up. I thought I'd get Ben back and I'd be happy and we'd all be rich and famous. Instead I was going to be murdered and he'd disappear into a lab and never see the light of day again."

I looked down at her. "So, now you want to make it up to him?"

She snorted. "I *still* want him. I told him that straight out, that if I was stupid enough to fall for all of that crap to get him, that now that I had a clear shot at him, well, I wasn't going to give up now. After all, I'd paid for the opportunity with my flesh and blood. But I was going to be honest and tell him everything. So, maybe we won't be rich and famous, but at least we'll be alive, and who knows? If we don't figure out how to make his theories work, maybe our kids will."

"There is that. Now, let's head back to the front and you can go back to bed."

"Thanks for listening, David."

"I just want the two of you to be happy. I want my brother to have the one thing he never had."

"What, a girlfriend?"

I chuckled and shook my head. "The freedom to live his own life. Ever since he published that paper, they've been watching him and telling him what he could and couldn't do. Now he gets to make his own decisions."

I walked her back to the mess, where she gave me a hug, handed me her mug, and headed back to her and Ben's room.

I put her mug in the sink, got another cup full of coffee for myself, and headed down to my own room—

—where a mostly naked Kei almost bumped into me as she came out of her room. Her eyes got wide as I looked her over and she blushed.

"Kei, put some damn clothes on"—I sighed—"or I will start fining your ass."

"Sorry, boss."

"Don't make me sic Hank on you," I grumbled and went inside my own room, closing the door behind me. Three weeks and we'd be home.

It was four more days after my conversation with Aurelia before we rendezvoused with the *Astro Gerlitz* at our usual location well above the plane of the ecliptic. She'd started to become a lot more relaxed in the last few days—well, at least to me it seemed that she had. She was no longer hanging off Ben like she needed to be with him every waking moment. Though she was still showing him a lot of affection when I saw them and whenever he returned it, she really did light up.

While Emiliana had managed to snag us a couple of TEUs with high-dollar cargoes, three quarters of what we were carrying was going to Marcus and his people. We'd fill most of the empty space with a load of ores from them, but this would be the last trip for probably a year. Marcus and his security people wanted to lay low for a while as they took some time to install and use all the stuff we'd shipped them over the last year. Also, we really had cleaned out most of the precious metals, leaving them without much to trade until they started mining again.

Though I had a few ideas I'd thought about on the way here that I was going to share.

"Captain Grohl," I said, coming into the mess on the *Gerlitz*.

"David! What brings you aboard? Not that I don't mind seeing you of course."

I sighed. "I need a favor, a big favor. From Marcus, from all of you."

"Sit, take a load off. This have anything to do with your brother's rescue?"

"You know about that?" I asked, a little surprised.

"Of course. When Paul contacted us to let us know you'd be late, he gave us all the details."

I nodded; it made sense.

"So, what do you need? You want us to try and help you keep an eye on the folks trying to grab your brother?"

"Actually, I want to send him and his fiancée back with you."

"What?" Captain Grohl replied, his eyes showing his surprise. "Why?"

"Because no one knows where you are and he'll be safe."

"Dave, that's a lot to ask! And you'd do that to your own brother? Maroon him out there with the rest of us?"

I had to chuckle at that. "Captain, I'd hardly call it being 'marooned.' Plus it'll only be for a year or two, until folks have forgotten about him."

"We're not a hotel, David, we can't just take in guests."

"Yeah, I get that. He'll have to work, and he'll have to contribute. I'm not worried about that. Ben's no slacker, plus I think Marcus will find him useful."

"Oh? What's so special about your brother?"

"He's a genius. You give him a problem, any problem, he'll figure it out. He's probably got more degrees than you guys have spaceships. That's why the McVay and Clark families want him so badly. Well, that and one other thing."

"What other thing?" Captain Grohl asked, leaning forward and scowling.

"Ben may have figured out the secret to faster-than-light travel."

"And you want to give him to *us*?"

The expression on the captain's face was one of disbelief.

"Look," I said, "if he really does figure this thing out, everyone is going to be looking to steal the secret; there'll be spies everywhere. I'm already planning on building a shipyard for constructing starships, if Ben does figure this out. My grandfather's put up the money for it.

"But, where are we going to build the engines? A nice secret facility out in the middle of nowhere sounds like a good idea to me."

"I think Marcus would be more afraid of the amount of exposure that could end up giving us. What with everyone looking for your 'secret' production base."

"True, but it would also give Marcus and the rest of you first pick on the drives. It would make it easier for you to get things from the rest of the system; it would give you a lot more money to use, because we'd be making a fortune as long as we keep the monopoly; and best of all, with the whole galaxy unlocked, you could all go places where the VMC would never be able to find you."

I watched as Captain Grohl chewed on his lip and nodded his head slowly.

"That... *that's* a good argument. We're so short on so many things still, that if this panned out, the resources we'd be able to bring in would guarantee our survival. Still, it's a lot to ask."

"No, it's not a lot to ask. Not yet. If he finds the answer, and I think we need to build the engines out there, *then* it will be a lot to ask."

"I don't know, David, it's still a lot to ask."

"Captain," I said looking him in the eye, "I'm not doing this because of any other reason than that you people are my *friends* and I need help! Do you think I'd be trusting my brother with you people if I didn't trust you? If you weren't people I can count on?

"I'm not doing all of this," I said, waving my arms back toward the cargo bay, "solely for the money. I like Marcus! I like all of you! You all got screwed, okay? And if there's anyone out there who knows all about screwing people over, you're looking at him! That's why I want to help, because I got a lot to make up for in my life. But right now, I need some help, so I'm asking. Help!"

He sighed and, leaning back, nodded his head. "Fine. We'll take them. I'll make sure Marcus understands everything you just told me. Like it or not, we owe you, and if your brother is half as smart as you make him sound, well, we can always use smart people."

"Oh, one other thing."

"What now?" Captain Grohl said, rolling his eyes.

"I'm probably going to be leaving the *Iowa Hill* soon to work up another ship. Nick, my assistant, will be sitting for his third-class certificate soon and once I'm gone, he'll need an assistant.

I'd rather that person was one of yours if we're going to keep using the *Iowa Hill* to ship your cargoes."

"I'm sure Marcus would want that as well. I'll let him know."

"Thanks," I said and, standing up, I shook hands with him. "Oh, and if anyone seriously messes with my brother, make sure they understand that I will personally come out there and teach them a lesson."

Captain Grohl laughed. "They're still more afraid of you than Marcus whenever they have to deal with Pam. Trust me, they'll behave."

"Great! Now, let me go wish my brother the best, say goodbye to him and his girl, and get them aboard."

Twenty hours later, we'd shipped all of the cargo. I'd hugged my brother and wished him well, then done the same with Aurelia.

"So, what next, boss?" Nick asked as we powered the reactors and grav drives up and headed for Ceres.

"Boredom. Lots and lots of sweet, sweet boredom," I said with a smile.

"Sounds good to me!"

EIGHT

Ceres

ROLLING OVER IN BED, I GLOMMED ONTO KACEY, WHO WAS sitting up.

"I need to go shower, Dave!" She laughed.

"Not if you stay here in bed another day with me, you don't!" I said, pulling her back across the bed.

"Don't you want to, oh, I don't know...eat?"

"Man does not live by food alone!" I replied.

"Yeah, well, this woman does! It's been two *days*, Dave! I think I'd like to rejoin the world for a little while."

"Crushed! I'm crushed! My woman would rather be in society than with me! Oh, how could you do this to me?"

I got a face full of pillow.

"We are going to shower. Also, I think these sheets are going to get washed too, now that I look at them. But that can wait until we after we eat and talk about things *other* than just how much we missed each other, killing pirates, rescuing brothers, and stealing cargo ships."

"What else is there?" I asked. I tossed the pillow on the floor and crawled across the bed to get out of it with her.

"I seemed to remember you handing me a couple of thick folders with some plans and agreements your grandfather wants to go over?"

89

"Why did he even print them out?" I mused. "I mean, why didn't he hand me a data stick or something?"

"Because most people don't know how to take paper and copy it into a computer."

"Really?" I asked looking at her surprised.

"Do you?"

"Ummm..." I scratched my head. "Shower?"

I got hit in the face with another pillow, then retaliated by tickling her when I finally caught up.

Eventually, we did make it into the shower and ended up downstairs in the Doyle family household.

"Morning, Mom," I said as we both walked into the kitchen.

"Morning was over a while ago," Jenny, my stepmother, said with a smile. "Sit down. I heard the shower so I've got something started on the stove."

"Have you and Dad started looking around for a place of your own yet?" I asked as I sat down with Kacey.

"Welll..." she started.

"My mom doesn't want them to move out," Kacey said.

"Oh?" I asked and looked at her. "Why not?"

"Well, I'm the last of the kids living here with Chaz having finally moved out, seeing as he and Hank got their own place. So there's a lot of room, they like having Dianne and your parents around, and most importantly of all!" Kacey grinned at me. "Your mother has been doing all the cooking and cleaning so *mine* doesn't have to!"

"Free maid service? Really?" I said, looking back at my mother, who was blushing.

"It's not *free*...well, not really," she said. "We don't pay any rent, we don't even pay for food, and honestly, David, I *like* being a housewife. Plus Maureen's kitchen is the kitchen of my dreams! You should *see* what she's got in there!"

"Plus your mom is a waaaaay better cook than mine," Kacey said and giggled.

"I thought you all shared cooking duties?" I asked, looking at Kacey.

"Yup, and when Sheila got married and left, there went all the fancy cakes. When Carl left, that was the end of the cookies! Dad'll cook steaks, and boil water, but that's about the height of his skills."

"And you?"

"I figure I'll get your mother to teach me. That or hire someone," Kacey said with another grin. "I mean, we're gonna be rich, right?"

"Technically we're already rich," I said, smiling back at her.

"There is that. So what does your grandfather want to do?"

"Well, first off, he wants us to start handling shipping for him."

"With only one ship? That'll be a trick."

"Maybe, maybe not," I said with a shrug. "I got the impression that he was concerned with certain specialty cargoes."

"You don't think he's doing anything illegal, do you?" my mother asked.

I shook my head. "I think it's probably more a matter of cargoes that he doesn't want the other families to know about—trade secrets, confidential deals, competitive stuff." I turned back to Kacey. "As for only one ship... well, I need to talk to Cheryl about the *New Market*."

"What for?"

"Because it's currently abandoned and I'm one of the few people who know its current orbit and location. It's brand-new, and except for a hole in the upper starboard cargo door and a few bent deck plates in the hold, in perfect condition."

"So you what, want to steal it?"

"I'm not so sure we'll be stealing. It was a pirate ship and we captured it and the crew. That's why I need to talk to her. Hank doesn't think that the McVays will file any sort of claim against it, seeing as it was involved in an act of piracy."

"That was a hundred million Earth-credit ship, if they bought it new," Kacey said, looking at me. "You really think they'll just let it go?"

"That's why I need to talk to Cheryl. She'll know the laws and what we have to do."

"Okay, and what's the other thing your grandfather wants?"

"Oh, this one is easy!" I said with a big smile.

"Great! Easy is good! What is it?"

"We're going to open up a shipyard!"

Kacey stopped and stared at me for a good twenty or thirty seconds.

"Hon, if I were a violent woman, I'd punch you right now. Are you *serious*?"

Taking a deep breath, I nodded and sighed. "I didn't threaten to punch him, but my reaction wasn't much different."

"Why does he want us to do that?"

"Because if and when Ben figures out FTL, someone is going to have to build the drives and the spaceships and he wants it to be us."

"Me and you 'us' or him 'us'?"

"That's what the thicker folder is for. I'm thinking we'll do it like we planned. A three-way ownership deal—us, him, and Ben."

"We get forty percent, the other two get thirty."

"Wow, that was quick!" I said as I laughed.

"We're going to be running it. Your grandfather will be paying for it, and Ben will be putting up the FTL drives. We can hold him off as a non-voting partner until such time as Ben has produced a drive, which will give *us* control."

"You mean *you*," I said with a grin.

"Well, I am the one in charge of business in this family, aren't I?"

"Umm, mostly. Oh, Hank thinks that we may need to change the name of our ship."

"What for?"

"Well, after what happened at the Lassell Orbital, he thinks we may have picked up a reputation for rich cargoes."

"Ah. Maybe after our next trip," Kacey said as my mother put two plates of food down in front of us. Whatever it was, it sure smelled good.

"Where are we going this time?"

"I got us a good contract to deliver spares and replacement parts to a bunch of habitats in the Jupiter region."

"What's the Jupiter region?" I asked as I started eating.

"Everything in the orbit from the L4 point to the L5 point."

I blinked. "That's a pretty large area. How many places are we going to be visiting?"

"All of them, I suspect," she said with a wink as she picked up her fork. "It's a yearlong contract, and if we do a good job they'll sign us to a longer term on the next one."

"Is this with Ceres Habitats?" I asked, a little suspicious.

"Yup! Mom was complaining last month about their current hauler. Some bright boy in Accounting said it would be cheaper to hire someone and not do the deliveries themselves and, well, there aren't a lot of reliable firms running the larger cargo ships looking for work. So Ceres was getting nickeled and dimed on costs by the multiple smaller cargo ships out there. I told her we'd do it, and we worked out a contract."

"Might I remind you of what my grandfather wants?"

"Weren't you just telling me about a brand-new but abandoned cargo ship in need of an owner?" she replied between bites.

I shook my head. "So how much is this making us? Because I'm sure there are a lot more places needing spare parts that I'm sure you'd like to take over the routes for."

"We'll clear about a million a year after salaries and expenses. Half of that will have to go to pay off our outstanding debt with our stockholders. But..."

"But?"

"If we make it to next year and get a five-year contract, I can go to the bank and see about securing a loan to buy another Argon-class ship. Mom's told me that the folks working the Neptune area contracts are just as bad and they want to replace them as well."

I nodded and swallowed what I'd been chewing on. "So we can build our fleet up with a dedicated set of contracts via your mom. I just hope you left enough open time for us to help out our friends."

"Yes, I took them into account, as well as the ability to bid on the occasional specialty high-end contract that doesn't pay enough for the bigger outfits, and is too much for the small fry."

"How long do you think it will take to pay off each ship we buy, then?"

"Ten to twenty years, depending on what shape it is when we get it. However"—she stopped to take a drink before continuing—"if we *are* going to build a shipyard, we can get a deal on ships that need either refueling or new reactors entirely. Then just give ourselves a deal on the cost of the repair work."

"Isn't that, like, illegal?"

"Nope! As long as the other stockholders don't complain, we can do whatever the hell we want. And learning how to refit ships will probably become a very important skill if Ben is successful."

"Huh. Maybe we should hit my grandfather up for the loan instead of the banks."

"You think he'd go for it?"

"If he's making money, he'll go for it. Especially if it's all part of building up the new shipyards. I doubt we'll be able to start off building new ships, so might as well start off rebuilding and refurbishing old ones."

"I really need to read those documents."

"I think what we really need to do is go to the park, maybe catch a movie, visit with some of your friends, and just be a married couple for a few days," I said, smiling over at her.

"Umm, you make a convincing argument. It can wait until later, I'm sure. If nothing else, I can corner Mom after she gets home from work and see if she knows of a good place to put our shipyard."

I smiled and we turned our attentions to our food. After we'd finished, we both gave my mom a hug and headed off to the park—after making sure we were both armed, of course. I didn't know what kind of response my rescuing Ben would elicit, but I wasn't going to assume there wouldn't be one and I wasn't going to take anything for granted.

"Do you really think Ben will solve the whole FTL thing?" Kacey asked much later as we just kicked back on a park bench, enjoying the scenery. The parks on Ceres were huge domed affairs that you could see the stars though when they were in "nighttime" mode. The purpose of the parks here were to keep the people of Ceres from becoming agoraphobic. Just as the city "streets" were all so wide with high ceilings to keep people from feeling claustrophobic. Both of these were serious problems out in the habitats and on a lot of stations and asteroids.

"I haven't got a clue. To be completely honest with you, hon, I'm almost hoping that he doesn't."

"How could you want that?" she asked, sounding a little incredulous.

"Think about it. You want to run a shipping line, I want to tune gravity drives. We both want to raise a family and just have a life, right?"

"Well, yeah."

"Instead we're now going to be building a shipyard. If Ben is successful, we'll have to build an engine-works or some such, for these new drives to be manufactured in. We'll have to manage that, the shipyard, provide security, and hire hundreds of people. Everyone will want a part of us, including the governments of every group in the solar system. We'll have to get our own security, we'll be traveling all over the damn place for business." I shook my head. "Our lives will cease being *our* own."

Kacey was quiet for a while after that. I was starting to wonder what she was thinking about when she suddenly spoke up.

"If Ben is successful, it'll take years to get any sort of meaningful production. Also, we have no idea just how it will work. It may replace grav drives, or it may require ships to have them. Yes, we will become very rich and probably very powerful. But we can and will stay home."

"How can we do that?"

"Simple, if they want to buy our stuff they have to come to us. We stay here on Ceres and we don't leave. If they don't like it, then we can sell to somebody else, or even not at all. If Ben decides to stay out with Marcus and them, once he does figure it out, it's not like we even have to *tell* anyone until we want to."

"And what do I tell my grandfather?"

"That if it does work out, you'll name a line of starships after him and the family so no one ever forgets who paid for it?"

I laughed. "Seriously? You think that'd do it?"

"David, hon, what do you give the man who already has everything?"

"I don't know, what?"

"Immortality."

I thought about that a moment. "Oh."

"But for now we have much more pressing things to think about."

"The shipyard?"

"No, the Jupiter run I contracted us for. Each leg is about a three-month cycle. Once you get your assistant Nick up to speed, we can hire someone to help him, and we can start dealing with other things."

"Such as?" I asked her.

"Buying a house, setting up your shop, getting us an office, wheedling your mom into coming to work for us." Kacey leaned into me. "Starting a family."

My eyes got wide at that.

"Umm, right, family."

"Which is all the more reason for you to stop shipping out and stay home."

Putting my arm around her, I hugged her close. "Yeah, it is. I never planned on staying a spacer any longer than I absolutely needed to. I'll have the hours I need for engineer second after the next trip. Then I just have to wait a few years to have the time in grade."

"What's it take to get to first?"

"Three thousand more hours, and only a thousand of those have to be from being shipboard. You just have to be doing actual engineering work as it applies to ships."

"Is there a time requirement?"

"No, but the test takes three days and is a complete bear. Honestly I'd never really thought I'd go for it, that second would be more than enough, but..."

"But if we're going to be running a shipyard, and possibly an engine-works, you'll need it?"

I nodded. "Yeah, that."

"Well, like you said, none of this is going to happen overnight. Now, let's go see what kind of trouble my brother is getting up to."

"Which one?"

"All of them!"

Getting up, we walked back to the entryway we'd taken. It really was a lot like being outside back on Earth. True, it wasn't as hot and there wasn't any kind of breeze, but it was still nice.

We got down to the "street" after passing through a series of "pressure ways" that were a series of "air gates" that kept the atmosphere up in the dome from interacting with that of the first level. It also was where the emergency pressure doors were located, which would seal the park from the rest of the upper level if there was any kind of leak or breach.

There were actually pressure bulkheads hidden all over the first level. As you went further down, there were less of them, but they were still there. The population of Ceres was well over twenty million at this point. As they continued to dig out more and more and build their "onion" of layer inside layer, eventually the amount of real estate would easily equal that of the Earth's. Which meant that the population would continue to grow as well. Making sure that any one accident or disaster was kept as local as possible so as to not endanger the rest of the population was important.

Though those methods changed the deeper you got. Or at

least that was what I'd been told as they were still working on the third level. However the fourth and fifth were already well past the planning stage.

"I wish your brother Ben was here," my mom said the next morning as we all sat around having breakfast.

"It's just not safe here for him right now, Mom. Besides, I think he could stand some private time with his girlfriend."

"Ben got a new girlfriend?" Dianne, my younger sister, asked.

"They dated some when he was at MIT. She was the 'bait' they used to get him alone so they could kidnap him."

"And he's still dating her?" Dianne said, surprised.

"They were doing bad things to her," Mom said, looking over at Dianne. "Dave told your father and me all about it. So you will *not* be bringing it up with her, understand?"

"Yes, Mom," Dianne said with a hint of embarrassment.

"Kacey, I'll need you to come in sometime today so I can go over the delivery dates with you," Maureen, her mother and my mother-in-law, said.

"I'll go in with you, Dad, and Kurt," she said, nodding toward my father, who'd taken a job with Ceres Habitats. "What are your plans for the day?" she asked next, looking at me.

"I'm going to go talk to Cheryl about salvage rights. After that, I'm going to grab Nick and go do an engineering inspection on our ship. We're coming up on our yearly soon. I'll be scheduling that for when we get back from our cargo run."

"I'll meet you out on the ship then after lunch and we can start going over the things your grandfather gave you."

"Are you really planning on building a shipyard here?" Rob, Kacey's father and my father-in-law, asked me.

"Looks like. I seem to recall there being a lot of talk of expansion in that area back when I first came here."

"There was and there still is. If you're looking to buy some land for it, you might want to move on that soon. The government is definitely getting ready to sell off more surface lots."

"Any idea how much we should be asking for?"

"I'd say a two- or three-kilometer square area would be big enough. Remember you're going to be building down and not just up, so make sure that you've got the rights to build down at least a half a kilometer."

"Down?"

"It's cheaper to quarry out your docks and hangers than to build them up on the surface. It's also easier if your workers are in a shirtsleeves environment than one requiring pressure suits and space suits."

"Hmm," I said as I thought about that. "Think you might want a job?"

"Hey! Quit trying to steal my best project manager!" Maureen said, looking up.

I smiled at her, "But, *Mom*, it's going to be called *Doyle Shipbuilders*—who else am I going to steal?"

"One of your brother-in-laws!"

"You know," Rob said with a thoughtful look in his eye, "we could bring my father in as the president, I could be the vice president..."

"You'd drag Grandpa out of retirement?" Kacey asked, looking over at her father.

"Oh, he'd love it! Starting a new company is right up his alley. Plus he still has a lot of clout. When we actually start doing business I could take over the day-to-day and you just kick him up to the board."

"Rob..." Maureen said, looking at her husband, who just smiled back at her.

"Yeah, I think that's my cue to go meet with Cheryl!" I said, getting up from the table. Taking a moment, I gave both moms a hug, then gave Kacey a hug and a kiss. Gathering up my things, I went out the front door...

...and right into an ambush.

"Mr. Doyle! It is true that you kidnapped your brother?"

"Mr. Doyle! Are you related to the Morgan family?"

"Can you please answer some questions for us, Mr. Doyle?"

I sighed and looked around at the small crowd on the street. There were a half dozen reporters and three or four cameramen. It was hard to tell, as the cameras some of them were using were small.

"What's going on here?" I asked, giving them a bewildered look.

"Haven't you read the news?" said one of them—a very attractive woman who was definitely too old for me, even if I wasn't married.

"Obviously not. You are?"

"Dara Knight, Ceres News System."

"And just what news are we talking about?"

"Earthgov is trying to have you extradited on charges of piracy."

"Oh? They are? Why?"

"They're claiming you boarded an Earthgov flagged cargo ship, then kidnapped the entire crew."

"Would this be the same ship that kidnapped a member of my family and a citizen of Ceres?"

That stopped her.

"They did what?" she asked.

"Several weeks ago, a citizen of Ceres was kidnapped by members of the McVay family, one of the very rich elite families on Earth. I think this is illegal even under the laws of Earth, not to mention our own."

"So you're admitting you attacked and boarded the ship?" one of the other reporters called out.

"The ship that ordered the *New Market* to heave to, and then fired upon her when she did not, was an *Earthgov* flagged destroyer. The captain an Earthgov officer. The captain ordered the boarding and the removal of the crew. I was there solely as an observer and concerned party."

"If that's true, why are they trying to have you extradited, Mr. Doyle?" Dara asked, getting control of the interview back.

I shrugged. "Not a clue. Obviously this is the first I've heard of it. Guess I need to talk to my lawyer."

"Would we be talking about the *same* family member they tried to charge you with kidnapping over his emigrating to Ceres?"

"Yes, and before you ask, no, I'm not going to tell you where he is. He's currently in seclusion after having dealt with that ordeal. Being taken by pirates is not a pleasant experience."

"Mr. Doyle, are you accusing the McVay family of *piracy*?"

"When you take someone against their will onto a ship and spirit them away, what else do you call it?" I asked with a frown. "Now if you'll excuse me...?"

"What about your relationship with the Morgan family?" someone else called out.

"What about it?"

"Is it true?"

"Hold on, let me ask all of my bodyguards, servants, and whatever it is you call those people that the obscenely rich always seem to have hanging around." And then I started looking all around me.

"Huh, guess I'm still just a working stiff like the rest of you!" I said, grinning back at them. "Now, I really have to go or I'll be late." And with that I walked off quickly.

"David! What brings you by? Oh, and I saw your interview," Cheryl said as I walked in.

"Already?"

"You're a client, as well as family. I have an app on my tablet that alerts me of these things."

"Oh! How'd I do?"

"Not bad, but in the future, you say 'No Comment,' or 'My office will release a statement once I have been made aware of all the particulars.'"

"I'll try to remember that. Are they really trying to have me extradited?"

"Probably, but they didn't have any success with the kidnapping case and after what you just said in that interview they'll have even less success with this one. Were you really on an Earthgov destroyer?"

I gave her a guilty smile. "My grandfather's yacht is a converted, modern, Earthgov Navy ship. According to the captain, the ship is part of the reserve fleet and can be recalled in case of an emergency, and he was also a reserve officer. So technically both of those statements are true. At least, that's what he told me."

"I'm sure your grandfather will grease enough wheels to make sure it's ruled that way," she said with a snort. "Now, is there anything else you have on your mind?"

I told her about the *New Market* and everything that had happened.

"Hmm, I'll have to look into that. If you'd brought it back here as a prize ship, you probably would have been allowed to keep it, unless the owners bailed it out. But you left it derelict, so that changes things. Their insurance company will have first claim on it, regardless of whether they filed a claim or not, and at a hundred million plus, they're going to want to exercise that claim."

"But no one other than me knows where it is," I pointed out.

"It's a lot easier to find a ship that close to Earth orbit. So they just might decide to launch a search operation of some kind."

"Doesn't their being involved in a criminal action change things?"

"Not really. The owners will claim that they had no idea what the crew was up to, and that they bear no responsibility for what happened. As it's an Earthgov flagged ship, that's for the courts to decide. So even if the Mars government finds the crew guilty of kidnapping or piracy, it won't have any bearing on what happens to the ship."

"So how long before I *can* claim it?"

"Probably a year. If they leave it derelict that long, then they've abandoned any claim. A lot will depend on whether they file an intent to salvage. If they don't, that makes things a lot easier. I'm guessing you changed the orbit on it?"

"I thought it wouldn't be safe to allow it to fly untended and uncontrolled into such a busy area as Earth space," I told her with a serious look on my face.

"Sure you did."

I laughed. "Well, it was traveling at a pretty good velocity when we took it. So that's not as much of a lie as you might think."

"I'll assign someone in my office to keep an eye on the claims statements coming out of Earth, then. Are you in any kind of rush to claim it?"

"Not right now. Plus it's going to need some repair work, so we need to save up some capital."

"Sure you don't want to sell it? A ship that new would bring in a fair bit of money."

"*That* decision I'll leave up to Kacey."

Cheryl laughed. "Can't say as I blame you, she's got her mother's determination and her grandfather's sense for business."

"That's good, because all of this is a bit more than I ever expected to deal with."

"Yeah, life's like that."

"You mean life with the *Doyles* is like that," I said with a grin.

"Well, yeah, that's us! Stirring things up is like the family motto. If there's nothing else, I need to throw you out as I have a legal brief I need to prepare for a case this afternoon."

"Nope, see you later, Cheryl," I said, giving her a hug.

"And I'll make some inquiries on the whole extradition thing, but I wouldn't worry about it."

"Thanks!"

Leaving her office, I caught a tram down to the spaceport and, after checking with the port authority office there, I went aboard the *Iowa Hill.* Nick, Yuri, Kei, and Paul and his wife Kat were all living on board, because it was free as they were crew members. Also none of them really wanted to make a home here, as that really was back on Eris, though it would be years before they got any opportunity to go back there and visit.

Stepping into Engineering, I took a moment to look around the place that had been my real home for several years now. It was old, it was outdated, the two Siz-gees were on their last leg and would need replacing in seven or so years—that or the ship would have to be scrapped. But at least it was clean and neat and it was mine.

I flashed back on the day before I'd sat the test for my own engineer third's certificate and, like Dot had back then, I turned to face my assistant.

"Come on, Nick, inspection time!"

"I was hoping to study for my test, Dave," Nicolas said, looking up from the book he'd been studying while sitting at the main console.

"Yup, everything we're going to do today will most definitely be on the test. Which I've already scheduled you for, tomorrow morning at nine."

"What?"

"Oh, and the panel refurbishing examination will be after that."

"But I'm not ready!"

"Hence why today is going to be a practical review of everything you need to know. Plus we're coming up on our yearly inspection and I want to make sure that everything and anything *we* can fix, is fixed. It's a lot cheaper for us that way."

"You're a slave driver, you know that?"

"Yup, learned from the best too! Now, let's get hopping, this is going to take all day and then some."

It took us till almost 8:00 P.M. to finish with the inspection, because we found a few things that did need replacing or repairing. Kacey had come aboard sometime after lunch and when I got out of the shower we went up to the mess to get something to eat. She'd already let her mother know we'd be staying on the ship tonight.

"So, what's the verdict?" I asked as I helped her make us dinner.

"The shipyard stuff is fairly cut-and-dried. There are a few changes I want made, like the percentage split I told you about. We will also be exercising control of Ben's shares until such time as he's able to buy in."

"You sure my grandfather would go for that? He's putting up a lot of money."

"Ceres won't sell property to anyone who isn't a citizen and when it comes to a corporation, it needs for the majority of shareholders to be Ceres citizens. Some of the other details are the Morgan family percentage gets a higher repay rate for the first two decades so they can recoup their investment faster, but there's an interesting part to that."

"Oh? What?"

"The accounts that the repayments are made into will be split between an Earth account and a Ceres account."

"Why does he want to do that?"

"Because the Ceres account is going to be controlled by you."

"Me?" I said, looking at her surprised.

"I think this is your grandfather's way of giving you your share of the Morgan family assets. If this thing goes belly up, well, you get nothing. If it's wildly successful, you get not only the company, but probably half the money he puts up to start it."

"And just how much will that be?"

"Four billion Earth credits."

I stared at her a moment, the only sound in the galley area being the fork I dropped hitting the floor.

"How much?"

"Your grandfather is putting a sizable amount of his operating capital into our business. But didn't you once tell me he's worth a couple *trillion*?"

"Still...that's a lot."

"Sure is. But we're putting up the skills and management to do it, and if your grandfather's gamble pays off, we'll be making that kind of money every year or two."

"How can we make that much money? The Xenon-class freighter we took was only about a hundred million! You could buy forty of them for that much money!"

"How much money do you think we'll be selling our starships for?" Kacey asked, turning to face me.

"Huh? I don't know, I guess it depends on how big they are?"

"Half a billion dollars apiece."

"What?"

"That's how much we're going to sell them for, until no one can afford it anymore. Then we'll start lowering the price."

"And just who would pay that?"

"Every government in the solar system. We'll probably be backlogged so bad we'll have to build another shipyard. Dave, we're going to be the *only* people building and selling these. Maybe we'll start selling the engines to another company after a while, if we can build those fast enough. But we'll be selling *those* at two hundred million apiece, I suspect."

I stopped and stared at her a moment.

"We need to build the engine-works on Eris, don't we?" I asked her in a soft voice.

"It would make the most sense," she agreed with a nod. "But if we do that, we're going to have to find some people we can trust to run it for us. Some people who will be happy to move there and *stay* there."

"That won't be easy."

"No, probably not. Besides, building these things may require a lot more equipment, and specialized equipment at that, than we can ship out there. So we may very well end up building them here. But until Ben figures it out, it's all just idle speculation."

I nodded and bent over to pick up the fork I dropped.

"What's the other thing, the shipping contracts?"

"That's actually a lot more reasonable. It's a cost plus, so we're guaranteed a good profit. In some ways it's not all that different from the contract I just signed with Ceres Habitats."

"So what are we shipping, and to where?"

"Food and supplies to a couple of dark habs that apparently your family owns."

"My family as in the Morgans?"

"Yup."

"Why do they own a couple of dark habs?"

"They're researching and building ship-based weaponry."

"What? Why are they doing that?"

"Because starships are going to need to be well armed to avoid being taken by pirates. Also because when the VMC finally pops, someone is going to need to build a bunch more warships than

Mars, Earth, Ceres, or Jupiter currently have. And those ships are going to need weapons. So your grandfather somehow either purchased, or built, two dark habs that are doing this. We bring food and parts in, haul weapons out."

"And just where are we going to haul them too?"

"I think our shipyard is going to have a very large weapons depot," Kacey said with a smile. "There is one drawback, though."

"And that would be?"

"We need to get our hands on a couple of Argon-class ships. They're old, so no one will think twice about them, they're small enough that no one will be surprised that they're running supplies to small or remote habs, and the cargoes aren't going to be all that large."

I nodded. "Makes sense. Oh, I asked Cheryl about the *New Market*."

"Oh, what did she say?"

I relayed the conversation we'd had.

"You know, if we sold it, we could easily buy several Argon-class ships."

"That's what I was just thinking. Also, I'd be afraid to fly that thing anywhere within Earth space. They just may decide that they want it back."

"Point."

"So what do we tell him?" I asked her as she started cooking.

"Yes. That's what we tell him, assuming he agrees to my terms on the shipyards. The shipping thing we won't be able to start until after we finish the first run for Ceres, because we'll have to salvage the *New Market*, then not only sell it, but purchase a couple of smaller freighters, hire crews, that sort of thing."

"Damn," I said, blowing out my breath. "Just how secret are these habs? Do we need crews that are sworn to secrecy? Or what?"

"As long as we don't tell the crews what's in the containers coming back, we should be okay."

"We may need to talk to the president's head of security," I said after thinking about that a moment.

"Why?"

"So if they decide to spy on us, they won't do anything to give it away to anyone else? I mean, I'd think if any pirate out there found out that there was a small freighter hauling weapons that they'd try to grab it."

"Ugh, yet another complication," Kacey said, shaking her head.

"Well, hopefully those habs are someplace nearby or at least not anywhere with a lot of piracy."

"We may end up paying the government for an escort. I better add a rider for that to the contract."

"Not to change the subject, but when does your mother want us to leave?"

"Six days. She's got plots for us, all of that."

"She does?"

Kacey nodded. "They've got a lot of high-end plotting computers at Ceres Habs. So they plot it all out to make it easier for you to get the deliveries on time. The whole route should run us about eighty days. Most of the layovers aren't very long as we're only off-loading a container or two."

"There are some bigger deliveries, though?"

"Yeah, there's two big ones that will unload several hundred containers each. Those are places that serve as local suppliers for all of the habitats and orbitals in an area."

"That's a lot of orbital parts."

"Some of them are huge, but it's not just stuff for the habs themselves, there's a lot of stuff that people put in habitats that Ceres also makes. They serve a fairly broad market."

"If you say so. I'm just the delivery guy," I said with a grin.

"Oh, is that so? Then how about after we eat you make a few deliveries for me?" Kacey said with a saucy smile as she leaned into me.

"Oh, I like the sound of that!"

"I thought you would..."

NINE

Ganymede Orbital Two

"WOW, THIS PLACE IS NASTY," KACEY SAID AS WE WALKED DOWN to the office for the company that was receiving our shipment. We were sixty-three days into our trip and the company that ran Ganymedes One, Two, and Three had their main parts storage here.

"Yup, this was the first place I'd ever been to when I shipped out with the *Iowa Hill*, and I gotta tell you, I was *not* impressed!"

"Do they always keep it this cold?" she asked with a shiver.

"Sadly, yes. The main concourse isn't much better either. Not a lot of people live here, so they cut costs wherever they can."

"Yeah, I can see they don't clean much either," she grumbled as we came to the end of the large docking arm. We went through the locks to the main concourse, which was positively balmy after being in the near freezing docking arm.

Kacey checked her tablet while I took a good look around to make sure no one was taking "too much" of an interest. The working girls, as well as the working boys, were lounging about and looking pretty. With the amount of traffic Ganymede Two got, I'm sure business was good.

Kacey looked up, got her bearings, and we headed off down the main concourse passageway. When we got to the far end, there was a nice looking door with the sign GANYMEDE ORBITAL CORPORATION – SHIPPING AND RECEIVING.

"Looks like the place."

"Sure does," I agreed and, opening the door, we went inside.

"Can I help you?" the receptionist at the front desk asked.

"*Iowa Hill*, we're delivering from Ceres Habitats," Kacey said, showing the woman her slate.

"Oh! Right. I think Doug just sent the crew out to unload. Let me take you back to his desk."

Getting up, she showed us into the back where a large man was on the phone with someone.

"Doug, these are the folks with the Ceres Habitats delivery."

"Let me call you back," Doug said and hung up. "You're early!"

"That's not a problem, is it?" Kacey asked.

"Thankfully, no. It's better than that last group who were always late."

"Yes, well, you'll notice we also have a much larger ship and we're hoping that, with us being a more dependable hauler, perhaps we could work out some agreements for any cargoes you may have going our way? Seeing as we're already on a fixed schedule, we could offer some very competitive rates on tonnage."

I watched as his eyebrows went up a hair. "Won't that get you in trouble with Ceres Habitats?"

"As long as their cargo is prioritized and reaches its destination on time, our contract allows for us to haul other freight. As we're already going to these places"—she showed him our schedule—"we can be *very* competitive."

"Sit, please, sit!" he said, smiling. "Anything that reduces our overhead is always welcome!"

We both grabbed seats and I watched as Kacey started horse-trading. She'd been doing this at every place we'd stopped that had regularly scheduled shipments. Because we had to make the movement for Ceres Habitats already, we could offer a lower rate than just about anyone else.

This had been a part of Kacey's strategy when she signed the contract with her mother: to pick up cargoes of opportunity, as these would have a very high-profit ratio for us. Showing up early would give us the time to load and the rates we could give for a haul back to Ceres would be the lowest out there. So by making introductions now and talking with those in charge, when the *Iowa Hill* came through on its next run, she could contact people like Doug a month or two in advance and maybe work out a deal.

This way the ship wouldn't be coming home empty, and a few extra stops along the way wouldn't hurt the bottom line either. What made it work was that while the Ceres Habitats cargoes had to be moved on a schedule, the stuff Kacey was hoping to pick up wouldn't. Or it would be a much looser one. It was sheer genius that she'd come up with this. The smaller concerns who'd been doing this job before us had smaller ships and hadn't had the smarts to take advantage of an empty ship dead-heading back to Ceres.

"You are a genius," I told her as we made our way back to the *Iowa Hill.*

Kacey smiled. "We'll see. He's definitely interested as we can help his bottom line. Once we've proved ourselves, then I'll see about enlisting his help for those times he doesn't have something for us, but maybe he has a friend who does? For a percentage, of course."

I laughed. "Of course."

Just then my slate pinged. I grabbed it and saw it was Chris, our captain.

"Chris, what's up?"

"Come back to the ship immediately. Bring Kacey and anyone else you see."

"On my way," I said but he'd already cut the connection.

"What was that all about?" Kacey asked.

"I don't know, but we're going to find out," I said and we all but ran back to the ship. We coded in through the lock, and immediately went up to the mess. Everyone was sitting there except for Hank, who I guess was overseeing the unloading.

"What's going—" I started to say and Chris pointed to the monitor on the far wall. The headline across the top identified it as a Ceres Government broadcast. There was a man sitting at desk who I recognized as one of the usual news readers.

"Again, Ceres is under attack. We have identified the ships attacking us as from the Venusian Moral Collective. They approached and without warning began bombarding the docking areas. Our patrol ships are on their way back to the area and our defensive systems have already destroyed two of the attacking warships. To all Ceres ships, *stay away*! I repeat, *stay away* from Ceres until such time that the enemy ships have either been destroyed or retreated. Only Ceres-registered ships with weapons are allowed into the area at this time. What's that?" he said, looking off to the side.

"We now have video from the surface!"

The view changed as he repeated his warning about avoiding Ceres. There were three ships, lined up nose to tail, firing rail guns at the surface, an occasional missile streaking down. There was a fourth ship, but it was drifting out of formation with a cloud of debris around it.

"I wonder where the other one they destroyed is?" Chaz asked softly.

Suddenly the camera pulled back, way back, and an ore boat came streaking across the view from the left side. Lasers on the lead ship immediately started shooting at it. You could see the metal on the front of it starting to ablate; ore boats had a fair bit of armor on them, because of the environment they worked in.

"What is that idiot trying to—" Chris started to mutter and then cut off as the boat slammed directly into the lead ship, tearing through the hull and exploding.

"Oh my god!" Emiliana said.

"Shit, there's *more* of them!" Chaz said, pointing.

Sure enough there were several more that were flying in. A missile came boosting up from the surface and while the second ship was trying to destroy it with its defense lasers, two ore boats flipped bow for stern and came at it. One hit dead-on, the other ripped across the ship's side, tearing it open, then tumbling out of the view of the camera just as the missile hit, breaking the ship in two.

The third ship started breaking orbit, but three more ore boats crashed into it, two of which had flipped before doing so, the third one just drove straight in.

"...all of the attacking ships have been destroyed! I repeat, all of the attacking ships have been destroyed! We need emergency personnel to head to the following areas that have been attacked and had their pressure containment breached!"

I stared at the screen as he listed a number of places, a few of which I knew, but most of which I didn't. None of them were where my in-laws lived, thankfully.

"To all those Ceres citizens abroad, we are now at war with the Venusian Moral Collective. We do not know why they launched this surprise attack! The attack began around two p.m. local. This presentation will now repeat for the next twenty-four hours!"

And with that it looped back to the newsreader, announcing that there had been an accident at the main port docks and for everyone to avoid the area. That was followed by two more accident reports, then the announcement we'd walked in on.

"How old is that?" I asked Chris.

"We're about an hour's transmission distance from Ceres right now. I'd just caught the end of general transmission on voice channels that Ceres was under attack when I messaged you. I don't think we saw it live, that was on a government shipping channel and we're picking it up off of the station's repeater."

I swore as I thought about what we saw.

"Why did they attack us?" Emiliana asked, looking around the mess.

"Because they believe that Ceres is harboring those folks we've been helping, that's why," I said with a sigh. "Kace, how many more stops before we can head home?"

"Just two, both are small."

"Shouldn't we just go home?" Emiliana asked.

"We're just a cargo ship. It's not like we can do anything. Plus with the main docks out, we may not even be able to land."

"Emil, how long until we're off-loaded?"

She looked at her tablet. "Eight hours."

"Okay, Chris, we're pulling out ten minutes after they seal us up. Make sure everyone knows if they're going ashore they need to be back here an hour prior."

Getting out my own tablet, I check to make sure the feed to the Ganymede message service was up. I opened up my mail program, made sure the encryption was on, and sent my grandfather a message.

Grandfather, we'll be pulling out of Ganymede Two four hours after you get this. Why was Ceres attacked?

I paid the fee to get it sent out in the next info packet and pressed SEND. I didn't know if I'd get an answer before we left, or if I'd get anything at all. But if someone had figured out what I was doing with the *Iowa Hill*, my grandfather just might know about it. I'd have to corner Paul at some point and ask him to check with Marcus and his people to see if they knew anything.

"Did you just ask your grandfather?" Kacey whispered to me.

"I'm worried that someone figured out what we've been doing," I whispered back. "He's got access to an Earthgov senator, so I suspect he'll know the reason soon enough."

"What happens if he says it's our fault?"

"Then I guess we'll be leaving Ceres and going someplace else," I said with a heavy sigh. "They'll probably let me take my panel-refurbishing shop back."

"You think they'd kick us out?"

"You? No. Me? Probably. I mean, this was all my idea, right?"

Kacey gave me a hug then and we all just sat there for a while, shell-shocked.

"I'll go out and give Hank a break," Paul said after long while.

"I need to check on things as well." Chris sighed and followed Paul a minute later. The rest of us all got up then, and went back to what we were doing, or took care of what we needed to do. We'd all be back in Ceres space in a little more than a week.

I just wondered what we'd find and what our reception would be.

"Damn, that doesn't look good," Chris said over the all-hands intercom as we approached Ceres. "The main docks are now just a big hole in the ground. A very big hole. There's a fair bit of traffic in parking orbits. Let me call Ceres Control, hold on a minute."

I looked at Kacey, who was sitting with me and Nick down in Engineering.

"*All* four of the major commercial ports have been destroyed. They even hit our naval yard."

Kacey reached over and hit the comm button. "See if we can land at Ceres Habs, we're on contract to them."

"Will do."

"Okay," Chris said a minute later, "we can land at Ceres Habs, but we're going to be landing on the surface. We'll have to suit up to go ashore. All of the docks that have ground power and boarding tubes are being taken up with official business, transports, or priority cargoes."

"Any word on the smaller ports?"

"Some are damaged, but not destroyed. The smaller cargo

ships of our class and some of the larger ones have places to dock, but right now those have got a waiting list, from the sounds of what I'm hearing.

"Prepare for landing, Dave."

"Everything's running, Chris," I told him and then kept an eye on the gear. I was surprised at how quickly he brought us down. Either space was crowded and they wanted it clear, or he was just as worried as the rest of us as to what we'd be finding.

I felt it when we touched down and then watched as the grav drives quickly powered down.

"Engineering, secure from flight."

"Securing. Should I take the reactors all the way down? We have enough fuel for the APU to keep the basic systems running for a month."

"I think that'll be yours and Kacey's call. Though I don't think we should leave anybody on board. If the VMC come back, sitting on the surface in a cargo ship probably isn't the safest place to be."

"Got it, I'll shut the reactors down, then. Attention everyone, we will all be going ashore. Those of you who need a place to stay, Kacey and I will take care of it. So don your pressure suits or space suits, pack whatever gear you'll need for now, and meet at the main lock in thirty minutes."

I let go of the intercom button and turned to Nick. "Go get your things and suit up."

"Will do!"

"I'll meet you in our cabin after I get all of this put to bed," I told Kacey as I set about powering down one of the reactors. I already had the APU running as we always had that on for takeoff and landing, so it was just a simple matter of making sure that Environmental and the ship's computers had power.

"All hands, gravity will be lowered down to Ceres normal in five minutes," I said, using the all-hands. The APU didn't have the ability to power the grav drive. So once I shut down the other reactor, I'd have to shut down the panels to avoid throwing any breakers. I had a suspicion that we probably would be here a lot longer than either Kacey or I had planned on.

When I finally had the reactors dialed down to their lowest level, I got up and went to Kacey and mine's cabin, where she was packing a number of things into airtight bags. Stripping down, I got into my pressure suit, then put on my parka and associated insulated pants. I made sure I had my tablet, and other than that there wasn't anything I really needed as I had extra clothes at Kacey's.

I led the way out to the air lock and waited for Chris and the others.

"Wait at the bottom of the ladder when you get out. I'll come out last," Chris told everyone. "It's easy to get lost out there if you don't know where you're going. Once I lock up the ship, I'll come down and show you where to go."

"I'll go first," I said and went into the lock with Kacey and Nick. We probably could have cycled more through, but this made it easier. When we got outside, I helped Kacey down as she had a couple of things she was carrying. Once we got clear I stood back a little and looked around.

Other than that one time we'd transferred to the *Iowa Hill* after Hank and Chaz had strung the lines to it, I'd never really *been* outside in a real vacuum before. I'd most certainly never stood on a planet or dwarf planet with no atmosphere and looked out at the plain grayish rocks and around at all the... "desolation," I guess you'd call it. I could see there were ships lined up beyond ours and someone had put down some sort of string light to define a path to where the air lock probably was.

"Follow me," Chaz said with a wave and we all trooped off after him with Hank and Chris bringing up the rear.

"Been here before, Chaz?" I asked over the radio.

"Yup. This is where they used to stage the ore boats. See that green beacon?" he said, pointing ahead.

"Yeah?"

"That's the standard marker for an air lock out here in the asteroid belt. Green is a pretty uncommon color out here, especially when it's that bright. It stands out."

"Learn something new every day," somebody muttered.

"If you start getting cold or hot, let me know. Those pressure suits don't insulate you much and while the parkas and the rest help, call out if you're having any problems."

"Just how far are we walking?" Nick asked.

"Five minutes. Not enough for any of you to get in trouble, but it still pays for us to be careful," Hank said from the back. "We're used to working in vacuum and understand all the dangers.

The ground you're walking on, for example, is leaching the heat out of your body. More so if it's in the shade. So before coming back out, you'll all want to buy a set of insulating overshoes to protect from that."

"We'll send you a link," Chaz added.

I found the beacon and kept my eye on it as we walked and Chaz and Hank kept up their banter. Which I was starting to realize was more to keep everyone's minds occupied and all of us moving forward. I could only guess that some people didn't do well in this environment and they were keeping us distracted to cut down on any possible problems.

When we got to the air lock, Chaz just waved us all in. It was a much larger one than on the ship, and we all fit in easily. Once inside, Maureen made a beeline for Kacey and hugged her tight.

I helped Kacey get her helmet off.

"Mom, I'm okay, I'm not the one who got attacked."

Chaz walked over and was immediately grabbed as well. At least he'd already taken off his helmet.

"Jeff's dead!" Maureen sobbed. The effect on Chaz and Kacey was immediate.

"What? What happened, Mom?" Chaz asked.

"He was working near the spaceport when they attacked it. The first missile barrage took out the tower and the defenses. No one knew what was going on and he ran in there with a bunch of enforcers to see who they could help. Then the second missile hit."

"And?"

"It was a small nuke. It vaporized several of the docked ships, as well as the roof structure. The shock wave blew out all the walls and everyone down there was killed instantly!"

"Oh my god! How many people died?" Kacey asked.

"So far they think we lost about fifty thousand, from the attacks on the ports, and the random attacks on some of the surface. They were trying to shoot their rail guns deep enough to breach the first level. They got through in a few spots, but the damage was minimal in most cases. Though they did hit a few structures with people in them."

Chris came over then and hugged Maureen—she was his aunt—and I joined him as well.

I gave them a minute to settle down. Emiliana had joined

us, as well as Hank. Paul, Katy, Yuri, Kei, and Nick were all looking a little lost.

"Kacey, you and the others take Mom and head back to the house. I'll take Paul and the others here and get them settled in at a hotel somewhere nearby. Okay?"

"I'll go with him and keep him out of trouble," Hank volunteered.

Kacey and Chaz both nodded and with Chris and Emiliana in tow, they headed deeper inside.

I looked for a sign pointing out the way to the tram station, and once I spotted that I led the others off.

"You don't think they'll blame us, do you?" Yuri asked in a soft voice.

"No, but don't go telling anybody where you're from either," I told all of them in a low voice. "Stick to your covers. My biggest fear right now is that the VMC knows about the *Iowa Hill* and they attacked Ceres because that's where she's flagged. If that's the case, we'll have to rename her, probably replace the transponder and maybe even paint her. Then again, they might just blame me for all of this, and all of you will end up with a new boss."

They nodded quietly and didn't say another word until after we'd gotten them checked in at a hotel within walking distance of the Doyle household.

"Are you really that worried?" Hank asked me after we'd left the hotel.

"I'm the only common thread here, Hank. I'm the one who pushed to help them. I'm the one who *has* been helping them. I don't see any other alternative here. If they don't come by and drag me off tonight, I'll just go down there and save them the trouble in the morning."

"And do what? Turn yourself in?"

I shrugged. "Right now I'm still a bit numb. Yeah, I'm pissed. They came here and killed all those people, and they did it without warning. Wouldn't mind doing the same thing to them. Just imagine what a ship like the *Iowa Hill* would do to one of their floating cities if we brought it down out of orbit and just crashed into it at full power, like those guys in the ore boats did to those warships."

"Do you think you could get that close?" Hank asked, giving me a look.

"Hank, nobody bothers the tramps. We're slow, we're unarmed, and completely harmless. We change the name, false-flag the transponder to show we're flagged with Earth or Mars, and they'd just ignore us until it was too late."

Hank nodded slowly as we walked.

"It's not a bad idea, Dave."

"It isn't?"

"No, but a very famous general once said: 'It's not the duty of a soldier to die for his country.'"

"It's not?" I asked giving him a surprised look.

"No, his duty is to make the other poor dumb bastard die for his!" Hank said grinning at me.

"Yeah, but how else could a tramp like ours destroy a city?"

"When you get the chance, look up 'Rods from God.'"

"Rods from ... what?"

"God."

"What are those?"

"Just the thing you're looking for."

We got to the house then and we went inside. The others were already here, along with the entire Doyle clan. There was a lot of crying going on. I knew that tonight wasn't going to be an easy one. Not an easy one at all.

It was hours later and I was lying in bed with Kacey, who had all but cried herself to sleep. Finding out her brother had died in the line of duty was hard. Just as hard as finding out several other people that she knew were now dead as well.

I had my tablet out and was looking at a picture, having looked up "Rods from God."

It was slang for a high-tech kinetic bombardment tool that had been invented about two hundred years ago. It was basically a tungsten "telephone pole," with a chemical rocket on the back that "launched" the rod at over twenty gravities toward the surface of the planet below, before burning out. A simplistic and minimal guidance system kept it pointed at the target as it screamed down at insane speeds, the gravity well accelerating it all the way until impact.

I did the math. One would almost guarantee the sinking of a Venusian city. Two or three would completely destroy it, and from the way Hank had mentioned it, apparently these things existed still.

My mail icon flashed then: it was a note from my grandfather. I read it and scowled a moment after I had, then sighed. Another score to settle. I thought about Dot for a moment and wondered just how much that would cost, but... but that was too crude. I wanted people to suffer.

Shutting down my tablet, I set it on the table and cuddled up to Kacey, who made a satisfied sound in her sleep.

I was starting to have an idea, and it had brought along several of its friends.

TEN

Ceres, Presidential Offices

I WAS SITTING OUTSIDE THE OFFICE OF THE PRESIDENT OF CERES. I'd asked to see either him or Jack—who was the head of security for Ceres, whatever it was that job entailed.

"Well, you have the look of a man who's waiting for the axe to fall."

Glancing up, I saw Jack was standing there looking down at me.

Sighing, I stood up. "I can't help but think that I deserve some of the blame for what just happened."

"Yet you still came down here and asked to see one of us?"

"I'm not in the habit of pushing my mistakes off onto others, and I'm a citizen now—what kind of one would I be if I ran away?"

"Come to my office," Jack said, so I followed him into the back and down a long hallway. Opening a door he stepped inside, and motioned toward a chair across from his desk.

"Make yourself comfortable," he told me as he closed the door.

"Do you have any idea why they attacked?" I asked as he went and sat behind his desk.

"Three days before the attack we received intelligence that the VMC had learned that there was a large number of their enemies, what everyone calls the 'Let-Bees,' living in a community here

119

on Ceres. We also obtained, from different sources, a track of a large fleet being sent here to destroy Ceres.

"Our navy intercepted them about ten hours sunward from here, and there was a standoff. Unbeknownst to us or our navy, four missile frigates and two bombardment frigates had split off from the main task force a couple of days ago and came around from a different vector. Of course when they attacked us, our navy engaged the task force and there was a vicious battle."

"Who told them that?" I asked, a little surprised.

"We're looking into that. But as far as any of us know, they don't know about your trading or any other of your activities. But honestly, even if they did, that doesn't give them the right to make war on us. It doesn't give them any right to bomb us and to kill civilians."

I shook my head. "I still can't shake the feeling that something I did led to all of this."

"David, I know this may sound strange, but you're not the center of the universe, or even our small corner of it. If they *thought* that their enemies were living here, then they should have sent in a couple of spies to investigate. The only thing any of us can figure is that they're so out of touch with the outer systems that they thought we were just another habitat and they could come in here and kill everyone, and nothing would happen."

"So when are we striking back at them?" I asked.

"That...that, is a problem," Jack said with a sour look on his face. "The battle with their fleet took a heavy toll on our ships. We don't have enough to protect ourselves from another attack while launching a response."

"Ummm," I said thinking about everything he'd just said. I'd come here with a plan to buy my redemption. Then I found out that I apparently didn't have anything for which I needed to redeem myself.

Still, they'd killed my brother-in-law, and a lot of—

"David," Jack said, interrupting me, "do you have something you want to say?"

I gave him my best innocent look, which wasn't very. "You wouldn't happen to have a dozen or so 'Rods from God' that I could buy, would you?"

Jack stared at me for a full minute.

Then he started to smile.

Evilly.

"Come," he said, getting up from his desk.

Standing up, I followed him out the door. We went down several flights of stairs, then came to a door with an armed guard. He waved the man back and, opening the door, almost dragged me inside.

"So our—Jack! What the hell? This is a secret briefing!" said some guy in a navy uniform with what looked like stars on his shoulders. I noticed that the president was there, along with the vice president, Rachel—who I now knew was the head of the treasury—several people who I recognized as being key representatives from our senate, and several other military members.

"Sit down, Lou. Now, some of you may know my guest here, David Doyle. Dave apparently wants to help us in our time of need. Now David, please, tell these men just what it is you're planning and why you want us to provide you with a bunch of orbital kinetic weapons."

"Orbital what?" Rachel asked.

"Rods from God," the president said.

"Oh!"

I frowned at Jack, who just smiled evilly at me.

"So, David, why do you want them?" the president asked before I could get started.

"I want to sink a couple of cloud cities—well, hopefully more than a couple."

"You do know that each of those cities has a population of millions?" Lou, the naval officer we'd interrupted, asked.

"And I'm supposed to care about them...why?" I asked.

"So, you're not bothered by the idea of what sinking one of those cities will lead to?"

"They came here to kill everyone. They did kill my brother-in-law, who was trying to save people when that first nuke went off. They think they can't be touched, they think they can do whatever they want, kill whoever they want, whenever they want, with no consequences.

"Well, I think it's time someone disabused them of that notion. So, how many do you have and how soon can I load 'em up?"

"And just how to you plan on delivering these weapons, Mr. Doyle?"

"I own a tramp freighter. Nobody looks twice at folks like

us. I'll just slip into orbit, open up the cargo bay doors, and open fire."

I watched as Lou thought about that a moment and then turned to Jack. "Is he for real?"

"I brought him here, didn't I?" Jack said, still smiling that nasty smile.

"Captain Williamson!"

"Yes, Admiral?" one of the uniformed men with captain's boards on his shoulders replied while standing up.

"Mr. Doyle here has carte blanche. Whatever he wants, you give him. From this point on, you don't tell anyone his name, his ship's name, or what he's going to be doing. This is a matter of extreme national security and classified to the highest levels."

"I understand, Admiral," Captain Williamson said and saluted.

"Follow me please, sir," Captain Williamson said to me, and walked toward the door I'd entered from.

I started to follow him, but Jack grabbed my arm.

"Make 'em pay," he whispered to me. "My son was flying the ore boat that rammed the lead ship."

"I always do," I told him. "I always do."

He let go of my arm then and I followed the captain out the door and down the hallway.

"So how big of a cargo ship are we talking, sir?"

"Argon class, and call me Dave."

"Call me Mike. Let's go talk to my munitions people and see what they can figure out."

"I've been led to believe that they come in their own launcher. Is that true?"

"Sure is. They even fit in the same footprint as a standard forty-foot cargo TEU. Makes it easier to ship them around that way. But you're gonna need a targeting system to aim them and a ballistics computer to program them. Probably going to need an interface to the ship's maneuvering computer as well, to help align the ship and improve targeting."

I continued to follow him as he talked. Obviously Captain Williamson knew a fair bit about weapons systems. Which was probably why the admiral had picked him. He led me down another flight of stairs and out to a tram station that I'd never seen before.

"This is the government's secure tramline," he said to me

as we entered one of the cars. "It connects several of the major government buildings, as well as the naval shipyards."

"I thought they destroyed that?"

"They damaged one of them. The other two are less obvious."

I nodded and sat down as he told the machine where we were going.

"I have to say, your idea has merit. Nobody looks at the cargo ships, especially the smaller ones. I would suggest you do something about your transponder. Seeing a ship flagged out of Ceres will draw interest."

I nodded. "Already taken care of. So how many of these things do you have?"

"I'll have to look at inventory. We don't carry a lot of them, for obvious reasons. But I'm sure we'll have more than enough to do the job."

"I just hope they get the message and leave us alone," I said with a heavy sigh. "However, I've been led to believe that they're a bunch of fanatics, so who knows?"

"Take out the cities they're using to build their fleet, and I'm sure that'll slow them down."

I thought about that a moment. "Can I get a list of cities where their 'exalted' ruler lives? As well as the ones building warships? If we can get him, I don't doubt that would put an end to all of it."

"I'll talk to the Intelligence section."

"Thanks."

We pulled into another station after that and I followed him through a number of corridors and checkpoints. I was handed a badge that said JOHN SMITH on it at the second one and where there was supposed to be your picture, it was blue with a red triangle pointing off a few degrees from straight up.

We finally walked into an office with a very bored-looking chief petty officer who was reading something on a monitor.

"Smitty!"

The man looked over at Captain Williamson and sighed. "And to think, I knew you when," he said.

"Oh, I got a good one for you this time!" Captain Williamson said with a grin.

"And pray tell, sir, what is that?"

"How many tungsten telephone poles have we got loaded and ready to go?"

Smitty looked at the captain, looked at me, then looked back at the captain.

"Who's that with you then?"

"Someone you're best not ever remembering, on Admiral Carstairs's orders. In fact, you're not going to remember any of what I'm asking you, what you're going to be doing for me, and just where all these wonderful stores we're about to expend are going."

"Twenty-three. We got twenty-three sitting out in stores."

"Great, now how are we fixed for targeting systems? I'm looking for something that'll pick out a city from orbit without giving itself away."

"Captain! I can't just give away ANIL-59s to jus— Wait, are we talking *floating* cities?"

"Yes," I growled.

Smitty sat up straight, clapped his hands together, and smiled. "Why, Captain, I just happen to have one ready and raring to go! Even got a WBY-20 ballistic computer to handle programming the launchers for firin'! Now, where are we putting them?"

"In the side of a cargo ship," the captain told him.

Smitty looked at me. "Can I come?"

"Sorry, no," I said with a shake of my head.

"Damn. Promise me you'll take pictures. Where are we loading?"

"The ship is currently in Ceres Habitats' surface parking area. If I bring it here, everyone—and I do mean everyone—who isn't working on the ship needs to be evacuated. I don't want anyone warning anybody that we're coming."

"That I can do. Secret projects come in here all the time. Let me get you a pilot to shuttle the ship over here. Cargo, you say?"

"GSD Argon class."

"Got it."

"How soon can you load it up?"

"How soon can you get it here? I'll need to have a couple of my guys set up the targeting system."

"I'll need someone to teach me how to run it."

"We can do that while we're doing the install."

"Great, get me your pilot, I need to recall my crew."

Smitty picked up the phone on his desk and dialed a number. "Rachet! Suit up and get your ass in here! Now! Got a hot one!" He hit the disconnect and dialed another number.

"Jenkin! Get the team in, got a black ops mission hot and heavy, get the loaders out and tell Winston to grab his gear. I got a magic box I need him to wire up. When? Now, of course! Move it!"

A slender woman in some sort of pressure suit ran into the room and slid to a stop in front of us, saluting the captain.

"What's up, Smitty?"

"Go with that man, move his ship here to the special projects dock. Understand, you talk about this and you will not just incur my wrath or the wrath of the good captain there, but of Admiral Carstairs as well, understand?"

"Got it!"

"Can you escort him out of the facility?" the captain asked Rachet. "I need to make sure all the proper paperwork is filled out and lost."

"Yessir, Captain!" Rachet said and saluted.

I followed her all the way out to a public tram, turning in my badge when we got to the last checkpoint.

"Where are we going?"

"Ceres Habitats, that's where we're parked," I told her as she got us our tickets.

I got my tablet out then and sent a message to the entire crew, informing them that we had a hot cargo, and to head back to the ship immediately. I'd explain all when I met them there. I sent a second one to Hank to grab my pressure suit and parka. That we had a very special delivery to make.

"Okay, Rachet, let's go," I said with a shake of my head as one of the tram cars pulled up, opening its doors.

I met Hank at the lock that led outside to the ship.

"Who's here?" I asked.

"Everybody just left a minute ago. What's going on?"

"We're flying over to a special dock to pick up something and she's flying us there." I pointed to Ratchet, who was looking curious but keeping her mouth shut.

Hank scowled.

"I will address everyone while she's flying us there. Is there a place to change around here?"

"Not that I've seen."

Shrugging, I stripped right there in the middle of the hallway, grabbed the suit and got into it.

"Not much for modesty, are we?" Hank said with a laugh.

"I think right now I'm not much for anything," I said with a snort as I donned the parka and put on my helmet.

"You gonna be warm enough in that?" Hank asked Ratchet as she put on her helmet.

"Oh yeah. Special issue."

He shrugged and put his own helmet on as she sealed hers. I stuck my important stuff in the pouch on my waist and balled up my clothes. Hopefully they'd survive. If not, I had more on board.

Cycling through the lock and walking back to the ship didn't seem to take as long as our leaving it had. Then again, I had a lot on my mind. When I cycled out of the air lock with Ratchet and Hank, I turned to them. "Hank, tell everyone to meet up in the mess in fifteen. Show Ratchet to the flight deck and tell Chris to answer any questions she has. She knows where we're going, but he can decide if he's flying it or she is."

"What are *you* going to do?"

"Start waking up the reactors and the drives. That's going to take a few minutes to get going," I told him and walked into Engineering. Nick was already there and had already started on getting the reactors back on line.

We spent the next fifteen minutes doing systems checks and running down checklists. We wouldn't need full power to move us in Ceres's gravity, especially as we were empty, but I still wanted us up most of the way before we took off. At least it was still warm enough inside that the gravity panels shouldn't be too hard to start bringing up.

"So, boss, what's up?" Nick asked.

"We need to move the ship to a special location, where we're going to pick up a special shipment. I'll go over all of it up in the mess in a few minutes. Let's start warming up the grav panels. Then we can head to the mess."

"You got it!"

A few minutes later, my intercom buzzed.

"Dave, everyone's in the mess but you and Nick."

"Okay, coming up."

"Where's Ratchet?" I asked when I walked into the mess, closing the door behind me.

"On the flight deck with the door closed," Chris told me. "Now, what's going on?"

"We're about to run a black op for the Ceres government," I said, looking around as Kacey came over and gave me a hug. "Now, I'll be asking for a couple of volunteers for the dangerous part, but for this part you're all drafted because I need the ship and the crew.

"We're heading over to one of the navy base depots or some such that is still intact. We are going to pick up twenty-three very nasty weapons. We're going to set them up in the cargo hold, along with some associated hardware. We are all going to pay very close attention to how this stuff is set up, because after we leave here, we'll link up with that Xenon-class ship I took. We'll mount the weapons on that, and that will be the ship that we fly. The *Iowa Hill* will return here.

"I will be the engineer. I need a pilot, and I'd like an able-bodied spacer. I'm not planning a suicide mission, but this is going to be dangerous. Deadly dangerous."

"What are you going to do?" Chaz asked.

"We're going to sink those cloud cities that are building the VMC's warships."

"I'm in."

"Chaz!" Hank said, surprised.

"Hank, they killed my brother! I'm in, and don't you dare try to talk me out of this!"

Hank swore loudly. "Guess I'm in too, then."

"I'll fly it," Chris said, surprising me.

"Okay," I said, raising a hand before anybody else could speak. "Start thinking about what we may need to do this. So we can order it and get it loaded. Hank, Chaz, you've both been aboard the ship we're going to, so if you know of anything we'll need, tell me so we can order it."

"What's our budget limit?" Hank asked.

"We don't have one. But this isn't a license to steal. We get what we need and then get the hell out of here. Now, I'm going back down to Engineering to finish getting us ready to move. I've pulled the repeater for your tablets. Understand right now, that none of you will be talking to anybody off this ship until you get back. The only way this will work is if no one knows we're coming.

"Understood?" I asked, looking around, and they all nodded.

"Thanks. I really don't want to do this, I really don't. But if we don't do something, they'll come back and try this again. These people are insane. They won't stop until they've killed everyone, unless we stop them. We're trying to slow them down so our own navy can rebuild, and maybe put the fear of Ceres into them."

Opening the door, I headed back down to Engineering, taking Kacey with me as she was still holding on to me.

"What brought this on?" she asked.

"I thought they were gonna blame me, you know that. So I figured I'd offer to 'make it right' by doing this."

"So they *did* blame you?"

I shook my head no. "They didn't blame me. As far as they know, it had nothing to do with me. But even if it had, they said they still wouldn't blame me. And as I was sitting there, thinking about that, thinking about all the people who'd been murdered, thinking about Jeff, I guess something must have shown on my face because that guy in charge of Intelligence or whatever for the president?"

"Jack Shian."

"So that's his last name. Anyway, he saw the look on my face and suddenly he wanted to know what I had planned. I asked for the weapons we're getting and he got this look and dragged me down to meet...I don't know, some big national security planning thing. I told them what I wanted to do and why I thought it would work and Jack vouched for me and, well, here we are."

"Why'd he do that?"

"You know that first ore boat that took out the lead ship?"

"He knew someone on it?"

"His son was flying it."

"Oh," Kacey said and looked down at the floor a moment. "I'd try to talk you out of this if they hadn't killed Jeff." Kacey shook her head and looked up at me. "Is it wrong of me to want revenge? To want to kill them all? To make them suffer?"

I leaned down and gave her a kiss. "If it is, then I'm wrong too, Kace. Trust me, they're going to pay, and they're going to pay lots."

"Just...just don't get yourself killed. I don't want to lose you, Dave."

"Yeah, I don't want to lose me either," I said with a soft chuckle.

"I have a plan and a bunch of ideas. I'll sit down with Chris, Chaz, and Hank and run them all by them. And see what we can come up with. The *New Market* still has an active lifeboat aboard. So if worse comes to worst, we can always use that to escape."

Half an hour later we raised ship, with Ratchet flying and Chris overseeing her. It was only a ten-minute trip and we landed in a hanger that they sealed and pumped an atmosphere into. As soon as the cargo doors had opened, they started loading the launch tubes for the tungsten rods.

"Okay, who's the one who's going to show me how all this fits together?" I asked as a couple of techs climbed up into the cargo hold.

"That'd be me, name's Winston," said a dark-skinned man who looked to be about thirty. "What do you want to know?"

"How to hook it all up, you know, in case we have to move it."

"Why would you want to do that?"

"You can either teach me and my guys here how to do it," I said, motioning to Nick, Hank, Chaz, Yuri, and Kei, "or you can come with me, just in case. But this is very much one of those 'don't ask questions' kind of deals."

Winston nodded slowly and looked around. "I think you're insane, but I also think you've got a point. Each rod has an address associated with it. They'll fire in any order you want. They're on a simple network bus so we can just daisy-chain the launchers on each level, run a cable to a switch, and run one from that to the controller.

"The controller has a detailed map of Venus in it. Once you get a fix on a couple of landmarks, or their satnav system if they've been stupid enough to leave it on, the targeting computer will give you every option you could ever want."

"Ever fire one of these before?" Chaz asked him.

Winston shook his head. "No, but I've seen the test footage. Open up the doors on the other side of the bay, because the backblast from the chemical rockets when they ignite is significant. They burn for forty-five seconds and will be moving at well over ten thousand meters per second by the time they burn out. From that point, gravity does all the work. They'll hit the ground about three minutes after you launch if you fire at the recommended range. They're moving that fast."

"Do you think one will do the trick?" I asked him.

"You're hitting them with a kiloton of force, so I'd be surprised if any city could survive a hit from one."

"How big are the rods?"

"Two feet in diameter and twenty feet long, or point six meters by six point six. They weigh about twenty-four tons."

"Won't they just punch through like a bullet through paper?" Yuri, of all people, asked.

"By the time they hit the target, they've heated up so much from punching through the atmosphere that the crystalline structure of the rod has passed the point of stability. They're superheated, so any sharp high-energy impact causes that energy to destroy the crystalline structure in an instant and it all goes boom. It's really quite impressive to see."

"Alright, you five go set it up. Winston, you supervise and tell them what to do," I said, looking around. "I need to go find Captain Williamson. I got a list of things we need."

"Yes, sir!"

ELEVEN

Somewhere in Space

IT WAS ALMOST EIGHT DAYS LATER WHEN WE CAUGHT UP WITH the *New Market*. It was easier this time as we had exact orbital data and hadn't just left the computers to run unattended for a week.

"Okay, Chris and I will go aboard with Hank and Chaz," I told everyone at the crew meeting. "Once we have the portside cargo doors open, Paul will come alongside, then move in close so we can tie off and start shipping cargo.

"Any questions?"

Everyone shook their head no. I was already in my pressure suit and had the few things I'd need in a pressure bag. The other three were also suited up and, after I gave Kacey a last hug and a kiss, we all trooped out of the mess, across the top cargo deck, and into the rear air lock, after put on our helmets and made sure they were closed and locked.

When the rear hatch opened, I could see the back end of the *New Market* about ten meters away. I looked it over and noticed the hole in the boat bay. I'd forgotten about that as the *Iowa* didn't have a ship's boat.

"We need to open that up and jettison the boat, Hank," I said, pointing toward the bay door. "No need in hauling any extra weight."

"Put a line on it and have the girls haul it into the cargo bay on the *Iowa*," Chris said. "It may be repairable. If nothing else, it can be sold as salvage to help pay for things."

"I thought Ceres was paying for this?" Chaz asked.

"They paid for everything up until we left. I suspect they won't be giving us any more cash when we get back. Remember, this entire endeavor doesn't exist, never happened, and isn't on the books."

"Chris has a point," I agreed. "Hank, make sure Yuri and Kei know what to do."

"Sure thing."

Hank went first, and got the air lock opened, then Chris and I jumped across, followed by Chaz in case there were any problems. Out of the four of them I was the one with the least amount of time in a suit in free fall. Chris had cut his teeth as an ore boat pilot and had probably as much free-fall experience as the other two.

I'd left the gravity on, if reduced, when we'd left the ship. I immediately headed for Engineering as Chris headed for the flight deck. It was cool inside, but not cold. I didn't want the matrices in the life-support filters to die and I didn't want any ice forming anywhere, as I'd been planning to come back and didn't want a mess to clean up.

When I got to Engineering I took a moment to look around. The layout was similar to that of the *Iowa Hill*'s but they had fusion reactors here, which were a different shape and size from the PWR fission reactors back on the *Iowa*. There were four of them here as well.

The main two were K-50s, five-hundred-megawatt fusion reactors. These were top commercial-grade machines and it took all of their combined energy to move this ship at point-one gravity when it was loaded to max weight. The third fusion reactor was a K-20. That provided two hundred megawatts. Its purpose was both to act as emergency backup in case one of the K-50s shut down, and to provide supplemental power for any maneuvering around gravity wells when the ship was at capacity.

Some cargo companies paid extra for a third K-50, but the K-20 was the common configuration. The fourth fusion reactor was an F-1000 auxiliary power unit that provided one megawatt of power. I'd left that one running, as with nobody on board it really didn't take that much power to run the ship.

Logging into the engineering console, I started the process to bring up the K-50s and the K-20. We'd be needing all the power we could spare.

"Dave, safe to open the port-side cargo door?" Chris called over the suit radio.

"Affirm. I should have basic maneuvering power for you in about twenty minutes. I'll be able to bring gravity up once we've finished loading the heavy stuff."

"Okay. I'll let Paul know he can start maneuvering then."

"If you get Chaz killed, you know I'll never forgive you," Hank said, coming into the room with his helmet open.

"Honestly, I'd been hoping for Yuri and Kei," I said, taking off my helmet and setting it on the chair besides me.

"Why in the world did you want them? Other than I'm sure they'd both be very happy to throw themselves at you."

"Because they're both really good at mayhem? If we get boarded, I figured those two would go into the whole 'save us poor damsels' act they do just before they killed everybody and blew up their ship."

Hank snorted. "Those two would probably get away with it, knowing the way they dress. Do you really think those EMP bombs will let us get away?"

I shrugged. "I don't know. If I'd remembered we had a boat bay on this beast I might have asked for a replacement so we could just abandon ship after we fire everything off. When do you want to run that code cracker on the ship's computers?"

"After we've got everything loaded and the doors closed. Too bad we didn't ask Melissa for the owner's codes before you booted her off the ship. Chaz is tossing her stateroom right now to see if she wrote it down someplace."

"He's doing what?" I asked, chuckling.

"He's got a low opinion of her, said she looked like the type. I bet him breakfast in bed for a week if he can find it."

I had to laugh at that.

"So, how are the starboard side doors? Can you fix 'em?"

"No, they took too much damage. We'll set shaped charges on all the hinges and cut them loose when the time comes."

"What about the interlock safeties?"

"Chaz and I will rewire them on the trip there. We're going to go string that tarp we had them make over the hole, so if someone does pass close by they won't notice it. So tell me, Dave, and be honest: Why are we here?"

I gave him a sidelong look as I checked that the core temperatures were coming up within specifications.

"Seriously, Dave, and don't feed me a line of Marsie loyalty shit or any gang-banger code. I've been a bosun long enough to tell when somebody feeding me a line grade-A unrecycled head-wash."

"Because it's my fault."

"And you told us that the Ceres Intelligence services said otherwise. Also that even if it had been because of you, they wouldn't have held you responsible."

I shook my head. "I got word from my grandfather not long after we got back to Ceres. He found out exactly what happened."

"And?"

"The McVays are really quite unhappy with me. And not just because I kidnapped my brother back from them and stole a hundred-and-twenty-million-dollar cargo ship in the process."

"Oh?"

"Apparently locking Melissa in with three very nasty men who apparently were not at *all* happy that she'd tried to throw them to the wolves to save herself didn't go all that well."

"They didn't?" Hank said, looking at me surprised.

"Oh, they very much did. But it gets worse."

"How could it get worse?"

"She's doing the talk-show circuit with her three new *husbands* and is apparently in negotiations for the movie rights about her *harrowing* ordeal and the *love* she found during it."

I stopped and stared at Hank, who looked like he was going to explode.

"She . . . what?" he said and started to actually *giggle*. Which was pretty damn disconcerting when Hank did it.

"They either broke something in her or maybe, I don't know, fixed it? In either case, it is the scandal of the damn century that this wealthy elie babe is now very publicly acting like some doler porn star. There's even rumors of a 'sex tape' out there, whatever the hell that's supposed to be."

I had to wait for Hank to stop laughing, which he did for five whole minutes.

"Okay, okay, that's messed up," he said, still giggling.

"Now you know why I left Earth. Anyways, the head of the McVay family damn near had a stroke because Melissa is his 'little girl' and *he's* the one who told the VMC that Ceres is not only helping the Let-Bees, but that they've set up a huge community there. Hundreds of thousands! He even paid some company to falsify all sorts of pictures and other evidence.

"So yeah, I think it's safe to say I caused this mess."

Hank blew out his breath and shook his head, a serious look on his face. "I'm not so sure I agree with you on that, but honestly? Someone really does need to knock the VMC's collective dick into the dirt."

"Yeah, that too. They killed a lot of people, some of whom I've met, and of course Jeff. Jeff alone really is a good enough reason to be out here, doing this."

"I'll give you that. But, what about the McVays? They own some of this as well."

I looked up from the console and into his eyes. "Who owns this ship again?"

That stopped him a moment. "You don't think they'll fall for that, do you?"

"The McVay family knew this war was coming, long before it did. How much do you think they made off of it?"

"They'd be that stupid?"

"They're greedy. After we make our attack, a whole bunch of stuff will happen to make it clear, to anyone who looks, that the McVays are war profiteering."

"And you've already got someone set up to look."

"You know, I was going to hire someone to kill the head of their family, but I think this is going to be just so much more fun to watch."

"Assuming we survive."

"Uh-huh. Now, get back to work."

I went out onto the cargo deck, as they got ready to string the cables. I wanted to watch them do it, and I wanted to be there to run all the diagnostics. Once that was done, we'd hook up the launchers for the EMP bombs—those had been a last-minute suggestion. All of our launches would be completed just before we launched them. They wouldn't be moving anywhere near as fast as the rods would be. We wanted to trigger those in the upper atmosphere, but we didn't want it to happen until everyone on the surface had gotten the alerts, seen the live imagery, and discovered they were under attack.

Then everything would go dark.

Smitty came up with that one, and I damn near kissed him for it. Because it would also make it harder for anyone to track us as we broke orbit.

It took another two hours to get everything hooked up and checked. Once that was done I sent Nick, Yuri, and Kei back and did a last check to make sure that we had everything we needed and hadn't forgotten anything.

When we finally untied from the *Iowa Hill,* I watched as it slowly floated away from us. I could see that they had put a line on the ship's boat and were resecuring the line on the cargo deck. I was surprised to see that other than a hole through it, it appeared to be in good shape. Chris must have hit the door retract because the cargo doors started to fold down, and a few moments later the *Iowa Hill* was gone from sight.

Saying a silent prayer to the god that watches out for fools and former gang members, I went back to Engineering and started checking panels and making sure that everything was running nominally. Surprisingly, Chaz had found Melissa's passwords, so Chris had reset everyone's shipboard passwords while we'd been testing the launch systems.

"Attention, all hands! Attention! Prepare for gravity! Prepare for gravity! Dave, Hank, Chaz! This means you!"

"I'm good," I keyed back.

"Hank and I are good," Chaz replied and I kept my eyes glued to the gravity generator feeds as Chris slowly brought them up.

"Looks good, Chris," I said over the intercom.

"Okay, I've got the course laid in, and I'm going to start us off at point two. Once we're on a track that makes it look like we're coming from Earth, I'll back us off to point one."

"What's our ETA?" Hank called.

"Six days."

"I'm heading up to the mess," I commed. "I can monitor everything from up there as easily as down here while I make us dinner."

"Won't get any complaints from me!" Chris replied, along with a couple of "Yups" from Chaz and Hank.

"The next six days are going to be boring," I grumbled to them as I got up.

"Considering you and Chris are going to be standing eighteen-hour watches, I don't see how that could possibly happen," Hank intercommed back.

"If this wasn't a secret mission, I'm sure my union would have serious words about the working condition," Chris added with a laugh.

I sighed. "Yours and mine both."

"Venus Control, this is the Earth cargo ship *New Market*, requesting clearance into standard approach orbit for the Canberra Customs clearing station."

"*New Market*, this is Venus Control. Canberra does not have you on their manifest."

Chris sighed heavily into the microphone, then said, "Understood, Venus Control. Can we have a holding orbit while I contact the shipping department at my company and get this worked out?"

"Affirmative, *New Market*, please be using Canberra holding orbit Delta. Have you a good day."

"Roger, *New Market* out."

Chris turned to me; I was sitting in the engineering jump seat on the bridge. I could run everything from up here if I needed to, and for the last six hours as we'd navigated the Venusian space lanes, I had.

Hank and Chaz were down for a nap.

"You know, I'm almost regretting you didn't get Kei and Yuri for this," Chris grumbled.

"Really, Chris, already thinking of cheating on Emil?" I teased.

"Please, we're about to go into combat, slaughter a couple million people, and probably die in the process. Like you of all people would be acting the saint."

"Nope! And thankfully I have been saved from that temptation. How long until we're in position?"

"Fifty-three minutes. I'll wake up Hank and Chaz, you might as well go take up your station. Just remember to hook up a static line."

"Got it."

I went down to my quarters, took a quick shower, and got into my pressure suit, along with my parka. I made sure I had my tablet and it was slaved to Engineering. Then I went out onto the bottom deck where we had the launch control and ballistic computer set up. The Rods from God containers were all two levels above me. The EMP bombs were on this level, but at the far end.

I strapped myself into the seat, after fastening a long static line to the eyelet at the door leading out of the small air lock onto the cargo deck. Chaz came out to join me just as I was getting settled in. Hank would be helping Chris as he could fly the ship, or run the engineering board for me, if either of us had to deal with something more important.

"Okay, let's go over the target list," Chaz said, slipping into the seat beside mine as I brought the consoles up.

"Fort Lewis, warship manufacturing site," Chaz read.

"Rods one, four, six."

"Compton Flats, warship manufacturing site."

"Rods two, five, seven."

"The People's Home, government capitol target."

"Rods three and eight."

"Columbus City, weapons manufacturing."

"Rods nine, twelve."

"Well's Home, government target."

"Rods ten, thirteen."

"VMC Naval Base Alpha."

"Rods eleven, fourteen, sixteen."

"Fort McKinney, naval base, warship manufacturing."

"Rods fifteen, eighteen, twenty."

"VMC Naval Academy."

"Rods seventeen, twenty-one, twenty-three."

"The City of the Most Holy asshole himself," Chaz growled. "Government and political target."

"Yeah, I hope we get the bastard too," I agreed. "Rods nineteen and twenty-two."

"Nine targets. I wish we could have spread them out more."

"We need to make sure those shipbuilders are put out of business—our own navy took too much damage and Venus still has far too many ships by comparison. I'm not even sure that three of these things will sink a city, much less two," I said as I checked our navigation feed to make sure that both we and the rod's targeting systems all knew where we were.

Then I started uploading the coordinates of the targets to each rod. We'd be launching one every thirty seconds, to cut down on the chances of any single rod interfering with another one. That was also why we would be stagger-firing on each target. After the chemical rocket package burned out, it fell away from the rod so as to cut down on drag. Ground targets, like cities, didn't move all that much, so terminal guidance really wasn't much of an issue.

"Open the portside doors and blow the starboard doors, Hank!"

The doors on my right started to split open, then there was a series of soft vibrations I felt through the seat and my feet on the deck. Looking to my left, I could see that the ruined doors were slowly moving away from us.

"I thought there'd be a lot more to that," I said, looking at Chaz through my helmet.

"It's a lot of weight," Chaz told me. "We didn't want to damage the collars the pins go through. When the backblast hits, it'll push it a bit faster."

"Just as long as it doesn't hit me."

"Yeah, we took that into account."

I turned to look at Venus, down below us as we orbited high above. I could see clusters of lights in the darkness of the night side as we sailed toward the terminator. Venus was a lot more "white" and "yellow" looking due to the clouds.

Definitely not as pretty as Earth.

"Ten seconds," Chaz said, interrupting my thoughts.

I flipped the guard off the first trigger switch and when the count hit zero, I pressed the button.

I barely felt it as a streak of light literally rocketed out of the hold and down toward the planet below.

I flipped up the cover on the next switch and waited for zero. Then pressed it and this time I looked out the other side and noticed that the doors there had started to tumble. When the exhaust from the second launch hit them, I noticed they got pushed back by that.

When I launched the seventh rod, I heard Chaz cheer.

"Take that, you murdering bastards!"

"Huh?"

"I saw one of them hit. Big bright flash." I noticed he had a digital camera out and was filming.

"Hope you're not planning on showing that anytime soon," I told him.

"Nope, this is for the archives. Plus I figure your friend Jack might appreciate seeing you avenging his son."

"Yeah," I said in a soft voice. "I think he will too."

It was both boring and terrifying as I worked my way through those buttons. I'd made it clear I didn't want anyone other than me to do it, because I figured I already had enough death and mayhem on my soul that I'd be unaffected by it. But when I caught the flash of a rod impacting one group of lights on a city that was still on the dark side of the terminator, and a lot of those lights went out, I realized that things were never going to be the same for me. I was killing millions. Every time I pushed a button I was sentencing millions to death.

Sure, they deserved it. Sure, we hadn't started it. Sure, there was no other way.

At least, that's what I'd been told. That's what we'd all been told. What we all believed.

But was it the truth? Were they all raving lunatics down there, to the last man, woman, and child?

Or were they just going along to get along? Were they just as caught up in this madness as the thousands who'd been killed on Ceres?

I pushed another button.

I had no idea. I didn't know. The more I thought about it, the more I *didn't* want to know. Ordering the deaths of millions was one thing, talking about it and cheering for it was even easier. But to be the guy actually doing it?

Yeah, it was starting to hurt when I pushed down.

"Twenty-three didn't launch," Chaz said.

I looked at the display: rod twenty-three had lost communication.

"Shit." I flipped up the guard for the EMP bombs and pressed it. The screen lit up with another error.

"We lost comms to the EMPs as well! Fuck."

"Dave, where are those EMP bombs?" Chris asked over the radio. "We need to get the hell out of here."

"We lost the network. I'm on it!" I said as I unbelted. "Don't close the doors! They could go off at any instant!"

I canceled the order to rod twenty-three as an afterthought. But I left the one to the EMP bombs active.

"Grab a network cable and get up to twenty-three and see what happened!" I told Chaz as I grabbed one of the other spares and started moving to the other side of the bay where the EMP bombs were located.

"On it!"

I hit the end of my line and swore, unclipping it as I fumbled for a minute and went back to moving to the far end. The launchers were all in a row, set to ripple fire. The network line from launcher twenty-three came down through the floor grates above. I took my cable and plugged it into launcher four. They were all daisy-chained so I could run this up the stairs at the end to Chaz and plug it into one of the other rod launchers.

"Found it! Launcher twenty-two had a minor rupture and it melted the cable, replacing it—"

"Wait!" I said as I was standing square behind the launchers. The EMP bombs used a compressed gas charge to blow out of their tubes before lighting their engines, but a compressed gas charge with enough power to move a two-hundred-kilo rocket is more than enough to knock an eighty-one-kilo man on his ass.

Four of them going off in low gravity blew me right off my feet. I hit the ladder with my legs and started to tumble. I grabbed on to the cable as I saw the open starboard side, the doors long gone from sight by now. Tightening my grip on the network cable I prayed it would hold, and wrapped my hand around it just as it jerked hard, and I kept going.

"David's gone Dutchman!" Chaz called out. "He just got blown out the starboard side."

"I see him; I'm slipping us toward him, hold on."

The pressure light in my suit helmet started flashing.

"I got a leak, guys!" I said as I tried to stop myself from tumbling and figure out just where my suit had gotten holed.

"Don't worry, we're coming," Chris said.

I had a thought then.

"How long until the EMPs detonate?"

"Don't worry, we got plenty of time, Dave."

"Hank, you listen to me! When it gets down to ten seconds, press the emergency shutdown! If the systems are up when that thing goes off, we're all fucked! You hear me?"

"Dave, calm down, we got plenty of time," Chris said again.

"I see him!" Chaz said. "I'm going after him!"

I could feel a burning sensation in my leg.

"I tore my right leg," I said, and curled up to do my best to clamp my hands over the spot that was starting to hurt. If I wasn't still tumbling, I'd have gotten out my patch kit, but I was really starting to have issues here.

"Give me a count, Hank!"

"Dave—"

"That's a gods-damned order, Hank! How long?"

"Fifteen seconds," Hank said.

"Hank, if you don't shut it all down *now*, God himself won't save you from what I'll do to you!"

It got quiet then, and I started to wonder if I'd feel it when I died. The suit was trying to keep up with the loss of air, but as it was more of a rebreather than a bottle-based suit; there was only so much it could do. Suddenly, the suit went quiet. The light went out. The little motor that moved the air shut down.

The EMP bombs had all detonated.

"Ooof!" I gasped as I got hit by something. Then I was being manhandled and something or somebody was prying my hands off my leg, and if I thought it hurt before it *really* hurt now! I was flailing a bit, then I felt myself spun around and heard a helmet *clunk* against mine.

"I got you. Your suit's patched, but the EMP fried it. Let me get a line on you, then we can head back to the ship."

"But your suit's dead!"

"No, I've got a miner's suit. Now we need to get you in atmosphere ASAP."

Things got a little squirrelly after that. Squirrelly, now there's a word for you. I remembered squirrels. Rats with fluffy tails. Damn things would get into everything. They say they used to live only in trees and shit. But I guess when they built the quads they decided to move in too. Damn things were always—

"Dave!"

"Huh?" I said weakly.

"Wake up! We need to power the reactors back up!"

"Oh...? Oh...! Right. Where am I?"

I felt something cool hit my arm, and then suddenly my entire body felt like that time I accidentally touched a live two-twenty feed during class. At least this time I didn't go flying across the room!

My eyes focused and I was at the console. It was black. Of course it was black. We'd been hit by an EMP...I think? Everything had this weird quality to it, like it wasn't quite real.

"Did the EMP do this?"

"No, I did this. Just like you told me to."

I told him to? I thought about that, then remembered doing just that.

"Oh, right," I said, nodding and looking at the screen. "These don't work without power." I pointed at the console.

"Yes, Dave, I know that. Now, how do we *get* power?"

"Oh, turn on the APU," I said and smiled at him.

"And how do I do that?"

"There's a big dial on the side. Turn it to E-M-G start."

He ran over to the F-1000, found the dial, and turned it. "Now what?"

"See that T-handle there by the front?"

"Yeah, what do I do, turn it?"

"Nope. You put your foot next to it, grab it with both hands, and pull it like you're trying to take a lottery ticket from a doler!" I said and laughed.

"You're shitting me, a pull start?"

"No batteries. They go bad..."

Hank pulled, the line coming out a good four feet, swore, pulled harder the next time, and the small propane turbine kicked in. I'd have to refill that tank. Where was my checklist...?

"Now what?"

"Press the big green button on top. The big, green, cheerful, Christmassy button!"

"Okay, I pressed it. Now what?"

"That's it, it'll all come up in three, two...ta-da!" I said as the board lit up.

"Is it safe for you to be running things like this?"

I snorted. "This shit is easy. It's the maintenance that kills ya!" And I started hitting the emergency start buttons on everything. "I tell ya, it's gonna take me a month to clean up this mess! Remind me to refill the propane tank on the F one tho-thousand.

"Chris," I said hitting the intercom. "Blast away! We got all the power in the world! Let's go hoooome!!"

"What the hell did you do to him, Hank?" Chris called back as gravity returned with a will and I slid out of the seat and onto the floor. I think I hit my head. But I wasn't sure. My leg sure looked funny, there was a big-ass bandage or something around it.

"I hit him with a painkiller and a stim! That's it."

"Oohh, you hit me with the big T, didn't you?"

Hank stopped and looked at me. "Don't tell me, you're a Tramadol addict?"

"Well, I don't know if I'd say *addict*, I haven't touched it since I was twelve, but it was such a fuuuuun drug. We used to do it, like, every day after school! Ben made me quit. Said it made me stupid. But look, I'm not stupid! I got everything all turned on, see?"

"Haul him up to the bridge. Chaz, go through the med cabinets and see if we got any Narcan."

"Oh, yeah. The bridge. Did you remember to pull the power on the transponder?"

"Yeah, that's off," Hank said as he picked me up and threw me over his shoulder.

"Hank?"

"Yes?"

"I did a bad thing today, Hank."

"Fortunes of war, Dave. Somebody had to."

"Yeah, but it was my idea. And I pushed the button."

"Uh-huh."

"It's funny. Those people I killed, back when I was a kid? Never bothered me. Nope, I was a cold, hard bastard. Do you know they *still* tell stories about me back home?"

"No, didn't know that, Dave."

"This...this was worse. Way worse. Sure, I didn't watch 'em die, I didn't see them suffer, I didn't hear their screams or any of that. Still, this was worse—evil maybe. Wanna know why it's worse?"

"Actually, Dave, yeah, I do. Because I *know* about your past."

"It worse because Kacey's pregnant and I'm gonna be a dad."

"How does that make it worse?"

"Because how can a monster who just killed millions of people be a good dad? How do you tell your child that you slaughtered more people than any man in history?"

"You don't."

"Huh?"

"Trust me on that one, Dave. Some things you don't tell your children until they're adults, and sometimes, maybe not even then."

I thought about that as I got dumped into a chair. I'd done a bad thing. Maybe the worst thing. I knew it had to be done. At least, everyone *else* said so. I felt something stab me in the arm.

I blinked.

I swore—damn, did I hurt!

"How are you feeling?" Chaz asked me.

"Like shit."

"Well, then it worked," Hank said with a smile.

"How fast are we accelerating?"

"Point three," Chris said. "Traffic control is offline. A lot of ships are offline. We may be the only thing moving in orbit right now. Chaz, get back on the radio and see if you can hear anything on the military frequencies."

"Shit, something just pinged us," Hank said from the radar console. He had it all on, but set to passive.

"How strong was it?" Chris asked.

"Not very. But their doppler is going to show just how fast we're moving and that's going to raise eyebrows."

"Only way we can pull point three is by being empty. Pull us back to point two before they ping us again," I said as my thoughts cleared.

Chris did something.

"Okay, we're down to point two."

"We just got pinged again," Hank said.

"We're lights out and all that, right?"

"So what do we do when they catch us?" Chaz asked. "Because we're the only thing moving."

"We could turn the lights on, make us nice and bright, then get in the lifeboat and head for one of the asteroids above the ecliptic," I said with a shrug. "Much as I hate to dump the ship, I can't spend it if I'm dead."

"I have a better idea," Chris said and hit a couple of switches in the overhead.

"Oh? What?"

"We make it *look* like we did that. I opened the hanger for the boat. The doors on the port side are still down, the other side's gone. I'll give the ship a Dutch roll combined with an actual slow roll. They'll figure we abandoned the ship and the ship's boat launching started it rolling. At point two, they won't be surprised to see the nose starting to hunt. Eventually it'll tumble and disintegrate."

"But what if they decide to board?"

"We still have one of those rods left. We wait till they come into sight, and launch."

"You'll have to stop the roll," Hank said with a thoughtful look.

"I'll keep it slow, so I can stop it quickly."

"Who'll fire it?" I said. "I don't think I'm in any shape to do it."

"Plus we had to cut your pressure suit off of you, so you don't have one anymore."

"Huh?"

"Those gases were hot, Dave. You've got plastic melted to your leg in places, second-degree burns everywhere, and a nice little case of frostbite around the melted spots."

I felt my stomach do a flip.

"You don't have any more of that Tramadol, would you?"

"Sorry, I don't want to hear any more confessions of a war hero," Hank said with a wink.

"If I had a cane, I'd hit you with it. Fine. Hopefully nothing breaks on the way home, because there's no way I'm fixing it like this."

"They're trying to raise someone in command," Chaz said suddenly. "They're saying they have a suspicious object boosting out at point-two gee. It's not running a transponder, and not responding to any hails."

"Which means they're too close for us to use the lifeboat, anyway," Hank said with a shrug. "I'll go down and get the system fired up and ready to fire the last rod."

"I'm surprised there's only one ship coming after us," I said after a few moments.

"I'm surprised they're even allowing it," Chris said. "The comms are jammed with distress calls. All of the habitats in orbit on this side of Venus have lost power, station keeping, everything. Any ships that were reentering to land lost power and a lot of them crashed. There's calls coming up from the planet from the cities you hit that didn't break up or sink outright, as they're starting to lose altitude. It's total chaos down there, Dave."

I swore silently and shook my head.

"I'm gonna hobble down to Engineering," I said, trying to get up on my one good leg.

"Dave," Chaz said, standing up to push me back down into

my seat. "As your brother-in-law, I'm pulling rank. Sit your ass down. Chris, let's not talk about it. I mean, yeah, part of me wants to dance, but part of me wants to cry. So, let's just leave it and leave here."

Chris looked at Chaz and then at me. He nodded. "Yeah, understood."

"Pulling rank?" I said, looking up at Chaz.

"Kacey told me that if you looked like you were going to do something stupid, I was allowed to stop you. I screwed up once already, I hadn't realized you'd undone your lifeline. I'm not going for two here."

"Uh-huh. Might as well bring up the rear camera and see how fast they're overtaking us."

"Good idea...Damn, they're haulin'," Chaz said as we watched. "Now I know how they felt when we took this ship from the last crew!"

"Hank, they'll be here in a minute," Chris said on the all hands. "Plug into the intercom out there and stay off the radio."

"Roger that. Going out now."

"Kill the cabin lights," I said.

"Good point," Chris said and we were all plunged into darkness, only the light of the displays showed on the bridge now.

"Okay, they're slowing," Chaz said. "Taking up station just behind and to the side. Ah, they got a light on the back of us. I think it's safe to say they noticed the missing boat. Okay, they're displacing a little; they're shining that light around."

"I think they've noticed that the cargo doors are open," Hank said on the intercom. "They just lit up the other side as we rolled, so they've undoubtedly seen the missing doors, probably the damage to the decks on that side as well."

"They're trying to raise us by name," Chris said.

"They're reporting they've found the *New Market* under boost, but apparently abandoned." Chaz said. "The ship's boat is gone, one set of cargo doors is missing, and there appears to be some damage. The ship is rolling and appears to be uncontrolled.

"Okay, they were just ordered not to fire on it, they are to survey it, take a lot of pictures to gather evidence, and if they can do so, to board it and regain control. I'm switching to a side camera; they're coming up alongside."

"Get ready, Hank," Chris said.

I watched as Chris checked the two side cameras—he had them both up on his console and I could hear him counting off the time per revolution as he watched them creeping up.

"Now!" he yelled and I felt it when the ship suddenly stopped rotating and suddenly there was a VMC frigate maybe a hundred meters off the side. They had a spotlight trained into the cargo bay and as I watched the last Rod from God came blasting out of the hold, and punched straight through the side of the frigate. When the chemical rocket motors hit, they opened the hole wider as they broke off and tore into the insides of the ship.

"All communications have stopped!" Chaz said as Chris started moving us quickly away from the ship as an explosion suddenly broke it in two. The whole thing went dark then and the two pieces started tumbling in different directions.

"Let's get us on a new course so if anyone else comes out to look, they don't find us," Chris said and went back to flying the ship.

"Good shooting, hon!" Chaz called out over the intercom.

"Does this mean I don't have to bring you breakfast in bed for a week after we get home?"

"I said good shooting, not *fantastic* shooting!" Chaz said, laughing.

"Fine, be that way. Chris, when should we change the transponder and hang those plates with the new name?"

"I think we've all had enough excitement for today," Chris said. "That can wait until tomorrow."

TWELVE

Ceres—Doyle Household

IT TOOK US FIVE DAYS TO GET BACK AS WE BURNED AT POINT-two gees the entire trip. We did burn out four panels at that speed, especially after all the point-three hijinks the ship had been through. As the hold was still in vacuum and I didn't have a pressure suit anymore, I had to talk Chaz and Hank through replacing all of them over suit comms. Thankfully, the ship had sailed with twelve spares, so it wasn't like I had to rebuild them.

I'd been hauled off to surgery within hours of our landing. My leg was definitely messed up, and I'd be healing for quite a while. They did say I wouldn't have a limp, just scars, once I finished physical therapy.

I was sitting on a couch in the living room with my leg up, my mother was playing at nurse when she wasn't cooking or cleaning house, and everyone else was off at work. Kacey was off talking with her grandfather about coming to work for us.

"David?" my mother said, coming into the room, "there's a Jack Shian at the door to see you?"

"Send him in, Mom, he's a friend," I told her as I set my tablet down.

"David! I'm happy to see you made it back!" Jack said, coming into the room.

"Excuse me if I don't stand," I said, motioning to my leg, which was in a cast from just below the hip to the tips of my toes.

"Yes, I heard about that."

"Mom?"

"Yes, David?"

"This is going to be one of those private confidential conversations. Jack's from the government."

"Oh! I'll go into the kitchen then and make some noise," Mom said, smiling. She knew I'd done something important even if she didn't know what. But that was enough for her.

"Good woman there," Jack said after she'd left.

"Yeah, my dad really hit it big when he met her. So what brings you by?"

"I wanted to thank you, personally. I also wanted to convey the thanks of... well, everyone that was in that room when I brought you in. You impressed a lot of people, Dave."

I sighed and shook my head. "I'd rather everyone forgot I was ever there."

"You did a great thing, Dave."

"No, *your son* did a great thing. So did all those other men and women who gave their lives for Ceres, for our people. Me? I just went and killed millions of people, some guilty, some innocent."

"It had to be done, Dave, you know that."

"Yeah, I think I do. They needed to finally suffer some sort of consequences for all the people they've murdered. Doesn't make it any easier.

"What are they doing now? I've been out of the loop since it happened."

"They believe that the McVay family of Earth was either behind it, or involved."

I smiled at that. "Nice to see that worked. Still, I'm surprised they bought it."

"They just can't believe that Ceres is big enough or powerful enough to have done it. We've learned recently that it was the McVay family that was behind the information that led to the attack here as well."

"Hence my involvement, I—"

Jack held up a hand, stopping me. "I told you once already: this is on them, not you. Getting back to the point, the McVays were found to have profited from the exchanges, so obviously they had ulterior motives. The factions on Venus, from what little we've been able to gather, have split into two groups, though both of those groups agree that the McVays are culpable in the attack. They either planned it, or they caused it to happen with their lies about Ceres."

"So they won't be coming back here?"

Jack smiled. "They most certainly won't. However, we're still going to improve our navy and our defenses, just in case they change their mind."

I gave him a weak smile. "Well, at least we got that."

"Yes, we got that. We also got that all of the other governments now understand that if pushed into a corner, Ceres is capable of unleashing hell on them. Mars has just approached us with a mutual defense treaty and closer economic ties."

I just nodded.

"So everyone of course wants to know: what do you want, Dave? What can we do for you?"

"Honestly?"

It was his turn to nod.

"Forget it was my idea. Forget that I did it, or at least forget my name. Forget all of our names. Tell everyone we were an elite team of Ceres Navy personnel who went above and beyond for their country. Don't build us any monuments, or memorials. We didn't do it for fame. We did it for our home."

I watched him as he thought about that.

"Worried about retaliation?"

"No, I'm worried about my soul. Regardless of whether or not what I did was right or justified, I don't want to be remembered as the man who slaughtered millions. I sure as hell don't want to be celebrated for it."

I started shifting on the couch. "Help me get up for a moment."

Jack came over and helped me up onto my good foot. I grabbed my crutch and went over to the chair my gear bag was on. Unzipping the side pocket, I got out the memory stick with the copy of Chaz's video.

Hobbling back over to Jack, I handed it to him.

"What's this?"

"Watch it in private. Show it to whomever you think deserves to see it. Try and keep it off the nets for at least a few years. Maybe save it for a documentary after we're all dead and gone," I said.

"Thanks, Dave." I could see he was starting to tear up at that.

"Convey my thanks to Captain Williamson and tell him to thank Smitty and his team for me."

"I'll do that."

Jack put the memory stick in his pocket, then pulled out an envelope and handed it to me.

"What's this?"

"Due to matters of national security, the Ceres government has had to confiscate the ship you recently salvaged. While the government does not pay top dollar, we do try to reimburse fairly."

I snorted at that. "Well, Kacey had been hoping to sell it," I said and tossed it by my tablet. "Thanks."

"You're more than welcome, Dave."

Jack shook my hand, then turned and left while I carefully got back on the couch. My leg hurt like hell, and after my problems with drug abuse as a child I really didn't like taking painkillers. My little episode aboard the *New Market* was still fresh in my mind.

"Hi, hon!" Kacey said, coming into the living room and giving me a hug. I yawned and stretched, then tried to sit up. I'd mostly been sleeping.

"Hi, Kace," I said and pulled her down so I could give her a kiss. "Wha'cha been up to?"

"Getting the corporation documents written up, talking to banks, all the stuff we need to do to get the business up and running. Grandpa's agreed to come on as president."

I'd noticed her grandfather, John Doyle, the family patriarch, was standing behind her. So, smiling, I reached up and shook hands. He pulled me up onto my good leg and clapped me on the back. Kacey's grandfather was a *big* man. A bit over two meters tall, and he had shoulders like a linebacker. He'd started out as a welder, then built his own company, sold it to what eventually became Ceres Habitats, then repeated the process a few more times until one day he'd ended up *running* the place.

He had fists the size of my head and a reputation for using them as well.

"Heard we almost lost you," he said, pulling me into a hug.

"Well, I did have a few bad moments there," I said and hugged him back. "Sure you want to do this?"

"If you think I'm gonna let you start a company called Doyle Shipbuilders and not put my hand in, you're even crazier than you look! I still regret not changing the name of my last company."

I laughed at that.

"So, any idea where we want to start looking for land?" he asked.

"There's a naval shipyard not too far from here. The infrastructure we'll need already runs out to it and there's a lot of restricted airspace out there along with the weapons to back it up. The port and docks there are dual use, though we'll have to pump a bunch of money into them and expand them. But we'd have to do that anyways, and it'll be cheaper as the basic infrastructure is there.

"We just need to convince the government of Ceres to sell it to us," he said and smiled at me.

I sighed. "You obviously know something I don't."

"Willie T used to work for me as a boy."

"Willie T?"

"William T. Sanford is our president," Kacey said, giving me a look.

"Oh, I had no idea what his name was!"

"So when a man with a proven track record walks up to him with a proposition, I think it's safe to say he'll listen to what I have to say."

"Ah," I said, nodding. "I thought it was about something else."

"Oh, I'm sure that your being married to my granddaughter and being the one paying for all of this won't go unnoticed either," he said a with wise-ass grin on his face.

"Okay, so what's our next step?"

Kacey helped me sit back down on the couch and get my leg up on the ottoman. "Well, tomorrow you need to come with us to sign all of the corporate paperwork as you're the CEO and majority share holder. Then we go to the bank and open up a bunch of accounts so we have someplace for your grandfather to send his money that he's investing in us."

"Have we gotten anybody to help Nick on the *Iowa*?" I asked. "Because I'm not going to be sailing for a while with this leg."

"Yes, Nick has an old friend that's agreed to help. He's got his engineer fourth certification, but my mom has put our contract on a two-month hold as there's just too much cleanup and repair work going on right now for them to ship out any parts."

"Well, I wanted to start working that shipping contract with my grandfather. If there's something Ceres could use right now, it's what he's got for us. We'll need a warehouse to put the stuff in, of course, but if we can get a deal on that land soon, we could build that *first*. That or rent space from the government or the navy."

"Well, before we do that, I think we need to put that ship you brought back, up for sale."

"Can't," I said, shaking my head.

"Why not?"

"The government confiscated it. Something about 'matters of national security.'"

Kacey said some very unladylike words, and her grandfather laughed.

"They can't do that to us!"

"Sure they can," I said and smiled. "Take a look in that envelope over there," I said, pointing.

"What's that?"

"Our compensation."

"How much did they give us?" she asked, grabbing it.

"Beats me, you're the one handling the money."

Kacey gave me a look while rolling her eyes, then tore open the envelope and pulled the check out. She looked at it and smiled.

"They give us enough?"

"I probably could have sold it for more, but after broker's fees? And repairing all the damage? Yeah, they gave us enough." She passed it to her grandfather, who looked at it and passed it back.

"So, do we have enough to buy a couple of old Argons?"

"Yup, I'm gonna need your help with that."

"I'm gonna need a wheelchair or something, then. Oh, I've been looking at the price-break points on K-20s and K-30s."

"Oh?"

"We can fit three K-20s into an Argon-class ship easily. Three used K-20s cost a lot less than two K-30s and unless you're running a heavy load, you don't need all three of 'em running. We could even get away with putting only two in, as long as we made sure to placard the decrease in ship lift capacity. They also won't be able to land in any kind of gravity well."

"We're nowhere near retrofitting the reactors on ships, Dave."

"Yes, but we may want to start keeping an eye out for deals

on any fusion reactors coming out of ships that are being sent to the breakers. I'm sure any Argons or similar-class ships that we look at are going to have PWRs that are in their last ten years of life, if that."

"That's a good point, Kacey," her grandfather pointed out. "We know what's coming; right now, nobody else does. So they'll be more than happy to unload stuff to us figuring we'll be stuck with paying a fortune to use it. Prices only go up when people know they can get more out of ya."

Kacey nodded. "Yeah, you're right. Once word gets out we're building a shipyard, everyone's gonna try to swindle us."

"So, when are we talking to the government about buying some property?"

"Anytime after we sign the papers and get our bank account," Mr. Doyle said. "I can call up Willie T tonight and find out if we could see him in the afternoon."

"Won't he be tied up with all the rebuilding?"

"Right now, I think all of the executive-level decisions for rebuilding the mess and dealing with the survivors have been made. Besides, if he doesn't have time, he'll tell me."

"We hope," Kacey said, looking up at him.

"I'm not the president of the preeminent shipyards on Ceres yet, dear."

"And you won't be until after we start producing actual ships," I said.

"How sure are you that your brother can put this rabbit out of his hat?" he asked me.

"If he can't do it, then it can't be done. The only question is how long will it take him. I got him off incommunicado until a certain group of rich assholes on Earth stop trying to make him their slave."

"Want me to bring that up with Willie?"

I shook my head. "Not yet. First let's get the shipyard started and start shipping this stuff from one of my grandfather's habs."

"What is it, exactly?"

"Ship-mounted weapons."

Mr. Doyle nodded slowly. "Yeah, I can see where the Ceres Navy might be interested in buying a bunch of those. Why are they building them out in hidden habs?"

"Because Earth?" I said with a shrug.

"Might want to see about moving them out here, where we can keep an eye on 'em."

"*That* might be an idea. But first I want to fly out to each of them and see what they're doing and what they got to offer."

"Only smart. Well, I'll let you get back to resting. Kace, Dave, see y'all in the morning!"

"'Night, Grandpa!"

"Later, Mr. Doyle."

"You're family now, Dave. 'Grandpa' will work just fine."

"Thanks, Grandpa!"

I watched as he left and then, yawning, I leaned into Kacey. "Jack stopped by."

"Is that who gave you the check?"

I nodded. "I made it clear that I didn't want any recognition for what I did. I wanted all of us to remain anonymous."

"Yeah, that's for the best, I'm sure."

"I gave him a copy of Chaz's video."

"Why'd you do that?"

I gave a slight shrug. "Maybe it'll make it easier to bury his son? You know what? We should name our first fighter that we build after him."

"Yeah, I think folks would like that."

Signing all the incorporation paperwork was boring and took a lot more time than I would have thought. The bank was a lot easier, they knew who my grandfather was and that I'd be moving a lot of money here. So the last thing that they wanted was to make my life difficult.

"So, what's for lunch?" I asked.

"We're having lunch with Willie," Mr. Doyle said.

"We are?"

"Yup. For some reason there's a lot of folks who want to shake your hand. No idea why, though. Probably because of all the money you'll be bringing in."

I stared at him for a full minute. "If you're really that clueless I'm going to fire you before we even get started."

He laughed. "Someone"—he looked at Kacey—"has made it more than clear that you don't want to discuss certain topics. Not that I blame you. But like it or not, you did these people a service. You bought them some breathing space and gave them something to cheer about when their world had all but fallen apart. Now, you may not like that, Dave, but you're going to be polite, shake their hands, say thank you, and not bitch—or I'll break your other leg."

I snorted. "You would too."

"'Course I would. Even the high and mighty need their heroes and while it may suck to be you, they don't know that and they *certainly* don't need to know that. Leadership three-oh-one: Sometimes ya gotta put all yer bitchin' behind you and smile as you take one for the team."

"Just as long as they keep it to themselves," I grumbled.

"The more you don't want any recognition or fame, the more these people will respect you. These folks hate gold diggers and con men."

"I just don't want them treating me like some hero, regardless of what they think. I'm not role model material."

He laughed at that. "Yeah, sure you're not."

Kacey wheeled me inside and we ended up in a large conference room, one that I didn't recognize. I did, however, recognize a lot of the people who were there. They all smiled, came up to me and shook hands, thanked me for stopping by, and didn't say anything else.

I liked that last part. I guess Jack had warned them.

After everyone got seated, a couple of waiters started serving us. I couldn't help but notice that all of them were armed. I guess folks were still worried about what might happen next. Suddenly, Mr. Doyle's words started to make sense.

"So, John, what's this I hear about you starting a new business?" President Sanford asked.

"Yup, my granddaughter and her husband there have been looking at this for a while now, and we've been hammering out the details. As you probably know, my grandson-in-law there has ties to some serious money back on Earth, and he's talked them into investing in a shipyard here on Ceres."

"Is that so?"

"Yup, sure is. You may have heard that he's got some people doing research in some new technologies as well?"

"I do seem to recall hearing something about that. Think it'll pan out?"

"Well, Willie, you know how it is. Everything's a gamble."

"Yeah, until *you* invest in it, John," the president said with a smile. "So, what are you looking for?"

"There's a piece down by the Besua Naval Shipyard I've been looking at. With the dual-use docks down there, I was thinking it would be a good place for us to build—especially as we're hoping that if things work out, the good folks in the Ceres Navy might have an interest in some of our products."

"Lou?" President Sanford asked, looking over at the admiral, who had a thoughtful look on his face. "Got something to say?"

"With the new shipyard you just approved yesterday, we've started looking at shutting down one of the older ones. Besua is as good a choice as any to shut down. We could keep an office over there, to help with any future work we might want to contract, but maybe they'd be interested in *buying* the shipyard? Then we wouldn't have to move a lot of that equipment out and sell it to the scrapyard."

"Dave, Kacey?"

"I'd have to look it all over. How much area does it cover? We want to make sure we have room to expand," I said.

"We've got four square kilometers fenced off. We have a couple of weapons ranges there."

I looked at Kacey. "How much would you be looking for to sell it to us?" she asked.

"That would be Rachel's department," the admiral said with a smile. "Just understand that we'll be moving out in stages; it won't happen overnight."

Kacey smiled at him and then turned and smiled at Rachel. "So, after lunch, how about we talk a little business?"

"I'd be delighted!"

THIRTEEN

Iowa Hill

"FEELS WEIRD," I SAID TO HANK AS I SAT IN THE MESS WITH MY tablet on the table while drinking a cup of coffee.

"You're still the chief engineer for the ship," Hank said with a chuckle.

"But I'm used to actually *doing* the job! Not supervising while sitting on my ass in the mess."

"How much longer are you going to be in that cast?"

"Was supposed to be another week. But seeing as the doc wants to be the one to take the cast off, probably not until we get home."

"We could have waited, you know."

I shook my head. "We need to have the *Iowa* ready to go back to work for Ceres Habs as soon as they get things sorted out. Kacey and I also need to check out these two habs as soon as possible to find out what we're dealing with."

"Grandpa Morgan wouldn't tell you?"

"All he said was 'bring a pressure suit.' So I just wasted good money on one that I can fit my cast in."

"You can always get it retailored."

"There is that. So, any idea what's up with these places?"

"Nope. You're sure they're making weapons?"

159

"That's what I was told. You're not gonna tell your buds to attack 'em or anything, are you?"

Hank gave me a look. "You got something to say there, Dave?"

"Eh, just been trying to figure out how to politely ask how long you've been working for Mars Intelligence without getting into some kinda fight."

"Because of your leg?"

"Because I like to think you're a friend," I said, picking up my coffee and taking a drink. "They still let you have those, right?" I asked, grinning at him as I set my cup back down.

"Ass. I'm not *exactly* working in Intelligence."

"So you're telling me you can be a 'little bit pregnant'?" And I leaned back as he took a half-hearted swipe at me.

"Don't quit your day job, Dave."

"Well, at least you're not denying it."

"How'd you figure it out?"

"Back when you told me you knew *all* about my past. I never told you the nitty-gritty, so the only way you'd have known was if you'd been briefed, and...well..." I gave a quick shrug of my shoulders.

"I thought you were so far out of it that you'd have missed that slip."

"Nope. So is that why you're out here roaming the spaceways?"

"No, that story is the truth. The first time we touched down on Mars? A couple of old friends paid a visit—word had gotten around from some old frigate captain who'd retired out on Ceres that I was involved with some young kid with a storied past who seemed to be deep in the center of things. So they figured maybe I'd like to regale them with a few tales."

"Gonna tell 'em about our little trip to Venus?"

"They figured out that one all by themselves. If you come with me next time I make it to Mars, you can help me lie outrageously and drink all the free beer your bladder can handle."

"Well, tell 'em that if they've got a problem with this place, to talk to me about it so we can work it out. Right now, Ceres needs all the weapons it can get its hands on."

"Seeing as they're working on a mutual defense treaty, I don't think they'd have any issues with doing that."

"I hope you didn't clue them in on where Marcus and his folks are."

Hank shook his head. "Wouldn't be fair to them or you. Not that I figured it out. Chris is pretty tightlipped."

"Think Paul knows you're working intel?"

"As Mars is one of the groups looking the other way and trying to slip whatever covert support they can Marcus's way, I don't think he'd care."

"That's good, because I pay both your paychecks so I get first crack at your loyalty, remember that," I said with a chuckle.

"Okay, what *else* aren't you telling me?"

"How'd you like to manage Doyle Shipping for me and Kacey?"

"Wait, what?"

"Hank, we just *bought* a shipyard! We signed the paperwork before we took off two days ago. Sure, we got Kacey's grandfather running it, but right now it's just the three of us and we're going to be up to our ears just getting it into some semblance of order. Plus we're gonna need a lot of help finding crews for those two ships we just bought."

"What do I tell Chaz?"

"That he's your assistant? I doubt this is something you can do without help. Also, I'm sure you're going to want to sail with each crew as we bring each ship into service, to make sure we're getting what we hired."

"Are you going to pull Chris?"

I shook my head. "Right now, the *Iowa* is the ship we'll be using for our special projects. Chris is in the know and he's family. So he can be trusted." I smiled again. "And once you and Chaz get married, you'll be family too."

"What makes you think we're going to get married?" Hank asked, giving me a *look*.

"I think he mentioned something to Kacey about a conversation on commitment?" I replied, looking up at the ceiling while trying not to smile and failing, miserably.

Hank just shook his head and sighed. "In my defense, living with all these couples on board does tend to get your mind thinking."

"Also those Doyles are all awfully quick to grab on when they find something good."

"Yeah, there's that," Hank said with a laugh. "I guess I'll talk to Chaz about it. After shipping with you for the last few years, I suspect life on a regular ship just wouldn't be all that much fun.

"So how goes the studying?" he asked, motioning toward my tablet.

"That's probably the only good thing about the cast, it's giving me the time to actually sit down and go through all this stuff. I'm not looking forward to finding someone to do the apprentice hours with, though."

"How many is that?"

"Couple hundred. If I'm lucky, I'll get through it in a few months."

"There's that much work?"

"Yup, that was why I wanted to get the cert. Lots of work and you can charge top dollar. 'Course with us opening a ship-yard, it'll end up saving us a ton of time not having to wait for someone else to get the job done."

"Sounds like you're going to be busy."

I shrugged. "Being busy was always the idea. It'll be years before we're building anything new, I'm sure. Kacey may think that we'll be cranking out ships in a couple of years, but I know a lot more about what's involved in just designing one. That part right there can take years."

"Which is why *I'm* planning on licensing our first design from General Ship Designs!" Kacey said, coming into the mess.

"Ah, speak of a sexy devil," I said, smiling up at her, "and she appears!"

"How's the leg?" she asked, coming over to me.

"Fine."

"What are you going to license?" Hank asked her.

"Argon Twos."

"What's an Argon Two? Can't say I've heard of those."

"They only made a few, the Kryptons pretty much killed them."

"Still doesn't tell me what it is."

"It's a wider version of the Argon," I told him. "You can get a version that can land on Earth; the standard model, however, can't. Mars is about the strongest gravity field it can handle. Originally they were also point-oh-five gravity ships, which made them slow, but they only needed one fission SS18G PWR reactor, called a 'Pig-gee' that was rated at four hundred and fifty megawatts. So they were cheap, but they were slow. They also ran with a much smaller crew."

"How much smaller?"

"Two pilots, two engineers, two able-bodied spacers rated as watch-standers."

"They were mostly used as bulk haulers," Kacey added. "I think they only built one breakbulk type with decking. The design is cheap, because there weren't a lot sold, and with a few updates, we think it'll fit a niche in the market."

"Like a faster grav drive?"

"Exactly. We'll make them point-one ships, put in two fusion power plants, add a couple cabins, improve the mess, and we'll have a ship that hauls seven thousand TEUs, fits in every hanger any of the smaller-class cargo ships fit in, and costs less to operate than even the old Argons."

"It'll definitely be cheaper in the long run to buy one of these than to buy an older Argon that needs its fission reactors swapped out," I pointed out.

"Does this mean you're gonna buy up all the old Argons when the price crashes?"

"Maybe if they're cheap enough," Kacey said with a shrug. "And well kept up like the *Iowa* with grav drive upgrades already installed. But there's only so much refit work we'll do after we start building new ships."

"This first design," I said, "is mainly for us to find out just *what* is involved in building something from scratch."

"So did Dave ask you about helping with our shipping business?"

"Yes, he did."

Kacey spent the next fifteen minutes asking Hank his opinions on hiring a crew and then went on to other subjects as I went back to studying. For me this was going to be an incredibly boring trip as I couldn't work and my leg still hurt enough that hobbling around wasn't much fun at all. I wasn't looking forward to the inspections and the rest of the things we'd be doing at the two habs, but it did have to be done.

"Dave, we're being hailed by Saint Lazarus Habitat. They want to know why we're here."

"I'll be right there," I said and, grabbing my crutch, I hobbled into the bridge and donned a headset.

"Saint Lazarus Control, this is David Doyle, Alistar Morgan's grandson. We have a shipment of foodstuffs and other items you've ordered. I believe you were notified of our coming."

"One moment, David, please do not approach any closer while I check."

"Sure thing." I turned to Chris. "Hold us here."

I looked out the windows of the bridge. I could see the habitat fairly clearly; it was painted white and well lit.

"What are those markings?" I asked Chris and motioned to very large colored squares laid out in a row. The pattern repeated every one hundred and twenty degrees around the rim.

"Plague warning," Chris said. "It's also why their beacon is flashing the red-white pattern it is."

"David, you are cleared to approach. The transshipping will take place in vacuum. You are cleared to dock your cargo bay only. You are not to dock your air lock with any hatch. If you are coming aboard, you are to remain in pressure suits at all times."

"I copy, Saint Lazarus Control." I turned to Chris. "You heard the man."

"Kat, could you open the portside cargo bay doors?" Chris said and slowly brought the ship closer. I could see the doors for the habitats cargo bay opening. A beacon appeared on Chris's navigation screen as they did.

"Guess I need to suit up," I said. "Let Kacey know to suit up and make sure everyone understands they're not to crack their suits if they should go into atmosphere there."

"Will do, Dave."

I carefully made my way down the stairs, which on the ship were more like ladders; with my leg I didn't slide down as fast as I normally did. By the time I got to my room, Kacey was suited up, though her helmet was off. I'd need help getting into my suit because of the cast on my leg. At least the crutch was aluminum and wouldn't be affected by the vacuum of space.

When we finally made it out onto the cargo deck, I looked around and saw that there were several suited people inside the cargo facility of the Lazarus. So sticking to the edge of the cargo ramp we were now tied to, I made my way off the *Iowa* and inside.

"Can I help you?" a woman asked as I approached. She wore a pressure suit with the visor darkened.

"I'm Dave Doyle, Alistair Morgan's grandson. I'd like to speak to Mr. Constantine."

"Follow me, please. Just remember not to remove or open your helmet. You will need to dial your pressure up by ten percent, in case of leaks."

Kacey and I both took a moment to make the adjustment to our suits, then followed her. When we got to the air lock going inside, I was surprised that there was a man there who inspected our suits and checked our pressure settings. "Those will have to stay out here," he said, pointing to the airtight pouches on our suits that were normally used to carry anything you didn't want exposed to vacuum.

"Afraid we'll take something?" Kacey asked with a chuckle.

"Something you most certainly do not want," he replied and held out his hand.

We passed our pouches over and stepped inside. I was surprised as we went through a decontamination protocol.

"We have sick people onboard," the woman explained. "So just as we don't want anything getting out, we also don't want anything new getting in."

We both nodded at that.

"This way, please," she continued when the door opened, leading us out and down a well-maintained and clean passageway to a hatch labeled HABITAT CHIEF. She opened it, waved us in, then closed the door behind us.

"Ah, David, it's nice to meet you. Who is your companion?"

I looked at the man sitting behind the desk. He was wearing what looked like a long-sleeved sweatshirt, which was pretty common wear in a lot of habitats, especially by the outer segments where they tended to be cooler. However, his sweatshirt also had a hood on it, a rather large hood, that was pulled up and forward so it was hard to see his face. He was also wearing gloves.

"This is my wife, Kacey. Are you Constantine?"

"Actually, I'm Bill," he said, sticking out a hand, which I shook. "That's just the code to let me know it's okay to load you after we're done unloading. What happened to you, if I might ask?" he said, motioning to the overly thick leg of my pressure suit.

"Broken leg in a shipping accident when a tie-down failed," I lied. "I didn't want to delay the trip. I had no idea if you were desperate for supplies or not."

"Ah, well, we weren't. But it's the thought that counts."

"So why the quarantine?" Kacey asked.

"Didn't the name cue you in?"

We both shook our heads.

"We're a leper colony."

"What?" I said, surprised.

"Leprosy still exists?" Kacey said, equally surprised.

"Technically, we have Haloday's Syndrome, but it's pretty much the same thing. It's rare, but it can be contagious. Or at least a lot of people on Earth believe it is. So your grandfather set up this habitat as well as the Kalawao Habitat anti-spinward from here in a trailing orbit."

"And the weapons?" I asked. "Why the hell are you making ship-mounted weapons?"

"Well, we have to do *something* for money," he said with a shrug. "We get all the basics from your grandfather's endowment, but a fair number of us are technicians and engineers and there was a time when we were a little bit paranoid that someone might try to kill us. If you look carefully when you leave, you'll see we're fairly well armed."

"I guess I need to find out what I owe you for the weapons, then," Kacey said. "We weren't told that we had to pay you."

"Oh, Alistair took care of that."

"Still, I'd like to know the costs, so I can pay him. After the attack on Ceres, the government is going to want to buy a bunch of these for the new warships they're building in case the VMC comes back, and, well, Alistair shouldn't be bearing the cost of that."

"Don't argue with her," I told him. "You'll lose. She's really quite the stickler for making sure people get paid."

Bill laughed and held up his hands. "I'll send you the prices when I transmit the manifest. Be warned, all of these weapons ship in sixty-foot TEUs. Rail guns are long. Also, all the containers are in a vacuum. There's a decontamination protocol for them, I'll send that to you as well. While they should be safe, nobody here wants to take any chances."

"So is that all you make, rail guns?" I asked.

"Along with the control interfaces, yes, that's it. Kalawao does both short- and long-range lasers. We thought about missiles, but the fuel and the explosives for the warheads were too problematic and too likely to cause accidents."

"Smart. I wouldn't want to deal with anything like that either. Anyway, we were hoping for a tour of the facility?"

"The *entire* facility?"

"No, no, not all of it! Just the weapons production lines."

"Ah, better. It's not our privacy so much as not wanting to see you puking in your helmets. The effects of Haloday's Syndrome can be...*disconcerting*, to put it mildly."

He stood up slowly then and I got a brief glimpse of his face, or what was left of it.

I didn't try to look inside his hood again.

"I'm looking forward to this, to be honest," he said as he led us out of his office.

"Why's that?" Kacey asked.

"Because I haven't had the chance to show off our production line in years. It really is something to boast about. You see, we don't have any contractual obligations, so we are never in a rush. This allows us to not only see that every job is done right, but to make sure our working conditions are always top notch."

The next hour was educational. Everyone we saw was dressed the same as Bill, but the entire facility was spotless. The production line was also nothing at all what I expected. Each weapon was built by a team, who did everything from start to finish. Everything was inspected not just by a team of inspectors, but each team inspected the others' weapons at the end of the shift.

But what was even more interesting was that they were engraving artwork down the rail barrels. Each one had a dragon along its length and it didn't look like any two of them were the same. The dragon artwork definitely took your breath away.

"Pretty, aren't they?" Bill asked as we stood there admiring the barrels.

"That had to have taken a lot of time," Kacey said.

"Time is the one thing we're rich in. Come, let me take you to the test stand and show you how they work."

When we left two hours later, I was definitely in need of getting out of the suit. The decontamination process was a little more involved, our pouches were returned, and when we got back to our quarters the first thing we did after stripping out of our suits was hit the bathroom. After that, we hit the showers.

"So how was it?" Hank asked when we finally made it up to the mess.

"We are going to be charging a lot for their weapons," Kacey said. "They're works of art. Literally. When we get home we'll uncase one and show you."

"They're also really anal about quality," I added. "They're not in a rush as they're not on contract. So they want theirs to be the best—and honestly? I think they are."

"I saw we were loading," Kacey said. "How long until we're done?"

"Another hour, I think," Hank said. "You going to inspect the other place as well?"

"I'm afraid if we don't, they'll feel insulted," I said with a sigh. "But if it's anything like this place, I don't think we'll regret it."

"Did you ask them about moving?"

"They can't," Kacey said.

"Why not?"

"Most of their patients come from Venus and Earth. They only have one specially outfitted ship to transfer patients and it doesn't have the ability to navigate the ring."

"So, what are we going to do about security?"

"Get the Ceres Navy to provide us with an out-of-sight escort."

"You think they'd do that?"

"As we're getting weapons for them? I don't see why not."

"Good point. Well, I'll leave you two to get something to eat. I need to suit up and check with Emil on our load and balance."

I watched as Hank left, then turned back to Kacey.

"You know, I'm going to miss sailing on this ship."

"After all this time, I'd be surprised if you weren't."

"Well, I'm going to hobble back down to Engineering and check up on the new guy before getting back into that pressure suit," I said, wrinkling my nose. "I'm not looking forward to another two hours in that thing. My leg itches like crazy after thirty minutes and there's not a damn thing I can do about it."

"I'll be sure to cut the inspection short."

The only real difference we found between the Kalawao Habitat and the Saint Lazarus one, was that the people of Kalawao were a lot more colorful in the decoration of their habitat's walls. Also, they didn't carve dragons into the laser emitter barrels.

No, they used anodized aluminum in multiple different colors, shades, and hues to put very colorful birds of types I'd never seen before. I had no idea if they were real, mythical, or perhaps both. Otherwise they were just as quality conscious and proud of their work as the others had been.

Obviously my grandfather had put some care into just who he picked to come here. Which made me wonder if there was a third habitat that was filthy, ill kept, and full of lazy degenerates and social misfits.

After I remembered my brief glance of Bill's face, I decided I truthfully did not want to know.

FOURTEEN

Besua Naval Works

BESUA GOT ITS NAME FROM THE SURFACE FEATURE IT WAS BUILT in and under. Having a crater of sorts meant you could put your docks in the wall and that made it cheaper for ships to fly into a sealable and pressurizable environment. It was always cheaper, safer, and easier to have your workers in a shirtsleeves environment than working in a pressure suit.

Because when you're working with lots of sharp metal objects, welders, and other such things, a slice in a pressure suit could mean death. Whereas a tear in someone's pants, shirt, or coveralls was just an annoyance.

The "navy" side of Besua had twenty separate docks and only one of them currently had a ship in it, and that was a test-bed ship used for testing new systems or providing research for the folks doing systems and weapons development. As more than half of the base wasn't being used, I could see why Admiral Carstairs wanted to sell it to us. This way he got some budgetary advantage out of closing down a base, above and beyond not having to maintain it anymore.

"Damn, this is big," I said, looking around the first hanger.

"Yeah, we easily could fit two *Iowas* in here," Kacey agreed.

"You could fit two of those Xenon-class ships in here," Chris said, looking back and forth with a critical eye, "and still have space left over. Are they all this damn big?"

"Not according to the documentation they sent us," Kacey replied. "They only have two this large. When this place was originally built, there was talk about getting either a few of those ship carriers the Mars Navy uses, or some of those larger cruisers that the Earth Navy flies.

"The rest are smaller. Six were built to handle cruisers, and all the rest handle destroyer length ships, though all are wide enough you could still stick any of the same-length cargo boats inside."

"And Ceres has, what, two cruisers? They've raised almost an entire navy based around destroyers."

"Well," I said, "they're building cruisers now, as well as refitting one of those Mars ship carriers and building a slew of small frigates to fill it."

"The problem," Kacey said, picking the conversation back up, "is that if we want to *build* in here, we're going to need a lot more gantries and lift cranes. Also, how are we going to set up any sort of production line? It's a lot cheaper to build in segments, with a dedicated hanger building each segment. Then you just use a transfer system to move them to where you're assembling your ship."

"What's wrong with the system they have already?" Chris asked, motioning to the front of the hanger where there was a pressure door leading to the existing transfer system to move in materials.

"Not big enough. The ships will be built in cross sections, then those sections will have to be moved. We're talking ten-meter-long cross sections as wide as the ship," Kacey said, looking over the hanger. "The existing transfer system can handle the materials we need to build those cross sections—things like hull plating, decking, gravity drives—but that's it."

"Let me see those plans," I said and held out my hand.

Kacey shrugged and handed them to me, and I started walking over to the south wall. All of these hangers were in an east/west configuration; we were at the northernmost point. I stopped when I got to the wall, looked at the plans, looked at the wall, then looked at the plans again.

"These aren't 'as-builts,'" I told her.

"What are those?"

"Something you need to bug them for: detailed engineering drawings," I said. Turning back to the north, I paced off counting until I came to the center, where the main equipment entrance was.

"Follow me."

I went out to the delivery rail system. Then I started counting paces again until I came to the entrance to the next hanger.

"Okay, what was that about?"

"Those hangers are one hundred and fifty meters wide. Each of my strides is a meter. From center to center it was one hundred seventy meters, which means there's twenty meters, probably of stone, between each of the bays, assuming they spaced them evenly."

"Okay, and why is that important?"

"We'll cut a passage through the wall separating the first eight bays and build a gantry across the front of all eight, through those passageways to service all of the large moves. We'll have to put in a series of pressure doors and folding bulkheads, for whenever we need to launch a ship, but I don't see that as a problem."

"That isn't going to be cheap."

I shrugged. "We're still saving a fortune by not having to build everything from scratch. But we use the two large bays to build our cross sections and other major frame pieces. We then lay the keels in each of the six remaining cruiser bays and do final assembly there."

"What about the other smaller docking bays?"

I shrugged again. "Once the reactors and the drives are in, we can always fly the new ships into one of those to do all the final outfitting. I think it's time we stole your father away from Ceres Habitats. We're going to need his input on this before we build it, or we may end up with a costly remodel."

"Mom's gonna hate me for this." Kacey sighed.

"Well, we could always make her a competitive offer as well," I said, grinning.

"She's a vice president. We'd be wasting our money because there's nowhere near enough for her to do here."

"We're going to need steel for the hulls, decking for the habitation areas, for the cargo decks. Aluminum for the grav-panel fixtures, and that's not even getting into the hundreds of subsystems we'll need to buy," I said, shaking my head. "We have a dozen shops to set up here. All of that is going to need stuff, lots of stuff."

"I'm tapping my sister Sheila for the former and my brother Carl for the latter."

"Wait, don't they work for your mother?"

"Sheila does. Carl works for Dad."

I sighed. "I'm doomed when your mother gets her hands on me."

Kacey snorted. "I'm planning on buying a *lot* of materials from her as we get set up."

"Why would you do that? Why would she want to sell to us?"

"Because Ceres Habitats needs a huge financial shot in the arm right now. One of the main habitat assembly buildings got destroyed during the attack. So they have not only the building to replace, but all of the finished and in-process components that were in it. They also need to replace the people they lost and train them up."

"Don't they have insurance?"

"Insurance doesn't cover acts of war," Kacey said, shaking her head.

"Well, let's go track down the actual engineering diagrams for this place. You can call your dad while we're doing that and let him know he starts tonight. Then call your mother and start locking up resources on everything we need, I guess."

I had a thought then.

"Hey, do you think we could hire people from Ceres Habs to do the work here we need done?"

"Why would we want to do that?"

"Because if Ceres Habs has some of its production shut down, they've probably got a lot of workers who are staring a furlough right in the face? Plus they're all in construction, right? I wouldn't be surprised at all to find out that they've got people who can help with the work."

"I think you just might have something there," Kacey said with a smile and got out her tablet.

"Hello, Mom? We gotta talk! What? No, this isn't about Dad—well, not yet. But I heard a rumor you're gonna be laying people off? What? Things get around, Mom. Now look, we're gonna need some rebuilding done in here and I was thinking..."

"So," Chris said, coming over to me while Kacey talked to her mom. "Want to come over for dinner tonight?"

"Huh? Something up?"

Chris laughed. "Maureen Doyle is about to be strung over a barrel by her daughter. Trust me, we don't want to be around to see any of that."

"What? You don't think Kacey will take advantage of the situation, would she?"

"If she doesn't, her mother will probably disown her. Word of advice: do *not* play bridge with them."

I looked at Kacey, whose voice was now all sweetness and light, and I shivered. She was in full horse-trading mode. With her *mom*, the undisputed queen of horse-trading on Ceres.

"Thank god I don't know how to play."

"So, how'd it go?" I asked Kacey later that night while we were lying in bed together.

"Mom put up quite a fight, but in the end she had to admit that selling everything to me at cost was worth it, as we would be keeping her workers from being poached or finding other jobs if they were working for us, instead of being furloughed."

She rolled over and kissed me. "I even got her to agree to handle payroll for them."

"Why'd you do that?"

"Because they all get to keep their benefits and their time working for us counts toward their seniority. Sure, it means we pay a little extra for them, but that was how I got Mom down to selling us everything else at cost." She grinned widely then. "It was *glorious!*"

"Yeah? And how'd your mom take it?"

"Bitching and complaining and fighting every step of the way! But I had her dead to rights and I wrung every concession I could think of out of her. Nope, she won't be making any money off of me *this* time!"

"I take it she has in the past?"

Kacey nodded. "More than once. When it comes to making deals and all that, Mom's always been hard on all of us. She knows that there's people who'll try to take advantage of her kids because of all the trading and negotiating she does. Ceres Habitats is one of the major corporations here, and she can be ruthless when it comes to business. So there's always people with scores to settle."

"And of course how well you all do probably reflects on her, right?" I teased.

"Yeah, there's that too. I think that's why both Jeff and Chaz decided they didn't want to go into business. Oh, and Dad starts tomorrow. Along with Sheila and Carl."

"Oh?"

"They can't do anything with the line down anyway. Like you said, we need them. Dad thinks we can take the dock all the way down by the one the navy is still using and set that one up to do the reactor swaps and other upgrade work on those two Argon-class ships we bought."

"Why set up a dock? We're only doing the two of them, right?"

"Dad pointed out that there are a *lot* of those ships out there as well as other old cargo ships that companies would be more than willing to pay us to do the same swap on. *If* we can get the cost down and keep it down. He's already got some ideas on how to do that and is planning on using our two conversions to test those ideas out."

"Do I want to know?" I asked, a little worried.

"He's got a line on one of those enormous plasma cutters that the breakers use. He's going to *cut* the entire engine room out of the ship, while building a new one, that he'll then just jack up into position and weld into place."

I blinked at the sheer audacity of the idea.

"That's . . . outrageous," I told her.

"That's my dad. Think it'll work?"

"Maybe? Yes? I'll talk to him tomorrow. But for now, come here, my little conquering hero, and let's celebrate your successful night of wheeling and dealing with the best of them!"

"Yes," Kacey said, preening, "let's!"

FIFTEEN

Doyle Shipyards—Besua, Ceres

I LOOKED OUT AT THE ARGON-TWO—OR, AS WE WERE NOW CALLING it after the design changes, the Besua-class—cargo ship that had taken shape on the floor of the hanger below me. We'd just laid the keels for three more now that this first one was almost complete. Tomorrow it would start its trials.

"Wow, we built a ship," Kacey said, leaning into me.

"I know, right?" I said with a laugh. "You'll never guess who called me about them."

"Alistair?"

I shook my head. "Damascus Freight Lines, my old employer. Apparently, Steve Roy, the *Iowa Hill*'s old captain, contacted them after that tour we gave him when he came through here last month. A lot of their old GSD Argon-class ships are getting to need new reactors. They are wondering if they could work some kind of a deal for a lower price if they trade us the ship that needs work."

"It would be cheaper for them to just have us replace their old Siz-gees with the K-30s."

"The crew requirements for our Besuas are less, and they haul more. Plus they're new."

"I seem to recall they don't fully crew their Argons?"

"They crew them with three pilots, two engineers, two spacers, and a cook. The Besuas only crew with six."

"Still, it's a lot more."

"Well, I may have dropped a hint or two with Steve that if they book us before anyone else did, I might give them a bit of a discount?" I said with a grin as Kacey turned and frowned at me.

"You what?" she said.

"Offered them fifteen percent."

"Fifteen percent? That's our entire profit margin!"

I nodded. "I'm aware of that, Kace."

She looked at me, took a couple deep breaths, then looked back out at the ship.

"Okay, why?"

"They fly to the kinds of places where all our potential customers are. Or go. They fly all over the solar system. We cut them fifteen on the first three, then ten on the next three if they decide to order more. After that, we'll give them a two percent on everything for being first."

"That's a pretty good deal," Kacey said slowly. "I can't fault your logic either. I've been working with Dad and Grandpa for weeks now to come up with an advertising campaign."

"I know. But until we get something out there, for people to actually *see* all the advertising in the world isn't going to help us."

"What about number one there?" she asked, motioning her head toward our first ship.

"With all of the 'learning experiences,'" I said while making finger quotes in the air, "we had while building it, I don't think I want it to be representative of our work. I was thinking we have Hank get us a crew for it, let them beat on it for a while, and see what breaks."

"I'll talk to Emil about setting them up for the 'bunny run' in the belt. Might even want to talk to Hank about finding a less-than-perfect crew. That should put it through a rough environment."

"Just might have to double-up on the safety gear, though," I said thoughtfully as Kacey's tablet pinged. I looked at her as she pulled out her tablet.

"Chris just got back with the *Iowa* from their latest trip. They're docked down at Ceres Habitats; they brought back a fair amount of raw materials. Also, Emil is making dinner and would we like to stop by?"

"Sure! Let me tell my mom. Check to be sure we can bring the baby."

"He says yes and to be there at seven."

"Ah, life after having children," I said with a laugh. "Dinner's always at seven and never at nine anymore!"

"Well, Jeff is coming up on a year old, so maybe we should start thinking about number two?" Kacey teased.

"Won't get any arguments from me! Well, let's check in with your father to make sure things are on track, then we can go home and get ready for tonight."

She put her tablet away and I slid an arm around her as we walked down the observation catwalk back to her father Rob's office. Our offices were a bit closer to the main entrance into the complex, though I had a workshop back here where I kept all my tools for tuning and working on the grav drives.

"It's not even two years," Kacey said with a shake of her head, "and we've already got our first ship done and three more started."

"Yeah, it's been busy as hell though. Having a kid, getting certified, sitting for the engineer second test..." I gave her a hug. "I saw how hard it was for you, having Jeff in the middle of all that. Thank god for our moms or I don't think we would have made it!"

Kacey laughed and leaned into me as we walked out of the docking bay. "I think your mom gets the lion's share of the credit on that. Though even mine surprised me with how much time she was willing to take off."

We walked into her father's office and were surprised to see Rob and several supervisors standing around and staring at the large wall display we normally used for meetings and reviews.

"What's going on?" I asked as we stepped in.

"The VMC just attacked Earth."

"*What?*" I exclaimed. "Why in the hell did they do that?"

"I still don't know why they attacked *us*! But they attacked Mare Imbrium on the Moon and the navy base there, then immediately launched attacks on Boston, Chicago, Los Angeles, Osaka, Wuhan, Mumbai, Lagos, Madrid, Berlin, and London."

"Damn! How bad is it?"

"Wuhan and Chicago are *gone*, several of the others suffered near misses, whatever that means, and the rest were intercepted. But there's a battle going on—they didn't send one ship to launch the missiles, they send over twenty, according to the reports we're getting."

"What kind of missiles, Dad?"

"Nukes, Kace, they used nukes. There's reports that they're landing troops as well, but"—Rob shook his head—"no one knows for sure and all of this is old news. We're getting it on a relay via Mars."

"Dad, you know that four-man fighter/bomber we've been working on?"

"Yeah?"

"Have Grandpa kick it over to President Sanford. *Tonight*."

I looked at her father as his eyes widened a hair and then he got a thoughtful look on his face. "Yeah, I think that's a good idea. I think come tomorrow we may find ourselves with a new contract. If they've got the balls to attack *Earth* we may find ourselves up next."

"Chris just got back with the *Iowa Hill*," I told him. "We'll be over there for dinner if you need to reach us."

"What about your family back there?" he asked me.

"They're in the Midwest, so hopefully they're well away from it. But I guess we're going to find out just what kind of shape Earth's military is in."

"I suspect no one is going to like the answer to that, whatever it is," said Barbara, the supervisor in charge of the cargo cross sections.

"Yeah, probably not," I said while looking at Kacey, who nodded. We left and headed home.

The trip there wasn't a long one—Chris and Emil's place was within walking distance, as were both of our parents'. Mom was still helping Maureen Doyle take care of her place, though she and Dad did have their own home now where they lived with Dianne, my younger sister.

"I take it you've seen the news?" Chris asked when we got to their place.

Kacey and I both nodded as we stepped inside. I was carrying Jeff, as well as the diaper bag. Mainly because, to my continuing dismay, not only was Kacey a better shot than I was, she could draw faster too. So much for my vaulted elie genetics.

"Think it'll affect us at all?" he asked.

"I don't know if it'll have an effect on our shipping schedules as we never get any closer to Earth than Mars," I replied, "but it's definitely going to affect our shipbuilding."

"Why's that?"

"Because we've been working up a design on a new fighter/bomber," Kacey said, taking Jeff from me as I set down the diaper bag.

"Why would anyone want a bomber?"

"Because no one likes the term 'missile boat,' apparently," I said. "The idea is, we built it so it can carry four very large missiles, or twelve smaller ones. You launch the missiles first, then go in with a couple of rail guns and finish off what's left."

"It's not all that different from those small frigates that the Mars Navy uses, we just pulled out all the crew quarters, boarding parties, etcetera," Kacey said, picking up the conversation. "Because they'll primarily be fighting out in the belt, there'll always be some sort of support facility in the area. So we went for speed and maneuverability and got rid of the ability to do long patrols."

"Yeah, twenty-four hours is about the longest you're going to want to be in one of these. We're treating them a lot more like the old military fighters than we are naval ships."

"And you think they'll go for it?" Chris asked.

"Compared to even those small frigates, they're cheaper and faster to build. They should be incredibly fast due to the lower mass, but with those missiles, they'll still pack a hefty punch."

"And," Kacey finished, "we can easily field a dozen of them for every ship the enemy shows up with. In short, we can swarm them and overwhelm their defenses."

Chris thought about that a few moments, then nodded. "And we're fighting here at home and they have to travel a long way to get to us. Yeah, I can see your point. So when did you show this to the navy?"

"My dad's probably sending the proposal over as we talk. We really wanted to get the cargo line going before we opened up a second one, but..." Kacey shrugged.

Emiliana came in then carrying their daughter, Afrie.

"Stop talking shop!" she said, smiling. "I get enough of *that* at work!"

"Hank and Chaz coming over?" I asked.

"Not tonight. I wanted something a lot more relaxed than Chaz would enjoy," Emiliana said with a smile.

"You got that right!" Kacey laughed. "So how's Afrie doing?"

We sat down and chatted for a few minutes before Emiliana passed Afrie off to Chris and went back to the kitchen before calling us in to eat. Dinner, as always, was good.

"You know, sooner or later we're going to have to open up a restaurant for Emil," I said to Chris as I helped him clear the table after dinner. "Honestly, I'm surprised she hasn't opened one already."

"After the next one is old enough that she can leave them with a nanny for eight hours a day and not feel guilty about it," Chris said with a chuckle. "Bad enough I'm gone for months at a time."

"Honestly, I'm surprised you're still with us. I'd have thought you'd gone back to the larger ships now that you've married Emil."

Chris shrugged. "I'm getting a lot more hours on my license here, the pay's good, it's the family business, and now that we've got three ships, I'm the chief pilot!" he finished with a laugh. "I will admit that it will be nice when we have enough business to get some larger ships. The big haulers tend to mainly do 'out and backs.' So I'd have more time at home."

"Well, when we get enough of those Besua-class ships, we could move you into one of those if you want? 'Out and backs' are really what those are being built for. Just targeted at smaller markets."

"I've seen the design specs, Dave. You'd have to do some upgrades if you wanted to stuff one of those with enough refined ore to make the Mars run, or the Ganymede run."

"We've already had this discussion, believe it or not. Once we've gotten the standard design shaken down, we're going to do a heavy-lift version with an increased weight limit."

Chris nodded. "Oh, I got this when we made our last delivery to our good friends," he said and pulled out an envelope that he passed to me.

Taking it, I noticed it had my name written on the front. I could recognize my brother's handwriting. We'd gotten Christmas cards from him for the last two holidays—he'd sent one to me and Kacey, and a second one to our parents via Chris. From the notes inside it seemed that he was quite happy with his current situation. As we were nowhere near the holidays, and this one didn't feel like it had a card in it, I was immediately curious.

"Why'd you wait so long to hand it over?" I asked, looking back up at him.

"Because I didn't want you to spend dinner reading it?" Chris said, grinning at me.

"Dick," I grumbled. "But yeah, I probably would have." I put it in my pocket.

"Such restraint! I'm surprised you didn't tear it open immediately."

"It took weeks to get here, a few more hours won't change anything."

"Think he found the answer?"

I shook my head. "Not really. If he had he would have come back here instead of sending me a letter. I suspect it's a list of stuff he needs for his research that he can't get there."

"So, what do you think is going to happen with Earth?"

I shook my head. "I honestly don't have a clue. But someone once told me that these kinds of people have to turn their hate on somebody, or they'll start turning it on each other."

"Yeah, I get that, but *Earth*?"

I looked around and lowered my voice. "After what we did to them, they have to do *something*. I just wonder how they managed to build enough ships to do this, because I can't see them leaving their homes undefended after that last spanking."

"Well, I've told Emil that I don't think we should be doing any runs to Mars unless folks are willing to pay a premium, and I'm not flying them."

"I'll make sure Kacey and Hank know," I agreed.

We chatted a bit more then about how the different stations and habitats they'd been going to were faring, as well as some of the side cargoes they'd picked up and what they'd been learning about possible commerce opportunities in Jupiter space. To be honest, it was a welcome change from the kinds of things I'd been caught up in when I'd first started out. None of us were looking to change the world, we were just trying to make a living and build up the family company.

When we said our goodbyes and headed back to our house, I was honestly feeling pleasantly mellow. Kacey told me what she'd been talking about with Emiliana. Nothing really but mundane stuff until we'd gotten inside.

"So, what were you and Chris really talking about?"

"He doesn't want to go as close as Mars until the war settles down, and he's hoping for something in the future that'll let him be home more. You?"

"Some of that, some of the trading trends she's been seeing, though those will probably all change with the attack."

I went and checked our security system, then for any kinds of listening devices and such. We did discuss confidential company business in the house, so we'd learned to be a little paranoid. I pulled out the letter from Ben and showed it to her.

"Gonna read it?"

"Now that we're home I will."

"Well, let me put Jeff to bed and you can show it to me after I'm done."

"Okay," I said as I ripped open the end. Sitting down, I unfolded the paper inside.

Dave,

As I've mentioned in the previous letters, things have been going well for me and Auri. I've been doing some experiments in my spare time to try and validate some of my hypotheses. There have been a few incongruities, but I think I'm making progress. There is, however, a few things I need that are not easy for me to create or build here. That's what the attached list is for.

Life out here is actually pretty good—we've fit in well enough at this point that the idea of staying is an attractive one. I definitely prefer doing my research out here, even if I can't put as much time into it as I could back home on Ceres. There are a lot fewer distractions here, and I don't have to worry about any of those idiot elies interfering with my work. There are still a few things I'd like to learn, and out here I'm getting that opportunity.

I've asked Marcus if it would be okay to invite you out to visit. He said he didn't have a problem with it, as long as you don't show up like you did the last time, whatever that means. So yes, I miss seeing your smiling face and it's not like I can just send you a message or call you on the phone. So when you get the chance, come visit for a few. I'm sure Kacey would enjoy meeting her new sister-in-law.

Yes, you heard it here first, your little brother is getting married! So now you have to come and see us!

Best Wishes,
Your Brother,
Ben

I stopped, blinked, and reread that last paragraph.

"So what's Ben got to say?"

"He wants me to visit," I said and passed her the letter.

I looked at the list of stuff he'd asked for. Some of it I understood, some I didn't. I doubted any of it mattered.

"Is that the list?" she asked.

I nodded and passed it over to her.

"When's our next scheduled delivery with them?" I asked.

"Couple months. There's a bunch of stuff to sell yet, then we've got an order to fill for them."

"Pay for everything out of our account and have it shipped over to Besua. We can stick it in a corner and either use it or sell it later. Take care of their order as quickly as you can without drawing attention. Don't worry about the best deal. Again, cover it from our accounts if necessary and I guess get that list filled as well."

Kacey frowned at me. "What am I missing?"

"'*There are still a few things I'd like to learn*' is from our old code. It means 'the sooner the better.'"

"Is that bad?"

"It used to be, but he didn't end it there, he added that extra bit about 'getting the opportunity.' He modified the line, so I think he's being honest about wanting to stay out there, though probably not for the reasons he's giving in the letter. So we need to get out there, and the sooner the better."

"What about Earth and the VMC?"

"I think that makes it even more urgent. The only thing is, how do we let Marcus and his people know we'll be there early?"

"Oh, we worked out a code for that a while ago. But what do we tell everyone?"

"Huh?"

"Dave, we've got a one-year-old and suddenly we both disappear? People are going to know we're visiting Ben. What conclusion do you think they're going to come to?"

I smiled at her. "It's in Ben's letter, plain as day."

"Oh? What?"

"He's getting married. We're going to meet his fiancée, our future sister-in-law, go to the wedding and congratulate them and all that stuff."

"Okay, but just how do we let them know that, without telling them, whoever 'they' are?"

"The secret isn't that I've stashed Ben someplace. The secret is where I've stashed him. We just make sure a few people know that Ben's getting married. When suddenly we're not around, maybe they'll figure it out, maybe they won't. But when we get back? I'll put up a picture, on my desk, of Ben and Aurelia, like a wedding pic or such. We just have to make sure there aren't any clues in it. We then let it slip we were there for the wedding."

Kacey pondered that a moment. "It could work, but I think we might need a little help on selling it."

"Jack Shian has a room full of people who do that kind of thing. We tell them we're sneaking out for the wedding, not because there's been a breakthrough or any of that, and ask them to cover for us because we're worried people might draw the wrong conclusion."

"That could work. So, what do you think the real reason is?"

I snorted. "Knowing Ben? It could very well be that he just wants us there to see him get married."

Kacey laughed. "Well, he is your brother, so I wouldn't put it past him. I'll get to work on this list as well as Marcus's in the morning. For now, how does bed sound?"

"Bed sounds good!" I said, taking her in my arms and giving her a nice long kiss.

Being married to Kacey had the single life beat in spades and then some. Tonight would be a good night to show her that once again.

"John, Dave, Kacey, Rob, I'm happy you could make it here on short notice."

John snorted. "Willie, we sent you those drawings because we know you're looking for options."

"Still, this is pretty impressive," Admiral Lou Carstairs said. "Who came up with the concept?"

"That would be Dave," John said, nodding over at me.

"Ah, should have guessed," Lou said with a smile. "So, tell me, why fighter/bombers? Why not frigates? Like, say, those small ones Mars uses and that we're currently building?"

"Because we can build six of them for every one of those frigates. They're faster, more maneuverable, require less crew, cost less, and take less time to construct. We're not trying to cover the amount of empty space they are. We're not looking to project force as much as protect our homes. Well, we can base these here at Ceres, we can build a number of cheap outlying bases for refueling and rearming. We put six-twos in them and no one is gonna be able to catch them, the targeting computers won't be able to track them, and they can be on the scene before anyone else gets there."

"Six-twos? Won't that be rough on the crew?"

"Not during combat it won't. They can push up to three gees acceleration and still only feel a little over one onboard."

"Well, I guess that explains why you've made these so small."

"That and you can't put too many six-two panels in a ship without tearing it apart and having all sorts of cascade failures. As it is, they'll probably be burning out grav panels every ten or twenty hours of combat flying. So they're going to *need* a base of operations. These are not patrol boats, they're hunter/killers."

Lou looked thoughtful.

"So how much are these going to cost?" Rachel asked.

"Fourteen million each," Kacey said and slid a folder over to her.

"*Fourteen?* But they're so ... *small.*"

"They mount two rail guns, each powered by its own F-800 fusion reactor. The fighter itself will be powered by a single K-30. That actually takes up two thirds of the body of the fighter and accounts for more than half of its weight."

"Only one? But what happens if it gets damaged?"

"With the speeds we project them engaging an enemy, anything that hits them hard enough to damage the reactor will certainly kill the crew, so there's no point," Kacey said.

"The primary purpose of the crew," Rob said speaking up, "is to deliver the missiles it is carrying on the target. It can do that at speed. The rail guns are for when they run out of missiles or to finish off an already damaged target."

"Why'd you name it the Shian?" Jack asked, looking up at me.

"Because I wanted the crews to understand they had a standard to live up to. You have to go out. You don't have to come home."

"Lou?" President Sanford said, looking over at Admiral Carstairs.

"I want half a dozen to see if these live up to their specifications and if I can find people crazy enough to fly 'em and fight in them."

"And if they do?"

"Then I'm gonna want as many of them as Rachel will let me buy. At least a hundred."

"And just where am I supposed to find one point four billion dollars, Lou?" Rachel asked.

"Put half of those small frigates on hold. If these pan out, we won't be needing 'em." Lou turned and looked at me. "And I like the name. We need to celebrate our heroes and remember them. So if it ever comes to it, others won't be afraid to make the sacrifice."

"So, John," President Sanford said, looking over at Mr. Doyle, "how soon can you start?"

"Already have. We're working up the numbers for a test bed, we're gonna need you to send over a bunch of your weapons systems people. We haven't brought in anybody for that yet as we only just started working the numbers on this last night."

"I'm surprised you even had something like this in the works."

John shrugged. "Let's just say that we're all still feeling a bit antsy about what happened two years ago. We wanted something we could come up with in a lot less time than it takes to build a warship, and, well, Dave knows grav drives. When he suggested the idea of a small, fast missile boat"—Mr. Doyle shrugged—"we were sold. Look at what those ore boats did to them. He just refined the idea and gave 'em teeth."

"He certainly did," Jack agreed.

"Well, let me get a contract written up for an initial order for six," President Sanford said, "with an option for an additional sixty if those meet Lou's needs, and an open line for additional lots as well as spares. We'll come over, say, at four and sign them at your headquarters?"

"Works for me," Mr. Doyle agreed.

"Then it's settled. Thank you for coming, folks."

We all stood up then and shook hands.

"Jack, got a minute?" I asked and motioned off to the side.

"Sure, what's up?"

"This is kind of a strange request, but you know my brother Ben, the one I set up in a hidden lab?"

"What, did he figure out FTL already?" Jack asked with a surprised look.

I laughed and shook my head. "No, but he is getting married and me and Kacey are going to be sneaking off for the wedding 'cause he wants *somebody* from our family to be there."

"So what's the problem?"

"Could you keep an eye on our kid? My mom will be taking care of him, but I'm worried that if people notice us missing they're going to think that Ben figured shit out and is going to start making drives next month, when the truth is he's nowhere close. That I just want to be there for his wedding."

"That's a good point, people *are* going to think that. Aren't you worried about them guessing where you stashed him?"

"Those dark habs my grandfather has building those weapons for us aren't the only ones he's got. Obviously he built a special one for Ben's research and we just hid it in the belt somewhere."

"Oh, obviously," Jack said with a smile. "Don't worry, I'll make sure people don't get the wrong idea."

"Thanks, Jack," I said, sticking out my hand.

"Thank you for naming that thing after my son."

"I told you before, Jack, your son was a hero. A real honest-to-god one. I want the people fighting for us to try and live up to the standard he set that day. After all, my kid lives here too, right?"

"Right."

"So, Jack's gonna cover for us while we go to the wedding?" Kacey asked as we rode the tram back to work.

"Yup. How long until we can leave?"

"Everything should be ready next week. Didn't even have to pay extra. Though I did have to make a few promises."

"We just need to be back here when they start installing the drive on our test bed. That thing is going to be a nightmare to tune."

"Shoulda thought about that when you helped design it!" she teased.

"I didn't think we'd be building one for another couple of years and that I'd have all the bugs worked out by then," I said with a sigh. "Your grandfather is gonna kill me if we lose this contract."

"Yeah, I think that's a safe bet!" Kacey said, smiling at me.

SIXTEEN

Astro Gerlitz—Rendezvous Space

"WELCOME ABOARD, KACEY, DAVE, NICE TO SEE YOU BOTH AGAIN," Captain Grohl said, shaking hands with us as we took our helmets off.

"Thanks for having us," I said. "I take it you know why we're here?"

"To visit your brother and be his best man at his wedding."

"So he hasn't gotten married yet?" Kacey asked with a chuckle. "We thought that was just the excuse he was giving to make sure we'd visit!"

"No, he really does want the both of you there. He also wishes he could have got your mom and dad as well, but was worried that would probably have been asking for too much."

Kacey and I both nodded.

"Yeah," I agreed. "To be honest, it was tempting to send them in our place, but I don't think Marcus would have been pleased!"

"Got that right. Well, find a seat and make yourself comfortable. We should be done shipping cargo in ten hours. Once your ship is out of here, we'll get you moved."

"Moved?" I asked, surprised.

"It's gonna take us a couple of weeks to get home. So we're going to pack you onto one of the destroyers that came out with us so you can get there faster."

191

"Wow, that was nice of Marcus," Kacey said.

"They're heading that way regardless, so might as well take you with them," the captain said with a shrug.

"So why is it going to take you so long to get back? I thought the trips took less time than that?"

"We have another stop that we have to make, obviously."

"Oh, not my business, then," Kacey apologized.

"And another reason for you not to be aboard when we do," he said with a smile.

"So what's your take on recent events?" I asked.

"The Earth thing?" He shook his head. "I'll be honest with you, Dave. A lot of us weren't happy with what you did to them after they attacked Ceres—"

"What makes you think I had anything to do with *that*?" I protested.

Captain Grohl gave me one of those long-suffering looks like I was one of the slow children. "Please, David, we know you."

I felt my face flush guiltily.

"As I was saying, we weren't happy, but we all knew it had to be done. We'd *hoped*, all of us had *hoped*, that this would have curbed their willingness for slaughter. After all, if Ceres could deliver such a response, then obvious Mars or Earth would do even worse."

Shaking his head, the captain sighed heavily. "We were beyond shocked at what just happened. While Earth is being slow to respond, we do not doubt what that response is going to be. At least they appear to have stopped their search for us. However, I suspect we will get all of the blame they can give us, come what may."

I honestly didn't know what to say in response to that. The first interplanetary war was now a thing, and there was every reason for me to believe that *I* had caused it. While I was sure the historians would all cover for me, after all who was I? Nobody special, that's for sure. No, they'd probably give the credit to the McVay family for their obvious attempts at profiteering off of the gullible VMC.

For once, I wasn't at all unhappy at the prospect of an elie family taking credit for something someone else did. Especially when that someone was me and that credit was starting a war.

I was already having enough trouble sleeping some nights, even this long afterward.

"So, got any *good* news?" I asked, trying to change the topic.

"Actually, yes, I do. My youngest just turned one! Now I get to subject you to lots of pictures and you get to make appreciative noises!" he said laughing.

"Hey, we're parents now too!" I replied with a laugh of my own. "Bring it!"

"We'd appreciate it if you stayed in your quarters for the trip," said the crewman who showed us to our room. "If you hear the drive alert, be sure to secure yourselves as this ship can pull quite a few gees if necessary."

I nodded and looked at the room, then at the location of the bathroom in relation to the room and smiled slowly.

"Got it," Kacey said and I followed her into the room and closed the hatch behind us. It was almost completely filled with by the bed.

"And why are you looking at me like that?" Kacey asked, smirking.

"Strip."

"What?"

"Strip!"

"Dave..."

"It's our second honeymoon," I said, grabbing and kissing her.

"Well, if you insist..."

The first time they knocked for dinner I told them to go away.

By the next time, we'd run down enough to hit the shower and head up to the mess. I think I recognized some of the crew, they all smiled and nodded hello as we sat down to eat.

"Not complaining, mind you," Kacey said as I slid over until my leg was pressed up against hers, "but I have to ask just what's gotten into you."

I smiled at her. "Ever have a memory that was so good you felt guilty about it?"

Kacey blushed. "Oh yeah..."

"Well I just replaced it with a better one." And I picked up my fork and started eating. It took me a moment to realize she was staring at me.

"What?" I asked, looking at her.

"You're telling me that you and Pam Wells...?"

I nodded.

"And I did better than *her*?"

"Yup. It wasn't even close."

I suddenly found myself being hugged. Tightly.

I smiled and, putting an arm around her, I hugged her back. I'd been worried, honestly. Pam had been a total animal in bed, that bed. We both had been through a lot and the adrenaline dump on top of not going to die or any of that had really made it something special.

But dammit if this really hadn't been better.

"Obviously, all those stories about love being better than raw lust are true," I whispered to her. "Not that we didn't engage in some of that in there."

"Eat!" Kacey said, letting go of me. "If you thought that was raw lust, you're about to get an education!"

I almost blushed at some of the looks we got. It's not like the small mess on a destroyer is all that private. But Kacey was still as hot-looking as ever and it was clear that we were very much a couple. So instead of feeling embarrassed I felt proud. When I'd been here with Pam, I'd been like the kid who'd won a prize. Now? Now I was a grown man who'd won life's lottery.

And I would do *anything* to protect that. To keep my wife and our children safe.

I had an epiphany suddenly. Everything I'd ever done, every act of violence that is, had all been done out of anger. Every fight, every killing, going to Venus, even standing up and protecting Pam had been done because I'd been pissed at her for falling to pieces on me, and at our old first mate for abandoning us.

But now? If I ever had to go back to Venus and show them the error of their ways again, it wouldn't be out of anger. It would be because I was a man doing what he had to do.

Suddenly, I understood exactly what had motivated Pat Shian, Jack's son, to do what he'd done.

"Something on your mind, hon?" Kacey asked, pausing from eating to look up at me.

"Just you," I said, smiling back at her as I went back to eating.

"Damn, what did you do to me, woman?" I complained as we left the ship.

"Oh, I'm not taking all the blame for this one!" she teased as she held on to me. "I can barely walk!"

"Dave! Kacey!" Ben said, running over and giving us both a hug, then looked surprised as we winced.

"What happened?" he asked, looking worried.

"Four days in a private room with a big bed, no children, no interruptions, and nothing else to do but each other..." Kacey said, snickering. "What do you think happened?"

Ben laughed. "Well, at least you enjoyed the trip! Here I thought you'd be bored!"

"Trust me," I said with a mock groan, "after you've started having kids, time alone with your wife will never be boring!"

"Well, let me get your things, I'll show you where you're staying."

"Which is...?"

"Same place you stayed last time," Ben laughed. "If you thought Marcus wasn't going to get some mileage out of your visit, then you honestly don't know the man."

"Well, I guess you can carry our bags, I think I can still find my way there. Where is Marcus, by the way?"

"Working. Dinner tonight will be at his and Pam's. Aurelia will be there as well."

"Where's she at?" Kacey asked.

"She didn't want to intrude on a 'brother's bonding moment' but I don't think either one us realized you'd have reduced him to a cripple," Ben said laughing.

"Come over here so I can hit you," I grumbled and waved a hand at him as I headed off to the shop I'd lived at. "So, you look happy and from the tone of your note, I guess you like it here?"

I glanced back at Ben as he nodded. "Yeah, it's nice. It's a lot more of a community than I'd have expected. It's also a lot bigger than I thought it would be. I also like the work."

"You do?"

"Yeah, because I'm making a difference. I can see the effects of what I do often enough. I'm contributing and, well, people appreciate it. I mean, sure, the pay sucks!" Ben said and laughed, "but we're all equally poor, I guess you could say."

"What do they have you doing?" Kacey asked.

"A couple of things. I'm teaching an advanced physics course a few hours a week, a couple of mechanical and civil engineer classes too. I work with Mabel reviewing her plans, and offering suggestions. I also do inspections with her—oh, and I've designed a new line of fusion reactors for them that they can build here."

"You did *what*?" I said, stopping to turn and look at him.

"What? The technology is well understood and when you're building them nice and big, instead of those small ones they put on the ships, it's actually not all that hard."

"Not all that hard, the man says," I said, looking at Kacey, who just laughed.

"Look, a civilization is always defined by how much excess power it has."

"If you say so."

"I do. Mabel and Marcus were looking at buying a couple more fusion reactors and trying to figure out how to get them here without anyone tracking them. So I just told them, 'Why not build your own?'"

I just shook my head and went back to heading to the apartment.

"Only you, Ben. Only you," I said while still shaking my head.

When we got to the shop, I was surprised to see two of the guys I'd taught working there, plus two more, who I didn't know, assisting them.

"Gerald! Thomas!" I said as they both came over to shake my hand. "How goes it?"

"It goes well, Dave, really well. So well that I'm hoping you'll teach these two who've been helping us and see if maybe you can give them your blessing?" Gerald said.

I looked at the two new guys, who both looked a little worried.

"Been telling stories about me, have you?" I asked him.

"Since you've started trading for us, you're damn near a legend down here," he laughed. "But we'd all appreciate it if you could take some time to teach them and review their skills. Thomas and I've been doing it, but well, you've got the actual certificates."

I nodded. "Sure, I guess I can do that. I also want to check the factory and make sure things are still good there too."

"Oh, Mabel and your brother Ben there have been running that place with an iron fist!"

"Really?" I said, glancing back at Ben.

"Yeah, they had a panel blow out spectacularly, and several people got badly hurt. So now we pull every tenth panel off the line and test it, and we test every one hundredth panel until it fails."

"Now I'm definitely going to go by there. But not tonight. Now, Gerald, Thomas, and you two"—I motioned to the new guys—"this is my wife, Kacey, one of the two reasons I left. I think you've already met the other one?" I motioned toward Ben. The two new ones nodded.

"Just remember, I'm far more protective of Kacey than I ever was of Pam; however, it might be wise to keep one thing in mind."

"And what would that be?" Thomas asked with a grin.

"She's a faster draw and a better shot than I am," I said, shaking my head. "So odds of anything being left alive for me to kill are pretty damn slim."

Gerald and Thomas laughed at that while the other two seemed unsure of what to do.

"Well, let's get settled in, I guess." I turned to Ben. "Come get us for dinner?"

"Of course."

"Did anybody think to put anything in the fridge?"

"Yup. Auri and I came down and cleaned up and stocked it. The extra beers belong to the guys, though."

"Eh, help yourself," Thomas said. "Not like you haven't earned it."

"Thanks, guys," I said, and picking up the bags I led Kacey into the apartment. I went all the way into the bedroom and set the bags down, as I looked around. The place hadn't changed much at all, though the sheets and blankets on the bed were obviously fresh.

I heard the sound of a zipper being pulled down then. Turning, I looked at Kacey, who was getting naked rather quickly.

"Kace?"

"What do you say to replacing a few more memories while waiting for dinner."

"Oh, I like that idea..."

Dinner was nice. Kacey and Aurelia got on well with each other, and when we sat down to catch up on things, we were all such obvious couples that it made me smile. Ben and Auri were very much in each other's space and Pam all but curled up in Marcus's lap when we sat down in the living room.

"Did my brother actually design and build a fusion reactor for you?" I asked once we'd gotten settled.

Marcus laughed. "I was going to tell him no and then I remembered whose brother he was and figured if I didn't say yes, he'd go off and build it anyway on the sly."

"Why does everyone act like that's such a big deal?" Ben protested.

"Now you see what I had to put up with for years," I teased and Marcus, Pam, and Auri all laughed. "And you're right, he would have done it anyways, just to prove that he could."

"You're not still upset over that itch gun, are you?" Ben asked.

"What's an 'itch gun'?" Pam asked.

"You point it at someone and as long as you hold the trigger, they itch," I said. "Don't ask me how it works, hypersonics or something like that."

"And what, he used it on you?"

"Worse, he used it on a teacher in school and I had to cover for him. Got detention for a *week*," I grumbled, "and I never said no to him again." They all laughed at that.

"So when's the wedding?" Kacey asked.

"Tomorrow, after work," Aurelia said. "There's a few folks who want to be there."

"How many is 'a few'?" I asked.

"Less than 'a lot,'" Ben joked.

"As much as I hate to ask, because I'm enjoying the vacation," Kacey said, "how long are we here for? We just signed a contract for a new fighter for the Ceres Navy and, well"—she pointed to me—"he's the one who needs to figure out the grav drive."

"What's wrong with the grav drives?"

"I'm using a bunch of six-two panels on a ship not much bigger than a K-30. I don't want the ship tearing itself apart if they lose one while under max thrust."

"Six-twos? Why are you doing that?"

I explained the design to him, only going over the high points. I could see that Marcus was interested as well.

"How many generators are you going to put in the ship?"

"I was thinking something like a single two-twenty. It's more powerful than something that small would need, so there'd be plenty of headroom for any spikes."

"Have you thought about two smaller one hundreds?"

"I'm not sure how that would help."

"Wire the top panels to one, the bottom panels to the other."

"What? How am I supposed to do *that*? They're not made to work that way!"

"Actually," Ben said in his best "nerd" voice, "they are."

"Huh? Then how come no one ever mentioned it when I studied for my cert?"

"Because it's easier not to do it that way on the bigger ships. Which is stupid because it cuts down on cascade failures, which are enhanced by the resonance feedback through the—"

"Ben," Aurelia said putting her hand on his arm, stopping him. "You don't have to explain it, we already know you're right."

I watched as Ben blushed rather brightly.

"Looks like somebody met his match," Kacey teased.

"About damn time too, if you ask me." I smiled and gave her a kiss on the side of the face.

"Getting back to my original question, how long?" Kacey asked, looking back and forth between Marcus and Ben.

"A couple weeks?" Marcus said, looking over at Ben.

"Okay, why is this Ben's decision?" I asked, rather curious.

"Weeellll, I wanted to go over my research with you and, umm, show you something?" Ben said, with an ear-to-ear grin.

"You didn't!"

"Well, not quite, but we're almost there," he said, giving Aurelia a hug when he said *we're*.

"Oh?"

"Yup. One of the things I discovered when I started setting up some simple tests to check my theories is that the Sun's gravity well has a much larger effect on what people like to call 'subspace.'"

"Just how big of an effect?"

"Big enough that no FTL drive is ever going to work inside the Kuiper Belt. I've got a test rig that Marcus is going to let me put on one of their frigates, then we're going to fly out past the belt, and if my theory and Aurelia's math are all correct, I'll have cracked it."

"Damn...that was a lot faster than I thought it would be! Even for you, Ben!"

Ben laughed. "If you hadn't stuck me out here, I'd still be scratching my head. But we're out so far now that that there's an observable difference."

"At first he thought I'd screwed up on my math," Aurelia said, giving him a look that made him blush all over again.

"Which is why I proposed," he said and then kissed her.

"Okay, why did that lead to you proposing?" Kacey asked.

"Because she was right and I was wrong and where else am I ever going to find that in this life?" Ben said, grinning again. Only this time, Aurelia was grinning too.

I had to laugh at that.

"So, if this experiment pans out, what does that mean as far as building an actual drive to take advantage of it?"

Ben frowned. "That's going to take quite a few more experiments, and they're all going to need to be done out there as well. I mean, I can build everything here, but someone has to take the test rigs out there and run them."

I turned and looked at Marcus. "What do you need?"

"Captain Grohl mentioned your idea of building these new drives out here. I want that as well as a percentage ownership of the company that builds them."

I felt Kacey stiffen, so I gave her a hug before she could say anything.

"Before I turn the negotiations over to Kacey, I gotta ask: Why?"

"Because we need the money? Look, Ben shows no signs of wanting to leave and you did tell Grohl that this probably would be the best place for you to build them. So if you're going to build them here, I want part ownership for the government here, not me personally. I can use those profits to build up our defenses and, yes, I want to buy some of those fighters once you get production up and running.

"Because sooner or later, someone is going to guess we're on Eris or one of the other dwarves and they're going to come looking. So I want us to be prepared. I also want us to have more of the things we need to guarantee our survival. Just the small amount of what you've shipped for us so far has made a major difference. With more money, we could not just improve that, but improve all of our day-to-day lives significantly."

"Okay, that makes sense."

"Kacey, negotiations can wait until tomorrow," Pam piped up before Kacey could get started. "It's after hours and we're *not* here to work."

"Fine," Kacey grumbled. "Take away my fun!"

I laughed and gave her another kiss. "So, Ben, when are we making this trip?"

"Tomorrow's the wedding, then I need a day to prepare, so any time after that."

"Make it three, then, I need to help out the guys in the shop and I am *definitely* going to spend a day going over things in the factory."

"Heard about that, did you?"

"Yeah. I want to take another look at it. I've learned a lot more about engineering and production lines since I set that place up, could be I didn't do as good a job as I thought. Not that the testing you're doing isn't a good idea, but one in ten is a pretty bad sign. If I can get that up to, say, one in a hundred before I leave, I'll sleep better at night."

"Well, far be it from any of us to turn down free help, but I do believe I said something about not discussing work?" Pam said, giving me the eye.

Kacey laughed and gave me a kiss. "See? It's not just me."

"Well, I don't think anybody wants to talk about what certain idiots are getting up to."

"Oh! I finally got to watch *The Iceman Chronicles*!" Pam said, laughing.

"Uh-oh," I mumbled.

"How'd Dave stack up?" Kacey asked.

"They were right to be afraid of him," Pam said, still giggling. "He's an elie gone bad with an Adonis girlfriend and has a genius for a best friend!"

"Other than being six foot two, blond, blue eyed, with a love of overcoats and hats, that guy could have been you, Dave."

"Really?" I asked.

"So how do they get him in the end?" Kacey asked.

"They don't! That's the best part! He goes off to avenge the death of his girlfriend and blows up some big elie estate, killing hundreds of them, and they all just *assume* he's dead!"

"I think they were hoping for a sequel," Ben said.

"Have any of you seen *Walking Out*?"

"Kacey!" I complained.

"Can't say that I have," Pam said as the others all shook their heads, except for Aurelia, but she'd told me she'd seen it when we first met. "What is it?"

"Someone made a documentary about Dave springing Ben and everything around it. Dave *hates* it."

"Have you seen it?" Ben asked.

"Nope, I refuse."

"Any idea who made it?"

"I think my grandfather ordered it made for PR reasons. But I'm afraid to ask."

"Why?"

"'Cause I might punch him? Auri's seen it."

"You have?" Ben said, looking at her.

"Umm, yeah. You're in it. So are you, Pam."

"What?" Pam said, her eyes wide.

"It's a documentary and they used a lot of file footage from some of the port security cameras. Also, they had the picture from your piloting license."

"They're not very good pictures," Kacey said. "Though they did play up the 'saving the damsel from the deadly pirates' angle a bit. They sensationalize his past a lot, then talk about him cleaning up and leaving that life style behind. There's a fair bit on some of the 'problems' he faced, then the capture by pirates, the arrest when he made it back, the betrayal by an old gang member, smuggling his brother out and setting up the gang member to take the fall for betraying 'the code'—whatever the hell that's supposed to be—and then his going to jail on the Moon.

"It's kinda engaging. Yeah, they took some liberties with the truth, but it's all a top-notch production and was quite a hit on Mars as well as a lot of the outer worlds."

"I had to go around hiding my face for months after it hit Ceres," I grumbled. "At least it doesn't mention me changing my last name."

"How'd they explain all the assassins?" Ben asked.

"They avoided that completely," Kacey replied. "Though there are a few stories about things he did to 'protect and rescue crew members who got in trouble.' They definitely played up the tramp cargo ship aspect and made it look a lot more romantic than it is."

"Are you in it?"

"Nope. Nothing about his life on Ceres or his getting married. They don't mention his parents or his sister leaving either."

"Well, that's good," Ben said.

"Which is why I think my grandfather did it." I sighed. "Leaving them and Kacey out makes it harder to connect the documentary David to the real David. So if you're filming your experiments, just leave me out of them, okay?" I grumbled. "I've had enough fame to last me a lifetime."

We talked a little more about how things were on Eris now, since when I was last there. Things were definitely better than they had been and not all of that was my fault. Mabel's expansion plans were proceeding quite well and some of the people who'd finally made it out here to be with their friends and families had brought some valuable skills.

By the time we got back to the apartment, both of us were exhausted and actually spent the entire night sleeping.

The next morning was a little surreal at first. Waking up there, and still half-asleep walking out into the kitchen to find Kacey there making breakfast literally threw me for a loop, and I think I stood there dumbfounded for a minute until I finally woke up.

"What? You've got work today and I'm not going to be doing anything beyond harassing Marcus after lunch."

"Umm...Nothing, nothing at all..."

"Pam never made you breakfast, did she?" Kacey said, catching on quickly.

"No, no, she didn't. For a moment I thought I was back working off our rescue."

"Now why in the world would you have thought that?"

"Umm...All the awesome sex?" I said and grinned at her.

"Sit down," Kacey said, rolling her eyes. But she was smiling all the same. "This is almost done. Any guidance on dealing with Marcus?"

"We own the rights to the drive and the tech. Well, you, me, and Ben. Mostly Ben. Give him a good stake in the plant, though. Maybe a three-way split? Us, Ben, and Marcus's people?"

"But Ben lives here."

"Yeah, but if we start having issues with Ben, then maybe we're the ones who need to think about what we're doing. But make it clear that they can only sell or give the drives to us, Doyle Shipyards. Nobody else. Also make it clear that they can examine the books whenever they want and that the price of the drives will clearly be called out on the invoices. We don't want anyone cheating them."

"And if they want drives?"

"Cost. They get 'em at cost, but limit them to a percentage of production and they're only for their own use, and they can't go selling used spaceships or any of that to get around it."

Kacey nodded. "Okay, fairly standard stuff."

I nodded. "Mostly, but use your own judgment. Find out if they'll need anything from us to support Ben's research. Only fair we foot the bill on that."

"Got it."

She set a plate of food in front of me, then took a second one and sat down across from me as we ate. I had to smile. If we didn't have our child back on Ceres, and, well, a big-ass shipyard, it would be tempting to stay. Life had certainly been much easier living here, and now that I had both Kacey and my brother, I'd accomplished everything I'd wanted to since the last time I'd sat at this table.

Finishing up, I got up, kissed her, and went out to see how things where holding up in my old shop after three or so years. Maybe the next time we visited we'd be able to bring my parents and the kids.

Stepping out the door was another feeling of déjà vu, as no one was here just yet. I went over to my old toolbox and started to inventory the tools. There were a couple that were missing and I made a note of which, as well as which needed replacing due to wear and tear.

I put that up on the side of the toolbox with a magnet to hold it in place. I'd get either Gerald or Thomas to order some replacements from the machine shop that had made all the copies.

I then went and inspected all the panels that were complete and ready to be delivered. I was still doing that when Thomas, Gerald, and the two "new" guys showed up.

"How's the work look, Dave?" Thomas asked.

"Good, the work looks good. Have to say I'm pleased you're all taking the time to do it right."

"Thanks. We do worry about it. Todd and Clay come by once a week and do a check on our work as well. And we head over to their shop about as often to check on them."

"They opened up another shop?" I said, surprised.

"Yup. They're also training up two new guys like we are. Our workload has been increasing, albeit slowly, because of all the new areas Marge has been opening and our ships having to go pick up cargo runs from some crazy guy who wants to help us out."

I laughed at that. "Well, that's good. I'm gonna spend the day going over the basics with your two helpers and get an idea of where they are and what they know. Maybe I can run them as well as Todd and Clay's guys through all the tests to certify them. If not, well, at least I'll know what to focus on to try and help bring them up to your level faster."

"Thanks, Dave."

I shrugged. "I still think of this place as my shop; I did build it. So I got a responsibility to see that folks here know their craft."

They all smiled and nodded as I said that. I don't know if they believed it or not, but I knew I was going to act like I did. Because I was now a Second Engineer and I took pride in my work; I could see that at the very least Thomas and Gerald were as well. I guess the engineering bug had really bit me, because it wasn't just about fixing things and being able to look at a job well done—it was about building things too.

I had built this shop. In a way it would always be mine, and I was proud of it because it was the first big thing I'd ever built and I'd done it by myself. The closest I'd come since doing that had been the drives for the new fighter. The rest of the ship, even the shipyards themselves, had been a collaborative effort. I'd actually cornered my father and gotten him to help me with the cockpit design of the fighter and laying out all the instrumentation and the cableways.

We'd both enjoyed that a lot.

"Dave, we need to get ready for Ben and Auri's wedding!" Kacey said, calling to me from our apartment's doorway.

I looked up from the work I'd been doing with Parath.

"Oops, gotta go. You can finish up here. Have Jerry check it out when you're done. Looking good!"

"Thank you, David," he said with a nod of his head. Putting my tools away, I headed into our apartement.

"Hit the shower, I laid out some things for you to wear," Kacey said.

I gave her a kiss, showered, shaved, got dressed and then we headed off to City Hall, where the wedding was going to take place.

It wasn't hard to find when we got there and I noticed Mabel, Miguel, Greg and his wife, Walt, Marcus and Pam, and several others that I knew, even if I couldn't remember their names. There were another dozen there as well, including Ben.

"Where's Aurelia?" I asked.

"She comes in after everything's ready," Ben said, smiling.

"So when are we starting?"

"Now that you're here, immediately," Ben said.

"This way, please," Marcus said and he led us into a large

meeting hall. There was a minister of some sort standing up front as we walked in.

"Oh here, hold onto this," Ben said, handing me a small box.

"What's that?"

"Wedding rings."

"Wedding rings? I thought that was the best man's—" I looked at him.

"See, you're smart, you figured it out with my having to tell you!" Ben said and laughed.

"I'd hit you, but then you'd have a bruise on all of your wedding pictures," I grumbled. "You know Mom is going to kill you."

"Why's that?"

"Because now she's missed *both* of our weddings."

Ben swore. "I'll have to figure out something to make it up to her."

"Grandchildren work," I teased and surprisingly, he smiled.

"Now, if you two are done?" the minister asked, making us both blush.

Everyone found their seats, and after a minute there was some music and we got started. Aurelia came in, all dressed up and looking a lot more beautiful than she had back when I'd rescued her. I knew she was supposed to be a good-looking woman, but this was the first time I'd ever seen her showing it off and, well, she had a lot to show off.

But that still couldn't stop my eyes from sliding over to Kacey, who was her bridesmaid, and staying there. Not because I was afraid to be seen looking over Ben's future wife, it was because I still only had eyes for her. She looked as lovely and radiant as ever and how I'd gotten so lucky was one of those mysteries that only God could explain.

The ceremony wasn't a long one, but it was still nice. It was clear, standing up there in front of everyone, that Ben really did have a thing for Aurelia now, and from the look in her eyes I think she had even more than that for him.

I passed him the rings when the time came. Applauded when he kissed the bride. Smiled when they turned and faced everyone as husband and wife. Then leaned in and said in a voice that only he and Auri could hear:

"Ben if you mess this up, as your older brother I will seriously pound you into the dirt because you'll never find a better woman."

Aurelia smiled and laughed. Ben just rolled his eyes.

"I'm a genius, Dave, give me some credit for figuring *that* one out."

Smiling, I shook hands with my brother, kissed his wife on the cheek, and then watched as they went and met the folks in the audience as I put my arm around Kacey and hugged her.

"It's nice to see I'm not the only one who got lucky," I told her, still smiling.

"Yup, she worships Ben just like you worship me." She giggled and gave me a hip check.

I stood and looked thoughtful for a moment.

"Hmmm?"

"I'm trying to think of a witty comeback, but it's hard to contest the truth!" And then I turned, pulled her close, and kissed her until the minister started to cough.

"What? We're already married!" Kacey said, looking over at him when we stopped.

"Yes, but you're standing on the ceremonial rug and I *really* do need to roll that up."

"Oh!"

I laughed and led her off to follow Ben and the others as they headed off to the reception.

"Well, that's one thing achieved. Now to see just what he's discovered, I guess."

"I guess," she agreed.

SEVENTEEN

Beyond the Kuiper Belt

"SO, READY TO MAKE HISTORY?" BEN ASKED AS I STUMBLED INTO
the mess and headed straight for the coffee.

"After I've had my coffee, eaten, and woken up a bit more.
You know, I have to wonder if anyone's been out this far before."

"They've sent probes out past the heliopause, more than once,
but I'm not sure anyone has gone out past the Kuiper Belt."

"We're going to have to secure everything before we can even
start so Captain Morrison can power off the grav drives. Probably
should get everyone into their pressure suits as well."

"Dave, it's just a simple experiment."

"That's what you said when you made that cayenne pepper trap."

"I was only eight then, Dave!" Ben said laughing.

"The alarm bell silencer?"

"I was ten!"

"The pneumatic push-up bra?"

"Umm, okay, pressure suits," Ben said, looking embarrassed.
"At least she only had her dignity hurt."

"And you got a black eye."

"You didn't have to hold me still for her, you know!"

"Ben, trust me, I did," I said and gave him a look, causing
him to sigh.

"Anything else you think we should do?"

"Honestly? I'd like to shut down the entire ship. If the test runs with no problems, we bring some of the systems up, and do it again, see if it changes anything."

"The extra data wouldn't hurt," Ben agreed.

"I'm also curious to see if this test of yours has any effect on the systems onboard."

"Do you think we should try it with the gravity drive on?"

"I don't know. I mean, you said gravity messes with this, right?"

"Gravity *wells* mess with it. I'm not sure the amount of a gravity the panels create would cause enough of an effect."

"Yeah, still, maybe we shouldn't. It's a long walk home."

"Point. I'll go tell the captain to suit everyone up and that we want to totally down the ship, or at least as much as he's comfortable with. Once you're done eating, suit up and meet me in the aft hold."

I nodded and, setting down my coffee, I went and got some food. It was probably going to be a long day.

When I caught up with Ben down in the aft hold, he and four other crewmen were suited up, each of the four stationed behind a camera that was on a tripod securely mounted to the floor. I put my helmet on, but I left the faceplate open. The cameras weren't running yet, but I wanted my hands free. Ben was giving his test equipment a final check.

Just then Captain Morrison came on the all-hands.

"All hands, all hands, now hear this! Now hear this! Suit up! We will start testing in thirty minutes! Repeat, testing will start in thirty minutes! All gravity will cease, all major systems will be shut down or put into standby. Life support will be on, but beware of dead areas. If there is an accident we will close the airtight doors!"

Satisfied with his gear checks, Ben started flipping switches.

"Turning on the monitoring equipment," he said. "Current position is..." He turned and read the display on the navigation repeater he'd had installed in the small hold. The main device itself was on a three-by-five-meter pallet and was a bit taller than I was, maybe two and a half meters. There was a smaller testing unit that would be used first set in the middle of the bigger unit, in what Ben said was an "unused area." The entire testing framework also had its own power, two one-thousand-watt auxiliary power units.

"Power it up, Dave."

"Starting power unit one," I said and watched the display for APU one as it came up. Once it was fully up and had settled into an even rhythm, I went to the breaker box and grabbed the handle.

"Isolating from ship's power." Pulling down the handle, I locked it into place and checked to be sure that the test bed was no longer connected.

"Isolation is complete. Starting power unit two," I called out and pushed the button to start it.

"Okay, all of the onboard monitoring equipment is up and running," Ben said. "Turning on the cooling gear and setting the Newtonian ring gear to standby."

"Power looks good," I told him as I saw the APUs pick up the small load.

"Plasma generators to warm-up."

"Still good."

"Gravitron injector set to warm up..."

We worked our way slowly through the preparation checklist. As each system hit its operating temperature I confirmed his observation. Once we had it all up, we stepped back and took a break.

"So, what, ten minutes to reach steady-state on the temperature?"

"That's what it took in the lab," Ben said with a nod.

I stood there and stared at the test bed and the machines on it. The first test wouldn't even involve most of it. Ben was going to create some sort of field effect—I honestly didn't understand the science at all—then shoot a stream of gravitrons through it and take a bunch of measurements.

The second experiment, the one that created what he'd been calling the "test gate," was the one I was concerned about. That was the one that needed the full two megawatts of power.

"Okay, everyone hook up," I said as the temperatures evened out. We all took out lifelines and clipped them to the nearest bulkhead. With the test we were doing, anybody bumping into things after we lost gravity could ruin the measurements and possibly even skew the results.

"Captain, zero gee, please," Ben called over his suit comm after he'd put his helmet on.

"All hands! Zero gravity in twenty seconds!"

I counted the seconds in my head. At five seconds the zero-gee horn sounded twice and then we were weightless.

"Well, let's see what we've got." Ben gave a little push and floated over to the test panel. "Okay, turn on the high-speed cameras!"

Each of the four crewmen triggered the cameras they were stationed at.

"We're good, Ben," the guy in charge said.

"Alright, test sequence in five... four... three... two... one." And he pressed the green button on the touch screen. There was a brief flash and then a steady stream of light came from the small apparatus on the near end of the test bed.

"Power looks good," I said, looking over the display from where I was standing.

"Wow, it didn't self-terminate!" Ben said in an excited voice. "Shutting down in three... two... one..." He pressed the red button now blinking on the touch screen. There was a loud *crack!* and that was it.

"Cameras off!"

"High-speed cameras are off!" the guy in charge replied.

"Slight power surge," I said, looking at the graph on the display. "But it's all good."

"Captain, you can bring the gravity back up for a short time," Ben called.

Morrison called the all hands, gave the warning, and then ten seconds later we were all standing again.

"So, how's it look?" I asked Ben.

"It fucking worked, Dave!" he said, turning to me and smiling through the open faceplate on his helmet. "All these years and it fucking *worked*! The math proofs were correct, the theory, all of it! I was right! Me, a stupid, clueless fifteen-year-old know-it-all figured it out! I can't believe I got it *right*!"

"Ben, chill. No, twenty-year-old you got it right. The fifteen-year-old pain in my ass just had the idea."

Ben laughed and shook his head. "That was just doing the math and creating the theories until I could figure out how to actually *prove* what I'd theorized. How to actually get my *hands* on the physical effects! Now, let's shut this down and power up the test gate."

"I was afraid you were going to say that," I said, shaking my head.

"Anything goes wrong, just cut the power. The field will collapse as soon as the Newtonian rings lose plasma, or stops circulating, or gets too hot and the magnets kick out and the plasma disassociates."

"Yeah, yeah. So you say. Start the checklist."

It took another thirty minutes to get everything powered up and warmed up. This test involved a lot more equipment and the machine to run it was larger. A lot larger. It occupied most of the test bed.

"Captain, zero gee again, please," Ben called and we all checked our tethers.

"Okay," Ben said to the five of us in the room. "This test is to open an actual gateway to another spot in the galaxy. If I did the math right, it should open a portal to a spot about five light-years from here. You do *not* want to get anywhere near it, even if it will be only twenty-five centimeters wide. The gateway should open up one meter in front of the projection ring. It will be on for five seconds, then I'll shut it down. If I don't, Dave will cut power.

"This will be something to tell your kids about," Ben added with a grin. "Everyone ready?"

"Yes, Ben!" they all called out.

"Dave?"

I sighed. "If this screws up, I will never let you live it down."

"But if it works, you can't hold the babysitter incident against me anymore."

"Which one?"

"All of them, of course!" Ben said with a laugh.

"Let's make history," I said with another, more dramatic sigh. I could tell that Ben was excited, about as excited as I'd ever seen him. It wasn't just that he was about to make the history books. No, it was that he was about to be proven *right*. If there was one thing Ben had never gotten over, it was being able to say "See? I told you so!"

"Cameras!"

"Cameras are on!" the guy in charge called after a few seconds.

"Bringing the rings to active! Setting the activation charge!"

"We're at eight-nine percent of capacity on power," I told Ben. "Activation capacitors are charged."

"Activating in five... four... three... two... one!" And he pressed the button.

There was a strange sound like I'd never heard before, and I felt a jolt from the system as I was holding on to the power control panel.

"Yes! It works!" Ben all but screamed out.

I turned and looked, and sure enough there was a small black portal floating on the end of the test bed. I took a moment to look at it, really *look* at it... which was when I noticed I could see what looked like stars.

I could also see that there was a glowing field surrounding the area from the portal all the way back to just behind the projection ring.

And it was growing.

"Ben!"

"What?"

"What's that?"

"Holy..." Ben reached forward to hit the red terminate button just as the field reached him. He got knocked back, spinning, toward the bulkhead as the stand the panel was on got pushed down and under the expanding field, the panel itself shattering.

"Cut power! Dave! Cut power!"

I hit the emergency scram button on the APUs and watched as they cut off and spun down immediately. Just as the field got to me and knocked me back until I hit the bulkhead as well.

"Dave! Power!" Ben yelled.

"It's off!"

"What?" Ben said as I got my bearings back and looked at the test bed. The small testing unit in the center was starting to lean toward the portal, I could see it all but *stretching* as it *bent* toward the opening—and then suddenly, with a loud tearing sound, it broke free and was *squeezed* so it could fit through the portal.

The field was still expanding—it wasn't getting any longer, but its diameter was slowly increasing. The floor of the test stand underneath was crumpling and being pushed down into the deck beneath it. It didn't take long to figure out that if we didn't do something soon, we'd have to leave the hold or be crushed.

"Ben! Better think of something quick!" I yelled as I saw the deck plates start to deform under the unit. One of the tool kits we'd been using was now slowly being crushed into the floor as well.

"I'm thinking! How the hell is it even running without power? Shit! Dave! *Do something!*"

"You're the genius here, Ben!"

"But I don't know what to do!" he yelled back. I could hear the fear starting to take hold in his voice. I triggered my comm.

"Captain, bring up the grav drive! Full power!"

"What?"

"We got a runaway! Do it! Engineering! We need it and we need it now!"

"Bring up the grav drive!" the captain called. "All hands! Prepare for gravity and maneuvering!"

I heard Craig, the chief engineer, swearing loudly and I watched that field getting closer and started planning my escape, when I quickly dropped to the floor as gravity came back. I saw the portal starting to waver and distort.

"It's working! More! Ramp it to max!" I called and suddenly I got flattened as gravity peaked, followed almost immediately by a bright flash and a very painful electrical feeling, followed by a loud explosion that made my ears ring.

Then everything went completely black.

Which was when I noticed the bane of ship engineers everywhere: total silence.

"Sound off!" I heard someone groan. I listened as first Ben, then each of the camera operators, called out their names. That was when I realized I'd been the one speaking.

"What happened, Ben?" one of the crewmen asked.

"It collapsed when the gravity got too strong and the effect couldn't sustain itself anymore."

"I meant after that."

"EMP shock wave, I think. My suit is dead. I think it's fried."

I gathered my wits and checked myself. "Yeah, suits are dead. Everything electrical in the room is fried as well."

"What about the rest of the ship?" the crewman asked, sounding worried.

"Hopefully all the breakers tripped before there was any damage," I said as I tried to stand and noticed I was floating.

"Ah, shit. Gravity is out." I sighed. "I hope I don't owe Marcus a new frigate on top of everything else."

"Do we go to the bridge, or Engineering?" Ben asked in a weak voice.

"Engineering." I started patting myself down, looking for my flashlight. After what had happened last time, I got an old-fashioned one that ran off chemical batteries. EMP didn't affect them—at least if they were off, it didn't. Apparently all miners carried one as a backup.

Turning it on, I shined it around the hold until I got my bearings.

"Let's go," I said and carefully launched myself to the hatch out of the hold.

It took a bit longer to get there, as all the pressure doors had been armed and when power had gone out, they'd all banged closed. We had to crank two of them open before we got to Engineering.

Craig was swearing up a storm when I got there.

"How bad is it?"

"I can get fusactors one and two fixed. Three's gonna take a yard and I haven't looked at four yet, but all the batteries burst and the APU and the emergency APU are both gone."

"So we have no power and no way to restart the fusactors," I said, looking around.

"Looks that way. If the lifeboats are okay, we might be able to pull the power plant out of one and use it to get things started."

"Any idea what killed the APUs?"

"We had everything up to emergency power so we could max out the gravity. When that EMP shock hit, well, we spiked into over capacity. The fusactors tripped as they're designed to, but..." He sighed.

"The spike drove into the batteries and APUs that are normally offline," I said with an answering sigh of my own.

"What about the APUs on the test bed?" Ben asked.

"Huh?"

"The field didn't push forward or back and, well, those were at the back. One of them might still work."

I looked at Craig, who just shrugged. "Might as well go take a look."

So Ben, Craig, and I returned to the aft hold while the other four got grabbed by the assistant engineers and put to work.

"You were right, they don't look damaged at all," I said to Ben. "But I think we'll need a torch to cut them off the test bed. The frame they're on is mangled."

"First, let's see if we can get them started," Craig said. "Ah, good, you left the pull-start on them."

"Too lazy to take 'em off," I said with a shrug. I went over to the other one and managed to get it going while Craig got the first one up.

"We're gonna need to run a cable," Craig said, looking at the transfer box. Two megawatts would melt it.

"I'll disconnect these from the test machinery while you set that up."

Half an hour later, we had everything up but the grav drives and the fusactors. We were sitting down in Engineering so Craig could keep an eye on his team, who were just finishing up on the number one fusion reactor. The ship had four F-50s and as soon as this one was up, we'd get back partial gravity and they'd start on repairing the next one.

"So what happened?" the captain asked Ben.

"I'm not exactly sure, yet. However, I was able to review some of the video on the cameras; fortunately the EMP didn't scramble the memory. What happened was an event horizon wrapped itself around the gateway focusing ring all the way forward to include the gateway. By the time Dave had cut power, it wasn't using any from the power units anymore. One of the high-speed cameras showed that display: sometime after the gateway opened, the gateway machine stopped drawing any power from the two power units.

"It was in some sort of self-sustaining mode, and no, I don't know how or why, yet. It looked like the entire emitter system was trying to rip free of its mounts however."

"Why would that happen?" Captain Morrison asked.

"Because that's how the system is supposed to work. You open up a gateway; once it's stable you travel through it. Apparently after the gateway has been opened, there is an attractive force that develops between the portal and the projection hardware?" Ben said with a shrug.

"So it would have collapsed after the hardware went through?"

Ben shrugged again. "Maybe? I know that, right now, I wouldn't want to depend on that. Something was keeping that portal open, and until I know what it was I think any future tests are going to be done remotely, very remotely, and not aboard or anywhere even *near* a ship."

"You got that right," the captain growled.

"Look on the bright side," I said with a big smile, automatically sticking up for Ben.

"There's a bright side?" Craig, the chief engineer, said, giving me a look.

"We just proved that we can travel to other star systems."

Captain Morrison snorted, then laughed. After a moment we all joined him, the stress getting to us a little.

"Yeah, I guess you did, Ben," the captain said when we'd all settled back down. "But right now we've got a ship that's dead in space. How bad is it, Craig?"

"I won't know until we get that reactor fired up and I can run the test on the gravity drive. Give me a couple of hours, then I'll know."

"Okay, I'll move this up to the mess and get out of your hair. Ben, Dave, let's go."

"If it's all the same, Captain, can I hold on to David there? He's rated on these units and I can use the help."

"Sure! Come on, Ben."

"Let's you and me get started on number two while my crew finishes on one."

"Sounds like a lot more fun than sitting in the mess being bored!" I said with a smile.

"I also wanted you down here for when I do the testing on the grav drive," Craig confessed after the captain had left.

"Why's that?"

"I'm pretty sure we blew out a lot of panels when that gateway collapsed. I'm not sure if it was the EMP or the explosion that came right after it, but there was a surge in the grav drive just before everything went dead."

"How many spare panels do you have?"

"Six, and I've got a feeling that we lost a lot more than that."

"Do you carry any of the equipment to repair them?"

Craig snorted. "Nobody aboard is rated for it. But I know you built the factory and trained our rebuilders, so if anyone knows how to deal with it, I figured you would."

I nodded.

"So"—Craig lowered his voice as he grabbed a toolbox and we headed over to the number two fusactor—"did Ben *really* open up a gateway through space?"

"I could see stars through it, Craig. *Stars!* Yeah, it was wild."

"Too bad it blew up," Craig said, shaking his head.

"Eh, it's Ben. I've seen him blow up experiments dozens of times. But by the third or fourth try, he always nails it. Always."

"Think maybe you coulda warned the rest of us about that accident record?"

"But where's the fun in that?" I asked, chuckling.

"You're crazy, you know that?"

"I thought my coming back here and helping you all out had already proved that!"

"We blew out twenty panels. We've got replacements for *six*."

We were up in the mess, Craig and I, and he was making his report to the captain.

"That bad?"

"That EMP, combined with the physical blast, interacted with the coils above and below the explosion."

"So, what do we do to get moving again?"

"Dave here tells me he can repair them."

"With what?" the captain asked, looking at me.

"With what we have. I've done this before. It'll be messy and I've already let Craig here know that we'll need a kiln built to fire the paste back into ceramic."

"I thought we didn't carry any of that paste?"

"We can recycle the broken panels. I'll need a solvent to turn the powder back into paste. I'll get Ben here to help me figure out what we can make while Craig gets the kilns built."

"Oh, right, you built the panel shop here and taught our repair techs," Captain Morrison said while looking both embarrassed and relieved.

"I'm also certified to tune grav drives, so if we need to work on those I can, but so far those look fine."

"That's a relief," the captain said. Then he turned to Ben. "Before I forget: *You* owe every man and woman on this boat a beer when we get back to port, understand?"

"Yes, Captain."

"Beer? Screw that, I want a bottle of scotch," Craig said with a laugh. "Damn near gave me a heart attack when all four fusion reactors and the APUs scrammed at the same time!"

"Well, let's you and me find me a spot to do the rebuilds," I told Craig, "then we can get started on this. I'd like to be back underway in a few days."

"You and me both," Captain Morrison agreed.

Breaking down the coils was the easy part; with the help of a couple of crewmen we got that done in an hour. Ben quickly came up with a solvent for us using cleaning supplies, of all things. Mixing the powder with solvent was tough at first, until the cook gave us one of his heavy-duty blenders.

Then it was a long and messy grind of refilling the tubes, wrapping them, and firing them. Craig and the captain made me sleep while they were being baked in the kiln, because I was the only person on the ship who knew how to put the panels back together so they'd work.

Four days after the accident, we were back underway, running on just three of the fusion reactors, which was more than enough as we didn't need to power any of the weapons systems. The captain had us running a little slower, just in case there were other problems, I think he wasn't all that trusting of my using reconstituted superconductor material in the grav panels.

"So, what happened, Ben?" I asked as we were sitting on our racks down in the crew quarters.

He shook his head. "I'm still not sure. I need to take that test machine apart all the way down to nuts and bolts and check everything—the video recordings, the telemetry recordings, the sensor logs, everything. That event horizon that was pushing out? I don't know where that came from and I haven't had the time to study the videos to see exactly when it started, if it came up with the portal, or formed a short time afterward. But I'm starting to think that perhaps it's a worthwhile side effect."

"Oh? How so?"

"Say you're under attack. How'd you like to be able to throw up a shield and jump away?"

"Would be useful. But we could see through it, so laser weapons would probably still work."

"That's why I need to take the entire test bed apart. You

saw how the other test apparatus was torn up. There were a lot of forces going on in there, maybe even enough to bend light."

"And turn anybody in a ship using it into paste."

"Like I said, I need to study this. The next test unit is going to be a lot more involved. And like I told the captain, it's going to be remotely operated."

"And you're positive that if the test machine had ripped loose, when it flew forward toward the portal, the portal wouldn't have moved with it?"

"Like that old theorized drive where you use a black hole generator to pull the ship along?"

I nodded. "Yeah, that."

"The portal is a fixed relative spot. Part of why the test bed has to be bolted to the ship so it has all the same relative behavior. When the grav drive was activated, that started to collapse the portal. Then, as the ship started to move, a series of events took place that accelerated the destabilization as the positional framework shifted around the portal. When that happened, it collided with the event horizon as they were no longer locked into the same frame of reference. They then canceled each other out and the power was all dumped into that blast as they simultaneously collapsed."

"You know, I always thought this was going to be some new kind of drive thing where you flew through space, or something like space. Just being able to jump instantly, anywhere, seems kinda...I don't know, like cheating?"

"There's a limit on the range, Dave. Based on how much power you have and how much mass you're moving. It's going to take a series of jumps to get anywhere. So it's not going to be as cut-and-dried as it might appear."

"So what are these things going to look like? What sort of allowances should I be making when it comes time to build a ship?"

Ben shook his head. "I don't quite know yet. Until I've flown something through one and seen the effects on everything inside, I can't say."

"And just how are you going to get it back if it's a couple light-years away?"

"I have some ideas, but until I'm actually able to push something through, I won't be able to test them."

"Well, good luck."

"Thanks for coming, Dave. If you hadn't have been there, we probably all would have died."

"Oh, I don't know about that, Ben," I said, giving my head a slight shake.

"You made the call on using the gravity drive, Dave. If you hadn't..." Ben shook his head. "I don't know what would have happened, but it probably would have damaged the ship and again, we would have died."

"I don't know if we would have died, Ben. It hadn't gotten big enough to trap us, but sitting in a ruined frigate waiting for help to arrive would not have been fun."

"Still, you don't panic, Dave. Me? I was panicking. I was losing it. Then there was what happened afterward! If you hadn't have been here, who would have fixed those panels? The drive? No one here knew how to do that. We would have been, what, weeks waiting for rescue? Or months making our way home? Sure you don't want to stay and help me with this? You've got a quick mind, a steady hand, and probably know more about engineering than anyone else on board!"

"There are times when it's tempting to run away from everything and just hide out here, Ben. But I've just got too much going on now, and Kacey is in love with building that shipyard. She and her grandfather are definitely cut from the same cloth.

"Just promise me that you won't do any more tests with you or anyone else anywhere near the testing gear, okay? When it gets to the point where that might be safe? Then I'll come out to make sure you're not deluding yourself."

"You've got a deal. I'm definitely not cut out for a life of adventure," Ben said with a laugh. "I prefer my office and my lab."

"You did something out here that no one else has ever done before, *and* you lived to tell the tale. You're going to be in the history books, Ben. Just make sure to name the drive after yourself. Okay?"

"You sure you don't want me to mention you?" he teased.

"Positive. After some of the things I've done, trust me, I'm better off forgotten."

"Someone had to do it, Dave. You know that."

"Yeah, I do. I understand that, especially now. But for some things, it's better that no one remembers who did it, just that it had to be done, and was."

"So how much longer you going to stay?" Ben asked, changing the subject.

"I think I want another week once we get back. I want to spend some time on the factory. I think I see some spots where we could add some inspections to cut down on failures and maybe a process change or two to improve quality.

"You know, we're going to have to find some sort of production quality expert if we start building those drives out here, right?"

"Dave, that's going to be years from now. We got time."

"Exactly, we've got time. So maybe you should talk to Marcus about training one up out here? Somebody local? They could cut their teeth on the panel factory, then when it comes time to start building another factory, they'll have the experience."

"And this is why you really should just move here," Ben said with a laugh. "You figure out these things that never occur to me."

"That's because you're a researcher and a scientist. You're always looking to make new things. Me? I'm an engineer. I just want to make the same thing, cheaper and more reliable, again and again and again."

"Sounds boring."

"Yeah, you'd think so, but for me, it isn't." I smiled at him. "Well, I'm going to bed. Tomorrow we get back and I fully expect Kacey to drag me off and have her way with me."

"I'm sure you'll be kicking and screaming every inch of the way."

"Yeah, well, don't think your Auri doesn't have plans for you!"

"Ummm... 'Night Dave."

"'Night."

EIGHTEEN

Eris

WE JUST MANAGED TO GET BACK BEFORE THEY SENT OUT SOMEONE to look for us, or rather to see what was left. Our mission only ran three days over what we'd told everyone was the longest we should be gone. Ben had been hoping to do several days' worth of tests. He also hadn't expected to have the level of success he'd gotten.

Needless to say, Kacey and I disappeared for a good twenty-four hours of private time.

"I'm going to miss this," she sighed as we cuddled in bed.

"Yeah, all of this opulence and wealth is tempting, isn't it?" I teased.

"I was thinking more about the privacy. Nobody bothers us when we don't want to be disturbed. No work, no parents, no family, no baby..." She shook her head. "Am I a bad mother for wanting a break?"

"Then I'm a bad father," I laughed and hugged her.

"So what are your plans today?"

"I'm going to check out the panel factory I helped build and see if I can use some of the things I learned helping to set up our shops back on Ceres, as well as some of the things I learned while studying for my certs to improve the quality of the yield."

"Sounds hard."

"Oh, I don't know, I know a lot more now than I did then. I'm sure there has to be at least one thing that can be done better than I set it up. Quality issues always creep in over time if you don't set up a process to prevent it. That part I didn't do, because I didn't know any better."

"And how long will this take? For all that I'm enjoying our little vacation, I very much want to head back home soon."

I shrugged my shoulders. "A couple days? Mabel's coming down in the morning and we'll go over all of it together. How'd things go with Marcus?"

"Surprisingly well. He knows we don't have to do this here, that we could do it back home. With the war that's going on, he believes that when it's finally over, the folks here won't have to worry about reprisals ever again. So he's a lot less worried about this place being uncovered eventually."

"Especially if he can afford to put in more defenses, right?"

Kacey laughed. "Right. I also have a sneaking suspicion that he wants to put in at the very least a repair yard, if not an actual shipyard."

"Well, if all of this pans out, maybe we can go into a partnership with him."

"Why would we want a second shipyard?"

"Because we could do all of our new ship design and testing out here, away from prying eyes?"

"We'd need to send someone out here to represent our interests," Kacey said, cuddling up to me. "Someone who'll be more than happy to live this far out away from everything.

"And before you suggest it, no, not Ben. Your brother may be smart but he's definitely *not* management material."

I laughed. "Yeah, he's not. Also he sucks at business."

"I thought you said he's a genius?"

"If it bores him, he ignores it until it goes away. Business, finance, those things bore him."

"Guess I need to have a long talk with Auri in the morning about managing their money."

"Probably. Now, how about we get at least some sleep?"

Kacey yawned. "I like that idea..."

✧   ✧   ✧

We were up and dressed and eating breakfast when Mabel showed up.

"So, ready for this?"

I nodded. "Looking forward to it, actually."

"Well, just go easy on them. They still remember what your favorite method of 'correction' is."

"Was, Mabel, was. I don't do that anymore."

"What'd he do?" Kacey asked, with a hint of a smile.

"Laid a guy out with a spanner for not taking his job seriously enough."

"He also mouthed back to me," I pointed out.

Kacey laughed. "Wait until Grandpa finds out!"

"His or yours?" Mabel asked, looking back and forth.

"Hers," I said. "He's got fists almost as big as my head, and the stories about him using them are the kind of thing people *still* regale me with."

"Sounds like you married into the right family, then," Mabel said with a chuckle.

I gave Kacey a hug, put my plate and glass in the sink for later, and followed Mabel down to the factory. Going inside, I was struck by how much, and how little, it had changed. The walls were no longer just sealed stone. In some areas they'd been painted and there were posters and personal items everywhere.

You could tell that people worked here.

On the other end of the spectrum, the workbenches and the roller conveyors to move finished subassemblies to the next build area looked almost the same as when I'd left. It was nice to see that standards were being maintained.

"Hey, everyone! Look who's here!" Mabel called out as I stood there looking around. It got very quiet then as everyone looked up and saw me.

"Uh-oh," I heard someone mutter.

Shaking my head, I had to smile.

"Yes, I'm here because of the quality issues, but!" I said and looked around the room. "It's as much *my* fault as it is yours! Maybe even more so!"

"Wait, how's that?" asked one of the techs working there. I recognized the face but couldn't place the name.

"There's processes you're supposed to put in place when

setting up any kind of factory line to help keep quality from degrading. I didn't know about those when I helped set this up. Now I do. So me and Mabel are going to review the entire line today. Tomorrow we'll sit down with the supervisors and start talking about implementing those processes. Then I guess after that we'll go over it with all of you."

"Well, I know one thing I'd like to see!"

I looked up and saw it was the guy I'd laid out way back when I'd been helping to set this place up.

"What's that?"

"Weekly inspections of all our gear! Especially the templates and the metal brakes. By the time we realize they've become worn, who knows how many mistakes have been made?"

I turned to Mabel. "We're doing that from now on. Make sure he gets credit for suggesting it."

Mabel made a note on her table.

"Okay," she said looking around. "Anybody else have any suggestions?"

I almost laughed as half the people there raised their hands.

"Well, come over here, line up, and share," I said as we found a couple of seats.

"That was a lot of good feedback," I said, looking over the notes with Mabel when we broke for lunch.

"Tracy's breaking the ice helped, as well as your taking his suggestion seriously," Mabel said. "I gather he's been complaining about that for a while now and the supervisors still remember your 'correcting' him."

"Yeah, we need to put in a review system as well for employee feedback. Make sure it all gets looked at. Most of this," I said, tapping the tablet, "probably won't make any difference, or really isn't worth considering. But some of these are gold, I'm sure, and we still have to go over the line and figure out where we want to implement our quality checkpoints."

"I'm just happy that they're onboard with fixing things," Mabel said, looking up at me.

I looked back at her and sighed. "I would not be surprised to find out that somewhere there is a manager who is more concerned about production quotas and schedules than he or she is about quality. If I had the time, I'd stick around and find them and give them a gentle reminder of the dangers of faulty gravity panels."

"You mean you'd lay them out with a spanner!" Mabel said with a chuckle.

"Hopefully I wouldn't have to. But you may want to talk to your people and set the tone with them about remembering what's important."

"You know it's only going to get harder if you build that factory out here."

"I know," I said, shaking my head. "I'm going to have to find someone to run it. Someone experienced who I trust. I know you have some good engineers on duty out here, but from what I've seen they're all working aboard your ships or on maintaining your defenses."

"That or they're working for me on construction, or that fusion-works your brother designed. We have far too many 'necessities' when it comes to jobs that have to be filled. Thankfully, as more of our people find their way here, we're getting more folks who are trained engineers, but you're going to need someone with a lot of years' experience, and those kinds of folks are in short supply around here."

"I may end up having to set up a rotation among my own people. Have them come out and do a year, maybe a year and a half, here, then come home and someone else gets the job. It's not just the lack of people here, but no offense, Mabel, this factory is going to belong to me and Ben. Sure, you'll all have a piece of it, but I want whoever runs it to remember they report to *me and Kacey* first. Everyone else is second."

"You can always come back, you know!" Mabel said, finishing up her lunch.

"Maybe once we get the shipyard up and running," I chuckled and, getting up, followed her back to work.

"Yeah, I tell my son that every time he asks when I'm gonna retire: 'Well, maybe when I get the habitat finished!'"

"Well, be sure to let me know when that is, maybe I'll have a job for you!"

She snorted and I laughed.

"Get cleaned up, we're meeting your brother, Auri, Marcus, and Pam for dinner tonight," Kacey said when I got back.

"Where at? Marcus and Pam's?"

"Nope, there's a small restaurant that they want to take us to, to celebrate Ben's findings as well as to thank you for your work on the factory."

"There's still the meeting to go over what Mabel and I talked over today."

"Mabel told Marcus that the two of you had finished the plans, you just need to show the supervisors their part."

"Pretty much," I said to her as I headed to the shower. "Most of it wasn't really that hard. Though it is going to slow production down a little bit. We just need to get everyone on board with our new safety standards."

"Oh, I'm sure Marcus will make sure that they understand. Now, go get clean!"

"Yes, ma'am!"

The walk to the "old district" was interesting. Pam and I used to come down here about once a week to shop for food or the occasional little thing to brighten up our apartment.

While some of the food places where still there, most had moved into new quarters due to Mabel's expansion plans. In their place were a lot more shops selling goods that were either locally made or imported. There were also a number of small restaurants as well.

When we got to the one we were all meeting at, we went inside to see that Pam and Marcus already had the table.

"Wow, this is nice," I said, looking around. "Everything has grown so much in the last three years. I can just imagine what this place will be like ten years from now, or even twenty."

"Yes, and you've been a big part of that, the both of you," Marcus said, raising his glass and tipping it to Kacey and me. "We really need to do something to thank you, just none of us can really think of what that would be."

"Just keep Ben from doing anything too stupid," I said with a laugh as Ben and Aurelia came over and joined us at the table.

"That's a full-time job if ever there was one," Aurelia said, smiling at Ben.

"It's the peril of genius," Ben said with a mock sigh. "The rest of the world just isn't up to my standards!"

I snorted, Aurelia smacked his arm, and the others laughed.

"Have you figured out what went wrong with the test gateway?" I asked.

"I have a theory, but I won't know for sure until I build the next test generator."

"And that theory is...?" I prompted.

"The area I had the gate opened to was at a lower energy level than where our location for the test was. That was why there was that flow through the gate—it was an energy flow from higher to lower potential, and it was so strong it started to form a gravitational effect. It was also generating enough energy to keep the Newtonian ring operating."

"Is that a good thing or a bad thing?" Kacey asked.

Ben pondered that a moment.

"I'm not sure," he finally answered. "I mean, I think it's a bad thing and I'm going to add some shielding to the ring so we don't lose control next time, but what if we'd opened that gate to a place with a higher potential energy?" Ben shook his head. "*That* could have even more problematic, perhaps even disastrous. I need to find a way to deal with that before we even try sending anything through."

"I didn't know there were areas of differing potential energy in space," Pam said, looking thoughtful.

"Neither did I!" Ben said with a laugh. "Obviously space isn't as empty as we thought. But these are really just mechanics problems. I'm sure the solutions will present themselves as I come to understand the problem. Now that the hard one's been solved," he finished with a genuinely happy look on his face.

"So, which was better, discovering this, or getting married?" Pam asked with a mischievous look.

"Getting married wasn't the big thing," Ben said and I noticed Aruelia suddenly frowned. "That was realizing that I *wanted* to marry her!" He turned suddenly, grabbed a very surprised-looking Aurelia, and *dragged* her into his lap as he kissed her.

I was shocked! That was the most un-Ben thing I'd ever seen him do.

"Oh, and opening the gateway was cool too," he said with a smile when he'd finished kissing her. Aurelia was holding onto him, trying to catch her breath.

"Okay, where is my brother and what have you done with him?" I asked, only half joking.

"I've been thinking about what I've done—what I've discovered, what I've proven. I realized last night, while I was lying in bed with Auri, that I will never in my life, not ever, make a bigger discovery. Things like that only come once in a lifetime. I may do other things that are great or big and important, but that's the *one*.

"So as I laid there thinking about it, I realized that for all that it was an important thing, people hundreds of years from now won't care who did it or why. They may not even remember me. So just how important to my life was it? I mean, I did it, Dave, I did it! But now? It's over. Sure, I get to play with it, but it'll never be the same.

"What's important, what's really important, to me and to my life is the person I've chosen to share my life with. The family I'll make with them. Ten, twenty, thirty years from now, Auri will be here, with me. She'll be the focus of my life. She'll be my 'present.' My discovery? It'll be in the past. As far as I'm concerned, it'll just be another one of those things I did."

Aurelia grabbed his head and laid a kiss on him then like it was the most important thing she'd ever do in her life.

"Why do I feel like standing up and applauding?" I said, looking at the others.

"Poetry, sheer poetry," Marcus said and, leaning over, he kissed Pam. "I could not have said it better myself and the good lord knows that I've tried."

I had to laugh, as I hugged Kacey. "Only Ben could put the biggest discovery in the universe second to his wife."

"Well, he *is* a genius," Aurelia said, coming up for air. "And here I thought my announcing I was pregnant was going to be the highlight of the night."

"Aaand we lost them again," Pam laughed as Ben kissed Aurelia.

"I just want to get back home before the morning sickness sets in," Kacey admitted. "We started on number two before we left."

"Well, we've started on number one," Pam said, looking at Marcus with a hungry expression.

"Well, congratulations, Pam, Marcus!" I said, raising my glass. "And you too, Auri, Ben. Now how about taking a break long enough so we can order dinner?" I asked, winking at them.

"Yes, dinner would be good," Ben agreed.

✧   ✧   ✧

Dinner was nice. The food was good, my brother and his wife were happy. My ex-girlfriend and her new husband were happy, and I was beyond happy being able to share all of that with Kacey. We mostly made idle conversation and didn't talk about anything important beyond each other. I had to admit that for the first time in a long time I was happy with my circumstances. Sooner or later Ben would figure out the drive. Sooner or later Kacey and I would be building starships, or if not us our kids would.

The rest of the solar system was watching the war between Venus and Earth, and no one was thinking about me. Especially not the Clarks or the McVays.

"So, what's next for you, Dave?" Ben asked as we stepped out of the restaurant. Pam and Marcus had already said their goodbyes and left, so it was just the four of us walking down the street deep inside Eris.

"My next thing is building that drive for those fighters," I told him. "After that? Well, we do want to design a larger cargo ship. Though I wouldn't mind getting some sort of insight as to how the drive of yours will perform. Say, five or six years from now? So we can start figuring out how to put it on a ship?"

Ben was about to say something when a man came up to us.

"Excuse me; you're that Walker guy, aren't you?"

"Please don't tell me this is about that documentary..." I groaned.

"You killed my brother!" he yelled.

"What?" I said, shaking my head and putting my hands up. "What in the hell are you talking about?"

"When you destroyed the city he was living in! When you destroyed all of those cities! You're a gods-damned monster!" he yelled even louder. People were stopping and starting to watch.

"Wait, what makes you think I did that?"

"Because you're the Iceman! We all know what you did! We saw it all! And then you come here! You take care of Mr. Diebold's problems! Kill them off! Everyone knows you did it! You're the devil!"

"Whoa, whoa, calm down, I think you got me confused with someone else..."

"Well, you took away my brother, so I'm gonna take away yours!" he screamed and, pulling out a pistol, he pointed it at Ben!

I threw myself at the guy! I couldn't let him kill Ben! I

couldn't let anybody hurt my brother! That was the one thing I'd never messed up in all of my screwed up life! I'd brought him here to be safe!

The gun went off, again and again. It felt like I was getting punched; I lost count after the second shock. He stepped back, pushing me away as I stumbled, and raised the pistol again, but suddenly he was falling back as the back of his head came off, his body twisting back and forth.

Gasping, I collapsed and grabbed my guts, instinctively. Everything felt numb, I couldn't even feel my hands grabbing myself.

"Dave! Dave!"

I looked up, it was Kacey.

"I...I'm shot?" I said and swore. "All these years, and I get killed by some lunatic?"

"You're not dead, you're not dying, hold on, Dave! Hold on, don't you die on me!"

It was weird then, I was having trouble hearing, or remembering what I was hearing. Everything seemed to start happening at once as my vision shrunk to a small circle. There were people, and things going on, but I couldn't feel anything, I couldn't see anything and suddenly...

Everything stopped and it all went dark.

NINETEEN

...?

"SHAKE IT, FEEL THE WEIGHT IN IT," KAUF SAID.

I shook it. I could feel something moving back and forth inside.

"Okay, so there's a weight inside. Big deal."

"But it is, my young friend, but it is."

He set a block of... something on the table. It quivered a little like Jell-O, and you could see through it.

"Stab that with your pick."

I drew out my pick in one fluid motion and stuck it in the cube. The pick went in until the broader piece was stopped by the surface of the block.

"It feels like a person!" I exclaimed.

"Good, it's supposed to. Pull out your pick."

I did so, and you could barely see the wound that the four-inch pick had made.

"Now, strike it with the other one."

I looked at the other one, with its shorter pick, shrugged and, swapping weapons, I jabbed it hard into the block.

It was like *magic*! Before my eyes a bubble formed almost instantly in the center of the block! The block itself bulged.

"How did that happen?"

"That weight you feel moving back and forth?"

235

"Yeah?" I asked as I pulled out the pick. While the hole the tip had made closed up, the bubble stayed there.

"When it slams forward, it injects air out the tip of the pick."

"Wow..." I said, eyes wide as I stared at the cube. "I could kill somebody."

He smiled at me. "That's the idea, my young Mongoose. That is completely the idea. You're good. Very good. But this would make you better."

I nodded slowly and spun it in my hand. The weight must have had a spring on it, pushing it to the end of the handle, because I didn't feel anything shift.

"Why me?" I asked suddenly, looking Kauf in the eyes.

"Because, you, Mongoose, have a gift."

"A gift? What, are you talking about my flat-heel elie mom and how I can't go to jail because of her?"

Kauf laughed. "That's helpful, but no, that's not your gift."

"Well, then what is it?" I asked with the impatience of twelve-year-olds everywhere.

"You're angry. You're always angry. The world owes you and you're gonna make it pay. Every way you can. That"—he pointed to the new pick in my hand—"is how you're gonna collect."

"What about Koosh?"

"Koosh won't be coming back from jail. Not anytime soon, if ever. That was his. Now it's yours."

"You want me to take over for *Koosh*?"

"Yes."

"What about Big Jim? Is he with it?"

Kauf nodded. "Big Jim's with it. After all, you're from his quad."

I nodded, handed him my old pick, and slipped the new one into my pocket. Koosh was the head picker for the Howlers in the city. He was the guy who dealt with the *real* problems.

"Thanks, Kauf," I said and we hand-bumped and did the Howler hand flick.

"Embrace that anger, Mongoose. Let it run, and trust me, they will learn to fear you, and respect you. You've got the power now, use it."

"I will, Kauf, I will..."

"Goose! Good work down on the doler's side. Those Silvertips, you sure taught their boss a lesson!"

"Thanks, Big Jim! But he was easy. He shoulda had him some boys who knew how to fight instead'a just how to pose and look good."

Big Jim laughed. "So I hear, Goose!"

I walked out of the gang's clubhouse and looked around, smiling.

"Goose!"

"Hey, Merks!" I said and waved. Merks was fifteen, and one of the senior members in our quad. Only Big Jim, who was two years older, was bigger.

"So, I hear you put it to Flash and a couple of his boys over on doler turf?"

I shrugged, playing it cool. "Wasn't no big thing. Big Jim said he had to go after some things he done. So, he's gone."

Merks laughed and shook his head, "Damn, Goose, that's bagging it alright. What about his boys?"

"They'll have regrets. The ones I didn't down, that is," I said with a sly smile.

"Shit, you've only been doin' this a year and you got Koosh all beat. I mean, he was good, but *damn*...That's what, twenty now?"

"I don't keep a count."

"Why the hell not?"

"I liked Koosh. He taught me a lot. I don't want people thinking I'm better. That bro deserves respect and I'm gonna give it."

Merks gave me a look and, after a moment, he smiled and threw a sign. "Howlers for life, right? Gotta keep the faith."

"Yup," I said and threw the sign back at him as I nodded. "Koosh will always be ours."

"So Big Jim is out, and Merks is in," Kauf said, ignoring the dead body on the floor. "But he left us with some *things* we gotta clean up."

I nodded. "Sure think, Kauf. Just tell me who and when."

"You know me, Kauf, Howlers for life," Merks said.

"Okay, here's how it is..."

I looked around me. There were a *lot* of dead bodies. At fourteen, I was a force all unto myself. The other gangs feared me. I was fast—unnaturally fast, some claimed. I wasn't afraid of the cops. They didn't even bother to arrest me anymore, because I'd be back out on the streets before they even left the building.

I looked around, K-man and Gigs were both standing. Clean was down.

"Clean alive or dead?" I asked.

"Dead," K-man said. "He tried to take on Ranger."

I looked at Ranger, who was lying dead at my feet. "Idiot."

"Yup. What about him?"

I looked over at the kid standing behind the counter, eyes wide in surprise, his hands on the counter in clear sight.

"He attack anybody?"

"Nope."

"Then leave him alone."

"Goose, he saw everything!"

I turned and looked at K-man. "He didn't attack us. I think this is enough." I motioned to the dead bodies on the floor. "Leave him be and let's go. The cops won't bother me, but you ain't got that kinda cover." I turned to the young man looking at me. "Best be gettin' scarce."

"Thanks, I owe you one."

"Yup, bye." I turned and left with the other two leading the way.

"Hey, David."

I turned and looked at the two suits who were walking up to me as I cut through the alleyway to my quad.

"Whadda ya want?" I mumbled at them as I turned and went back to heading home. It was late, I was tired. We'd had something of a party back at the clubhouse. Celebrating another one of our wins. My wins.

"Oh, this won't take all that long. Your grandfather sent us."

"My who?"

I turned to look at him and got stuck in the back with a shocker. My whole body spasmed as every nerve lit up on fire! I don't know how long they held it there. Long enough that I saw the guy pull out a pair of gloves before I fell to the ground. Stunned and helpless, I watched him put them on. I could see they were weighted. I knew Kauf carried a pair like that.

So had Big Jim.

I flashed back then to just what had been done to Big Jim with them.

He bent over then and slugged me, hard, in the gut. I tried to roll away, but somebody had my arms...oh right, he had a partner. He hit me again then, and again, and it just...didn't...stop. Every time a spot started to become numb to the pain of the blows, he moved to another one. He worked all the way down my body to my calves, then I got rolled over onto my stomach and he worked all the way back up.

I started to understand exactly what Big Jim had felt and wondered if I'd even feel it when the end came. With all the pain I was feeling, would I even *know*?

The man causing me all that pain spoke then, whispered in my ear:

"Your grandfather is very unhappy with how you're living your life. The Morgans, they don't do things that way and you, Dave, are bringing shame to the family."

I tried to say something, anything, but it simply came out as a gurgle.

"If you don't change your ways? If I have to come back here? The next beating you won't be waking up from." And with that I felt a pain in the back of my head and everything went blank.

I spent almost a week in bed. Too hurt, too sore, too stiff, and pissing blood every time I went to the bathroom. Surprisingly, I didn't have a single bruise on my face. Ben covered for me with Mom and Dad, but I couldn't get it out of my head: Why hadn't they killed me?

My mind kept coming back to what he had said, just before he knocked me out. I'd been given a message. One that somebody had made damn sure I would get.

"You're quitting?" Merks said, looking at me in a combination of shock and surprise.

"It's time for some new blood, Merks. I've been doing this too long and I don't want to end up like Koosh."

Merks winced. "Yeah, can't blame you for that. I know you looked up to him. So, you leaving us?"

"Who said anything about leaving?" I said with a smile. "Howlers for life, Merks, you know that. I mean, yeah, I'm gettin' older and the Prof has got me looking at a sweet gig working on spaceships that lift out of where our dad works."

"So why do you want to go to space?" Mr. Hobart, my guidance counselor, asked, looking up from my records.

"Well, I gotta do something, and with Ben going to MIT it looks like something I'd like."

"Being an engineer?"

"My dad's been teaching me his job, but the tech stuff isn't challenging enough for me. Besides, I got the grades, so what's the problem?"

Mr. Hobart looked at me over his glasses. "David, I'm quite aware of your past with certain *juvenile* elements."

"Yeah, past, as in I don't do that anymore. So what's the issue?" I said, frowning and leaning closer.

"The issue is this device right here. Normally, the PWR relief valve keeps the pressure regulated when the entire system is under gravity. But in zero gee, the Backens-vacuum stop comes into play as the whole system, while still under pressure, undergoes a pressure differential shift as the water pressure at the bottom of the stack is no longer higher than it is at the top."

I stopped and looked around. I was in a stairwell. Looking up between the stairs it went up out of sight. The same for when I looked down. I didn't see any doors, anywhere.

So I sat down and checked my pockets for my tablet. Then I could call up a map and find my way out of here.

"Dave Walker?"

I looked up, there was a guy standing there. Someone had shot him in the eye. Probably me.

"Nope."

"You sure about that?"

"Are you?"

"We need to walk up the steps."

"Why?"

"Because we're sinking, but if we keep walking we'll be okay."

"What happens if we don't?" I said, getting up.

"I don't know, I didn't ask. But if you don't go..."

Suddenly, Dot Briggs was standing there, smiling. "You *will* regret it!" she said in that happy voice of hers.

Sighing, I put my tablet away, stood up and started going up the stairs.

"Am I dead?" I asked her.

"Do you want to be?"

"Not really. Kacey'd be pissed."

"Damn right I would be!" I looked and Dot was gone, but Kacey was now there.

"Where am I?" I tried a little harder. *"Where am I?"*

"Dave?" I heard Kacey's voice but everything was sort of white. But not exactly?

"Where am I?" I groaned. Something hurt.

"Dave, can you hear me?"

"Yeah, I think so. Are you real?"

"Of course I'm real!"

"So where am I?"

"Ceres. You're on Ceres."

"Oh god, another hallucination..."

"Dave! It's Kacey and we're on Ceres, dammit."

"Huh? How'd we get here?"

"You were in a coma. They couldn't treat you there, so they packed us on a destroyer and flew here."

"Why would they do that?"

"Poison bullets."

"What do bullets have to do with it?"

"Do you remember getting shot?"

Suddenly I remembered. I must have flinched.

"Take it easy, Dave."

"Why can't I see anything?"

"You're in a trauma tube."

"What the hell is a trauma tube?"

"The only thing saving your life right now. They're going to be pulling you out of there in a few minutes. It's not going to be pleasant. Don't panic."

"Well, that doesn't sound good," I said with laugh. Or tried to at least. "Are you okay?"

"I'm fine, Ben's fine, Auri's fine. Okay, you're coming out. Brace yourself, they had to cut your meds, it's probably going to hurt."

"Right. Probab—"

I took a deep breath, clamped my mouth shut tight, and tried not to scream. I think I whined. My guts were on fire. My head hurt, I had to close my eyes because the light hurt. My skin hurt. Everything *hurt*. I could hear people talking urgently, about move him here, hook that up there. Don't use that. What a mess that is. Get some painkillers!

"Tram addict!" I grunted between gritted teeth.

"No Tramadol!" I heard someone yell. A moment later, it felt like someone stuck a spike in my arm, and suddenly everything started to fade out again.

"Mr. Doyle?"

"Hmm?"

"Can you hear me, Mr. Doyle?"

"Ummm..." I opened my eyes and everything looked blurry. "Hi," I said weakly.

"Hello, Mr. Doyle. What do you remember?"

"Getting shot. Oh, and something very painful. And I think I'm on Ceres?"

"Very good, Mr. Doyle."

Everything came into focus then, and I saw there was a nurse standing next to me, checking a bunch of machines.

"So where am I?"

"You're in the secure wing of the Ceres Naval Hospital, Mr. Doyle."

"Dave, call me Dave. Why am I in here?"

"Because Admiral Carstairs as well as President Sanford offered, and your wife accepted."

"Why'd they do a thing like that?"

"Because you're a very wealthy man and it has been hinted that you have performed several critical services for Ceres."

"So how long have I been here?"

"Five days."

"Why so long? I mean, I just got shot, right? Why didn't they just fix me where I was?"

"You were shot four times. You've lost a kidney, a part of your stomach, part of your liver—that will grow back at least—half a lung, several of your ribs were broken, your large intestines were perforated, and you lost ten feet of your small intestines."

"Eww."

"Also, the bullets you were shot with were poisoned so your surviving kidney shut down, and your nervous system was paralyzed for several days so you had to be put on an external pacemaker as well as a ventilator. You also ended up with blood clots forming throughout your body—a side effect of one of the poisons—and suffered a stroke before the doctors could figure out how to deal with that.

"All of this was well beyond the facilities of the place you were visiting. Someone tried very hard to kill you, Dave. So they stuck you in a severe trauma tube as soon as they could and shipped you here."

"What's a trauma tube?" I asked as I'd never heard of them.

"Basically you can think of it as a giant refrigerator. They lower your body temperature to as low as they can safely go. They pump you full of blood thinners, put an oxygen mask on you, insert an IV full of oxygenated artificial blood, and a neural device that puts you in a deep sleep. About the same as a medically induced coma."

"Huh, never heard of those before."

"Yes, they're very new."

"How new?" I asked, giving her a look.

"Yours was custom-built to send you here. They're still very much in the research stage."

"Ben," I sighed.

"Who?"

"My brother."

"Oh," She shrugged. "In any case, you're alive, even if you shouldn't be."

"So how long until I'm up and about again?"

"As you still have a few more surgeries to go through, I can't answer that question."

"Wait, you're not done cutting me open?"

"There's a good chance you're going to need a pacemaker. They put several filters inside you to clean up any blood clots that they might have missed. They're looking into whether they can make you a replacement kidney, and they want to take another look at your heart—from the inside, using a camera probe."

"They can do that?"

"Oh, and one of the ribs that was shattered beyond repair still needs to be replaced."

"Damn."

"Yes, so do *not* try to get out of that bed. Not until they've finished working on you."

"When can I see my wife?"

"As soon as we're done here."

"Oh, go get her, please?"

"There's one last thing before I do."

"What?" I sighed.

"Don't go making any important decisions. You may feel fine but there are a lot of drugs in your system right now and your blood chemistry is all out of balance. So don't do anything rash."

I tried not to laugh. "You just described my entire life, you know."

"Yes, and that's why you're here. Now, give me a moment and I'll show your wife and parents in."

"David!" Mom said, running into the room, followed closely by Kacey, Dianne, and then my father.

"Hi, Mom. Guess I screwed up."

"You were protecting your brother, but next time, try not to get yourself shot!" she said, starting to cry as she gently hugged me. "I don't want to lose either of you, understand? So next time, push Ben out of the way or something!"

My right arm was free, I'd discovered my left arm wasn't, so I hugged her with it. Dianne was next—she didn't quite cry, but I could see she was upset. Dad also gave me a hug.

"I thought we were done with these kinds of things, David?" he said, giving me a look.

"Sorry, I just wasn't expecting it. I mean, they wanted to shoot *Ben*! Who in their right mind wants to hurt him of all people? Totally messed with my head."

Kacey came up to me then. "*Next* time, give me a clear shot! Don't try to wrestle with the guy with the gun, okay? You wouldn't have gotten shot so many times, if at all!"

I winced. From the look in her eye and the sound of her voice, she wasn't at all happy.

"Sorry, Kace. I just wasn't thinking."

"Damn right you weren't thinking!"

She gave me a look, then a hug and kissed me. "You scared the *hell* out of me! Don't you ever do that again!" Then she started crying and after comforting her for a minute the best I could, she let me go. I spent the rest of the visit talking with my mom and dad and Dianne, who told me a little about the college she was now going to, and how much fun it was.

When they finally left, Kacey came back over, gave me another hug, and looked at the nurse, who smiled and nodded, then left the room.

"So, how long have I been out?"

"You were shot almost three weeks ago."

"What? That long?"

"It took them several days to get you stable because new things keep happening. It wasn't until they examined his gun that they discovered he'd put a different poison on each of the bullets. *Then* they had to figure out what each one was."

"But why'd they send me home? Why not fix it there?"

"Because their medical facilities aren't all that good yet? Also..." Kacey lowered her voice and looked around. The nurse was standing outside the door, well away from us. "Marcus was worried that there might be copycats."

"Huh?"

"There are a lot of people upset over what happened, and some of them even blame you. Marcus had to make a public announcement that while you were drafted by the Ceres government to bring supplies to the team that carried out the attack, you had no part in the attack and don't know anything about the people who did."

"Where'd he hear that?"

"I told him. I told him you offered to take them to a derelict you were planning on salvaging so they could use it. That they then drafted us to take a team out to it, which we did, and that they wore hoods the entire time and we never even got to see their faces."

"Oh." I thought a moment. "What about Ben?"

"He then went on a very long rant about all of the work Ben has done for everyone there and rather than kill him, suicide would be the better choice because Ben's been doing more for their survival than you ever did, and everyone knows just how much you did. He then went on another rant about gratitude and how people needed to show it and that no, the whole 'Iceman' thing was a bluff you pulled because you were trying to protect Pam and on and on."

"Wow."

"Yeah, Marcus was pissed. The whole time he gave that speech Pam was sitting behind him *crying*. As everyone there knows just how important she is to their survival, yeah, people got the message.

"So, Ben built that container with the help of some of the doctors, Marcus had it loaded on his fastest frigate, we put in to one of the hangers at our shipyards, and you got brought over here."

"That was a hell of a risk."

"The navy is still keeping Besua secure and not allowing anyone to fly by there. There's also a heavy naval presence in orbit and they don't allow anyone they don't know to hang around up there. So, not as big as it might have been."

"If there are people that upset, maybe we should have brought Ben back with us?"

"He was torn, but I told him to stay there. Though I did get Marcus to assign him some bodyguards. Aurelia too."

"Why'd you tell him to stay?"

"Because it's still the safest place for him right now. I suspect the McVey family is every bit less happy with you than before, because you put the VMC on their asses."

I snorted. "I did no such thing."

"Un-huh. My mom and dad, along with my sister and brothers, will be by after dinner. I didn't want to tire you out."

"What about Grandpa?"

"I think the only reason he hasn't shown is that the war is still going hot and heavy."

"I meant yours," I said with a slight grin.

"What do you want to see him for?"

"'Cause I need to have him hire me an assistant so I can have them draw up the plans for the grav drives on the new Shian fighters?"

"You're supposed to be resting, David!" Kacey said with a note of warning in her voice.

"That's why I want an assistant who knows about grav drives, so I can just lay here in bed and tell them what I want done, and they can draw it up and show it to me and I can tell them where they screwed up," I said, smiling.

"I'll ask your doctors."

"Kace, I'm gonna go stir-crazy if I don't have something to occupy my mind." I raised my right arm and motioned at everything under the bedsheet. "Besides, those ships ain't gonna build themselves and both Ceres and our company needs those to work, and to work right."

"If your doctor says you can, I'll talk to Grandpa and Dad about getting someone to help you."

"Let them know that I'll be going with two of the one hundreds, instead of the one two-twenty that's in my notes. That's going to affect the design."

"So you're going with Ben's suggestion?"

"I don't want to beat my head against the wall only to have him tell me 'I told you so' when I finally do it his way."

"I gather that's a thing?"

"More than once. I just need someone to go through all the specifications on the different makes of the one hundreds until I find the ones that do what Ben was hinting at." I yawned. "Damn, I'm tired."

"Yes, well, you've been dead on your back for weeks now," Kacey said, smirking at me.

I stuck my tongue out at her, then yawned again.

"I'll come back tonight with my family," she said, then leaning over the bed she kissed me and left.

I was asleep before the she got out the door.

TWENTY

Ceres Naval Hospital

"I FEEL FUNNY TODAY," I TOLD THE DOCTOR WHEN HE CAME IN
to examine me.

"Oh, that's because you went through surgery last night after
your family left."

"I . . . *what?*"

"Surgery. We did a full examination of your heart with a
camera in a catheter and put in a pacemaker. We're still not sure
you need it, but right now we'd rather err on the side of caution."

"What? Why wasn't I told!" I said, trying to sound angry and
instead sounding something a lot more pathetic.

"You were. Or at least I think you were."

"Then how come I don't remember it?"

"Side effect of the anesthesia they used."

"Was my wife told?" I said, lowering my voice.

"Yes, she was told and she approved."

"I'm Dave, by the way."

"I know."

"Great, and you are?"

"Dr. Vincent, and I told you that when I came into the room."

I stopped and looked at him. "Dammit. Is that the anesthesia
as well?"

"Yes. It takes a long time for it to purge out of your system due to your current condition."

"Can't you use something else?"

"Your records say you're addicted to Tramadol?"

"Not quite, but as a young teen I abused it pretty heavily."

"Then sorry, we can't."

"So, how many more operations do I have scheduled?"

"One today, another tomorrow, two days after that we'll hopefully be cutting you open for the last time."

I sighed. "Man, did I fuck up."

"You saved someone's life. It's not always easy, you know."

"Definitely a lot harder than taking it," I said, giving my head a slight shake.

It was the doctor's turn to sigh. "Yeah, isn't that the truth."

"Can you really replace kidneys?"

"Yes, actually. Growing them isn't all that difficult; however, it does take time. Your new one won't be ready for eight months."

"Is that usual?"

"Normally we'd do it in four, but the recent attack has put a strain on our resources."

"Oh." I paused a moment and waited for him to finish. Then I said, "Can I get an assistant in here so I can start somebody on the work I'm supposed to be doing?"

That earned me a look.

"Doc, my company is building the new defensive fighter for the Ceres Navy and I'm the guy who did the basic design as well as the drives for it. I was supposed to be finishing up the drive design before all of this happened to me. I need to tell someone what's in my head so they can draw it up and test it."

He shook his head and gave me a long-suffering look. "The only thing worse than engineers is flight crew. Next week. But you'll have them an hour at a time."

"How many times a day?"

"I was thinking two or three a week."

"Doc! You're killing me here!" I groaned.

"If you follow instructions and don't give your nurses a hard time, we'll try once in the morning and once in the afternoon. But if the nurses or I think you're overdoing it..." He gave me a warning look.

"Any chance of untying my left arm?"

"It's not tied."

"Huh? Then why can't I move it?"

Dr. Vincent closed his eyes for a moment. "This is the second time I've had to tell you this, so don't go panicking on me again until I'm finished."

"*What?*"

"You had a stroke, actually more than one I suspect, due to one of the poisons on the bullets you were shot with."

"And?"

"Your left side is paralyzed."

"What!"

"Temporarily. For now."

"What's 'for now' mean?"

"It means that you're young, you were in intensive care when the strokes happened, so you got immediate medication. Your prognosis for a full recover is good. You'll be put through physical therapy once it's safe to start letting you get out of bed."

I swore, loudly. "I hate this medication. When did you tell me last? This morning?"

"No, yesterday morning. I think I'll have to talk to your anesthesiologist about dosages going forward. Any other questions?"

"None that you can answer," I said, shaking my head.

"Get some sleep. This is a long process and you're not going to be able to concentrate on anything until your body is able to purge some of the drugs we have you on."

"Thanks, Doc. Sorry for yelling."

Dr. Vincent smiled. "You've been through a lot, it's fine. Sleep."

I yawned and found I was tired. Sleeping sounded good.

Monday morning, I was waiting for my new assistant to show up when my sister walked in.

"Dianne? What are you doing here? Don't you have school?"

"Oh, I got a work-study program for extra credit."

"So, you were in the neighborhood and thought you'd stop by?"

"Nope, Kacey hired me. I'm your new assistant!" she said, grinning at me.

"And what do you know about gravity drives?" I asked with a frown.

"Not a lot. I read a couple of books on 'em over the weekend. But she said I shouldn't worry about it, you'd do most of the thinking. I'm here to take notes, draft up diagrams, and find answers to questions."

I would have facepalmed if I had the use of my left hand.

"Read a few books?" I asked. This was always when Ben was his most dangerous—for all you knew he'd read the theory book, the textbook, and then the design specifications. Which meant his technical knowledge was perfect and his practical knowledge was nonexistent.

"Well, okay, I read the theory and I went over a couple of books on practical application so I'd know what you were talking about. Ben's already given me the 'technical versus practical knowledge' lecture."

"He did?" I asked, surprised.

"Yeah, he said I probably wouldn't want to do cannonballs in the bathroom after the third time I'd failed to listen."

I snorted at that. "It only happened once."

"Yes, well, I'd rather not have it happen at all. I know I'm not as smart as him, but I'm still smart enough that I needed to learn some of the things you taught him and he eventually figured out, in order to stay out of trouble at school."

"The trouble he used to get *us* into, until I joined the Howlers and he started paying attention to what I was telling him," I said with a chuckle. "So, let's start with running down the specs on all of the hundred-rate gravitron model grav generators. After we review each one, you get to put all the specifications on a spreadsheet, including price."

"Price? Why do we want that?"

"Because the number one rule in Engineering is cost. Engineers who are cost-conscious are engineers who keep their jobs and their companies afloat. Only safety trumps price breaks."

"Because dead engineers can't cash their paycheck?"

"Exactly!" I said with a smile.

I watched as she got out her tablet and started doing a search on it.

"There are a lot of these. Are there any features we can use to filter by?"

"They need to be able to daisy chain, serial link, or parallel link."

"With the panels?"

"No, with other grav drives. Ben had an idea and I've been thinking about it."

"If you say so."

"Just wait until I make you go research gravity drive buffer theory."

"Did you just make that up?" she asked, looking up at me and scowling.

"Thankfully, no," I said, smiling back.

"Finally, I get to go home," I said as Chet, an orderly, helped me out of the bed and into a wheelchair.

"Trust me, I've been looking forward to this as much as you have," Kacey said. "Sleeping alone after seeing you all but dead hasn't been easy."

"Same," I said and then sighed, as I got comfortable in the wheelchair. Feeling had returned to my left side, which was good, but I was still having a lot of trouble moving my arm or leg. It would probably be weeks before I'd be able to walk again, but at least I could sit up during the day and actually *do* things.

"Ah good, you're checking out," Dr. Vincent said, coming into the room as the orderly put my feet on the footrests. "Start off slow. You've been in bed for the last six weeks and you're going to quickly find out that your body isn't used to sitting up anymore.

"Kacey?"

"Yes, Dr. Vincent?"

"Don't kill him in bed."

I laughed as Kacey turned the brightest shade of red I'd seen in a *very* long time.

"Umm..."

"Give him a few days to adjust. If he pushes himself too hard, or if you push him too hard, he's going to get sick, and then he'll be right back here. So go slow, start off easy.

"And I was talking to you too, Dave, so don't go trying to claim innocence if I find you back here, understand?"

"Understood, Doc," I said.

"Great. I'll see you here next week for a checkup and a physical. So misbehave too much and I'll put you back in that bed," he warned.

"I love you too, Doc," I said with a chuckle.

"Yes, well, you don't have Admiral Carstairs breathing down your neck."

"He's been doing that?" Kacey asked, a little surprised.

"He *really* wants that fighter. Told me that some of the Marsies are pretty interested in it too, since he shared the design specs."

"Why's that?"

"The VMC have pulled two nasty surprise attacks now. One on us, one on Earth. Nobody wants a third. Not from them, not from anybody."

I nodded; it made sense.

"See you in a week, Doc," I said with a wave as Chet pushed the chair out of the room. On the way to the elevator I waved to the nurses, who all waved back. Then it was down to the main floor and outside where a much fancier wheelchair was waiting, along with a man I'd never seen before, who was wearing what I'd best describe as "average" clothing. He was strong looking, had eyes that I could tell were checking out everything, and I noticed a faint bulge under his shirt that hinted at a gun. There was also something causing an outline in his pocket, which made me think he had a backup.

"Thanks, Chet," I said to the orderly as he and the new guy helped me into the new wheelchair.

"Thanks, Chet," Kacey also said and waited until he left, then motioned to the new guy. "Dave, this is Taylor. He's going to be your attendant and aide while you're in the wheelchair."

"And bodyguard," I said.

"Yes, bodyguard. And no, you don't get to argue about it. Several people, myself included, have decided that, right now at least, you need one."

"Where's yours?"

"Trust me, we've been having that discussion too," Kacey said with a sigh. "For the moment, there is someone, but I don't want to point them out because they're being discreet."

"Ah." I turned to Taylor and stuck out my hand. "Hi."

"I've got a third one on a left-hand draw," he told me as we shook.

"So you noticed me looking."

He gave a curt nod, retrieved his hand, and went back to looking around. "It's a holdout piece. I'm more here to discourage than to get into any gunfights. But you never know. Especially when you're guarding the rich and famous."

"Oh gods, I'm famous now?" I said, looking back at Kacey.

"Word's gotten out that we helped the special teams group

that went to Venus," she said with a nod of her head. "As well as the new contract we just got *and* that we're naming our first fighter after the hero of the First Battle of Ceres."

"That's all?"

"Well, they know about your grandfather."

"How'd that happen?"

"He's *here*," Kacey grumbled with a shake of her head.

"Problems?"

She sighed. "I don't even know where to start. He and Grandpa have been going out drinking, whoring, starting *fights*, you name it! The enforcers even brought them home once!"

I started laughing so hard that I had to grab my sides as it *hurt*.

"Your grandfather I can believe, but Alistair?" I said between gasps.

"Apparently he's in a lot better shape than he looks. They're as thick as thieves and I think Alistair wants to send some of his other grandchildren out here to 'learn how to grow a spine' and to see how 'real men and women live.'" Kacey said with another sigh as Taylor started pushing the wheelchair.

"He mentioned that to me once before," I said, trying not to laugh as my sides ached. "Anything else I need to know?"

"They've laid the keels for the first six fighters; the test article is almost done having all of the main spars, stringers, and other structural elements built. Next week they're going to start installing all the electrical and gravitron runs. After that, they'll start installing the electrical, navigational, and control systems while building the cockpit.

"The schedule currently says that in five weeks they'll complete the waveguides for the gravity panels and start on the installation of the gravity drives and the panels.

"Ideally, they're hoping to get the fusion reactor in and start skinning it four months from now."

"What about the weapons?"

"They're not going to put any rail guns or lasers on the test article. They are putting on the four pylons, so they can do tests with different loads on them. There's also been some debate over pulling out one of the rail guns and adding a second laser into the tail section to increase missile defense on the final design."

"Whose idea is it to pull out the second gun?"

"Dad's after talking to Lou and a few other people. The rate on those guns we're getting is higher than the standard rail guns by twenty percent. Also, removing the second gun and all the support for it lightens the overall weight by ten percent, and that's a lot."

"True."

"There's also been some ideas kicked around about a two-person, long-range recon version."

"Ugh, that's a very small space to be cooped up in for a long period of time."

"Hey, I don't fly 'em, I just sell 'em," Kacey laughed.

"So how's the family?" I asked as we approached the tram station, switching the conversation away from business and giving Kacey's belly a look. Her pregnancy was finally starting to show.

The ride home was peaceful. It was early enough in the day that everyone was at work, so the tram was mostly empty. When we got home, the first thing I did was spend some time with my son. By the time that was done, I was so exhausted that I took a nap. Dr. Vincent had been right: just sitting upright was tiring after all that time lying down. It was over two months since I'd been shot and I'd be healing for several more months to come.

The next day, I woke in bed and started to think of my options. I wasn't going in to work today. I definitely wasn't up for that yet. I couldn't even get into the wheelchair by myself—well, not yet at least—and I was definitely going to need help taking a shower.

The thought of that was almost as bad as getting a sponge bath!

"Ah, you're awake," Kacey said, coming into the room.

"I need help getting into the wheelchair, then help getting into the shower, then getting back *out* of the shower, getting dressed..." I sighed and shook my head. "This is going to suck."

"Yes, it will suck, but you'll get through it. May I remind you that the alternative was a lot worse?" she said, giving me one of those looks.

"I need to start exercising to get my strength back. I also need to do the exercises the physical therapist wants me to do. And I need to do them more often than just twice a day."

"Are you sure that's wise?"

"Well, if it's not, Doc Vincent will yell at me when I go back next week. But I can't stand being helpless. I think if I start off slow, maybe with a couple of one- or two-pound weighs and work my way up? If nothing else, moving my arms and legs will help me with relearning how everything works on my left side."

"True. Well, let me get Taylor. Part of his job is to help with these things until you can do them yourself."

I nodded. "Once I'm done, breakfast would be nice. I'm going to see if I can get any work done from home. Maybe next week I can start going in a couple days a week."

"We'll see..."

It took me an hour to get showered and dressed. Someone had thought ahead and put a seat in the shower and I was infinitely grateful for that, because I couldn't stand, especially not in a shower. Taylor had offered to help, but I refused. I wanted to start reclaiming my dignity, and if I had to do it an inch at a time, well, then that was the road I'd be walking.

Getting dressed wasn't all that hard when you're really just wearing a loose pair of sweatpants and a sweatshirt. I needed help with the socks, which sucked. Then again, I'd needed help with the pants. But I'd managed the shirt by myself.

When I drove the chair into the dinning room using the little control stick on it, I saw that my grandfather was already there.

"Dave, you've looked better," he said with a wink.

I rolled my eyes and looked him over. He honestly looked a lot more relaxed than the last time I'd seen him.

"You're looking good, at least. Enjoying the colonies, are we?" I asked with an exaggerated British accent like they had on those old vid comedies.

He laughed as I stopped at the table and raised the seat a little to make it easier for me to eat.

"Yes, I am, honestly."

"How goes the war?" I asked as Kacey served first me, then Alistair, then she pointed Taylor into a seat as well as Havier and a woman I didn't recognize, and served each of them. I guessed they'd already been read the riot act, because they all sat down without protesting.

"Best damn thing that's happened to Earth in a hundred years!" Grandfather said as he picked up his fork.

"What? But they're saying millions have died!"

"A billion plus, last time I checked," he said with a shrug.

"And that's a *good* thing, how?" I asked as I picked up my own knife and fork and started cutting up my omelet.

"Half the population is dead wood, you know that. With the war, they're the ones that are taking the brunt of it, and of course they're all inflamed now, so we're training 'em up and we're going to send them to Venus to take over all their cities."

"They're going to invade?" I said, surprised.

"Wasn't my idea, but I can see the brilliance of it. We get rid of even more of our useless population, cutting down on our debt. Also, there's a movement among some of the dolers to learn a skill to 'help with the war effort.' Five major cities got destroyed and a couple dozen smaller ones. So they're going to need a lot of workers and it'll take a couple decades to rebuild everything."

"Do they really expect to get that many dolers?"

"They got over five million already. A lot of the smarter ones see this as a way out of the slums and because of the war and the whole push to 'do your duty!'" Alistar laughed a moment. "Anyway, right now it's acceptable to move up and out. And they are. Jefferson told me that the government thinks they can shrink the doler population by at least a third by the time this is all over."

Harold Jefferson was an Earthgov senator, and the current husband of my bio-mom, Eileen Walker. Technically, my stepdad. We didn't talk much.

"Yeah, but then what? Won't they just grow back?" I asked between mouthfuls.

Alistair shook his head. "They figured out how to keep their population steady decades ago. No one really wanted to cut it back, because they were too useful. But now that a lot of them are being killed off or moving up? The thought is to increase the number of the proles by as much as possible. Because we've got a lot of rebuilding to do. Once that's done and once we own Venus, we'll start shipping some of the proles and any doles who want to move up, as well as a fair number who don't, there to build that up as well."

I shook my head. "I don't see that working all that great, but hell, what do I know?" Kacey sat down next to me with her own plate and started to eat.

"I'd ask how the shipyards are going," Alistair said, "but John's given me the run-down on that. Have to say, I'm impressed. The man knows his business."

"Which is why we hired him," Kacey agreed.

"So, how *is* the McVay family doing?" I asked.

Alistair snorted. "They still can't believe that you set them up."

"They set themselves up. They had to know that there would be some type of retaliation. It takes a special kind of stupid to set up a war and then try to make a profit off it before the war even starts, all the while claiming that *you had no idea!*"

"I still can't believe you did that, Dave," he said, giving me a thoughtful look.

"Who says I did?" I replied with a smile.

"Everyone—and by everyone I mean the governments, not the people—knows that *you* took that ship away from the McVay family when you rescued your brother and his girlfriend. So when word got out that it was the ship that carried out the attack on the VMC, well, let's just say you're known to be smart and quite ruthless when crossed."

"Does that mean the Earth government will be after us next?" Kacey asked.

Alistair shook his head. "They know better. Also, the truth is that the McVay family *did* start this and that sooner or later it *was* going to get out, because David's right: they were stupid and they didn't cover their tracks. Ceres *had* to strike back, and striking back hard was their only real option. Earthgov and the Earthgov Navy got a wakeup call that Ceres is a lot more powerful than they expected. And if a small planet like Ceres has that much power, what does that say about Mars? Or some of the Jupiter and Saturn governments?"

Alistair shook his head again. "No, they won't try anything, because while people like you may be rare, David, places like Ceres always have more than one."

I nodded as I finished up breakfast. I wasn't able to eat as much as I used to, but then my stomach had definitely shrunk from a lack of good food.

"So," I said, leaning back and stretching while the others finished up, "why did you come all the way out here, Grandfather?"

"Because I wanted to be sure you were okay and if necessary wave large sums of money around to make sure you got the best treatment."

"That's it?" I asked, a little surprised.

"David, you're *family*. Not only that, you're family that I approve of *and* you're a business partner in a concern that has the possibility of making this family more money than it has ever made before. More money *and* more power. If your brother is successful, all of your children are going to have the kind of power that human society hasn't seen in hundreds of years."

"That doesn't sound good," Kacey said.

"No, but sooner or later it was bound to happen, and I'd rather it was my descendants and family holding the reins of power than someone else's, wouldn't you agree?"

"Why does it have to be anybody?"

"Because that's what human nature dictates. But if you want a comforting thought, I do have one for you."

"And that would be...?"

"These people are going to be *your* descendants. They're going to be *your* children, or your grandchildren. Which means *you* get to raise them and hopefully determine just what kind of people they will be. Your family, the 'Doyle Clan,' already has some strong values. Those came from your grandfather. So it's up to you to continue with that, and make sure that the people who end up holding onto those reins are going to be ones you'd approve of."

I watched as Kacey took a deep breath and thought about that.

"Well, that's enough philosophizing for now. What are your plans for the day?"

"I'm going to try and get a little work done from my office here," I told him. "As well as start exercising so I can get my strength back."

"I'll be going into the office," Kacey said.

"Well, I have a few business appointments later in the day myself," Alistair said. "I also need to get ready to head back home. I don't like to leave the kids unattended for too long. You never know just what kind of trouble they'll get into!"

I snorted and Kacey laughed.

"You make them sound like ten-year-olds," she said.

"Sometimes I wonder. I do think I'm going to send some of your half sibs out here, David. They've had it too easy for too long. Time to kick 'em in the butt and let them make something of themselves."

"Just as long as they understand that they have to work," I told him. "If any of them turn into partying rich morons, I'll be shipping them back."

"Seeing as I won't be sending them out with any money, I think they'll learn pretty quickly. That or they'll starve."

"Well, I need to get to work," Kacey said, getting up and taking my and her plates. "The rest of you can bus your own plates. You know where the sink is!"

The woman got up to leave with Kacey; I guessed that was her new bodyguard. I'd have to wait until later to get introduced.

I smiled and kissed her. "I need to get to work too."

"Don't push yourself, dear."

"I won't. Promise."

"I need to take care of a few things as well," Alistair said, and got up to take his plate and glass into the kitchen. I'd thought he'd have Havier do it, but apparently my grandfather was more than capable of looking after himself.

I headed off to my home office then. I had a couple of conference calls I wanted to make with my father, brother, and sister-in-law. I also wanted to talk to the guys who'd be installing the grav drives so I could make sure everyone was clear on what we were doing. Because Ben was right: you could install them with one drive unit handling the top and the other handling the bottom. And on a lot of the freight shuttles back on Earth they actually did it that way, because it enhanced panel life when operating in a gravity well as deep as Earth's.

I was just getting ready to take a break, get some lunch, and then take a nap when Alistair walked in.

"Dave, got a minute?" he asked.

"Sure, Grandfather."

"A *private* minute?"

"Taylor, if you could give us ten minutes?"

"Sure thing, Dave," he said, getting up from the chair where he'd been reading some old Earther novel.

"I'll be glad when I don't need him anymore," I said with a sigh after he'd left.

"You'll never be rid of him now, David. He or someone like him is going to be with you for the rest of your life. Might as well start getting used to it," Alistair said as he got out a device and did a quick sweep of the room with it.

"Ah, I see you've been taking your security seriously."

"Yup. While industrial espionage isn't big on Ceres, it still happens."

"So, I have to ask: How is your brother, and how is he doing?"

"He's doing well. We really did go for his wedding."

I watched as Alistair nodded slowly. "So nothing on his other project?"

I smiled. "Oh, I didn't say that. We actually did some testing. I don't want to go into details, of course, but he did learn one thing."

"And that was . . . ?"

"His theories were right and yes, we proved that FTL is possible."

"Excellent! The next question is: How soon can you start producing it?"

"*That* is where the problem lies," I said with a sigh. "While the experiment was successful there were a lot of unexpected problems, one of which almost killed us. It did a number on the ship we were using as well."

"So, not soon then, I take it."

I laughed. "No, not soon at all. But Ben believes he has a handle on it. He's going forward with a new test regime to figure out just how to get control over this thing and make it safe. We're also looking at building the engine factory out *there* instead of here."

"Why would you do that?"

"Because no one knows where *there* is. It'll let us set up and start production and testing far away from prying eyes. Like you told me, the longer we keep this a secret, the bigger the advantage we'll have and the more money we'll make."

Alistair smiled at me. "I especially like that last part, David."

"Blame Kacey, that woman lives and breathes business. She told me we'll be charging a half a billion credits for our first ships and that we'll probably have more demand than we can ever meet."

"I do like that girl," Alistair said, still smiling. "So, when do you think you'll have something you can test?"

I shook my head. "Right now, I don't know. I got shot before I could talk to Ben about his test plans. He's methodical and thorough. He knows I'm going to need a lot of data before we even start building the drives so we can start looking at ship designs. Also, we're going to need to figure out just what we're going to need to be able to build the factory."

"What about the local government?"

"They're completely onboard. I sold them a third of the drive company. They need the money it'll provide them to continue to improve their lives. Also, they're going to want to buy a lot more defenses to protect our secret. Sooner or later, I'm sure everyone will figure out where they are. Once we start shipping drives it'll make it that much harder for them to hide. But by then, it looks like the VMC won't be an issue anymore and they'll be more than capable of defending their home."

"Thought about this, did you?" Alistair asked with a chuckle.

"A lot, Grandfather. I thought about it a lot. I've always wanted Ben to get the credit and his due. I very much want the people who are helping us and protecting him to be rewarded. And I want to keep as tight a hold on this for as long as I can. Because what you told Kace is the truth of things. I learned that back when I was running with the Howlers: If you have a monopoly on power, you get respect, and you get to set the terms of how you live. You get to keep the dogs at bay."

Alistair nodded slowly at that. "Very true, David. Very true."

"Oh, one other thing."

"Another surprise?"

"You'll like this one."

"I will, will I?"

"We're going to name one of the lines of our starships after *you*, Grandfather."

The look on Alistair's face was priceless: complete shock, which was slowly replaced by a look of complete joy.

"Why, thank you, Grandson, you have truly made this old man's day."

"You're paying for this, for all of this. It's only fair that people *remember* your name."

"Not unlike Mr. Shian's boy, right?"

"Very much, and for the same reasons when you think about it. Without you, I don't know if any of this would have happened, Grandfather."

"Oh, I'm sure someone would have come up with the funding."

I shook my head. "No, not that. If I hadn't gotten that beating all those years ago, I'd either be dead by now or rotting away in some jail someplace. I was going feral, Grandfather. Killing people no longer meant anything to me. *People* no longer meant anything to me. You literally saved my life. So when Kacey suggested doing this, I realized it needed to be done. Without you, I wouldn't have been there to help Ben get away. I wouldn't have been able to put him someplace where he could do the work he wanted, with people who could help. None of what I've done, none of that would have happened.

"So, thank you, Grandfather. I still stand by what I said when we first met. You made me the man I am today."

I watched as he came over and, bending down, he hugged me.

"You've made me proud, Grandson. Very proud. Now if you'll excuse me, this old man is going to shed a few tears knowing that he managed to do at least *one* good thing in his life."

I smiled and hugged him back, then let him go. He straightened up and left the room.

"Ah, one of those family conversations," Taylor said as he came back in. "I had no idea you and your grandfather were so close."

I smiled. "He made a huge difference in my life when I was a young man. A huge difference. I can honestly say that helped make me who I am today."

Taylor just nodded. "Well, lunch first or physical therapy?"

"Let's do the PT. I could use a little exercise after that."

I led the way out of the room in my wheelchair. That was safer right now for the other person as my control was still far from perfect and I didn't want to run into anybody. Again. It was just too embarrassing.

One of the many guest rooms—which I suspect Kacey was hoping to fill with our children—had been converted into an exercise room for me. Because my left arm as well as my left leg were mostly paralyzed, I couldn't do any kind of walking because I couldn't hold myself up.

Not yet at least.

I parked the chair and Taylor helped me out, or more exactly he picked me up and moved me onto the seat of the first exercise machine. It was a fairly simple arm-workout station, though there were no weights on it when I did my left arm. You'd think that with no weight on it at all, it would have been easy.

I was covered in sweat after two minutes and wanted to scream. I think I preferred the beating that Havier had given me over a decade ago. When Taylor called time, I had him put some weights on it and I used my right arm. That was hard, but at least I could *do* it.

Next came the leg machine, and while my right leg got a nice workout, I was barely able to move the apparatus, with no weight on it, an inch with my left leg. That was even worse than the right and I did scream. Or to be more precise, I swore.

A lot.

"The doctor said that your arm would come back well before your leg did," Taylor reminded me.

"That doesn't change how much it sucks," I all but growled.

"Well, one more, and you're done for now."

I sighed and did what I could to help as I got moved over to the pedal machine. The pedal machine was like a stationary bike, only it had a set you grabbed with your hands as well and it had an evil little device in it that *forced* you to apply pressure with the limb on the left, or the limb on the right wouldn't be able to turn the pedals. It also gauged just how much pressure my left leg or arm was providing and based on some medieval torture guide it constantly updated itself.

It could only have been made worse if they'd added a shock-collar to it.

In fact, I was kinda surprised they hadn't.

After ten minutes on that, I was soaked in sweat and almost limp.

"Shower?" Taylor asked.

"Give me some time to get my strength back," I said, panting. "It's not just that my left side is all but useless, it's that my right side is so damn weak! How'd I lose so much strength, so fast?"

"Being in bed will do that to you. But now that you're out of the hospital, we have some equipment that will exercise the muscles on your left side to stop the loss of mass there."

"Can we use it on my right side as well?" I asked, hopefully.

"That would be cheating," Taylor said with a smile.

"But I like cheating!"

"That may be, but your *wife* is the one who signs my paychecks. So *no*."

"Spoilsport."

"Yes, so I've been told. Now, let's get you cleaned up and then it's time for lunch."

"Starting tomorrow, I want to do this three times a day, every day. Not just two."

"You sure? That's not going to be easy on you."

"Nothing else ever was, why should this be any different?" I asked, looking up at him.

"Why indeed..."

TWENTY-ONE

Doyle Shipyards—Besua, Ceres

"AH, THERE YOU ARE," JOHN DOYLE SAID AS I HOBBLED OVER TO him using my cane. "How's my granddaughter and my newest great-grandson doing?"

"Both are fine. I even got to take a bit of a nap before heading over here. So how'd this morning's test run go?"

"Everything passed. We haven't seen any more issues with surges from the reactor popping the breakers. But then we haven't dialed up the internal gee to anything past one point three."

I sighed, shaking my head. "We're gonna have to pull that fusactor and put in another one."

"But everything on it looks right, David!"

I shook my cane at him and grinned. "You kids! You're always in such a rush! You need to slow down once in a while!"

John laughed at that.

"But that fusactor is getting replaced," I told him. "If we see the same problem with another one, then we'll buy a third one from a completely different manufacturer and see what *that* one does. But honestly, I just think that one's bad and no one at Mars Atomics cared because they don't expect their fusactors to see any gravity fluctuations over one gee and we've been pushing that one up to two."

John just nodded. We'd had this discussion twice already. John may know welding and a dozen other disciplines, but grav drives and reactors, both fission and fusion, were my domain.

"We can still get the initial testing done with the current fusion reactor," I continued. "We just need to keep the speed limited so the internal gees don't run too high."

"How's the leg?"

"Eh." I tapped on my knee brace with my cane. "It's only been six months. Right now I'm just happy I can walk and stay out of that damn wheelchair!"

"So you'll be okay for the test ride?"

"I'm the only one who still knows how it all works. So if anything breaks, I can fix it. Not like zero gee is gonna matter to my leg."

"True."

"How goes the production line?"

"Once we get the green light on the test and they release the rest of the prototype money from the navy, we should roll out the first ship of their initial six-ship order in three weeks. Then another one every three after that."

"If we win that full order we're going to need a lot of people in here." I looked down at the production floor where the initial testing article for the new Shian fighter was being prepped for a move down to one of the launching docks.

"And we'll have to train them, I know," John said with a shrug. "But if we offer enough money we can probably lure in enough folks from the small shops who are doing okay, but not doing great—"

"Or barely getting by..."

"—to help us get over that hump," he finished.

"Let's go round up our pilot and copilot for this test."

Three hours later, I was sitting in the back of *Shian Zero One*. There were a lot more displays here than the normal fighter would have. There were also a few more controls and even a large toolbox where the fourth seat went. The main test pilot, Jules Costell, would be flying the profile. Our secondary test pilot, Brea Barkley was primarily there as a second pair of eyes, but having another experienced test pilot there to give their own impressions would be useful.

Jules and Brea sat side by side up front, with enough space between their seats that they could easily come into the back. The seating positions back here were farther apart, giving those in the back a lot more room. The seat to my left that had been replaced with a toolbox and other testing gear was for the missile operator—it wasn't needed on this ship. Behind where I sat was the entrance into the ship, space for a possible small head on the production versions, as well as storage for gear and food. On this version, however, it was open all the way to the fusactor.

All of us were in space suits. This wasn't a job you could do in a pressure suit, and if something broke or went wrong, the extra life support could save our lives. Thankfully, the knee joints were reinforced, so I didn't need my brace.

"Okay, Dave, bring us up from standby on the power."

I dialed the fusactor up to fifty percent power, and engaged the grav drives, keeping an eye on the gauges to make sure everything was in the moving up into the green.

"You have power and the grav drives are now active," I replied after a minute.

"Great. Preflight checklist, please, Brea."

She went down the checklist, which was very long and full of challenge-and-response items for both me and Jules. There was a lot of testing gear that needed to be set, and because this was the first flight, we wanted to err on the side of caution.

"Test Control, you copy on checklist complete?" Jules asked when Brea had finished.

"Roger, *Shian Zero One*, we've got comms and we've got telemetry."

"Flight Control. Please evacuate the hanger."

"This is Flight Control, roger, *Shian Zero One*, pumping down now."

I kept an eye on my display. I had a pressure gauge there and I could monitor the pressure drop. It went quickly; for all that the docking bay wasn't all that small.

"*Shian Zero One*, you are in vacuum. Docking bay doors now opening."

Jules replied to him, then got the local traffic report. There wasn't anybody out there and our test range was clear, as expected.

"*Shian Zero One*, you are clear to maneuver," Flight Control finally called.

"Test Control, *Shian Zero One* is lifting," Jules replied. He slowly brought us up a few feet, and then took us out of the docking bay.

"Now that we're off the tethers, the controls are a lot lighter than they were in the simulator," Jules said. "We might want to turn the resistance up a notch."

"I'll make a note of it," I replied and did just that on my reporting console. As our intercoms were open mike to the people sitting back in the telemetry monitoring room, I suspected several other people were writing that down as well.

"Test Control, I'm going to do a couple of three-sixty yaws," Jules said, bringing us to a halt a hundred meters away from the docking bay.

"Reason for deviation from the test plan?"

"I want to be sure I've got a feel for the controls. Once I've done that, I want to do a couple of rolls, then have Brea repeat both maneuvers to get her feedback on the handling."

"Roger, you are cleared for the deviation."

I looked up at one point to confirm what my instruments were telling me: we were rolling at that point, but I couldn't feel a thing.

"Well, between internal gravity and the restraint harnesses I didn't feel any of that," I reported.

"Yeah, it's kinda weird," Brea replied. "Even in an ore hauler there's enough momentum from the size of the thing that you feel a little something. This ship is really light."

"Flight Control, we are proceeding to the range," Jules called out next and flew us out at constant velocity rather than a constant acceleration. Until we'd put the ship through some more flight tests, restraint and safety were the bywords we were living by.

"Roger, *Shian Zero One*."

"So, Dave, are we showing up on everyone's radar?" Jules asked as we moved off toward the block of space we'd be flying in.

"From the way the transponder is pinging, I'd say so. We don't have any of the detection gear on board, so it's hard to say just how many folks out here are watching us."

"I'm sure we're going to have a large audience. Test Control, *Shian Zero One* is coming up on the range. Is our chase ship ready to go?"

"One moment, *Shian Zero One*."

"*Shian Zero One*, the *York* has you on their radar and they are ready to proceed."

"Roger that, Test Control, request clearance on to the range."

"*Shian Zero One*, you are cleared on to the range."

"*Shian Zero One*, entering the range and engaging the drive at point-five gravities for test run alpha."

"Roger that, *Shian Zero One*."

"And now the boring part," Jules muttered. "At least I'm hoping so."

We flew for twenty minutes, going straight "up" in regard to the plane of the ecliptic. There was typically a lot less traffic up that way.

"Test Control, *Shian Zero One* is cutting acceleration to zero."

"Roger, *Shian Zero One*."

"How's it looking back there, Dave?"

"Looking great, Jules."

"Test Control, *Shian Zero One* is flipping and will be accelerating back."

"Roger, *Shian Zero One*."

"Stand by for zero grav," Jules said. I felt it and saw it on my board as Jules cut the gravity and pitched us up, to swap us nose to tail and get us pointed back the way we came.

"Shit!" Jules and I swore at the same time as the fusactor scrammed and shut down completely, leaving us on battery power, slowly tumbling nose over tail.

"*Shian Zero One*, *York* here, what just happened?"

"We lost our fusactor," Jules replied. "We're on battery power. We'll let you know our intentions once Dave tells me what to do!"

"Roger!"

While Jules was talking I was looking over my instruments. There were a couple of red lights on the fusactor's feed system.

"Talk to me, Dave."

"Looks like our fusactor fuel-system feed is suffering from a pressurization problem," I told him as I shut down the feed pumps. "I'm going to give them a minute to equalize and then see if I can restart them."

I listened as Jules relayed my message. While I was waiting, I reached for the APU control panel above my head to hit the start button.

"APU start," I called out.

"I was just about to suggest that," Brea said. "Guess I'll start writing up the fusactor out checklist while you work the problem."

When we hit a minute, I restarted the fuel-feed system on our K-30 fusactor. I immediately got an error.

"Well, shit," I said, running through the diagnostics.

"So, I take it that's engineer speak for 'it's broken'?" Jules asked.

"Sure seems to be. This looks like the problem we were seeing in the testing originally. Thought we'd fixed that. Obviously not."

"Any chance of doing something so we can stop tumbling?"

"Let me see what I can do with the APU. We're small and light enough that I should be able to patch it through to the main bus and send some power to the panels. Then I'll see what I can do."

"Test Control, Frigate *York*, we're going to try and stop the tumbling so we can be towed back to the barn."

"Roger, *Shian Zero One*."

"I'm glad we went a little larger on the APU," I said as I started going through control menus. "Though it would have been a lot nicer if we had the original two as planned."

"I'm surprised it didn't cut out when we were doing those maneuvers back at Besua," Brea said.

"You had the gravity on when you did the rolls," I said. I found what I was looking for and, unbuckling from my seat, I went over to the toolbox to grab a few things.

"Yeah, but we had the gravity off when we were doing the yaw tests."

I looked up at her. "Okay, that's interesting."

"We were still in Ceres's influence," Jules said, "so we still had some gravity."

"Huh. Let me get the relays swapped and then we'll try something."

Going into the back, where the main buses for the power lines were, I popped out the relays that connected the APU to the gravity drive bus, reversed them, and put them back in. The relays were current sensing on the K-30 side and would only close if there was power there. If the K-30 cut out unexpectedly while the APU was set to add its power to the gravity drive bus, the relays would open and prevent the APU from having a demand spike that could overdraw its limited abilities and possibly force it into a scram. Assuming something didn't burn out or blow up before then.

By swapping the relays around, they'd now be sensing the APU power instead of the K-30 power and would close so I could route APU power into the grav drives. The relays also had an over-voltage protection function that normally sat on the K-30 side of the bus, to protect both the APU and the relays from any K-30 power spikes should the grav drive suddenly fail. With the relays swapped around, that function should still protect the APU, but not the relays.

Crawling back to my seat, I reset the grav drives that had tripped off line when we'd lost power and brought them up slowly to point-one internal gravity.

"Okay, we got gravity. Now what?"

"Now I want to see if I can reset the K-30's fuel feeds," I said and, resetting the pumps, I started them back up. All of the red warning messages on my display suddenly cleared as the K-30 did a clean restart.

"Power's back!" Jules said.

"Don't touch anything!" I called out.

"Sure, what's the problem?"

"I don't want to blow out our APU bus relays. I had to reverse the bypass shutdown relays and now I need to go back there and pull 'em. When I tell you, bring the gravity up to point two. I'll pull them a couple seconds after, and hopefully we won't melt anything and the sudden shock as the gravity changes won't trip the fusactor."

"Sounds like a plan. Put your helmet on."

"Huh?"

"If those relays decide to rapidly disassemble themselves, it'll protect your face."

"Oh, right."

I listened to Jules call out our intentions as I got my helmet on, and made sure it was locked and engaged. Then I went back to the relays.

"Point two, Jules!"

"Executing!"

I gave it a three count and pulled out the two relay units. The first one felt fine, but I could feel the warmth of the second one through the gloves of my suit.

"We still good?" I asked.

"We're still good!"

"Give me a few minutes to set things back the way they were, then let's see if we can head back!"

"Roger that!"

Ten minutes later, I was buckling myself back into my seat as Jules got us underway again.

"So, no turning the gravity off when making maneuvers," Jules said.

"And that explains why we couldn't repeat the problem back in the hanger. It was the gravity surges from when we cut from two gees to Ceres normal. Not the being at two gees."

"So it would seem," Brea said. "I just wonder if this is an inherent flaw, or we just got a bad one."

"We're not the first ship to do that maneuver under zero gee," Jules pointed out.

"True, but how fast were we turning by comparison? Most ships do a very slow yaw or pitch over. Takes them an hour or two. We were doing it in ten seconds. So, by comparison, we were going pretty fast. That's a lot of angular momentum, Jules."

"Huh, hadn't thought about that."

"And that's why we're here, to look at these things," she said smugly.

"Guess the first round is on me tonight!" Jules said with a chuckle.

The flight back was thankfully undramatic, though the rest of the test runs for the day were canceled.

"So, what happens now?" John asked as we sat around the table after the debrief.

"I don't see any reason why we can't continue the test runs for the next few days," I said, looking up from my notes. "We just need to ramp down slowly from any gravities over half a gee, and not put the ship under zero gravity while maneuvering. True, we won't get all the data we want, but we'll get more than enough while we wait for a replacement. And we are definitely *not* buying any more Mars Atomics' fusion reactors until they can explain to us *why* this happened and show us what they're doing to prevent it from happening again."

"So, you think it's a design flaw?" Jules asked.

I nodded. "Like Brea said, nobody treats them like this, so it's not something they'd ever have had a need to test. So they probably didn't."

"Well, I for one am not looking forward to this conversation," John said.

"I am." I grinned. "I am going to take their head engineer and give him the kind of lecture he probably hasn't had since college."

"Is this another one of those 'engineer' things?" Brea asked.

"Yup!" I said with an even wider grin.

"You guys are weird, you know that?"

"Kinky too! That's why we get the hot women," I replied. "Speaking of which, isn't your husband . . . ?"

Brea coughed and blushed, causing several people around the table to snicker.

"Okay then, we'll pick back up with testing tomorrow just after lunch," said Rob Doyle—my father-in-law, the vice president, as well as the program manager. "I want the team leads to go over all the procedures and checklists to make sure they're updated with the new requirements until we get the fusion reactor replaced. I also want a *new* set of tests written up so we can test for this when we get the replacement in.

"We good?" he asked, looking around the table. Everyone nodded. "Okay, we're done. Back to work, people."

Grabbing my cane and getting up, I headed back to my office with Taylor following. I'd already told the techs that I wanted the breakers I'd used replaced with a reversible type, so the next time I could just set them how I needed them, rather than having to take 'em out and turn 'em around.

It was a long walk to the front offices where Kacey and I worked. Before getting shot I took the small powered walkway. Since then, I'd decided to walk every step of it, because I needed the exercise and my left leg needed the therapy.

"Hey, hon, how's it going?" I asked, sticking my head into Kacey's office. Joan, her personal minder, looked up and smiled at me as Kacey got up and came over to give me a hug.

"I heard you had a little excitement today?"

"Yup, but now at least we know what the problem was. Your grandfather send you the request yet?"

"For the new fusion reactor? Yes. I also saw the part where we're not buying it from our current vendor."

"Yeah, I'm going to call them up and yell at them here in a few."

"You know the delay to Mars is over four minutes right now?"

"Oh, I'm not going to let them talk, so that's not important," I said, grinning.

"Counting coup are we, dear?" Kacey asked, snickering.

"Just a bit. If they want that continuing production order for when we spin up the Shian production line, they're gonna have to earn it now!"

Kacey gave me a kiss, which I returned. "I'll leave you to it, then," she said and, letting go of me, went back to her desk as I went to my office next door. Walking in, I was surprised to see Dorothy Briggs, my old boss from when I'd first signed onto the *Iowa Hill*, sitting inside waiting for me.

"Dot!" I said with a smile. "What are you doing here?" Then I immediately turned to Taylor. "Put the gun away and understand that Dot here is on the preferred persons list."

Taylor looked at me; he had the gun halfway out. "But she's armed."

"She's also faster than you and a better shot. If Dot ever decides I'm better off dead, understand you'll just be the roadkill on the side of the road and I'll undoubtedly deserve whatever she's planned."

I turned back to Dot, who'd stood up and was all but laughing as she smiled at me. I stumped over to her with my cane and gave her a hug.

"How's things? It's been..." I paused a moment and tried to remember when I'd seen her last. "Too long. It's been too long."

"It's good to see you too, Dave. I heard about what happened. Well, some of it, not all. What's with the leg?"

"Asshole used poisoned bullets—each bullet with a different one. One of 'em caused me to have a stroke and...well"—I tapped the brace with my cane—"this is the lingering side effect."

"You know," Dot said tapping a finger along the side of her face, "I could have *sworn* that I told you about not letting yourself get shot."

I laughed. "Sit, sit. Do you need anything to drink? Eat? Any of that?" I asked as I dropped into the seat across from hers. My desk was on the other side of the office. I had a few chairs set up around a coffee table for more relaxed meetings.

"A drink would be good," she said and I noticed her eyes slightly flick in Taylor's direction.

"Tay, get us a couple of cold beers. From the shop out by the front gate. Walk slowly and knock before you come back in."

"Are you sure?" he asked me in a worried voice.

I turned and looked at him. "Dot's a very good friend. Yes, I'm very sure."

He gave me a look that spoke volumes and left.

"So, what's wrong and how can I help?" I asked as I turned back to her.

"Why would anything be wrong?" she asked, grinning.

"Well, I like to think that if you were here to kill me, it'd be done and over with by now. Though I'm kinda hoping that I'm on the list of people who you *won't* kill."

"You are," Dot said, still grinning.

"So, you turn up without warning, you're no longer flying with Captain Roy last I heard, and you show up *here*, which is a much more secure space than, say, our home. Now, I don't think I broke it, but hey, you're a friend—one of the few, to be honest, for whom I not only *have* killed, but *would* kill again."

"You know that documentary they made about you?"

I sighed and rolled my eyes. Dot laughed.

"I haven't seen it. What happened?"

"Well, it would seem that certain people who *have* seen it seemed to have recalled a thing or two about me and have this crazy idea that I may have done a bad thing. Or three."

"How long ago is this from?"

"Before I signed on with Damascus Freight Lines."

I winced. "I'm not even going to ask, but I think after Venus I understand. What do you need?"

"Think your brother could use an engineer?"

I stopped and thought about that a moment.

"You know where he is, don't you?"

Dot nodded. "He's with your friends. If the entire VMC can't find them, it's hands down the safest place out there. Pam's out there too, isn't she?"

"Yup, after I left she went back and married the boss. If I send you out there, there are a few things I want you to understand."

"Such as?"

"You'll be working for me. Well, me and Kacey, that is."

"Dave, I'm not a bodyguard, I'm sort of on the other side of that profession. Or was at least," she said with a frown.

"Oh, it's not that at all!" I said, smiling at her.

"It's not?"

"Dot, how would you like to be in charge of the factory that's going to be building our FTL engines?"

She stopped, thought about it a moment.

"Why me?"

"Because I need an engineer who understands the cost safety ratio, who is experienced, and who won't take any crap from anybody. Though go easy on my brother, he kinda gets lost in the moment sometimes."

Dot laughed at that. "What's the pay?"

"I'll pay you what we're paying our president here. You're going to be earning it, I'm sure, as we haven't even started to build our manufacturing plant."

"And here I'd been hoping just to get a job helping your brother do his research. So he found the answer?"

"Yes, but now he's stuck with trying to figure out how to make it work safely. Which is all the more reason why I need someone like you out there."

"I'll take it," she said and, reaching across the table, we shook hands.

"So, tell me what's new, and I'll catch you up on my end of things. After that, I gotta call Mars Atomics and read their head engineer the riot act."

"Oh? What'd he do?"

"Design flaw in the K-30s. Maybe even their whole line. We just found it during testing. After that, you're welcome back at the house for as long as you need to stay until we can send you out."

Dot laughed. "The phone call sounds like fun."

"You're free to stay and listen if you'd like."

"So, what's it like?"

"What's what like?"

"Being, you know— she winked at me—"one of *them*?"

"Damn, I had no idea you could be so cruel!" I said, laughing as she joined in. "But, seriously?" I shook my head as Taylor knocked on the door.

"Enter!" I called out and he came in with a couple of bottles of cold beer. I passed one to Dot, then took the other one.

"It's ... *strange*," I told her as I opened my bottle and she opened hers. "I've got a personal bodyguard"—I nodded toward Taylor—"and so does Kacey, the kids ... we've had to expand the house because we've got an entire team. People are always trying to hit us up for money now too, either because they have this great moneymaking scheme or they've got a sick kid, wife, mother, you name it. Everyone wants a piece of me, and for some people"—I tapped the brace—"that's literal.

"On the one hand, I love the work, I love the building and the designing, I love working with the grav engines. I love that Kacey's happy, Ben's happy, everyone's happy. But damn if there aren't times when I don't think about grabbing Kacey and the kids and running off to join Ben and just run a refurb shop."

"So the whole 'building the next generation of spaceships and helping humanity conquer the stars' thing isn't doing it for you?" she asked.

"Eh, Honestly? I couldn't care less. Building the ships will be fun and will be an enjoyable challenge. Again, everyone's happy and that makes me happy. But I was never cut out to be an elie, Dot. You know that. At least here, people are still free to tell me to fuck off to my face and they won't get in trouble for it. But it was all a lot more fun when nobody knew who I was."

I looked at my watch. "Well, I need to make a phone call and get my cheap thrills."

"I'll try not to laugh too loudly," Dot said with a grin and, hoisting her bottle, she saluted me with it and went back to drinking.

Standing up and stretching a bit, I walked over to my desk and hit the intercom.

"Stacey?"

"Yes, David?"

"Get me Carl from Mars Atomics, main office."

"Yes, David."

It was late and I was lying in bed with Kacey. We'd set Dot up in one of the guest rooms. I was wondering if I'd be getting a visit from Jack tomorrow, but then it did seem like Dot was doing quite the job of being anonymous.

"So, what's up with Dot?" Kacey asked.

"She needs a job where no one will find her and she matches up with what we're looking for, so I hired her. She'll be on the next delivery to set up our factory."

"Why am I not surprised that one of your friends is in trouble?" Kacey said with a sigh.

"Eh, birds of a feather, I guess. But Dot is a good engineer—better than me, I'm sure. She's got the experience, she's smart, she enjoys the work, and most of what I know about *how* to do the job, I learned from her. Plus, she's looking to settle down. I have a feeling she'll be there until she retires."

"Because she needs to hide out?"

"No, because the work is going to be hard and a challenge. Dot's always struck me as the type who needed a challenge. Which probably had a lot to do with why she was sailing on tramp cargo ships. They're old, the budget is thin, and you really have to be good to make it all work."

"How'd the call to Mars Atomics go?"

I smiled. "I had Dot and even Taylor in stitches. It was all they could do to keep from laughing out loud as I went over the problem we'd discovered with their fusion reactor and then carefully berated them for it. Every time they tried to come up with an excuse for why they hadn't tested that or designed for it, it just gave me another opportunity to make embarrassing observations about them, their history, their family, their schooling."

"And they let you get away with that?"

"I reminded them—more than once, mind you—that *I* was in the spaceship in question, and that *I* was the one who not only had to figure it out, but fix it, while we were coasting away from our homes at one very high velocity."

"Sure you weren't too hard on them?"

"If they want our business, they need to learn not to make excuses when they screw up. Pointing out that Alistair Morgan's favorite grandson and the head of his newest endeavor was going Dutchman in a ship, because they made a mistake, drove the point home, I'm sure.

"Plus, by now the word has gone around that we've got someone working on the whole faster-than-light problem whom everyone seems to feel can crack it. Which means we're probably going to be buying a lot of fusion reactors. So they know they need to keep me happy if they want our money."

"Hmmm, I wonder if I can get them to give us a discount—you know, to make up for *past mistakes*?" Kacey asked with an evil grin.

"Whatever the market can bear, right?"

"Right."

"I do need to send Dot off with a bunch of questions for Ben that I want some insight on as soon as he knows enough to give it."

"Such as?"

"Just how much power per mass is this drive going to take? What are my engine rooms going to look like? I'm pretty sure we're still going to have grav drives, so I know what they're going to need. I also need to know if I have to isolate power buses or any of that stuff."

"The first ships are going to be life-support intensive, you know that, right?"

I nodded. "Lots of explorers, scientists, that kind of thing."

"Then colonists with their cargo and belongings, so those will be even larger."

"But slower."

Kacey pondered that a moment, then nodded. "Yeah, slower. You think Ben's going to figure it all out soon, don't you?"

"Even if he figured it out tomorrow, it's still going to take several years to build the factory to build the drives. To train everyone. To send out all the special equipment they'll need."

"So why the rush to get that information from him?"

"Because," I said, turning to smile at her, "wouldn't it be nice if our first in-house-designed cargo ship could easily be modified to accept Ben's new star drive? It would cut down on the time needed for us to start producing ships if we already had something that fit the bill, and we could also charge outrageous amounts of money to retrofit our existing models."

Kacey laid there a moment, and stared at me.

"What?"

"Want to switch jobs? You're obviously being wasted in engineering!"

I laughed and kissed her. "Repurposing is big in engineering speak."

She sighed and cuddled up against me. "So, ten years until we have our first starship?"

"I'm thinking more like twelve. But I haven't a clue as to when we'll be able to start selling them to anybody but governments."

"You don't think there'll be a huge rush to migrate out to the stars?"

"Not at first. Not until people start to believe it's safe. Or at least safer than staying at home."

Kacey just nodded and I rolled over to face her and, yawning, put my arms around her. I was fairly certain we were going to win those government contracts. We'd retrofitted over a dozen GSD Argon-class cargo ships, the first of our Argon-Two cargo ships was complete and had finished trials, and we already had sold the three that we'd laid the keels down for months ago. We'd even laid the keels for eight more.

Life was funny. I wondered what fourteen-year-old me would have said if he could see where he was going to end up. Would he think it was cool? Or would he have just stayed in the gangs and ignored our Grandfather's warning? I do know that when he saw our company logo and noticed that the background was the Howlers logo he would have laughed himself silly.

I know I did.

Kacey had been right all those years ago: the fun really was only just beginning.